9/4/24

p 172, p 219, p 266,
p 267, p 268, p 280,
p 509, p 510,

To my dear l.. ..
m.. v.
..

THE NORTH STAR

ALSO BY KATHERINE GENET

The Wilde Grove Series

The Gathering

The Belonging

The Rising

The Singing

Wilde Grove Series 2

Follow The Wind

The Otherworld

Golden Heart

Wilde Grove Prayer Books

Prayers Of The Wildwood

Prayers Of The Beacons

Wilde Grove Bonus Stories

Becoming Morghan

The Threading

Non-Fiction

Ground & Centre

The Dreamer's Way (coming 2024)

Wych Elm Books

The North Star

KATHERINE GENET

Wych Elm Books

Otago, NZ

www.wychelmbooks.com

contact@wychelmbooks.com

ISBN: 978-1- 7386030-7-7

For all of us who would be beacons.

1

I AM MORGHAN, LADY OF THE GROVE. LADY OF THE Wilderness, Lady of Life. This is the vision given to me.

Awakening, I find myself on top of the great hill, looking down at the sea. This is the rise behind Wilde Grove, but now it is a tor, tall like a steeple of a great church. I stand upon it, the wind in my hair, and I look out to sea where the ocean churns and heaves itself in a maelstrom.

I am reminded of the vision the Queen gave to me months upon months ago. The vision that broke my sight so that I could see the web, the threads that bind us all together, the beauty of the world so exquisite it hurts my heart every day.

And beneath it all, spreading across our world like the great blight upon humanity that it is, the creeping darkness.

Not upon us. Within us. Our light dimmed, consumed by the world we have built ourselves.

But this hill, this tor, is mine, on land that I call my own. It is my home for I have built a relationship with it, and I love every stone, every blade of grass, every creature who shares it with me.

I stand upon it looking about, at the storms that rage, at the shadows that are dim at the edge of my sight, but that grow and spread like stains upon the land.

Grief cuts into me, sharp-edged, wounding. That we have come to this!

I want to close my eyes to the view, to the vicious storms, to the darkness waiting to devour, to the souls who have become unattached to the web, who wander in the night.

But it is not my job to look away. It is not my task, nor yours.

So do I stand and look, and a new sound comes to my ears. It rises above the wail of the wind, above the thrashing of the sea, the scream of the birds wheeling above the waves.

It is a song. Someone is singing.

There is more than one voice. I look down the grassy banks of the hill upon which I stand and see the track that spirals around it. A procession comes up the path, and it is they, walking single file, each lifting a lantern, who sing as they come.

I recognise those at the front, for they are people I know and love. Erin, who grows and matures, whose heart fills with more magic each day, and behind her the other women from the village. Clarice, my daughter. Winsome, friend dear to me, Lucy, Krista, Charlie.

Others.

Behind them, the men, lanterns also held aloft to light the way, though the darkness has not reached them yet. Their presence is a balm to my heart, lifting me to a sudden, wild hope. Ambrose, my dear brother, Stephan, Simon, Henry, Martin. More come after them.

The procession winds its way higher up the hill, voices lifted to the sky, to the world, until they come to stand behind me, their rows like sentries, their voices warding off the darkness, singing the truth out into it.

A subtle shift in the atmosphere, a slight pressure, and then beside me, flanking me, Ravenna, eyes dark, spiralling tattoos prominent upon her cheeks. She gazes out at the churning ocean, face impassive.

Upon my other side, Catrin, as muscular in spirit as ever she was in flesh, hand resting upon the hilt of her sword. She glances at me, then turns back to the view.

And so this is my vision. We stand, all of us, lifting the light to the world, the singing upon our lips. Ranged against the darkness.

Ranged against the darkness.

2

THE AOTEAROA NEW ZEALAND SUN PUSHED ITS LEMON-coloured light in through the flimsy curtains. Clover blinked at it, knowing from years of waking early that the colour meant the sun had not long lifted its bulk above the ocean and into the sky. She lay still, curled in the bed, watching the brightening eastern light slide over the windowsill and make the leap to the floor.

The dream clung to her, more real for the moment than her room, the chair where she'd flung yesterday's clothes, the small table next to the door with its untidy stack of tarot decks, the guitar leaning against the wall. Even the light at the window.

Clover pressed her lips together and slid out of the bed, feeling a momentary reluctance to leave its warmth. She padded bare foot across the floorboards to the door and out of the room.

'Rue?'

She touched her sister's shoulder gently but firmly. Rue's

room was darker than her own, the curtains thicker. The sun barely pushed past them, which was the way Rue liked it.

'I'm awake,' Rue said, and her voice wasn't muffled or clogged with sleep. She'd been awake for several minutes. 'What is it?'

Clover looked down at her, frowning. 'I had a dream,' she said.

Rue raised herself on an elbow and regarded her sister. Clover was twenty years old now, but the tousled hair and the cute PJs with a black and white panda face on the shirt made her look young again, made Rue feel protective, just as she had when Clover was a toddler and there was only Rue, her teenage sister to look after her.

Before Selena Wilde had arrived.

'Are you all right?' Rue asked, thinking she already had a good idea that something was brewing inside Clover.

Inside herself too, and the very air around them, which seemed to be filled with an unseen weight.

Because she'd dreamt as well. Although not so much dream, she thought, as memory, vision.

Portent.

'Did you dream about the Forest House?' Rue asked, looking up at Clover, a pale, golden blur in the dimness.

Clover nodded, then sat on the edge of the bed. 'You did as well.'

She hadn't said it as a question, but Rue nodded anyway.

'I think Selena did too,' Clover continued, and closed her eyes, checking the ripples of energy inside the house. She nodded. 'It feels like it.' Selena, who had been Lady of the Grove before Morghan, who had left Wellsford and

5

Wilde Grove and come all the way across a great ocean to find her and Rue when they had been children.

Come for them and stayed. Taught them much of what she knew.

'Probably,' Rue agreed, then pulled back the blankets when Clover shivered. The morning was warm enough, but Clover was often chilled, no matter the weather, and Rue had long ago come to believe it was because she was never properly in the world but walked instead some broad and far liminal space.

Where the weather was cooler.

Clover tucked herself into the bed next to Rue and closed her eyes as its warmth cocooned her. She relaxed slightly.

'I don't think I like it,' she said, opening her eyes to gaze at Rue. 'The dream.' She paused. 'Or the memory, rather, because that's what it was.'

Clover thought about it, about the way she'd felt as Rhian, the priestess she'd been in a past life, thousands of years ago, at the time of the Great Turning. There'd been something different about her this time. A sense of purpose, of direction.

Of a task.

In the dream, she'd been somewhere dark that smelt of smoke and fragrant herbs, and yet she'd had the sensation of the room — cave — whirling around her, and her mind had been filled with whiteness, a thick mist she'd waded right out into.

Clover stared at her sister, thinking. Rhian had been doing some kind of ritual, casting some sort of spell, but Clover didn't understand what it was. Only that there was a sense of urgency to it that hadn't dissipated when she'd woken. It still churned inside her.

Rue looked at her. 'You all right?'

Clover gave a tight shrug under the blankets. 'I'm not sure what was going on in the dream. It seemed just a glimpse, and yet...' She trailed off, not knowing how to put the sense of portent into words.

'What did you see?' she asked Rue instead.

Rue looked at her sister then turned onto her back and stared up at the ceiling. The room was brightening, despite the curtains, but it was still early. Six o'clock, perhaps.

Selena would be getting up soon to greet the day. Even at eighty years old, she still rose early. Rue knew that Selena slept little these days, bursts and starts only. A symptom of old age, Selena had said. Dandy had been the same. Rue felt a prick of loss at the thought of Dandy. She'd been surrogate grandmother to them, her warmth and wit a great balm. She'd been gone to her next adventure seven years now.

'Rue,' Clover said in a low voice, interrupting Rue's swerving thoughts. 'The dream.'

Rue wasn't sure she wanted to think about the dream.

It was going to change things. She felt it in the pit of her stomach, in the way her skin prickled.

She shook her head slightly. 'At the Forest House.' she said at last, and she sighed. The Forest House was the place Wilde Grove had used to be. Millennia ago.

'I was with the other priestesses, and the men too, standing on the grass and looking at the trees, as though waiting for something.' Rue paused, searching for more information. She shook her head.

'I don't know what. Something heavy, something really important. I felt like we'd been planning it for a long time.' She swallowed; her tongue stuck dryly to the roof of her mouth. The room was suddenly too dark, and she wanted to leap from the bed, fling open the curtains and flood everything with light.

'It felt like we were doing something that so much depended on.' She fell silent.

The glimpse she'd had of being Bryn again, the priestess she'd been far back in that past lifetime, was the first she'd had in such a long while that Rue had no memory of when the last time had been. She'd been back at the Forest House in the dream, and the feeling of reaching and striving and hot, hard determination, had been so strong, so consuming, that when she'd woken, Rue had cried out into the darkness of her room.

'There wasn't much else but that,' she said now, glancing over at Clover, and she frowned. 'You weren't there,' she said, and cast about in her memory for the reason why. 'Rhian wasn't there.'

In the dream she — Bryn — had been standing on the grassy slope below the low-slung buildings that made up the Forest House, looking down at the tree line. The other priestesses, and the men of the community, had stood ranged across the grass with her.

Except for Rhian. Clover.

The sun had been a silver disk in the sky, shrouded by thick white clouds. She'd stood on the grass, waiting, watching, an older Bryn than Rue had ever remembered before. She'd grown into a priestess of the Forest House for certain, a woman whose connection to her path, Rue could feel, had become something solid inside her, the driving force in her life, with a purpose that was, in the dream, about in some way to truly unfurl. Rue shook her head slightly; she didn't quite understand the sensation of heavy anticipation, except that it hadn't drained away when she'd woken up. It rolled around inside her now, as though her very organs had consumed it, were heavy with it. It sat in her chest, atop heart and lungs so that she could scarcely breathe.

She thought that if she was ever sent to war, that was how she would feel.

The thought frightened her.

'Where were you?' she asked Clover, turning her head to look at her. 'Where was Rhian? Why wasn't she with the rest of us?' Rue drew a breath. 'What were we doing?'

Clover considered the vision of her memory, the dream. 'I wasn't with you,' she said. 'But I could feel you.'

Outside the cave, magic was furled and waiting. Clover didn't know for what. Waiting for what?

A thin slice of light from between the curtains carved across the ceiling.

'I was — I mean, Rhian was — in the cave, getting ready to do some sort of ritual or spell.' Clover bit down into the soft flesh of her lip. 'You all were going to do a spell too, I think.'

Clover rolled onto her back as well, keeping a grip on the blankets. She glanced at Rue then looked back at the ceiling.

'We were...' She paused, frowning, trying to find the right words to describe what she wanted to say. 'We were preparing for something.'

Rue nodded. 'Something we felt very grim about.'

9

'But determined,' Clover agreed. 'It was a necessity.'

She rolled back onto her side and gazed in the gloom at the shadows on Rue's face.

'We need to go there,' she said after a few silent minutes had passed.

'I've got work,' Rue said, understanding straight away where *there* was. She didn't want to go to Wilde Grove. Not if it was that dream pushing them to, with its sense of heavy duty and grim necessity. Plus, to some extent, she'd grown away from all that, once she'd left school and did the fashion design course.

'It was just a dream, Clover,' she said. 'Even if it wasn't a dream, but a memory, then that's all it was — a memory.' She kept her gaze resolutely on the ceiling. 'It doesn't have to make us change anything.' She shook her head, waved a hand in the air. 'It's all so nebulous. A centuries-old memory, a heavy feeling. That's no reason to make us uproot our lives.'

She paused. 'Besides, it's been years since we were at Wilde Grove. Things have changed since then.'

Clover nodded slowly, reading the temperature of Rue's fears as they echoed her own. 'But they're going to keep changing,' she said, and stopped herself from burrowing deeper into the bed searching for comfort she wouldn't find. 'And we need to be part of the next step.'

Rue gave her a sharp look. 'Because of the dream? Why? It was just an old memory.' She found herself very much wanting to downplay it.

'An old memory that we happen to experience together now — why?'

'I don't know.' Rue threw back the blankets in a sudden

movement. 'I don't want to know.' She blew out a breath. 'I need to go to work.'

Clover sat up, looked at Rue in consternation. 'You can't go to work. This isn't an ordinary day anymore.' The whiteness of her vision in the cave filled her mind.

Rue tugged on her dressing gown and gave in, something collapsing inside her. She sat down on the side of the bed.

'I wish it was,' she said.

'It's not,' Clover told her.

'I don't understand though.' Rue lifted her eyes to Clover. 'Why isn't it? Because we had a dream, a vision of something — we don't even know what — that went down in the past? The very distant past, at that.'

Clover frowned and thought it over carefully. Then took a breath, shaking her head. 'It wasn't just a dream, or even a memory. It was — is, I mean — an, I don't know, an echo.'

'Even an echo, Clover, doesn't mean anything for us,' Rue said. 'Necessarily.'

'We have to go there, to Wilde Grove,' Clover said, feeling the stubbornness of her conviction. 'Echoes ripple down the timeline. We're living in one of those ripples.' She frowned, frustrated with her inability to express in logical terms what she felt inside. 'Especially if you think of ripples as unfinished business.' She sat back and tugged the blankets around her shoulders again, stared at Rue.

'Unfinished business?' The phrase made Rue uneasy. Bryn had been at the beginning of some sort of business. Something weighty, important.

She didn't want to have to carry on with whatever that task might have been.

'Why now?' she said, feeling a shroud of inevitability fall over her. She shook her head and picked at a piece of fluff on the blanket. 'Why now and why us?'

'We were there at the beginning, I think,' Clover said, remembering the cave, the feeling of being surrounded by magic.

'But it felt so heavy,' Rue said finally, and she found herself suddenly grappling to hold back tears. She shook her head.

'It felt like the beginning of a terrible burden.'

3

RUE AND CLOVER STARED AT EACH OTHER ACROSS THE BED.

'Well,' Rue demanded, 'Didn't it?' Her hand clenched against the blankets, making a fist. 'What do you see when you look at this — at what we're supposed to be doing?'

Clover pressed her lips together, shook her head.

'Nothing,' she said.

Rue looked at her in astonishment. Whatever she'd expected to hear as a reply, it wasn't this.

Clover always saw something.

'What do you mean, nothing?'

Clover closed her eyes, although that wasn't necessary to see into the deep and wide, into the warp and weft of things. The truth was, she didn't need to see — she felt it inside her as though she was this permeable thing through which the worlds hummed along their ways.

'Nothing,' she repeated. 'A fog. A great, blinding blankness.' She snapped her eyelids open and looked at her sister. 'I see the same thing Rhian did, in the cave, in my dream.'

'A fog? Is there anything in this fog?'

Clover pulled the blankets up over her head to make a hood and peered out at Rue for a moment, then closed her eyes to look inwards, to scan around inside that whiteness.

'Maybe there's something there,' she said at last, her eyes still closed. 'A lake, perhaps. But I can't see it – it's just more of a feeling.' She paused. 'Maybe it's a river.' She fell silent. 'I can't decide if it is a lake, or a river shrouded in fog...' She paused, feeling a reluctance to say the next words, even while she didn't know their meaning. 'Or just a white emptiness, like a hole in the worlds.'

And Rhian had been preparing herself to wade out into it.

Clover considered what she'd just said. When she looked for the meaning behind the whiteness, she couldn't find it. She knew only that it was there inside her, as though she had found a hole within her, and it was filled with fog. She almost pushed the blankets aside and looked down at her middle, but knew she would only see her white pyjamas with the panda on them.

The hole — or lake or river, it could still be those — it was inside her. And she didn't know what it meant. It had been inside Rhian, blocking everything else out, and now she'd woken up with it inside her.

But around that white fog swam the conviction that a return to Wilde Grove would give her the answer.

'We need to go there,' she said, dropping the blankets from her head and looking frankly at Rue. 'I need to go there, but I think you do too.'

Rue looked at her in consternation. The room had brightened, and a shaft of sunlight had wriggled its way through a gap in the curtains to shine like an arrow upon Clover's fair head, lighting her up as though her dark gold hair was a halo.

Or a beacon, Rue thought, and frowned. 'You know that if you go, I will too.'

Clover gazed at her, then nodded. 'I do. I know that.'

Rue was still frowning. She touched her middle. 'I feel some sort of weight,' she said. 'Here. I felt it in the dream too — as though we were about to do something I thought was risky and I didn't like the odds.'

'But we were going to do it anyway.' Clover nodded.

They were quiet for a moment, looking at each other. The shaft of sunlight moved on, settling upon Clover's eyes, brightening them, lightening them, making her blink.

For a moment, Rue thought in sudden, swift horror, it looked as though her sister was blind, the eyes white and unseeing. As though shrouded in fog. Then Clover shifted her head and Rue let out a breath.

'We're going to do it anyway this time too,' Clover said.

Rue paused before answering. 'But do what?'

Clover shook her head, feeling again the great white emptiness.

'Clover?'

Rue's voice was sharp, jerking Clover back to the present, where she blinked, disoriented.

Rue stood up and tugged the blankets off her sister. 'Come on,' she said. 'We'll get up. You need a cup of tea, something to eat.'

· · ·

'WHAT DID YOU DREAM?' CLOVER SAID AS SHE AND RUE stepped out onto the small courtyard behind Windswitch House. She was looking at Selena, who had her head tilted toward the sun, eyes closed. The curly hair sitting on Selena's shoulders was white now.

Selena turned and looked at the two girls she thought of as her own kin. For a moment they wavered in her sight, and she saw them as she had in her dream.

Bryn and Rhian.

She looked quickly away, unwilling to relive what she'd seen on Rhian's face.

She closed her own eyes against the warmth of the sun, letting it colour her lids orange and yellow.

'I dreamt of the two of you. At the Forest House.' She opened her eyes. 'It was later,' she said. 'Later than we've seen previously.' She paused, smiled a little. 'I was no longer Mother Wendyl, except in spirit, but I was watching, keeping an eye on you both.'

Clover's heart hammered against the ribs of her chest, and she went over to Selena and burrowed like a child into her side.

'We will have remembered you,' she said. 'Even so.'

'And I watched over you,' Selena said, wrapping her arms around Clover's slight body and smiling. 'Just as I do now.'

Just as she had, forsaking her home to do so, for more than fifteen years now.

'But what were we doing?' Rue asked, her frown not yet relaxed. She shook her head. 'I had the sense of something, but not what, exactly.' She looked over Clover's head at

Selena. 'Something momentous, though.' She blew out a breath. 'Something with consequences.'

'We have to go to Wilde Grove,' Clover said, straightening reluctantly from Selena's warm embrace. 'I feel strongly that we do.'

Selena gazed at her, taking in the morning-pale face, the light blue eyes that in her dream had been filled with mist.

She shook her head. Brought herself back to the courtyard outside Windswitch House. She did not know what magic Rhian had been spinning, what visions her gaze had turned to.

What visions now that Clover was destined to turn to see, her gaze blinded to anything else.

Selena swallowed, and it seemed to her for a moment, that time itself stuttered, that the deep past was reaching out to them, that it was not over and done with, but still alive within them.

Whatever they had begun then was not yet finished.

She thought of returning to Wilde Grove, made herself speak. 'How long has it been?'

Rue answered, a sigh on her lips. 'Six years. Not since the funeral.'

Clover's mouth trembled. 'That was an awful time. I can't believe we've not been back since.' She lifted her head toward the sun, feeling its growing warmth against her fair skin. It was six weeks past the spring equinox — Ostara, Seeding Time — and the sun's heat had grown.

'Clover?' Rue's voice was sharp.

Clover didn't answer. She could feel the seizure coming on, heading toward her with a booming rushing as though she stood on train tracks. She stared into the round, bright headlight of the oncoming train, unable to take her gaze away.

Rue clutched Selena's arm, digging her fingers in for a moment before she caught herself and relaxed them.

'She'll be back in a minute or two,' Selena said.

Rue nodded, but it was grimly. She'd never become accustomed to these seizures of Clover's. They'd begun when Clover was 14, few and far between, it was true, but Rue still didn't like them.

She fixed her gaze on her sister and waited for her to come back from wherever it was that she'd gone this time.

Because Clover always went somewhere.

CLOVER FOUGHT DOWN THE PANIC THAT THREATENED TO envelop her just as the white fog was doing.

She closed her eyes and breathed. In and out, she told herself; draw in a deep lungful of air.

Blessed is the breath.

Hold it. Clover counted to six, forcing herself to be calm.

Return the breath to the world. Clover exhaled slowly, relinquishing herself to the trance state.

And to being wherever she was.

She breathed again.

Blessed is the path of trust.

In. Hold. Out.

She opened her eyes, and the mist swam about her, thick, blank, white. She waved an arm and it shifted about her, sluggishly.

It was chill against her arm, for even in this state, she had the sensation of her body, even while she knew it was left behind, standing in the courtyard of the home she'd known for the last seventeen years, watched over by Selena and Rue — as always.

Clover closed her eyes, letting the surge of gratitude flood through her, holding onto it, and spreading out her arms, baring her chest — her heart — to the great white void.

'I'm here,' she whispered. 'Where you have led me.'

She tamped the nervousness down, held on to the gratitude, let each breath — in and out — swirl it around her spirit form, which was every bit as real to her as her physical body.

When she opened her eyes, there was movement in the fog, and it rippled about the figure coming towards her.

'Rhian,' she said.

Then, 'where are we?'

And then: nothing, because all Clover could do was stare.

Rhian's eyes.

'What's happened to you?' Clover whispered. She shook her head, refuting the evidence of her own gaze. 'What's happened to you?'

There was another movement in the fog, a smaller one, and Blackbird perched upon Rhian's shoulder, cocking his head to stare one-eyed at Clover.

Blackbird's beak opened.

'She has turned her gaze to the great flow of the world.'

'And been blinded by it!'

Clover put fingers to her mouth. She didn't like the shrillness of her voice, even as the fog dampened it. 'Why?' she asked, whispering now. 'How?'

She pressed her hand harder against her lips.

'Not blinded,' Blackbird said, his yellow eye steady upon her. 'The opposite.'

Clover stared at Blackbird, trying not to look at the horror of Rhian's eyes, both the same blank white of the mist.

Clover wanted to go home. Away from this mist, away even from Blackbird.

And away from the sight of Rhian in this state. With all its implications.

Rue, she thought. I don't want to tell Rue this.

'Breathe,' Blackbird said.

Clover nodded, sucked at the air.

'Blessed is the breath,' she murmured, her lungs full, even as she had no lungs, even as she was where she was in spirit only, attached to her body by the thinnest of threads.

'Blessed is the path upon which we walk,' Blackbird said as Clover let her breath go, steadied.

'Why do you speak for her?' Clover asked. A thought struck her, and she reeled back. 'She is not speechless too?'

Blackbird's head bobbed a moment, but his words reassured Clover.

'She speaks,' he said.

Clover made herself look at Rhian, whose lips turned up in a smile at her. Rhian inclined her head.

But still, it was Blackbird, the fog shivering in an unseen breeze about his feathers, who explained.

'Her voice is ready to speak the weaving.'

Clover shook her head. 'I don't understand any of this,' she said, and forced herself to look around. 'Where are we?

What is this place?' She paused a moment, then looked back at Rhian and Blackbird. 'Why is this place inside me?'

She didn't add her next thought. That this whiteness frightened her. Perhaps more than any other place to which she'd ventured in the Other Realms.

Blackbird spread his wings, flapped them twice, then settled back to his perch on Rhian's shoulder.

'This is the flow,' he said. 'We stand amidst it.'

4

'THE FLOW?'

Clover didn't understand.

Blackbird's head bobbed again, this time in agreement. Rhian too smiled, her blank eyes the same fogged white as swirled about them.

'The flow of all things,' Blackbird said. 'The flow in which the worlds are woven.'

Clover reeled back, flailed her arms, sending the fog whirling, then found her footing again, shook her head.

'You can't be telling me the truth,' she said.

Blackbird stared at her. Rhian too, looked in her direction, unblinking.

'What does she see?' Clover whispered.

Blackbird didn't answer straight away. He shifted again, and Rhian lifted a hand and cupped her fingers gently around his back before dropping her arm to her side again.

'She sees what you will see also.'

Clover stared at him. Finally, she shook her head, tears

starting at her eyes. Eyes that still had colour and sight. Surely Blackbird did not mean for her to lose her sight like Rhian?

'No. That's going too far.' She stared frantically around at the whiteness. 'The Council couldn't possibly have agreed to this.'

The fog hadn't cleared at all. Still was it thick, white, cold upon Clover's skin, against her face. Her eyes.

'No,' she said again, more feebly, and she looked at Rhian, spoke directly to her. 'We didn't agree to this.' Rhian's white eyes stared back at her. 'This is going too far.'

It was Blackbird who spoke in reply.

'My dear one,' he said, his voice filled with a sympathy that seemed somehow to Clover to make his words even more implacable.

'We go where and when and how far as we are needed,' he said.

CLOVER'S EYES FLUTTERED, BLINKED. SHE PUT OUT A HAND and Rue grasped it, holding it tightly. Clover licked her lips, blinked again, feeling her consciousness seeping back into her body.

She looked up at her sister, then around at where she still stood.

There was Rue, her dark hair short, fashionable, her forehead creased in worry.

There was the house, its solid bluestone rising into the day, warming in the sun.

There was Selena, gazing at her with tears in her eyes and an expression of aching sympathy.

Clover stared at her, licked her lips, struggled for her voice, was relieved when she found it.

'What did you dream?' she asked Selena. 'Did you see me? Do you know?'

Selena closed her eyes for a moment and Clover nodded.

'Know what?' Rue asked, still holding Clover's hand, and looking from Clover to Selena.

But Clover didn't answer. Her throat was dry. 'I need some water,' she said.

'Let's go inside,' Selena said.

Clover shook her head a little, but that made her stomach lurch. Still, she didn't budge.

'We haven't greeted the day.'

'The day rises without us,' Rue said, exasperation leaking into her words. 'It blesses us with its light whether we turn to it to see or not. One day without won't hurt.'

But Clover only turned to look at the deep green of the trees that surrounded their property, and the brightening blue of the sky above it.

'I want to,' she said. Stubbornly.

Rue gazed at her, confused. Clover was unsteady on her feet, her face was pale and sweaty, and yet even as she stood swaying there, she was insisting on the unnecessary.

'What did you see?' she asked again, and looked over at Selena, aiming the question at her also. She had something she wasn't saying, and it was to do with Clover. 'What's going on?'

Selena's gaze skittered away from her. 'Let's greet the day,' she said. 'It needn't take long.'

Suspicious still, Rue paused, then backed down. They

would tell her the truth. Maybe not this minute, but it would come out.

They didn't keep secrets in their family.

'Okay,' she said. 'Against my better judgment.' She let go of Clover's hand, then grabbed her by the elbow again when Clover staggered.

'You're in no state!' Rue cried.

'We'd best be quick then,' Clover said, still staring at the sky. What, she wondered, was that shade of blue called? Periwinkle? Cornflower? Why didn't she know?

Selena cleared her throat, looked up at the great blue sweep of the sky over the trees and drew breath. The scent of trees was sweet and earthy on the air.

'The world is deep and wide and vast,' she said. 'We walk our path through it, filled with grace.'

Rue looked sideways at Selena, wondering at the odd beginning, then glanced at Clover, saw tears on her cheeks and felt panic welling inside her chest. She wanted to know what had happened.

But she stayed still and quiet. It would be quicker just to let the greeting be done.

Then she would ask her questions.

'The sun rises,' Selena said. 'The sun rises and warms us and sets the seed to growing, the sap to rising, the bush to blooming. We feel its heat upon our cheeks and are warmed too, knowing that the day begins and we are walking our path, blessed by the light.' She paused, thinking of those places in the world where the sun didn't make it over the horizon for months at a time.

'Even in those parts of the globe where the sun is set for months at a time is the world still blessed by light, even unseen. We carry the light within us, we shine with it, we hold ourselves as a torch to the world in its darkened times.'

Selena slowed to a stop, not knowing quite where she was going with it.

But it was Clover who opened her mouth and spoke next, her voice ragged.

'The day dawns,' she said. 'We follow our path, wherever it leads us, for our kin walk with us, and our task is set.'

Clover closed her eyes and sagged against Rue.

'Right,' Rue said. 'That's it. No more. We're going inside and you're going to tell me what's going on.'

Inside the kitchen, Tara, just out of bed and having greeted the day in her own way, at her bedroom window and standing at the altar in her room, took a single look at Clover and knew what had happened. She filled a glass with water and brought it over to the table, slid it in front of Clover. Went for a warm throw, brought it back and tucked it around Clover's shoulders.

'I always hope you've stopped having these,' she said, her hands still on Clover's shoulders, willing warmth and steadiness back into her. Tara looked at the others.

'I dreamt last night.'

Selena nodded. 'We all did.' She looked at Tara. 'Will you share yours with us?'

Tara was silent for a moment, moving to sit down beside Clover, whose fair hair partially covered her face as she gazed down at the table, the water glass clasped loosely in one hand.

'I dreamt of Wilde Grove. Of you going there.'

Clover raised her head. Wet her lips with the water, then

nodded. 'That's what we're going to do. Go back to the Grove, where our path started.'

Clover looked inside herself where all was vast white fog. She took a breath, held it, blew it out.

Where the worlds are woven, Blackbird had said.

What business could she possibly have, Clover wondered, to wander about in that vastness?

Tara looked at them, her family. Her voice shook. 'Will you be coming back?'

Clover looked across the table at Selena and didn't answer. She didn't know the answer.

'Yes,' Rue said, pushing her reply into the silence. 'This is our home. Here, not there.'

She waited a minute, then when no one said any more, she shook her head, staring at the air above the table.

'Tell me what you saw,' she said. Then, more pointedly. 'What you both saw.'

Clover closed her eyes. 'You won't like it,' she said.

'I don't like it already,' Rue retorted, and glanced at Tara's confused face. 'They both have seen something that they don't want to tell us.'

Tara's expression turned to consternation. 'About your dreams?' she asked. 'About going back to Wilde Grove?'

'About the path I was set upon centuries ago,' Clover said, and she rested her head on her hands, hiding her face from her sister and the woman who had been as a mother to her.

'About the path I still have to walk.'

Rue digested this. A cold shiver went through her body, and she looked over Clover's head at Tara. Were they about to find out the reason behind Clover's prodigious gifts?

It was Tara who spoke next, her voice quavering. 'You make it sound ominous.'

Clover lifted her head and spoke, not looking at anyone, instead gazing inside herself at the whiteness, at the great spread of whiteness that waited to be filled with visions and the weaving of magic.

Visions of what, she didn't know, and she didn't think she wanted to know. Nor what sort of magic.

Not just yet.

'My vision is going to widen,' she said.

'What?' Rue squawked. 'It's not wide enough as it is?' She looked at Selena, but Selena stayed silent, hands clasped together on the table in front of her.

'Apparently not,' Clover said, then sat back with a sigh. 'There are things yet to be seen, and they've something to do with whatever happened in the past.' She paused, and now she looked at Selena, who nodded gently.

'And whatever is set to happen in the future.'

'I CAN LEAVE HAHANA IN CHARGE,' RUE SAID A WHILE LATER. They were still sitting at the kitchen table, working out the details.

It was settled. They were going back to the Grove. Rue wasn't sure why, not concretely, but Clover's insistence convinced her.

Clover had threatened to go on her own.

Which wasn't something Rue could let happen. They were in this — whatever it was — together.

In a little while, Selena would call Morghan and let her know.

Rue found her thought again. 'Hahana pretty much runs the business anyway.'

Selena smiled, knowing it wasn't true. The Stitch Studio was Rue's project through and through, one that promoted slow self-made fashion. She'd met Hahana though and agreed that she was perfectly capable of taking the reins for a period.

How long, though? The question rumbled around inside Selena, making her heart quicken. She was 80 years old now. She wasn't sure if she would be coming back.

Her own vision was clouded, the way forward unclear. But, Selena knew, it was in times like this that there was only the next step, and then when that was made, the one after that would become clear.

She thought of Annwyn, and all the others before her, and her heart whispered at the thought of returning home, of resting her bones there in the cradle of her homeland. She looked down to hide her thoughts, stared at the rings on her fingers, on the right hand, the one that Annwyn, then Lady of the Grove, had given her so many years ago — all those years ago, a lifetime ago. Selena rubbed a finger over the blue lapis stone, and let her eyes drift to the other, amber in gold, given to her by the woodcutter she had loved. He was as old as she now, his strength finally slowing.

Selena turned her attention back to the table, the conversation going on.

'Someone has to stay and look after the house,' Tara said. 'And I don't know that I could leave my mums.'

Selena nodded and reached out to put a hand over Tara's. 'Of course not,' she said. 'Not unless you really want to.'

Tara shook her head. Yes, she wanted to see Wellsford, and Wilde Grove, and meet everyone again, but on the other hand, she did important work here now, as a midwife.

And the way Clover had spoken, the sombre looks on Rue and Clover's faces — they frightened her. As much as she struggled not to admit it to herself, she would be out of her depth with whatever was going on, and it frightened her.

'I couldn't,' she said, trying to smile. 'It wouldn't be fair on them. I have a dozen probably, due over the next months.' She turned her gaze to Clover and felt the same maternal tugging that she always did, never mind that Clover was 20 years old now. 'But promise me you'll be all right.'

Clover nodded, but even as she did, she wondered how she could promise such a thing. If she was lucky, she likely had sixty or seventy years ahead of her. In a century that would see some of the greatest changes in millennia. Reaching twenty had been something of a trial, and she had the suspicion that it would only become more so as the years passed.

If she survived whatever it was they were heading into.

Heading back into.

But she loved Tara like a mother, so she nodded, even while thinking also about how the seizures were getting more frequent. When she'd first started having them, Rue had made her go to the doctor, just to make sure she didn't have something organic going on.

The doctor had called it Focal Onset Impaired Awareness Seizures, and Clover had heard the capital letters on each word as he said them.

Something to do with her brain, but not a tumour, thank the Goddess.

Clover could have told everyone that it wasn't a tumour. She didn't think it was much to do with her brain, either, but Rue had looked grimly relieved at the news.

And they'd all learnt to live with yet another of Clover's peculiarities.

'I'll be fine,' she said to Tara. 'I promise.'

She turned to Selena. 'We need to go soon.'

Selena drummed her fingers on the kitchen table. Nodded.

'As soon as possible,' Clover said, wishing even as she said it that they weren't going at all.

5

MORGHAN STEPPED OUT ONTO THE TERRACE AND TUGGED HER cloak tighter about herself. The year was moving along at what seemed to her to be a great pace — such a year it had been — and now here it was turning again toward Samhain, Last Light, and the wind had ice on its breath now.

Sometimes, Morghan wished she could escape the winding of time — each year it seemed to move more quickly, a little more tightly.

Perhaps this simply was part of getting older. If so, it was the way it was supposed to be, and so what if she felt the cold a little more with each passing year? She was still fit, healthy, able to bear the odd physical discomfort. There was much to be grateful for.

She walked across the lawn to the path between the trees. Soon she would be dancing the sun rising, and that would warm her up.

Morghan had never grown tired of this quiet space in the early minutes of the day, when her time was still her own, and nobody was there to make any demands on her. When instead, the spread of the world opened before her, and she could spin and dance and celebrate it.

The ground underfoot was damp from the night's rain and Morghan's footsteps were muffled. She paused a moment at the place where the path veered off towards the stream, but turned back again, and walked up the rising path toward the stone circle, listening to her breath as she walked, letting everything else fall away from her, all the cares and concerns, all the tasks and responsibilities.

This half hour belonged to herself and the spirits who walked with her. She dropped a hand outside her cloak and touched Wolf's fur. It was warm and dry. A smile curved Morghan's lips.

'My good and faithful protector,' she murmured to the spirit kin. She let her next breath out slowly and looked upwards, between the twigged branches of the trees, feeling Hawk's presence in the sky above. All around her, the woods glistened with life and light, the strands of the web crisscrossing everything.

Morghan walked the path to the circle of stones and upon reaching them went to the centre and bowed to the ancient stone dancers. She made an offering to Grandmother Oak, laying her hand briefly in greeting upon the tree's craggy old bark.

'Long have you blessed this circle with your presence. I honour you in turn.'

There was a song upon the fresh dawn air, played in the music of the world around her, the sighing of the wind, the rustling of the grass, the light thudding beat of her steps, the hum of trees and web, the glistening of water upon their leaves.

She stepped into her dance, feeling the life of the world all around her, encompassing her and everything within it. She danced with her eyes closed, still seeing everything, the trees of both Wilde Grove and the Wildwood surrounding her, singing their humming, drowsy song.

She danced, her thoughts returning to her after minutes of communion, and she thought about her vision, of standing on the hill that was a tor, watching the coming lights of those with whom she lived and taught.

As though she'd called her forth, the air rippled beside her and she danced then with Ravenna, the ancient priestess's eyes dark with knowing, the shadows playing over the spirals on her cheeks.

Morghan bowed toward her, and Ravenna led their steps in a new dance, a new pattern, Morghan nodding and following.

Hawk flew lower, circling over their dance and Morghan reached for her, leaping up to be caught in those large talons, then to share feather and wing and far-seeing eye. They rose upwards towards the clouds, then soared, wings spread wide, letting the wind carry them back down.

Back down to another time and place. Morghan watched through Hawk's eyes, saw Ravenna standing in front of the buildings that were the Forest House. She stood with her face tilted toward the sky, eyes closed, and all around her spun a web of magic, a conjuring that was being woven within her, that would spread out soon, Morghan thought, to encompass possibly the whole of the Forest

House, the whole of what, in her own time, was Wilde Grove and Wellsford.

She watched, circling on Hawk's feathers, examining the pattern of the magic, realising that in some way it echoed the steps of the dance that Ravenna had just led her in. Morghan didn't know how this was possible, but she was certain that she was right.

Where was everyone else? Hawk swooped around in a circle, lifting one wing so that they swung easily on the lift of the wind. Ravenna came back into sight, and now she was not standing alone with her staff planted firmly in the ground before her. Still she had her eyes closed, still her lips moved with her chanting, but in a loose circle around her now stood the others of the Forest House.

There was no Macha, red hair wild down her back, caught in beads and braids as was the fashion where she and Ravenna had come from, but there was Bryn and others, Ulla, Mairann, Awel, the rest of the priestesses, and the men too.

All were concentrating, and even tucked inside Hawk, Morghan knew what was being woven was vital to the well-being of the Forest House.

She dipped closer again, wondered where Rhian and Macha were, then turned her far-seeing gaze to the magic, that rippled on an unseen breeze.

A great blessing was being woven.

Hawk reeled away, making for the clouds, lifting higher and higher. When Morghan looked down again, however, the bright silver blue of the spell still glowed in the air as it expanded over the green hills.

Then, abruptly, the vision darkened, and Morghan

blinked, breathed, felt Hawk's wings still strong under her, and let the vision continue. Hawk circled a great spread of night sky, higher than before, higher than ever before, so that Morghan could see the curve of the earth below her, and across its length and breadth, beacons catching and burning one by one, their light spreading.

Ranged against the darkness.

Hawk tucked her wings away and once more Morghan was in the stone circle, in her own time and world, stumbling as she tried to regain the use of her legs, staggering to her knees, her palms planted against one of the stones, the ground's dampness seeping through the wool of her trousers to the skin underneath.

When she raised her head, Ravenna was there, looking intently at her with those dark eyes, then, with a nod, stepping back and vanishing.

Morghan bent her head, dizzy, feeling as though she needed to catch her breath, and she concentrated for several minutes on breathing slowly, deeply, in and out, regaining her equilibrium enough to get to her feet.

She thought of the beacons she had seen, riding the wind upon Hawk's wings. She'd been seeing the beacons for a long time now, she thought. More often in the last year.

This was not without meaning.

Morghan knew it was her purpose now, the weaving of the worlds, the reaching for each other, lighting the fires that would show the way, that meant that the next Great Turning would be a turning back.

A Returning, to a world where the truth lived, where each would be sovereign over their own life, and committed to the beauty of their neighbour's.

She closed her eyes, felt the worlds around her, singing around the great Wheel as they always did, and always had, and she admitted finally, irrevocably, that her time was not over and done with as she had hoped, as she had thought after all that she and Grainne had been through, had achieved.

Her time was just beginning.

Grainne had been private business, healing the wounds of her own past. Now, Morghan thought, opening her eyes to look at the gleaming gold of her hand as the rising sun lit upon it, another time had come, and another task was upon her.

Her lips twitched. But not just upon herself, she thought, recalling the women she had seen at the Forest House, who also had returned to this lifetime alongside herself.

The task was upon not just herself, but others too. Those whose names she knew, and probably, she thought, many whose names she had not yet heard of and perhaps never would.

This task was hers, but not only hers. The beacons across the land would need to be lit by many hands.

Morghan climbed to her feet, waited until she was balanced upon them, then held her arms up to the sky, the weak sunlight catching on the gold of her outstretched fingers.

'My Goddess,' she murmured. 'As you have woven the mantle for me, so will I put it on. It is time.'

She lowered her hands, and a curious flat sensation settled upon her. So, she thought, she had taken the last step.

She had accepted her fate, her next challenge. Committed to it.

Now all would be done in its advancement.

For a brief moment, she felt Catrin at her shoulder, felt the swirl of her approval. Then, like a breath, she was gone.

Morghan stood still a moment, remembering that Catrin had been at her side on the tor, in her vision.

Ravenna to one side, Catrin on the other.

Morghan nodded. She would follow the path of the North Star and do what had been appointed her.

For what purpose had she otherwise?

She thought finally of the other priestesses of Forest House, of the finely spun filigree of the blessing they had been weaving, and wondered over it, over the care taken with it, the intention behind it, and she wondered then, brow knotted, where Macha and Rhian had been.

Then Morghan doubled over again as the world wavered and blinked in premonition and the images of Clover, Rue, and Selena rose to her mind.

MORGHAN CLOSED THE DOOR TO HAWTHORN HOUSE BEHIND her and shrugged off her cloak, catching it haphazardly on the coat hook before going in search of Mrs Palmer. She found her in the kitchen, with Winsome also seated at the scrubbed table. Morghan gave her a wide smile in greeting then lifted her gaze to Mrs Palmer.

'We're going to have visitors,' she announced.

Elise Palmer was surprised. 'Have you finally taken to carrying your mobile?' she asked.

Morghan stopped in her tracks toward the kettle and

frowned. 'My mobile?' she asked, the words not making any sense to her. She looked at Winsome, but Winsome just grinned.

'Your mobile,' Mrs Palmer repeated. 'Your phone?'

'Oh.' Morghan's face cleared and she shook her head. 'No,' she said. 'Or at least, not during my morning prayers.'

'Then how do you know they're coming?'

Morghan put the kettle down and turned slowly to face Mrs Palmer. 'They called?'

'Who called?' Mrs Palmer shook her head. They were getting their wires crossed and she ought to know better. Morghan had other means of communication than a telephone. She cleared her throat. 'Selena called.'

Winsome nodded, having crept up early through the morning from Blackthorn House, knowing Morghan would be up, if not about straight away. She'd heard Elise's side of the conversation, had just been asking what Selena was like.

Morghan bent her head down, closed her eyes, and took a breath before looking at Mrs Palmer again. 'They are coming,' she said. A sudden glow of warmth suffused her, and she smiled. 'It's been so long.'

Mrs Palmer agreed. 'Years,' she said.

'At least six, I think.' Morghan said, knowing full well it was. She turned to pick up the kettle, filled it with water. It was warm in the kitchen, and she smelt fresh bread baking. 'She asked me to call her back?'

Mrs Palmer shook her head. 'They're leaving soon. They were already packed, ready to leave.'

Concern flared inside Morghan, and she stilled, frowned, wanted to check. 'Selena's all right, isn't she?'

'Yes. It's not that.'

Morghan nodded. She knew that. She flicked the switch on the electric kettle.

Mrs Palmer moved to the oven and took out a tray of buns, their warm yeasty smell making Morghan's mouth water.

'I'll make up their rooms,' Mrs Palmer said. She put down the hot tray and straightened, looked at Winsome, then Morghan. 'Something big's happening, isn't it?'

Morghan filled the teapot, sat down at the table with Winsome, and eyed Elise, who had taken over the running of Hawthorn House from her mother when Christine Parker had grown too frail to manage.

'Yes,' Morghan said at last, touching the tips of her fingers to the sides of the teapot to warm them and frowning at the powerful magic Ravenna had been weaving in her vision of the past. What had been the purpose of that? She suppressed a sudden shiver. 'I think so, yes.'

Elise nodded. 'Seems to me to be good timing, what with the state of the world and all.' She stifled a sigh. 'It's going to get worse before it gets better, isn't it? All the political messes, on top of rising sea levels, heat waves, polar vortexes, and all the rest.' She shook her head now. 'And this incessant rain. Going to get a lot worse.'

Winsome closed her eyes at Elise's pronouncement. The state of the world worried her. There was war impending, she knew it, where Russia gathered its troops along certain of its borders.

Yes. She was worried, and right to be.

Morghan nodded slowly, thinking then of the Fae, of their determination to pull the rest of the veil down and make their presence known, perhaps even taking back their rightful place in the world. That would bring chaos to the human race, the majority of whom no longer believed in the Fair Folk.

'Yes,' she agreed. 'It will get worse.'

There was silence in the kitchen for a long moment, broken only by the clock ticking on the wall, and a bird outside who chirruped, then bent to the bird feeder Elise kept sheltered out there.

Finally, Elise brightened. 'But it will be lovely to see Selena and Rue and Clover again.' She rubbed her hands together and turned back to the buns. 'Clover will be all grown up now.'

'Yes,' Morghan agreed and looked at Winsome, then back at Elise. 'She's twenty now. In our last conversation, Selena said she's doing very well.'

'Maybe,' Elise said, sliding hot buns onto plates and putting them in front of Morghan and Winsome. 'But something's got them on their way here, hasn't it?'

Morghan nodded.

Yes, she thought. The Priestesses of the Grove were returning.

The only question was why? Things were coming together, being woven into creation.

Morghan could feel it in body and spirit.

6

'I HOPE YOU DIDN'T MIND ME JUST TURNING UP AT YOUR breakfast table,' Winsome said.

Morghan looked surprised. Her mind had been miles away, thinking about Selena and the girls getting on a plane to come back to the Grove. She drew herself back to the present with a shake of her head. 'Of course not,' she said. They skirted around the well on Hawthorn House's lawn and made for the trees. 'You're always welcome — as you well know.'

She looked at Winsome, noticing, unable to help it, the murkiness that swirled around in Winsome's aura.

'You're looking at my colours, aren't you?' Winsome said. She shook her head.

'It's very hard for me not to,' Morghan answered, her voice apologetic. 'Something's bothering you.'

She said it as a statement rather than a question as they ducked between the trees onto the path that led down to Wellsford village. She would walk Winsome home, and then what?

This was the question Morghan had been asking herself for the last four months. Not so much what she ought to be doing — but how? How to become the pear tree planted between schoolhouse and church? How to do Queen and Goddess's wishes?

Now, today, it was more urgent than ever. The time for brooding upon it had come and gone. She'd committed herself to action.

But for this minute, she needed to give Winsome her full attention.

Winsome drooped a little, then laughed at herself. 'I thought I'd be better at all this by now,' she said.

'Better at all what?'

Winsome waved a hand about. 'All this,' she repeated. 'Living.'

'Ah.' Morghan breathed deeply of the damp air. That it was the Season of Last Light, of the Ancestors, again was hard to believe. Time flowed so swiftly.

She tried to still her shiver of disquiet.

'I have many moments, you know,' Winsome said. 'Of joy. All around me is the mystery of the world, the great spread of it, and I see so much more often how it really is now...' She trailed off.

'And yet?' Morghan inquired.

'And yet.' Winsome's mouth turned down and she hunched into herself.

Morghan frowned. 'All is not well with Ambrose?' She lifted her gaze from the state of Winsome's aura and looked around the woods as though Ambrose would appear.

Which was altogether possible. He walked these woods

as often perhaps as she did herself. She ought to seek him out after walking Winsome home. He would want to hear that Selena was returning. And she needed to tell him of her vision. She looked back at Winsome. Perhaps though, she thought, Ambrose might well feel their presence within the woods and find them instead. With Erin's arrival in the Grove, the magic seemed to have grown stronger for all of them.

Morghan frowned at the thought, realised it was true, and tucked it away for later perusal. After finding Ambrose, she would also go to Erin, let her know the news. She nodded to herself, then turned her attention back to Winsome, corralling it in and chastising herself briefly for letting it wander. Again.

'All is wonderful with Ambrose,' Winsome said, then sniffed slightly, tucking her chin down and telling herself it was the cold that made her do so. 'When I let it be, I suppose.' She glanced at Morghan, unsurprised to see those grey eyes regarding her steadily.

'You make me feel I'm being ridiculous,' she said.

Morghan laughed. 'I'm doing nothing.'

Winsome conceded that with a nod. 'All right then,' she said, and she drew a breath to bolster herself into speaking the thought that was really on her mind, that niggled away at her so often that it spoiled her joy. 'I worry that Ambrose doesn't see me as I really am.'

Morghan's brow rose in surprise. 'Winsome,' she said. 'I assure you he sees you very clearly indeed.'

'He thinks I'm wonderful,' Winsome said miserably.

'You are,' Morghan said, and now she shook her head,

all thoughts of other events fallen away. 'Winsome, what is the matter?'

Winsome took a breath and her answer gushed from her. 'I worry that he's in love with a fantasy version of me.' She flicked a glance at Morghan then looked back at her feet, feeling her cheeks grow scarlet. 'I'm very much more settled than I was a few months ago.' She shook her head. 'But temperamentally, I'm pretty certain I'm always going to be a bit of a whiffle waffle.'

'A whiffle waffle?'

Winsome laughed at the bafflement in Morghan's voice, and the sound of the nonsensical words coming from her lips, and some of the tension inside her broke. She shook her head. 'Don't mind me,' she said. 'I'm being silly. I even know I'm being silly.' She paused. 'Let's change the subject. Tell me why Selena and the others are coming here?'

Morghan looked at Winsome a moment longer, then let the subject turn. They could talk on the other later, if Winsome wished.

'They're needed,' Morghan said, letting the words slip from her lips without conscious thought. 'There are things we need to do, to decide upon.' The quiver of unease again. Why had Ravenna shown her the weaving of such a strong piece of magic?

A weaving of blessing, of all things?

She slowed her pace, thinking upon it, a frown between her brows. They were at place where the paths in the woods crossed, and where the boundary of the Grove was. In a moment, she would step across, out of the umbrella of the wards she and Ambrose had put there — and would again after the Samhain celebrations.

45

Just as she had done her whole life at the Grove, as Selena and Annwyn had done before her.

Protection spells.

And yet — that had not been what Hawk had shown her Ravenna weaving. That had been for blessing, not protecting.

'Morghan?' Winsome asked. 'Are you all right?'

Morghan drew herself back to Winsome's question with an effort. What had it been?

'It is time to begin lighting the beacons,' Morghan said, finding a smile for Winsome and nodding. This was also true, the other part to what Hawk had shown her. 'But first, we must know how we mean to do that. It is my apprehension that something about us coming together will bring the answer to that question.'

And the answer, perhaps, to the first part of her vision, her memory of the Forest House and their strange business.

And where, she wondered again, had Macha and Rhian been?

Morghan sighed and looked across at Winsome. She smiled.

'Some of these first priestesses — and the men of the Grove — are returning, Winsome,' she said. 'For the Grove is to be rebuilt.'

Winsome frowned. 'But it doesn't need to be rebuilt,' she said. 'You're here. It exists.'

'Not as it needs to,' Morghan said. She turned on the path again and crossed the invisible barrier, drawing Winsome along with her.

'But,' Winsome said, hurrying after Morghan. 'I don't understand.'

'The coming storm grows nearer,' Morghan said, seeing the spreading darkness from her visions. 'We've no choice anymore but to take action against it. I've been trying to decide, since Erin's initiation, what sort of action that ought to be. As you know.'

Winsome bowed her head as they followed the path. She did know. And she knew also, without having to ask, what Morghan meant by storm. Everywhere she looked she could see it brewing. Tension tugged her muscles taut, and she blew out a relieving breath through pursed lips.

'They're — Selena and the others...'

'Rue and Clover,' Morghan said.

Winsome nodded, wishing Morghan would slow down just a little. Of the two of them Morghan had the longer legs.

'Yes,' she said. 'Rue and Clover. They're returning now to help this rebuilding?'

'I believe so.' Morghan stopped and turned to Winsome, who stared back at her, eyes bright with concern. 'At least to help figure out what this transformation must look like. It will be a relief for me to have them here.' She reached out and touched Winsome's shoulder.

It was a little like an electric shock, Winsome thought, and she shook her head, feeling taller suddenly, more capable as her spirit unfurled itself under Morghan's magic.

'How do you do that?' she gasped.

'You're part of it,' Morghan said, her golden hand still on Winsome's shoulder, her gaze far away as she ignored the question.

'Part of what?' Winsome gasped as she felt herself sway under Morghan's grasp, the world opening around her.

Cù appeared at her side.

'Part of the plan,' Morghan said, looking at the web, looking for connections, seeing the work of spirit, of the gods and goddesses everywhere.

How much easier things were now that she had grasped the meaning and use of the hand the Fae Queen had given her. It was the hand she used to touch, to direct the elements, to do magic, to sift through the worlds.

To light the beacons.

Winsome licked her lips, trying to maintain her balance while everything in her vision widened and swirled. 'Me?' she squeaked and peered between the trees where she thought for a moment that she'd seen her ancient goddess, her sow beside her.

Morghan let go of her shoulder and Winsome shuddered, drew in a breath, drew herself back together. The world came back into focus, although Winsome thought, gazing about her, it still looked deeper, more real than before and Cù still grinned at her. She turned to stare at Morghan.

'You should give a person a little warning before you do that.'

Morghan looked abashed for a moment, then she smiled ruefully. 'I'm sorry,' she said. 'I forget that the ability has grown so much.'

Winsome nodded, then turned to walk. She stumbled for a few steps, then regained a measure of her equilibrium.

'That would send some people crazy, you know, having the world blown open like that.'

Morghan stilled, looked at her, thinking. 'Yes,' she said

finally. 'It is what I fear as the veil is brought down.' She considered it.

Why had she been shown a blessing weaving? Why not then, the protective wards they used now?

Morghan wished she knew. Wished that those in spirit would speak plainly, instead of always in symbolism and vision, which might be the language of the soul but was sometimes very hard for the rational mind to interpret.

Winsome glanced at her. 'I think we have enough chaos as it is, with more coming down the road. I don't think we need every Tom, Dick, and Harry having their perception blown open like that.' She could feel the after-effects still. The woods around her held pockets of reality in each shadow, shimmering large and deep in her mind and vibrating against her spirit. Her colours likely wouldn't be murky right now, she thought, and neither would her spirit be tight against her. Morghan's touch as she'd looked into the web had opened her wide.

Winsome stood straighter as she walked, feeling the power of that web humming around her. Seeing the truth of the world, Winsome thought, would either make saints or lunatics of anyone who hadn't been prepared for it.

So she'd best make the decisions she needed to and prepare, she decided and swallowed, nerves prickling under her skin.

The storm was coming, Morghan had said, and Winsome knew she was right.

They parted where the path branched to go down to the vicarage, and Winsome nodded at Morghan. 'Erm,' she said. 'See you soon, then?'

'Of course.' Morghan paused before she said the next words. 'Winsome,' she said. 'You're doing fine.'

Winsome looked at Morghan, startled, then huffed out a breath. 'Yes,' she said. 'Maybe you're right.' She suppressed a sigh; she could see that Morghan was preoccupied this morning, and that today wasn't really a good time to tell her what was going on. 'Will you keep me abreast of developments?' She shifted slightly on the dirt path. 'I think I would like to meet Selena and Rue and Clover.'

Think? Winsome knew she did. On this topic, her curiosity burnt inside her; yes, she wanted to meet another Lady of the Grove. Would Selena be like Morghan? Selena must have taught Morghan after all.

It was all very interesting, and Winsome's spirits lifted. She gave Morghan a broad smile when Morghan answered.

'Of course,' Morghan said. 'You are important to all of this, Winsome. You are the bridge.'

Winsome nodded, feeling her face fall once more. The bridge between Grove and village, Morghan meant. She still wasn't a hundred percent sure what being the bridge entailed, but like all of them, she thought, she needed to follow the breadcrumbs and do the tasks as they came to her.

The thought made her lift her chin and she summoned a smile for Morghan.

'May your day be blessed,' she said.

Morghan returned the smile and bowed slightly to her friend. 'The Goddess shines her light upon us.'

7

When Winsome returned, Veronica was in the vicarage kitchen putting the kettle on and tugging her dressing gown more tightly about her.

'Why does everyone have to get up so early in this god-forsaken part of the world?' she asked, making a clatter with the crockery.

Winsome's brow rose as she stilled for a moment before turning and closing the door behind her. She peered out into the churchyard, where the old gravestones rose from a sea of wet grass and St Bridget's looked forlorn and neglected in the grey air of the early day.

'Are you talking about me?' she asked.

Veronica shook her head and tugged down a new jar of marmalade from the cupboard. She plonked it on the table.

'No,' she said. 'Julia was prowling around looking for you.'

'Julia?'

'I told her you'd be at Ambrose's.'

Winsome's heart sank, and she refused to look at Cù. She knew he'd have that wrinkled frown on his forehead. How a dog — and not even a real one, for heaven's sake — could manage to look so disapproving when he had a mind, she didn't know nor appreciate.

She knew she was not performing well.

'I wish you hadn't done that,' she said.

Veronica stopped, kettle in hand and peered at her. 'You weren't at Ambrose's?'

Winsome shook her head. 'No,' she said. 'I mean, I was, I just...'

Veronica rolled her eyes. 'Why you don't want everyone to know what everyone already does, is beyond me, Winsome.'

Winsome slid into a chair and resisted the urge to hang her head upon her hands. 'Not everyone knows,' she said.

Veronica just raised an eyebrow and poured the steaming water into the teapot.

'Very well then,' Winsome said. 'Not everyone needs to know when exactly — which night — I spend with him.' She pressed her lips together.

Veronica replaced the kettle and sat down opposite Winsome. She'd moved into the vicarage three months ago now and found that she and Winsome rattled along together very well. The place was big enough that they both had their bedrooms and another for their private sitting rooms — although mostly they hung out in the kitchen — and downstairs the big reception rooms had been turned over for community use.

It was working very well indeed, she thought, still surprised at the turn her life had taken, still very surprised that she was yet in Wellsford, and moreover, quite happy there.

'Which nights, you mean,' she said now, looking at the pot and stifling a yawn. She preferred lingering in bed of a morning, but that didn't seem to be how this village worked. People thought nothing of knocking on the door before eight in the morning. A barbaric practice, Veronica thought, but one she couldn't seem to cure anyone of.

Perhaps, she wondered, that was why Winsome liked to slink home before the sun had even lifted its bulk above the hills.

Except, she didn't think that was the entirety of the reason. Hence what she was about to say. Because they were friends now. They'd become friends, as well as business partners of a sort.

'Why are you trying to keep it a secret?' She leant forward over the table and zeroed her gaze in on Winsome.

'I'm not,' Winsome said, flushing. 'It's just...it's just private.'

That made Veronica laugh. 'This is Wellsford, population a dot and a squeak. Nothing is private.' She reached out and patted Winsome's hand. 'Come on,' she said. 'What is it, really? You should be all glowing with love, and all nicely sexed up — he is good in the sack, isn't he? He looks like he'd be good.'

Winsome's eyes widened, and she felt her cheeks grow even warmer. 'He's erm, just fine in that department, thanks.'

Veronica wrinkled her nose. 'Just fine isn't much of an endorsement of a man's prowess,' she said, but decided, judging from Winsome's mortified expression that she ought to move on. 'So what's the deal, then? Why do you try so hard to give everyone the impression that you don't spend more than half your time at Blackthorn House with the handsome wizard?'

Now Winsome's face paled. 'What did you call him?'

Veronica's shook her head. 'A wizard,' she said. 'What's wrong?'

'That's what is wrong,' Winsome said.

'But everyone and their dog knows Ambrose is part of the Grove. He's Morghan's right-hand man, for heaven's sake. There'd barely be a Grove without him.'

Veronica closed her mouth and looked at Winsome, who seemed to have shrunk in her chair as she'd been talking.

'No really,' she said finally. 'I think you'd best tell me what's going on.'

'It's this bridge business,' Winsome said, drawing the words reluctantly from inside her secret heart.

Veronica frowned with incomprehension. 'What bridge business? Who's building a bridge?'

'Me,' Winsome said. 'Or rather, I'm supposed to be the bridge — between village and Grove.' She shrugged help-lessly and glanced outside a moment. Cù had gone to stand at the window gazing out — he was tall enough to do it without even standing on his hind legs.

There was nothing there but the grass and the wind and the church. Winsome shook her head and made herself look back at Veronica.

'Like at the Midsummer celebrations,' she said. 'I'm the one who bridges the gap between us both. The one who whiffle waffles back and forth.'

'Whiffle waffles?'

Winsome shrugged. 'You know what I mean.'

'I don't see you whiffle waffling anywhere,' Veronica said generously. 'Except when it comes to Ambrose McKeon. There, you're decidedly whiffle waffling.'

Winsome sighed, reached out and poured the tea. It was dark and strong in her cup and she stared down at it. 'Something's coming,' she said dredging the words from deep inside her.

'Something's coming? What do you mean?'

Winsome pressed her lips together for a moment. 'I mean that Morghan's preparing to make a move.'

Veronica's brows rose.

'Goodness,' Winsome said. 'I'm making a hack of this.'

Now Veronica's eyes narrowed.

'I mean,' Winsome said, trying again. 'I mean that Morghan is going, in some way soon, to make the Grove a more public thing.'

'A more public thing?'

'Yes,' Winsome said. 'Of, erm, some sort.'

'You mean their website?' Veronica shook her head. 'That thing's been live for months.'

'More than that, I think,' Winsome said. 'I don't think she knows the details yet, but she's serious about opening her teachings and way to, well, to the public, I guess.'

Veronica picked up her cup and leant back in her chair. She frowned at Winsome. 'This isn't news,' she said. 'Erin has been talking of barely anything else for months now.' She cocked her head to the side. 'What does this — specifically, mind you — have to do with you and Ambrose, and the fact that you're hiding that you love him madly and treating him like he's some dirty little secret instead?'

Winsome stared at Veronica, her body turning alternately hot, then cold. 'I don't treat him like a dirty secret,' she said.

Did she?

'Don't you?' Veronica shook her head and changed tack again. 'Tell me about this bridge business. And why Morghan doing finally what we've known for months was coming, is such a big deal for you personally.'

'I'm a vicar,' Winsome said helplessly.

That stopped Veronica short. 'Are you?' she asked. 'Are you still?'

'Technically, yes,' Winsome said, and she thought miserably of the email lurking in her inbox like a potential bomb. 'Still,' she added.

'Huh. I didn't know that.' Veronica took a swig of the tea and considered the matter. 'How does that fit into things?'

'Exactly,' Winsome said. 'How does that fit into things?'

'Much the same as it has been?' Veronica ventured, then glanced outside as a particularly heavy gust of wind buffeted the old house, making the glass rattle in the window. She rolled her eyes as she heard the first bullets of rain.

More rain, she thought. They'd have to get around by canoe soon.

'Can't you continue to be a very modern sort of retired vicar?' Veronica asked. 'Not predjudiced against her pagan neighbours?'

'I'm a vicar forcibly retired in disgrace,' Winsome said. 'For consorting with said pagan neighbours.'

'And bonking one of them,' Veronica added.

Winsome yelped and gripped the table. 'I wasn't bonking him then,' she said.

'You are now.'

Winsome sighed. 'Yes,' she admitted. 'I'm bonking one of them, to use your charming term. And...' she paused. 'I think I might be actually part of the Grove. Ambrose says I am.'

She paused. 'I don't know what to make of that. I don't know what to do with it.'

Veronica pursed her lips and nodded. 'Part of the Grove, part of the village. I can see why you're the bridge, then.'

WINSOME CRINGED UNDER HER UMBRELLA, HOPING THIS particular shower would run its course sooner rather than later, and made her way up the path to Julia's front door.

When she knocked, there was no answer.

Cù started off around the side of the house, the fluffed and upright tail of a cat disappearing in front of him. Winsome sighed and erected her umbrella again, and followed him.

Julia looked up from the potting bench inside her garden shed. She was fussing with the stock of roses that hadn't sold over the spring and summer, making sure they would last the coming cold months, snug and warm. She waved at Winsome, standing up and dusting her hands off.

'You tracked me down,' she said.

Winsome looked at Julia's beaming face and nodded. She still couldn't believe the transformation in the woman. Gone was the perpetually pinched look about Julia's mouth and nose, replaced by upturned lips and the beginnings of fine smile lines around her eyes.

'I did,' Winsome said, stepping into the warmth of the shed and shaking raindrops from her umbrella. 'Veronica said you'd been looking for me.' She cleared her throat. 'I'd been out for a walk.'

Julia stared blankly at her for a moment, then nodded. 'Okay,' she said. Veronica had told her that Winsome was with Ambrose, but perhaps she'd been wrong. It didn't matter anyway.

'I heard from my solicitor,' she said. 'You know I've been trying to do something about Mariah's house.'

'Oh yes,' Winsome said. 'Have you made any progress?'

Julia hitched her hands onto her hips and gazed down frowning at the roses she'd rooted from the ones in her garden. All the best of them. She was planning to sell them come the spring, was already setting about making her name as a consultant for plant health, specialising in roses.

A rose-whisperer, people were calling her. It quite pleased her, actually.

'I want to sell it, of course, but he says that to even try to do that I have to apply to the High Court to be some sort of guardian, which will give me the rights to take care of things.' Julia paused. 'It's been over 90 days since she, you know, disappeared, so I can go ahead and do that.' She drew a breath, looked at Winsome.

'I was just wondering, I guess, if you'd help me do it.' She blinked. 'Come with me to the hearing and things.' A shudder went through her body at the memory of what had happened to Mariah, of that terrible night when the Fae Folk had come walking through the woods, shining and beautiful and terrible. She closed her eyes. 'I just don't think I could quite manage it all on my own.'

Winsome nodded immediately. 'Are you still having dreams about them?' she asked.

Julia wiped a hand across her forehead and looked out at the rain. It was easing, which was good. The back garden was quite waterlogged. She'd have to think about better drainage if this kept up year to year.

'Not as often,' she said, and looked reluctantly at Winsome's dog, then at the cat who, although not real, had moved in to live with her, for all the world like a flesh and blood animal.

Except, of course, it was very cheap to feed and didn't have kittens every six months. Or not, Julia thought, that she knew of.

'Not as often is good,' Winsome said.

Julia nodded. 'When does the church go up for sale?' she asked.

Now Winsome took a breath. 'Soon,' she said. 'Really soon.'

'I miss it,' Julia sighed. 'I know it will never be the same — nothing will ever be the same — but I miss the actual building. Being able to sit inside her, soaking up that peace.' She lifted her shoulders. 'I miss that.'

'I do too,' Winsome said. Sometimes, not often, but sometimes, she took the keys from her desk drawer and slipped inside the old church, just to do as Julia said. Sit there and soak up the peace. She checked her watch. There was enough time to have a shower and change before heading down to Banwell, if she hurried.

'Are you coming to services today?' she asked. 'We can go together, if you like.'

The church in Banwell wasn't quite as old as St Bridget's, but it was much larger, and still quite lovely.

Julia wrinkled her nose and looked out at her garden. Her cat sat in the rain washing a paw.

'I don't think so,' she said. 'It's not really doing it for me, to be honest.'

Winsome stared at her in surprise. 'What do you mean?'

Julia flicked a hand around, at the cat, at Winsome's dog, at the way her plants' auras glowed, even in the rain.

'I mean, it doesn't take any of this into account, which I've been trying so hard to adjust to, so it misses much of the point.' Julia shook her head. 'I never thought I'd hear myself say this, but the services are too dry. They're useful, but there's no mystery. I'm trying very hard to embrace the mystery of the world — since it won't leave me alone.'

Winsome nodded but made no reply and they stood there a moment, listening to the lessening rain and staring out at the dog and cat, both of which they could see perfectly clearly even though, according to most everyone, they weren't there.

There was nothing to say, Winsome thought. Julia was right. She herself only went, why? Because she had once found mystery there, in the church, even if she'd had to dig long and deep for it, and keep on digging.

But she'd found mystery in a lot of places since then, hadn't she?

Julia was speaking again and Winsome tuned back in.

'Cynthia is calling a special meeting — have you heard?'

'About the church?'

'That,' Julia said. 'And other things. You need to make sure you're there — you missed our last one.'

Yes, Winsome thought. She had. She'd been with a dying woman, holding space for her, singing her across, holding the mystery of the world in her own two hands.

Like a bridge, she thought suddenly. Between one world and another.

8

'Hey.' Ebony opened the door to the shop and held it wide for Rue. She saw the look on her friend's face and froze in place. 'What's going on?'

Rue shook her head. 'Can we go somewhere?' she asked. 'Talk?'

The door swung shut and Ebony followed Rue between the shelves of esoterica that made up Beacon's stock. They stopped at the display of crystal balls, and Ebony reached for one, cupping the heavy quartz in a palm. She knew she oughtn't, of course, should put the thing back on its little wooden stand, because judging by the look on Rue's face, the crystal ball was about to absorb a lot of angst.

She returned it to the shelf. 'Let's go into the reading room,' she said. 'I'll make you a cup of something.' Another look at Rue. 'A cup of something soothing.' Then Ebony paused, her head suddenly light. 'It's not Clover, is it? What's happened to her?'

But Rue shook her head. 'Is Anita here? Can she look after the shop for a couple hours? I really need you.'

That decided it for Ebony. 'Give me three minutes,' she said. 'I'll let Anita know she has to hold the fort for a few hours.' She raised her brows and Rue nodded.

'A few hours,' Rue echoed, then wrapped her arms around herself and gazed about at the shop while Ebony scooted off into the back.

Ebony owned Beacon now — just as she'd said she would years ago when she left school to work full time in the shop. Rue rocked back and forth a little. She was proud of the business that Ebony had built. Beacon was turning into exactly that — a real beacon in the local witchy and New Age communities.

'Okay,' Ebony said, appearing at Rue's side again, a bag slung over her shoulder. 'Where do you want to go?'

'The beach,' Rue said without hesitation.

'Cool. Your car or mine?'

'Yours.' Rue tugged open the shop door. 'I don't feel up to driving.'

'REMEMBER THE FIRST TIME I BROUGHT YOU HERE?' EBONY asked, kicking off her sandals and feeling the sand between her toes.

'Long time ago now,' Rue said, squinting up at the rock formation on the cliff that had been the reason they'd come here that day years ago. It was a giant Druid's stone, a hole in it big enough to stand inside.

Rue knew that, because that's what they'd done — climbed the rocks and stood inside it.

'I wish the others were here,' she said. Suze and Sophie. Friends since high school.

'Sophie's in Ukraine,' Ebony said. 'She says there's going to be a war there.'

'A war?' Rue turned and looked at Ebony. 'What does she mean?'

'She means that Russia is amassing troops all along the border. They're going to invade.'

'God.' Rue stood on the sand and stared at Ebony, whose white-blond hair hadn't darkened much now she was in her thirties, and was chin length and styled in a way that suited her oval face and great cheekbones. 'She's not going to stay there, is she?'

'She's met a guy,' Ebony said and raised her eyebrows at Rue. 'Seems pretty serious.'

Rue shook her head. 'I need to write to her. Sophie's really settling down? She's always seemed so serious about going around Europe collecting her stories.'

'She said it's time to put everything together into a proper book.'

Rue's heart swelled with pride. Sophie's blog was pretty legendary. A book was the next natural progression. 'But she'll get out of the country, won't she? If there's going to be a war?'

A war. Hadn't that heaviness she'd felt that morning seemed almost like a premonition of war?

Perhaps it was this one, this new one between Russia and Ukraine. Perhaps that was what she'd picked up on.

She felt awful that she was hoping so. The world did not need a war in the Otherworld, as well as the Ordinary.

Ebony was looking straight at her now. 'So,' she said, her words casual enough, on the surface. 'What's up?'

Rue shook her head, gazed out at the sea, watched a gull spread its wings, wheel over teal-coloured waves, tried to find the words for it all.

'We're going to Wilde Grove,' she said.

Ebony stared at her. 'What? Why?' She dug her toes unconsciously into the sand. 'That's sudden, isn't it?'

'Today sudden,' Rue agreed, then turned down the beach. 'Let's walk.'

Ebony hurried to fall in beside her. 'What happened?'

'I don't know. That's the problem.' Rue folded her arms over her chest. 'I don't know.'

'Okay. I'm listening.' Ebony's sandals dangling from her hand smacked sand against the shift she wore over her leggings, everything a pale creamy white to go with her hair.

'We all had this dream last night,' Rue said, then stopped walking to swing around to face Ebony. 'What did you dream about last night or this morning?'

Ebony searched Rue's face for clues as to what was going on. She shrugged. 'I don't know. I don't remember.'

Rue's shoulders sagged, and she started walking again. 'I thought you might have had it too.'

'No. I wish I had.' Ebony lifted her hair with her hand, let the breeze cool her neck. If she'd had the dream — whatever it had been — along with everyone else, then she'd be part of it. Part of whatever was happening.

'So, the three of us, me, Clover, and Selena, we all dreamt we were back in the Forest House.'

Ebony nodded. She knew that the Forest House meant Bryn and Rhian.

'Something...momentous...was going down there,' Rue said, and hugged herself tighter. For a moment, she thought she could smell the dampness of the Forest House's river, instead of the light salt of the sea. The river where the Fae had given her Rhian to take care of.

'Momentous?' Ebony looked at her, alarmed. 'What sort of momentous? This is new.'

'We were older than I've ever seen before.' Rue gave a tight shrug. 'So, you know, it was later on the timeline, I guess you'd have to say.'

'What happened?'

'Nothing,' Rue said. 'I didn't even see Rhian in it.' She stopped walking again and gazed up at the rock formation, where from this viewpoint the hole in the rock outcropping looked heart-shaped.

'In my dream,' she continued, 'I was standing on the grassy bank below the buildings. Just standing there. I think I was waiting for something.'

'For what?' Ebony asked, watching the expression on Rue's face.

'I don't know,' Rue said. 'Rhian and Macha weren't there, but Ravenna and everyone else was.' Ravenna had been their priestess leader.

'But I had such a heavy feeling — like Sophie must be feeling now, in Ukraine, on the brink of war. As though really serious things were happening.'

Ebony shook her head slowly, her hair swinging. 'I don't understand.'

Rue's answer was a howl of frustration. 'I don't either!' She brought herself back under control. 'We were doing something way back then, and Clover says that whatever it was, we've now got to finish it. Or continue it. Or something.'

'What was Clover's dream?' A thought occurred suddenly to Ebony — if Clover was going to Wilde Grove, all her appointments at Beacon would have to be cancelled, shuffled between the other readers. The customers wouldn't be too happy about that. Clover was the best tarot reader available at Beacon. Available anywhere, probably.

'She was in a cave, having visions of some sort.' Rue looked at Ebony, her face strained. 'But she says that her — what do we call them? Her own visions, her ability to see the Other Realms — that it's going to get stronger.'

'Stronger?' Ebony didn't know whether to be appalled or impressed. 'But it's already stronger than anyone's I've ever met.'

'I know,' Rue said mournfully. 'I've got the feeling she wasn't telling me the whole story — and whenever Selena looked at her, she was all round-eyed and startled.' Rue shook her head. 'There's something they're not telling me, and I don't like it.'

'But they tell you everything, don't they?'

'I guess so.' Rue sat down on the sand, turning to face the lowering tide. Watching the waves calmed her. It was like watching the world breathe. 'I thought so.'

Ebony sat down too, stretching out her long legs. 'Let me get this straight,' she said. 'Something went down — way way back when, during the Great Turning, practically.'

Rue thought about it, nodded. Continued watching the waves come in.

'But that something wasn't concluded absolutely, and now you have to go back to Wilde Grove and finish it.'

Her statement made Rue turn her head and look at her. 'How do you do that?'

'Do what?'

'Find the sense in what I'm trying to tell you?'

Ebony grinned. 'Well, I've been listening to you for a lot of years now. I'm an expert in Rue-speak.' Her grin faded. 'Is it dangerous, do you think?'

Rue took her time in answering.

'I don't know,' she said on a sigh. 'Maybe not dangerous, but taxing.' She frowned, beetling her eyebrows together. 'I think this, whatever it is, is Clover's reason for being the way she is.' Her expression clouded. 'I wish I knew what they're keeping from me.'

'If they're keeping anything from you,' Ebony said, her tone matter of fact. 'It wouldn't be like Clover or Selena to keep secrets from you. You're the great protector of the family.'

Rue shook her head. 'Don't be silly.'

Ebony laughed. 'I'm not being silly. Ever since you came back from Wilde Grove that first time, that's what you've been. Clover's protector. At a cost too, may I say.'

'Hardly any,' Rue said. 'I've been able to build up my business. I haven't missed out.'

'You've barely ever had a boyfriend.'

'You're single too,' Rue retorted.

'True,' Ebony said, and leant back in the sand. 'Touché.'

They were silent for a long while, watching the waves edge up the sand, froth like delicate lace, then slide back down the beach. The breeze tousled the waves, then came and whispered around their ears, hushing and shushing and trying its best to calm them.

'When are you going?' Ebony asked finally.

Rue looked at her, lips pale, arms around her legs hugging them. 'Tomorrow.'

That made Ebony sit up to stare at her in shock. 'Tomorrow?'

Rue nodded.

'And you only decided today?'

Another nod.

'But that's too soon.' Ebony was shaken. She paused. 'It's that serious?'

'It feels like it is, yes.' Rue tucked her chin down on her knees. 'Afterwards — the dream and when we were all up talking about it, Clover had a seizure.' Her face twisted in anguish.

Ebony looked at her in sympathy. 'You know they're not really seizures, don't you?'

But Rue shook her head stubbornly. 'She has no control over the episodes. That means they're involuntary. Seizures.'

Ebony lifted her eyebrows. Rue saw her do it.

'Fine,' Rue said and tipped her head back, squinting at the high blue bowl of the sky. 'Fine. They're not real seizures. It's more of Clover's general weirdness.' She managed a smile, softening the words with affection.

'What did she see in this one?' Ebony asked.

'You know what? — This is another thing that is worrying me,' Rue said. 'She didn't really tell me. But there were tears in her eyes when she came back, and she looked a bit sick.'

'What? Why?'

Rue stood up, dusted the sand off her clothes and looked down at her best friend. 'I think that's the bit about her vision widening even further. I think she was told about that.'

Ebony rose too and gazed out to sea, sandals in hand, shaking her head. 'Yeah,' she said. 'That would make me feel a bit queasy too.'

'YOU'RE GOING TO COME BACK, RIGHT?' EBONY LOOKED across at Rue in the passenger's seat. 'All of you. Right?'

Rue nodded. 'Definitely.' She paused, hand on the door, then sank back into the seat. 'Well. I don't know about Selena, actually.' The new thought made her want to cry. Selena had been teacher and grandmother since she was fifteen and Clover only three. 'She might want to spend her last years in Wilde Grove, where she really belongs.'

Ebony snorted. 'Selena belongs here, with us,' she said. 'This place is her home.'

But they looked at each other and knew that what Rue had said might be true, in the end.

'Fuck.' Ebony bumped her head lightly against the steering wheel.

'I don't like any of this.'

9

EBONY PUSHED OPEN THE DOOR TO HER SHOP AND BARELY heard the tinkling of the silver bell above it. There was a frown on her face, and she was shaking her head, preoccupied.

'Are you all right, Ebony?'

'What?' Ebony looked up, blinked, then let the door swing closed behind her.

'You look like something serious is on your mind. Is everything okay?' Anita frowned. 'Is Rue okay?'

'Oh.' Ebony nodded, threaded her way through the crowded shop, Anita at her back. 'Yeah, Rue is fine. She and Clover and Selena are going away for a little while, is all.'

'Away? Where to?' Anita pushed into the break room behind Ebony and watched as her boss flung down her bag and sank onto one of the chairs. 'I'll make tea,' she decided before Ebony could answer.

'Yeah, that would be great, thanks.'

Anita nodded. 'Something uplifting by the looks.' She

paused by the tea kettle, cup in hand. 'You said Clover too? She's fully booked here.'

Ebony covered her face with her hands. 'I know. We're going to have to shuffle those onto the others — if her clients are happy about that.' She dragged her fingers down her cheeks and looked at Anita over the top of them. 'I guess I ought to get onto that.' Clover had been giving psychic readings at Ebony's shop Beacon for the last few years. Selena had thought it would be a good way for her to learn to hone and use her talent with judicious discernment.

Which meant not blurting out everything that came to her.

And really, Clover hadn't been equipped for any other job. University was out of the question — she'd barely managed a few weeks at school until begging to leave before all her fuses blew. Clover simply couldn't function around a lot of people. Even knowing how to shield her energy hadn't helped enough.

Clover was a conduit too wide open.

Her clients adored her.

'After your tea,' Anita said firmly, and set about making it. She glanced at Ebony again. 'Where are they going?'

'Wellsford,' Ebony said, tapping her fingers against the arm of her chair now as she thought hard about what was happening. 'You know — Wilde Grove.'

'Wow. I'd love to go there. It sounds amazing.'

Ebony nodded. 'It is,' she said absently. 'It is an amazing place.'

She'd only been there once, but it had made an impression — Morghan had made an impression. She had been a

lot like Selena, but different too. Ebony had had stars in her
eyes every time she'd gazed in Morghan's direction.

'Anita,' she said now.

'Mmm?' Anita put the mug in front of Ebony and tipped
her head at the sound of the bell. 'I'd better get out front.
What is it?'

'Is Margie in?'

'Sure. She got in about an hour ago.' She paused. 'Do
you need anything else?'

Ebony shook her head. 'No. Thanks for the tea, Anita.'
She reached for it as Anita disappeared into the shop and
held it to her lips, letting the steam dampen her skin. Then
she stood up, walked through to the reading room and
checked the door for the Reading in Progress sign, saw it
wasn't there, and knocked softly.

'Come in,' Margie said.

Ebony cracked the door open and peeked in. 'Do you
have any time before your next appointment, Margie?'

Margie checked her watch, nodded. 'A good half an
hour, as it happens. It's always slow on Mondays.'

Ebony knew that, of course, and she slipped into the
room. 'I wonder if you'd give me a reading?'

Margie looked up at Ebony in surprise. 'Give you a
reading?'

'Yes. I'd draw the cards myself, but you know what it's
like — sometimes it's better if someone else catches the
vibes for you.'

'Of course, then. Take a seat.'

Ebony smiled her thanks and sat down opposite Margie
at the round table. She poked a finger at the cluster of crys-
tals on the table and brooded quietly.

'What sort of spread?' Margie asked, already shuffling the deck with practiced efficiency.

Ebony thought about it. She was tempted to get straight to the point with a three-card spread, but that might not give her some of the finer points of the situation.

'There's a challenge, a situation,' she said. 'I want to know what part I can productively play in it.'

Margie looked at her thoughtfully. 'All right,' she said.

Ebony nodded, tried to sit calmly in the seat, her gaze on the cards in Margie's hand. Margie used the Waite-Smith deck and Ebony didn't mind that at all. It was pretty much the classic, after all. She waited as Margie relaxed, shuffled, then laid out the cards on the table.

They both surveyed them without speaking.

'Well,' Margie said, brows raised. 'That's a lot of Eights.'

Ebony nodded. 'Eights are about overcoming obstacles, aren't they? Finding new paths.'

'Hmm.'

'What positions are they in?'

Margie began with the first card she'd dealt. 'This is the overarching issue. The one at the heart of what's on your mind.'

Ebony nodded. The Two of Cups. 'Harmony,' she said.

'Yes. Two parts of your life coming together, or the deepening of a relationship.'

Ebony glanced at the last card Margie had laid down, then forced herself to listen again to what Margie was saying.

She was pointing to the next cards. 'These next three I did simply as past, present, future.'

That had been what Ebony was afraid of. 'Past,' she said.

'Six of Cups. Harmony again, but in a bigger context. Contentment, roots.' She paused, thinking. 'The ancestors.'

Margie glanced at her. 'Perhaps,' she said. 'And now, moving into position representing the present, we begin our journey with the Eights.'

'Yep. We sure do.' Ebony buttoned down the sigh that wanted to escape.

'Eight of Pentacles in the present position. The need to develop a new skill set to deal with what is coming.' Margie glanced at Ebony, then moved to the next card. 'Eight of Swords in the future position. Restriction, often from the demands of others. But restrictions that you can overcome, yourself, if you use your head to face down your fears.'

Ebony's mouth was a tight, flat line.

Margie moved to the last card. 'I did a really simple spread for you — an overview, as you asked. So this Eight of Cups is in the position of the final outcome. The grand resolution of the situation, if you like.'

Ebony didn't like. Not at all. 'The Eight of Cups,' she said. 'Indicating moving away from a situation in a relationship...'

'Or matter of the heart — not necessarily a relationship.'

'Perhaps,' Ebony said. 'But it's certainly moving away to a new and difficult phase of things.' She pursed her lips. 'Or even accepting that some particular affair of the heart has run its natural course.'

Margie nodded, then, keeping her voice casual, asked the question that the cards begged. 'Is this about a love affair? Have you been seeing someone?'

But Ebony shook her head. 'Not recently, no. This isn't about a relationship — not one like that, anyway.' She pulled out her phone and opened the camera app. 'Do you mind if I take a snap of the spread?'

'Go for it,' Margie said, and sat back so that Ebony could hold her phone over the cards. 'Do you want to talk about this?' she asked. 'The situation behind these cards? Whatever you're going through, it doesn't look like it's going to have the happiest outcome.'

But Ebony shook her head, even as she smiled at Margie. 'Thanks, but I think I'm just going to brood on it for a while.' She laughed and put her phone away. 'Oh, that reminds me — Clover won't be able to do any of her bookings for the next...' Ebony thought on it. 'However long.'

Margie was alarmed. 'Clover?' she asked. 'Why not — is she all right?'

'She's fine, but she and Rue and Selena have to make an unexpected trip back to the UK.'

Ebony, standing, drummed her fingers against the table. 'In fact, would you be able to get the others together and divvy up her bookings, give the clients a call and see if they still want to go ahead?'

Margie nodded but she looked bemused. 'What's going on?' She sat back a little and narrowed her eyes at Ebony. 'Are you going too?'

Ebony sat down again. She should have known there was no masking everything in front of Margie who was used to reading people.

'Maybe,' she said.

Margie looked pointedly at the spread of cards on the table. 'I don't think it's going to end well,' she said, then frowned. 'This isn't talking about your friendship with Rue, is it? I'd hate to think that might break or change the way these indicate.'

Ebony shook her head, hair swaying, as she looked at the cards again. 'No,' she said. 'Or at least, if it does, it will only be as a side-effect of something bigger.'

'That somehow sounds even worse.'

Ebony laughed. 'There is movement in the flow of the world,' she said. 'That's what Rue has said that Clover has seen. Things are changing. Something may be coming.'

Margie nodded, but her face was bitter. 'Things are coming, all right. Changing — definitely. We can't expect to have ground Gaia to pieces without there being some conse-quences.' She blew out a breath and looked at the cards again. 'I don't see much chance of success here, if these cards are about bigger things, about the state of our rela-tionship with Gaia and all others who live here with us.' She looked over at Ebony with raised eyebrows. 'But we're going to try, aren't we?'

Ebony nodded. Looked at the last card, the Eight of Cups.

'Even if it breaks our hearts.'

10

Stephan flung himself down on a kitchen chair and wrestled with Burdock, who grinned a wide doggy smile and squirmed, trying to lick Stephan's cheeks.

'It's so good to have a day off,' Stephan said, giving Burdock a final squeeze. 'I feel like this is my first day off in six months.'

Erin laughed. 'Not quite,' she said, bringing a plate of buttered toast to the table and pursing her lips. She'd worked the whole weekend and now it was Monday and she was grateful to have the day off too. 'Do you know it's been almost exactly a year since I came here?'

She shook her head in wonder.

Stephan reached out an arm and gathered Erin to himself, so that she sat on his lap for a moment.

'A year?' he asked. 'A whole year?'

'Almost,' Erin said, and laughed when Stephan tugged on a strand of her red hair which hung loose down her back in a wild tumble.

'When is it exactly a year then?' Stephan asked, and he twirled the strand around his finger.

'Next Sunday.'

Stephan rested his head on Erin's shoulder, and Burdock pushed his nose onto her lap. 'We shall have to do something special, then,' he said. 'Something to celebrate.' He nodded his head slightly, breathing in Erin's scent and letting his eyes close in bliss.

Erin smiled down at him, and stroked his head, dropped a kiss on it. 'Do you have anything in mind?' she asked.

'Several possibilities.' Stephan looked up at her, drunk upon her scent and feeling the energy rise between them.

Erin laughed and smacked another kiss on his lips, before extricating herself from his lap, breaking the entwining rising of their energy. Burdock bounced back, ears alert, eyes shining. He loved it when his people laughed and played.

'We did that already this morning,' she said, blowing out a breath. 'It's a fine day — and I don't trust the rain not to come right back again. I thought we might do something outside. Go for a walk, perhaps.'

Burdock got even more excited. He knew the word walk. It was one of his very favourites.

Stephan groaned. 'Walk? I've walked about a hundred miles this week, what with finalising the rewilding plans for the far farm.'

'A drive, then?' Erin plucked up a piece of toast and bit into it, stepping around to the other side of the table to keep some distance between them so that she could think clearly. She closed her eyes in delight. She was getting good at baking bread.

Everything in fact, was good. She opened her eyes again and looked at Burdock, standing there with his goofy grin, then at Stephan, whose dark curls gleamed in the early morning light, and she looked around at the cottage too. Her cottage now, but still with her grandmother's artwork on the walls, and her plants hanging all through the place just as they had on the day that Erin had arrived.

On the day almost exactly a year ago that Erin had arrived home.

She closed her eyes, hugging her happiness to herself, then drew back to the matter in hand.

'A drive, then?' she said. 'I promised Mum I'd pick up some stuff for her if I went into Banwell this weekend.'

'Shopping?' Stephan asked dubiously.

Burdock's tail drooped. He knew that word too. It wasn't a favourite.

'No,' Erin laughed, seeing the twin looks of disappointment on man and dog. 'Just a quick pop in to pick up some more printer ink. I promise. Then we could go for a picnic or something.'

Burdock's tail gave a hopeful wag.

Stephan nodded. 'Sure,' he said easily. 'It's a plan.'

BURDOCK SPREAD HIMSELF AS BEST HE COULD ACROSS THE back seat and grinned, waiting for the adventure to begin. They'd done the shopping bit and now he was waiting for walk and picnic to happen. He wanted to stick his head between the two front seats, insert himself in the bubble of energy that surrounded and joined his two people, but he'd have to twist himself into an impossible knot to do it.

Stephan swivelled around in the passenger's seat and looked at him, stretched out to give him a pat, bringing their energy with him and spreading it over the back seat.

'All right there, boy?' Stephan asked. 'Not too squished back there?'

Burdock gave a woof in reply and licked his hand, grinned when Stephan laughed.

'It's not that bad back there,' Erin said. 'He makes out it's a lot worse than it is.' She laughed too, looking in the rear vision mirror and catching sight of Burdock smiling, tongue out.

'Let's have some music,' Stephan decided, leaning forward to turn the radio on. He punched the button and sat back, watching the road unspool as Erin headed for their favourite spot in the hills.

'Change the channel,' Erin said, when she heard the news being read. She was in the mood for music. The news was never good these days.

Then she shot out a hand and stopped Stephan when he moved to do so. 'Wait,' she said. 'Isn't that near here?'

Stephan dropped his hand and tuned in to what the newsreader was saying.

'Yeah,' he said once the newsreader had moved on to other topics. 'The Brunton Bank Quarry is just over the other side of the hill.'

'We should go see it,' Erin said with sudden conviction. She glanced at Stephan and shrugged at his surprised expression. She nodded, the hair on her arms standing on end. Her heart knocked against her ribs.

Stephan frowned, shook his head. 'Why, though?'

Erin touched a trembling hand to her chest. 'I think we

need to,' she said. 'The story touched a nerve for some reason. I want to know why.' She felt the certainty of her intuition rise in a flush up her neck and across her face.

She nodded. 'There's something there.' A frown. 'Maybe. I don't know. I just want to see it.'

Stephan held his hands up. 'Fine by me. If you're getting some sort of feeling about it, then I want to see it too.'

Erin nodded. Was silent for a moment, checking in with her body to make sure she wasn't reading the impulse wrong. She was getting used to the idea that intuition wasn't something that necessarily flooded her mind but was more involved with the sensations in her body. As though it knew some things before her brain did.

'We take the next road on the left, then, true?' She flicked the blinkers on, saw Stephan's nod out of the corner of her eye and made the turn.

They were at the quarry ten minutes later and pulling off the road, the Mini's tyres crunching over the gravel. Erin got out, stared up at the sky for a moment then shivered. It had clouded over, grown suddenly cold. It was certain it would rain again for sure, she thought, frowning up at the roiling black clouds directly overhead. Something about them bothered her, but right now, she couldn't put her finger on it. Erin opened the rear door for Burdock to unfold himself and climb out, then snapped his leash on him, glancing over at Stephan.

'I don't feel good about letting him run loose,' she said.

Stephan was gazing about. He nodded. 'This place is a bit spooky.'

They walked together across the parking area and over to the lip of the quarry. Stephan put out his arm.

'Don't go too near the edge,' he said. 'We don't know how stable it is.'

Erin's mouth was dry. 'I don't want to go near the edge,' she croaked, and looked out over the abandoned quarry. 'Can you feel this place?' She pressed her free hand against her ribs, felt her heart's sudden thumping.

Stephan nodded, silent, staring out over the ravaged land. The cuts were deep into the ground, narrow terraces going down to the bottom of the quarry that was three-quarters filled with water greener than any he'd seen before. The wind rippled the surface, and Stephan huffed out a breath.

'They're supposed to — the company who owns it — they're supposed to restore the land when they've finished with it.' He put his hand on Burdock's warm head. 'You know, actually turn it into a nature reserve or something. Not just leave it as this giant scar on the land.'

'What did the newsreader say?' Erin asked. 'The company's in liquidation, or something.'

Stephan nodded.

Erin lifted onto her toes and peered downwards then sank back onto her heels, her mouth downturned. 'What a terribly sad place to end your life at.' She shook her head. 'I can pretty much hear the land screaming.'

Stephan nodded again and felt a bubble of anger burst inside him. 'It shouldn't be left like this,' he said, hands clenching helplessly. 'Company going bankrupt or not, the council should do something about it. Someone somewhere should do something about it. Things shouldn't always come down to money.' He closed his eyes for a moment, took a breath, then looked at Erin. 'We should do something about it,' he said.

'We?' Erin dragged her gaze away from the deep gash in the earth and looked at Stephan.

Stephan planted his hands on his hips and nodded. 'Yeah,' he said. 'We should. Look, this place needs some major healing. I mean it's so hurt that it's drawing wounded people to it. What did the lady on the news say? It's become a suicide spot. Three people.'

'It should be fenced off,' Erin said, patting Burdock's head. He was pressing it against her leg as though he too hated the place.

He did. It smelt sour, unloved.

'By the company or the council? They'd argue about that one.' Stephan tilted his head so that the wind blew back his hair and he could look at the sky for a moment. Even growing dark with tumbling rainclouds, it was a better view than the ferocious gash in the ground.

He listened. 'Do you notice how quiet it is here?'

Erin tilted her head. 'There's only the wind.' She shaded her eyes. 'I can't see a single bird.'

'Or hear them either. This place is truly blighted.'

Erin had to agree. 'Perhaps we could do a healing ceremony or something,' she said.

'Absolutely,' Stephan agreed, catching onto the idea with enthusiasm. The thought that they might be able to relieve some of the earth's suffering right there in that spot made him keen. 'And light a fire under the council to do something about it,' he added.

'Good luck with that,' Erin said. She took a deep breath, let it out slowly, and steadied herself to make that slight sideways shift that Morghan had taught her, to see the quarry with a gaze that saw energy and spirit as well as the physical.

She'd been right, she thought, unable to stop herself from cringing away from the deep hollow in the earth, tugging Burdock back with her. 'It's screaming,' she said to Stephan. 'I can hear the land and it's so hurt.' Erin took another breath and risked looking again.

Something shimmered on the far ridge opposite them, and Erin straightened slowly, not taking her gaze from it. Burdock whimpered at her side.

'Stephan,' she said, her voice low, urgent.

'What is it?' Stephan asked, seeing the look on Erin's face.

Burdock whined.

'Shift a little,' Erin said, 'and look over there. Right opposite us, on the other side of the quarry.'

Stephan wanted to know what had drained the blood from Erin's face, but there wasn't any point asking. She'd already told him what to do, where to look.

He did it, a breath, and a sinking into himself, then a spreading out, and a slight shift, perhaps sideways, perhaps just *deeper*.

And he saw them straight away.

'What are they doing here?' he said, his skin prickling even as his spirit flared wider. 'Are they...?'

His question trailed off.

'I don't know,' Erin said. She lifted a tentative hand in greeting to the line of Fae ranged up against the opposite lip of the quarry. She couldn't make out their expressions with any certainty from this distance.

'They don't look very friendly,' Erin said.

Stephan raised his head from the bow he'd given them, and he finished his earlier question. 'Are they...our Fae?'

'I don't know,' Erin said again. She hadn't been to the Fair Lands yet. Macha had taken her far and wide through the Otherworld, but not there. That was, she'd said, Morghan's task to accompany her there and make the formal introductions. Erin was unsure why Morghan hadn't done so.

'There are more than one, right?' Erin asked. 'More than one...tribe, or whatever?'

Stephan nodded, keeping his vision as wide as possible so that he could still see the Fae. There were six or seven of them, he thought. 'They don't look at all happy,' he said, and reached out to touch Erin. 'We should leave, I think.'

Burdock whined again. He didn't like this picnic spot. The ground wasn't happy, and the whole area was too quiet. Nothing to nose about or chase here.

Erin bowed her head to the watching Fae then backed up another few steps. 'I agree,' she said.

It was a relief when they were back in the car, heading away from the quarry and the impassive, unfriendly gaze of the watching Fae. They were past Banwell and heading back to Wellsford, their picnic and hiking plans forgotten, before they spoke.

'That place was awful,' Erin said, and she gripped the steering wheel tighter. 'What I really want to know, though, was what were the Fae doing there?'

'And were they our Fae?' Stephan asked, then winced at his words. 'I mean, we don't really have our Fae, but...'

'We do, though,' Erin interrupted. 'The Grove has had

an alliance with Queen Alastrina and her court for centuries, since the beginning, I think.' She frowned at the road into Wellsford. 'I need to go meet her, the Queen. Morghan needs to take me; it's time.'

She glanced over at Stephan. 'I'm going to ask her to.'

'And we'll tell her and Ambrose about what we saw,' Stephan said. 'They probably ought to come out and see for themselves. They'd know which Fae people they are.'

'If they'd be there again,' Erin said.

Stephan gazed out the window as they drove slowly past The Copper Kettle and Haven for Books. Would the Fae be there again if they took Morghan and Ambrose to the quarry? His chest tightened and squeezed the breath from him.

'I think they would be,' he said. 'I think they have something to do with what's going on there. The coincidence is too great, otherwise.'

Erin looked over at Stephan, then accelerated past the turn down to Ash Cottage.

'I agree,' she said after a moment. 'Let's go and tell Morghan right now.'

11

Winsome tucked the blanket around the barely conscious man, keeping her hands gentle, her touch loving, her focus radiating from her heart.

Near the door, the young man's mum sobbed around her white knuckles, while her own mother had her hooked in her arms. Winsome glanced over at them, smiled serenely and gestured them over.

'I couldn't,' Tonya said around her knuckles. 'I can't watch him die.'

'You don't want him to go on his own,' Winsome said kindly. 'You've already done the hardest thing.'

The life support machines had just been turned off. The hiss and rush of the ventilator was silent.

'He's not supposed to be here,' Tonya choked out. 'He's supposed to be going to work today, just like normal.'

Winsome took her elbow gently and led her beside the bed, giving Esther, the grandmother, a warm smile.

'Be here,' she said to the distraught mother. 'Take his hand.'

She'd left it outside the blanket.

Tonya took her boy's hand. Winsome could hear her breathing slow.

'Now,' Winsome said, her voice low and kind. 'Let's take care of him one last time, shall we? You'll always be his mother, but you can take care of him one last time while you tell him how much you love him.'

Tonya's breath hitched and tears streamed down her face. But she clung to her son's hand, eyes searching his face, pale except for the bruises from the accident. 'I do,' she said. 'I do love him.'

'Tell him,' her mother said, taking the place on the other side of the bed. 'Let's tell him what a joy he made our lives.' Her gaze flickered from her daughter to Winsome, and Winsome nodded at her.

'Remember when he was, what, three years old, Tonya? And he decided to buy you fish and chips for breakfast?'

Tonia smiled through her tears, her hands clutched around her son's. 'He stole my purse, the little bugger, and walked down to the corner to the chippie. We couldn't find him anywhere — we were running around looking for him like we were headless chickens.' She found a breath. 'I've never been so scared.' Her voice dropped. 'Until now.'

Winsome put a hand on her shoulder. 'It's going to be all right,' she said. 'In the end.' She'd wrung out a soft cloth and pressed it into Tonya's hand now. 'Let's bathe his face for him,' she said.

Tonya took the cloth, looked at it a moment, then

nodded and bent to the task, murmuring to her son as she wiped it gently over his skin and around his swollen eyes.

'My darling,' she whispered. 'My dearest boy.'

Winsome stepped back, giving mother and grand-mother time to be with their love in his last minutes. She concentrated instead on holding space for them all, the egg-shaped cocoon she'd woven for them. Egg-shaped for the new birth about to happen, and for the brightness of the soul.

'We are blessed in this space,' she prayed, her voice low. 'We are blessed to have had this young man in the world with us.'

Tonya dipped the cloth in the basin beside the bed and wrung it out again. She cleaned behind her boy's ears, smoothed his hair back, wiped his neck.

There were tears in Winsome's eyes as Kai sat up in the bed and looked around, saw his mother and beamed at her. Then he saw Winsome looking at him.

'I have to go now, don't I?' he said, then looked back at his mum and gran. 'They're going to miss me.'

'You'll miss them too,' Winsome said.

He nodded, climbing from the bed and walking around it to put his arms around his mother. Tonya paused in her ministrations, straightened a moment, and Kai pressed a kiss to her cheek.

Tonya touched her fingers to the spot, fresh tears on her cheeks, and looked over at her mother. 'He just kissed me,' she said. 'I felt him.'

Her mother leant over the bed, and they joined hands, smiling through their tears.

Winsome was watching Kai, whose attention was turned toward the doorway. He glanced at her.

'I go this way?' he asked. Then he looked back at his mother. 'Or can I stay with her?'

'You could stay with them for a little while,' Winsome said. 'Until the funeral.' She shook her head. 'But no longer, since you would start taking energy from them to do it, and that wouldn't be good for them.' She looked at the doorway of light. 'The way won't stay open forever, either,' she said.

Kai blinked at her, appeared to think about it, and nodded before looking at the doorway made of bright, clear light. 'My Auntie Sue is there,' he said. 'I see her waiting for me.'

Winsome nodded. 'You can come and visit your mother and grandmother in their dreams.'

Kai perked up. 'I can do that?'

'Yes.' Winsome smiled. 'Of course.'

BACK IN WELLSFORD, WINSOME TUCKED HER DIARY BACK IN her desk drawer, studiously ignoring her computer, and sighed. Kai's passing had been beautiful and terrible at the same time — so much of the world was, Winsome thought.

She stood up, looked for a moment down at Cù, then shrugged slightly.

'I need some fresh air,' she said.

Cù stood up, for all the world like a real dog, and went to the door, slipping through the wood grain without a second look.

Winsome followed, but she had to open the door first.

It was windy outside, and Winsome tugged her jacket

tighter, did the zip up. She glanced behind the vicarage at the little path that led into the woods and onto Wilde Grove land, thought of Ambrose somewhere up there, then turned her face away.

She walked across the cemetery beside St Bridget's, putting out a hand to touch the old stones of the church.

'I miss you,' she whispered, but she was unsure whether she was talking to the building, or her faith.

There was another path into the woods and Winsome took that one, making a deliberate effort as she walked to relax her shoulders, to slow her breath, to put her consciousness back into what she called heart-space.

It was a relief to get out of head-space.

Head-space, Winsome thought, could be a very cluttered place.

She breathed in the secret scent of soil, of the trees, and let the breath of the woods, damp and chill as it was, calm her. Here, she decided, she could leave all the problems behind for a moment.

She could just be Winsome in the woods.

The idea made her frown with frustration. The problem with being just Winsome in the woods was that she was still Winsome.

How did Morghan do this?

Winsome shook her head. She knew how. She breathed out, letting the frustration spill out on her breath, and she dropped back down into her heart, leaving her head alone.

'All shall be well,' she murmured to the trees and the drizzle that had started back up, more mist than rain.

'All shall be well, and all manner of thing shall be well.' So Jesus had said to Julian of Norwich when she'd been troubled as to why there was sin in the world. Surely there hadn't needed to be? Winsome didn't know why there was sin either, why there was so much corruption in the world, but perhaps it was as Jesus had said to the 14th century anchoress. Perhaps it was necessary.

Winsome stopped at a tree, tall and slender, and placed a hand against it, tipping her head back to look up at its branches.

'Do you believe that, tree?' she asked. 'That sin — corruption — is a necessary thing?'

The tree shivered under her hand in a gust of wind and Winsome drew breath. 'No,' she said, dropping her palm from the bark. 'I don't think so either.' She gazed at the tree, brow furrowed. 'I don't think we come here to suffer. Look at you — what suffering were you made for when only a sapling?' She shook her head. 'None. We brought suffering to you, and we bring it on ourselves.'

With a groan, Winsome turned her feet to the path again, thinking of Julian of Norwich's visions of Jesus. 'Joy in every circumstance,' she murmured to another tree, this one younger, who bent with the wind to listen. 'For the reason that all things will eventually be put right by Christ.'

Well, she thought. That was a reason to live in hope, if not action. Although, she supposed, joy was an action, wasn't it?

On the other hand — and Winsome seemed to have many hands when she argued with herself like this — just hanging around waiting for someone else to fix everything, even if that someone else was Jesus, didn't seem like a recipe for contentment in the world.

She reached the clearing where the summerhouse stood

and paused on the verge of the circle where the grass grew lower, and the trees stood back.

Winsome considered joy again, how different it was from happiness, and how really, it stood on its own. Not joy because something would eventually make everything right, but joy for its own sake, brought to be from the simple love of the world.

'There,' she said. 'That's our true nature, the reason we're here.' Tears sprang to her eyes as she thought of Kai, who had crossed over that morning from one world to the next. Kai's mother was suffering, she thought. How did she answer that, then?

'She's suffering from love,' Winsome whispered, and looked up again at the trees. Did they suffer the loss of their leaves? Perhaps they did, she decided, for the tree letting go of its leaves would know change was upon it.

But it did it anyway.

Winsome sighed. She was tying herself in knots and not getting anywhere. Perhaps, she thought, there were some things in the world that could only be found through the heart — here, she touched a hand to her chest.

Perhaps, if she just sat there for a while, she would find her answers.

She stepped into the summerhouse, the small faux temple that Morghan had told her was built for the use of the vicar. Winsome still didn't know if Morghan had been serious when she'd said that, but she was well past caring about it. The summer temple, as she'd come to think of it, was the perfect place to bring a heavy heart and a teeming mind, even in autumn. She faced herself towards the east.

'Light of the world,' she murmured. 'Rise and I will be strengthened by you.'

She shuffled in a semi-circle to the south, where she imagined the rest of the world spread out on its globe, thousands of miles of land and ocean she'd never seen.

'Breadth of the world,' she said. 'Full of the shining lights of souls.'

When she turned toward the west, she could hear the beating of her heart over the wind and the misting rain and her own breath.

'Light of the world,' she said. 'Here is your outward breath, your rest. Let me rest also.'

Finally, she faced north again, standing in the middle of the small temple with its compass points on the floor, placing her at her fixed point in the world.

'Pole Star,' she said, the words barely more than her breath on her lips. 'Light the way, guiding star.'

For a moment, the world seemed to swing around her and Winsome stood with closed eyes, her hands pressed against her chest, flattened over her heart.

'Jesus forgive me,' she whispered.

When she opened her eyes, there was movement across the grass, between the trees, and Winsome stared at the woman standing there, the air around her shimmering as though she'd parted the mist of rain to peer through at Winsome.

Winsome licked her lips, taking in the woman's slight smile, as though the goddess knew what consternation she was causing and was amused by it. Her pig wandered around her legs, nose wrinkling, and then it stared at Winsome also.

With a flick of her wrist, something appeared in the goddess's hands, and she held it out to Winsome.

A small bowl, Winsome thought, then corrected herself. No, not a bowl. A cauldron. She swayed where she stood, her mind threatening to glaze over. A cauldron? For her?

To do what with? Make potions, bubble bubble toil and trouble?

Winsome shook her head, shuffled backwards. This, she thought. This was what she got for her pagan prayers.

This weirdness. Bubble bubble. Trouble.

The goddess — Winsome, faced with her again, with the strangeness that all but oozed from her — couldn't remember what Ambrose had called her, had said her name was.

The cauldron gleamed in the goddess's hands. It was the size, Winsome estimated, of her medium mixing bowl at home, the one that hadn't had so much use since the end of lockdowns. Much to the relief of her waistband.

It was also gleaming bronze or gold. Some sort of bright metal. With a curved lip and the little tripod legs that made Winsome very sure what she was being offered.

Because she was being offered it. The goddess held it out in front of her, eyebrows raised, lips curved in a small smile. When Winsome didn't budge from her place upon the compass in the summer temple, the goddess bowed her head, made a movement that made Winsome stare in disbelief, because had that been a wink?

A wink?

The goddess bent, set the cauldron upon the ground,

then turned and disappeared with her sow into the trees. The air shimmered for a moment longer, then faded.

Winsome's mouth was dry. She wiped the palms of her hands on her hips and looked around, dazed and bewildered.

Cù wandered over to where the vision of the goddess had set the cauldron down in the grass and sniffed at it. Gingerly, Winsome stepped from the small temple and walked stiff-legged to join him.

For a moment, the cauldron was there in the grass, gleaming in Winsome's vision. Then it too faded away, and she was left staring at the wet ground.

12

Ambrose shook his head. 'Go through it again.'

'There's not much to it,' Morghan said.

'Nevertheless.'

Morghan nodded, her arms folded over her chest as she stood beside Ambrose's desk and gazed out the window of Blackthorn House. 'It's not over,' she said.

'What's not over? You say Ravenna was spinning a blessing — but that is not such a big event, is it? What could you divine of the purpose of this magic Ravenna and the rest were doing?' His brows beetled over his eyes. 'And why would they need to weave a blessing out over the Forest House? Surely it was already a blessed place?' He closed his eyes considering it. 'As it is today,' he said after a minute.

Morghan turned her gaze to him. 'It is a protected place — we weave wards out over the land, but do we spin blessings as they were doing?' She shook her head.

'The land of Wilde Grove is blessed by the work you do

here, that we all do here, walking the worlds, singing the Wheel.'

'Mmm.'

Ambrose looked at Morghan in surprise. 'You do not agree?'

'I do,' Morghan said, and shifted on her feet, turning from the view of the trees outside Ambrose's window. 'Which is why I am left wondering about the necessity for such a large spell of blessing.' She shook her head slightly. 'But that is not what I meant when I said it's not over.' She paused for a moment, considering. 'I mean that — I think truly for the first time — it has really sunk in that my task here isn't over.'

Ambrose looked at her, then shook his head. 'Morghan,' he chastened. 'Haven't we really known that for the last year?'

His words made Morghan sigh, then laugh. 'Some things take a while to sink in, my dear friend.'

'Hmm.' Ambrose studied her face, nodded. And let the conversation go where Morghan wanted. 'Tell me, then. Why has it sunk in now?'

Morghan tucked a strand of hair behind her ear and leant against the window frame. She had used to live in this house. She and Grainne and Clarice, when Clarice had been just a little girl.

Such a long time ago. An age ago.

A different age was upon her now.

She shifted, shook her head. 'It doesn't matter,' she said. 'Only that the path has been most pointedly marked over the last year, that I decided I had to give up the remainder of my resistance towards walking it.'

Ambrose laughed. 'Measure your resistance,' he said, quoting Morghan's oft-said words back at her. He reached out and caught her hand. 'She won't be any less with you, any less beloved, because you move on.'

Morghan closed her eyes, squeezed his hand and kept hold of it. 'You understand.'

'Of course. Grainne was the light of both our lives. She was the sun around which we revolved, basking in her love and strength.'

'And wild stubborn determination,' Morghan said, lips curved. 'Ambrose, how I loved her. How much I loved her.'

'And she you. You held her heart.' He paused. 'You still do, you realise that, don't you?'

Morghan let go of his hand, nodded. 'We bound ourselves together,' she said, remembering. 'Made promises that would last past this one lifetime.'

'So,' Ambrose agreed. 'That bond exists no matter what your attention is turned to here and now.'

Morghan looked down at Ambrose, where he sat behind his desk, his face clear and encouraging. 'You've become very wise on the subject of love,' she said. 'Winsome loves you dearly.'

Ambrose nodded, but there was a slight frown between his brows. 'We do not need, I think, to forge the sort of bonds that you did with Grainne, but I would, I think, forge one of marriage here within the next year or so.'

'But that is marvellous,' Morghan said. 'She is sure to say yes.'

Ambrose's frown deepened. 'Is she, though? I am not so sure.'

Morghan cast her gaze around, sat down in the chair beside the desk and looked askance at him. 'Why so?'

'She is not reconciled yet that we are from such different paths. It has of course, only been a matter of months, but still, she seems to be going backwards not forwards on the matter.'

It was Morghan's turn to frown. 'I don't understand.' She thought of her conversation with Winsome only that morning. She had been afraid that Ambrose didn't see her clearly. Had Morghan misinterpreted it?

'She isn't comfortable yet with the village knowing we are a couple.'

Morghan almost laughed. 'Which they all do, assuredly.'

'She will not present it to them in fact, however.'

Morghan was puzzled.

Ambrose cleared his throat. 'She scuttles back to the vicarage early each time she stays here, so that if someone needs her in the village, it will seem as though she spent the night there.' He paused. 'I don't see how we will continue when she wishes our romance to be invisible.' He smiled slightly. 'We tell her she is the bridge between Wilde Grove and Wellsford, but I don't think she knows what that means.'

Morghan shook her head slowly, considering Ambrose's words. 'We do tell her that,' she said. 'What do we mean by it?'

They looked at each other in silence for a moment.

'It's very easy to say things,' Morghan insisted. 'Especially things that have a bit of a catchy ring to them. But we do need to be sure of what we're speaking of, particularly to Winsome.'

'She brought Grove and village together at Midsummer,' Ambrose said. 'It was her doing more than anyone else's.' He paused, looked seriously at Morghan. 'That is what we mean. Winsome is the one who shows the villagers that the Venn diagram between Wilde Grove and Wellsford has a rather large overlap.'

Morghan's lips twitched in a smile. 'You are right, of course,' she said.

'She is also the figure who will allow us all to walk together into the future.'

'She is?'

Ambrose nodded. 'You walk the worlds, Morghan, but she walks *this one*.'

This pronouncement stopped Morghan short thinking about it. She nodded slowly. 'Yes,' she said. 'It's true — she knows much more about the state of other people's hearts than I do.' She drew breath. 'You've given me something to think about, Ambrose.'

Ambrose sighed. 'As for pondering marriage, these are very early days yet, and something that time will sort out.' He straightened in the desk chair. 'Now, back to the real matter in hand. The magic that Ravenna showed you. What was it?'

'A weaving of blessing,' Morghan said promptly, even though she had already told Ambrose this. She took a breath and turned her mind back the path she had now vowed to walk.

But still. Winsome the one to walk them into the future?

It was an intriguing idea.

'Why was it necessary?' Ambrose asked.

'That,' Morghan said. 'I do not know.'

'But she showed you the weaving, and then the lighting of the beacons?'

Morghan went to answer, then paused, considering. 'First,' she said. 'First, she showed me the steps of a dance.'

Ambrose waited.

'And then she took me back and showed me the priestesses weaving their spell.' Morghan's gaze was unfocused as she looked inwards. 'The dance steps were the same as the weaving.'

'What does that mean?' Ambrose asked, confused.

Morghan shook her head slowly. 'I don't know,' she said. 'I'll have to meditate on that one. It's curious, now that I think properly upon it.'

Ambrose nodded, shifted in his chair. 'Do you want to keep discussing it, or shall we give it a bit of mulling-over time?'

Morghan shook her head and sighed. 'I wish we could just settle on some specifics,' she said. 'How to become the schoolhouse and the church. How to return the flow of water to the fountain. How to be the pear tree.' She raised her gaze to Ambrose. 'Perhaps Selena and the girls coming here will give us some direction.'

After all, they were entwined in the mystery and the task. Somehow.

ERIN PULLED THE MINI TO A STOP IN FRONT OF HAWTHORN House and sat there a moment, hand still on the handbrake as she stared up at the house.

'You all right?' Stephan asked.

Erin gave a slow nod. 'Yeah,' she said and looked over at

him, a wincing smile appearing on her face. 'I just still can't believe it sometimes, you know? Even though it's been a year now.'

'Almost exactly,' Stephan added.

'Almost exactly,' Erin echoed, her smile widening. 'I could never go back now,' she said, looking back at the house. 'Not now I know.'

Stephan touched her hand. 'You never have to go back. In fact, I don't think you can.' He squeezed her fingers. 'Once you know something, you can't unknow it. Not even if you wanted to.'

'I don't want to,' Erin said. 'And I'm learning to trust it.'

Stephan nodded. He'd watched Erin the last year learn all she could and had seen the magic grow inside her. Had grown himself, right alongside her.

'Those really were Fae we just saw at the quarry, right?'

Stephan answered with a firm voice. 'They really were.'

'Okay.' Erin opened the car door. 'Let's do this, then.'

ERIN TREMBLED SLIGHTLY AS SHE KNOCKED ON THE DOOR TO Hawthorn House.

'Are you all right?' Stephan asked.

Erin nodded. 'I was just remembering the first time I came here.' She gave a self-conscious laugh. 'It's a day for remembering, I guess.'

'Almost exactly a year ago,' Stephan said, touching Erin's arm.

Erin smiled. 'Right. I was so confused back then.' She barked a laugh. 'It took a long time for the confusion to go away. I'm not entirely sure it all has, yet — new things keep coming along!'

Stephan slid his arm around her shoulder and she leant into him a little as they waited for the door to be opened.

'Why, hello you two,' Mrs Palmer said, beaming. She had grown very fond of the couple. 'I'm afraid Morghan isn't here — you'll find her at Blackthorn House with Ambrose.'

'Oh,' Erin said. 'All right.' She looked up at Stephan. 'I guess we can go there, then?'

'You can wait here for her, if you like,' Elise said. 'But I don't know when she'll be back.' She shook her head. 'And of course her mobile's here on the table. She just will not get used to carrying it around with her.' Elise laughed and gave an indulgent smile.

'But she's at Ambrose's?' Stephan asked.

Elise nodded.

'Thanks, Mrs Palmer,' Erin said. 'We'll go there, then.'

They let Burdock out of the car, and he shook himself then stretched first his front legs then his back and looked up at them, ready to go wherever they wanted to take him.

They led him to the path through the trees and he grinned at the prospect of some good exercise after all. Erin and Stephan walked in silence, letting the sounds of the woods surround them.

'It's getting colder,' Erin finally said, shrugging deeper into her jumper. The wind rattled about in the browning leaves.

Stephan nodded. It was probably going to rain soon. Again. It seemed this autumn that rain was all it did.

'It's not as stormy looking here as it was back at the quarry,' he said, peering up at the sky through the trees.

Erin glanced up and saw he was right. 'I knew there was something off about the sky while we were there — the way those clouds were boiling about right over the quarry. The sky cleared as soon as we were away from it.' She looked over at Stephan, eyes wide.

'I agree,' Stephan said. 'It was definitely unusual.'

Blackthorn House appeared at last out of the trees and Stephan jogged up the steps and knocked on the door, turning to look back at Erin as he waited for someone to answer. His lips curled in a smile.

'What are you suddenly grinning about?' Erin asked, her mouth tilting to its own smile.

'You're beautiful,' Stephan said. He smiled wider. 'Your aura matches the colour of your hair.'

Erin rolled her eyes but couldn't help her laugh.

The door swung open, and Morghan was on the stoop. 'Good,' she said. 'I need to speak to you two. Come in.'

13

ERIN AND STEPHAN FOLLOWED, GLANCING AT EACH OTHER with raised eyebrows. Burdock flopped down on the doormat and thought about taking a nap while he waited.

'What is it?' Erin asked, stepping into Ambrose's study and not able to wait any longer.

Ambrose was standing behind his desk and straightened as they came into the room. 'Ah,' he said. 'This is good timing. You two really should be part of the conversation.'

'Everyone should be,' Morghan said. 'We need all the input we can get.' She shook her head. 'I can't do this on my own. I'm not even supposed to do this all on my own.'

Erin gazed from one to the other. 'Do what?' she asked.

'Oh,' Morghan said, answering Erin's question. 'It's the same old chestnut — how to open the teachings of the Ancient Way to the general public.' She pushed a smoothing hand over her hair.

'See,' Ambrose said, leaning forward slightly, his hands planted on his desk. 'That's where I think we're going wrong. We're not going to appeal to the general public.' He shook his head. 'We've got to find the people who are seeking, and speak to them.'

'How, though?' Morghan was frustrated and took a breath to calm herself. Months she'd been puzzling over this, and little progress had been made. There was an urgency growing inside her that couldn't be dismissed. Yes, they'd achieved a lot for Wellsford, and soon the new medical clinic would open and Wellsford would have its own doctor for the first time in a great while.

Krista and Clarice, along with Winsome and Veronica, were building up the Wellsford website, all their classes streamed on it, plus lots of articles on all aspects of living in community.

But it wasn't enough. Was it?

She pressed her hand against her chest. The urgency was there inside her, a feeling that was gaining weight and dimension.

That was growing.

It was only part of the equation.

Morghan paused in her thoughts, stood still for a moment, chin tucked down, eyes closed.

When she opened them, it was to look at Erin. 'Selena is coming home,' she said. 'Selena Wilde.'

Erin was startled and looked for a moment wildly about the room as though someone would burst through the door. 'What?' Erin shook her head, the feeling deepening into shock. 'Selena Wilde?'

'You've never met her, of course,' Morghan said, and she looked at Stephan. 'Nor you, I think. The last time she was here was six years ago.'

'Just before my time,' Stephan said, already bursting with curiosity. He glanced around the room. 'Doesn't she live in Australia?'

'New Zealand,' Morghan corrected. Her eyes flicked to Erin. 'She's bringing Rue and Clover with her.'

Erin's brow puckered. 'She's bringing herbs with her?'

'We have rue growing in the garden,' Stephan said. 'It's good for keeping mosquitoes away. And evil.' He grinned suddenly. 'It used to be used as protection against witches.'

'And the plague,' Morghan said absently. 'But no, in this case, Rue and Clover are people.' She looked at Erin. 'Priestesses of the Grove.'

Erin's chest now felt suddenly hollow. 'Priestesses of the Grove?' she said stupidly. 'You mean our Grove?'

'I do,' Morghan said. 'The original members are returning.'

Nonplussed, Erin glanced at Stephan, then looked back at Morghan. 'I don't understand.'

'Not the original members from this era,' Ambrose said, seeing Erin's confusion.

'Although they are members of the Grove,' Morghan reminded him. 'I gave both the leaves.'

Erin's eyes went to the Wilde Grove leaves Morghan wore dangling from a chain around her neck. Were those what she meant? Erin touched the egg that she wore on its leather thong. Why hadn't she been given the oak leaf and acorn?

Why had these other two, with the plant names?

'I still don't understand,' she said to Morghan. 'Wasn't Selena the Lady of the Grove before you?'

'Yes,' Morghan said.

'She doesn't know the story,' Ambrose reminded Morghan gently, smiling at Erin.

Erin's eyebrows rose and she glanced at Stephan. What was going on? Why this sudden mention of people she'd never heard of, except from Stephan, who didn't know them either?

Erin was unsettled.

It seemed she was left out of a lot of things. She looked back at Morghan. Perhaps Morghan wasn't used yet to having a successor right there with whom to share Grove business.

Maybe she should broach the subject with her.

Erin reminded herself to pause before reacting. She drew in a breath and nodded to herself. Next time she and Morghan were alone, then. She would speak calmly and clearly of it. Perhaps that would be a better time to mention the Fae at the quarry, and the fact that she thought it was time that Morghan took her to meet the Queen.

There was a lot going on.

She cleared her throat and looked at Morghan, who was standing in the middle of the room, head bent slightly, a frown over her grey eyes.

'I really would like to know the story,' she said, and didn't manage to keep all the iron out of her voice.

Morghan looked at her, surprised for a moment. 'Have I really never mentioned Selena and the others?'

'Never,' Erin said, and she shook her head slowly for emphasis.

It felt to Morghan like a small rebuke, and she wondered perhaps if she deserved it. 'This last year has been extraordinarily busy,' she said and nodded towards Erin. 'My apologies for not sharing more of our history.' She paused.

'And the last time Selena and the girls visited, it was for my wife's funeral. I have perhaps not liked much to think of it.'

Erin froze, and for the longest moment there was no sound in the room but for the fire Ambrose kept blazing in the grate.

Morghan cleared her throat and broke the silence. 'Let's sit down, at least, shall we?'

There was a small sofa by the fire. Erin and Stephan sat automatically upon it, and Morghan lowered herself into an armchair.

'Selena was the Lady of the Grove when I came here,' Morghan said. She looked toward Erin. 'I was seventeen when I arrived. I've told you that, at least.' She smiled slightly.

Erin nodded. She remembered the conversation. They'd had it only a few months ago.

'Selena left the Grove in 2005,' Morghan said. 'The wind had been speaking to her for a while, and her dreams showed a child in need. One whom Selena had promised to help if her aid was ever needed.'

Erin frowned. 'Promised who? The child? How?'

'The child's mother. There was a soul bond there.'

'Oh.'

'The mother had died and left two children — Rue and Clover — and they were struggling on their own. Selena left Wellsford to go and find them.' Morghan shifted slightly in her seat and gazed at the crackling log in the fireplace. The year had certainly turned, she thought, and Samhain would be upon them again in a matter of two short weeks. It had begun to seem to her that the season of death took up more and more of the year. She needed to give thought as to what they would do for it. Perhaps something different this year.

'She went all the way to New Zealand?' Erin asked.

Morghan drew herself back to the room and nodded. 'Yes. Originally, we had planned that it would only be for a matter of weeks, but that turned out not to be. She was required to stay.'

'She found the kids?' It was Stephan who asked this time.

'She did. Rue was fifteen and Clover only three. Extraordinary children, both of them.'

'Extraordinary how?' Erin asked. The way Morghan had said it made Erin's heart thump louder in her chest. She resisted pushing a hand against her ribs.

'Rue was taking care of both of them, on her own and under very difficult circumstances,' Morghan said, looking back at the fire and remembering when Rue had first come to the Grove. 'And Clover is profoundly psychic.'

Is, not was, Erin noted. Her skin prickled with sudden jealousy. 'In what way?' she asked, then cleared her throat. Her mouth was dry.

'She sees the world of spirit as if there is no separation.' Morghan closed her eyes while she spoke. 'She sees also the past.' Her voice took on a faraway, musing tone. 'And perhaps the future.'

'The future?' It was Ambrose who spoke this time, looking at Morghan in surprise.

Morghan nodded slowly. 'I feel an affirmation when I

think of it, yes. Perhaps it has yet to bloom.' She looked at Erin. 'But certainly she sees the past.'

'Like I saw Kria,' Erin said, and wasn't sure if she said it to seek clarity or as a reminder that she had also been able to step back into the flow of her history.

Morghan's voice when she answered was mild, and Erin couldn't tell if she'd caught the undercurrent or not.

'Yes,' she said. 'Very much like that.'

Erin nodded.

'Why are they coming here now?' Stephan asked. Like Erin, he'd decided their tale of the Fae could wait.

'The ancient priestesses are returning,' Morghan said. 'The time we are in has called them.' She paused. 'Us.'

Erin was confused. 'But that's right. Aren't we the ancient priestesses?' she asked, looking at Morghan. 'You and I — Macha and Ravenna.' She glanced at Stephan. 'And Finn too, he was there at the beginning of the Grove, along with Ambrose.' A wave of dizziness swept over her as she said Finn's name, and she swayed slightly in her seat. She groped out a hand to clutch at Stephan. 'I feel a shifting,' she said, gasping out the words before she fell.

She tumbled, over and over, until she didn't know which way was up and which was down, and finally, she looked around for the red thread, found it, and travelled down its length.

Erin stood, as Macha now, staring out at the circle of women, knowing she'd arrived finally at the right place.

. . .

'But we heard no word of your coming,' one of the priestesses said. Bryn looked around her sisters, then more pointedly at Rhian. 'Did we?'

'No,' Rhian said, and a frown marred her brow, for she should have known of this. She should have dreamt it. She groped around the memories of her dreams, searching, but could not find the forewarning.

Bryn spoke again. 'Most new priestesses come because they or their mothers apply for them to. They do not simply arrive unannounced.'

Macha stood straight, feeling the grime of travel on her, wishing for a bowl of warmed water in which to wash. She'd attempted to clean herself at the stream before making her way into the Forest House, but she'd run out of the cleansing herbs long before.

'And yet,' she said. 'Here I am. Come from afar, to be one of your number.' She looked at each of the women in turn, then swept her gaze back to the one that had named herself Bryn, and the lanky girl Rhian with the big dark eyes beside her. She felt their suspicion roll off them in waves as they looked her up and down, gaze taking in the braided and beaded reddish hair, the markings upon her cheeks and collarbone. Did they recognise that they were the same as Ravenna's? Was there to be jealousy over it? Here, where they should know better? Macha sighed inwardly.

She bowed, making the gesture tight, respectful. 'I travelled with my presence veiled to the Other Realms,' she said, giving them a reason they had not seen her coming. 'For safety's sake.'

'For safety's sake?' It was another of the priestesses, her voice sharp.

Macha straightened but inclined her head in acknowledgment of the question. 'Yes, for some faerie do not feel as friendly towards us as they used to. I wished no trouble on my journey.' She turned to Bryn and Rhian.

'I ask now for your blessing upon my arrival,' she said, 'that we might be well met and bond as new sisters.'

14

Rue paced up and down the airport by their seats, arms crossed over her chest.

'Sit down, for goodness' sake, Rue,' Selena said. 'It's like watching a pendulum going back and forth.'

Rue shook her head but stopped her pacing, then dropped her arms, shaking her hands to get rid of some of her tension. She looked over at Clover, sitting next to Selena. Clover had headphones on, and was hunched over her phone, involved in watching something.

'She's all right,' Selena said.

Rue nodded, shook her arms again. Right now, Clover was coping better than she was. All her shields were up, and the headphones and video helped her block out — to some extent anyway — all the noise around her.

'Centre yourself,' Selena said with a sympathetic smile.

'I can't,' Rue said. 'Or not properly, anyway.' She paused. 'This was just so sudden.'

Selena nodded. 'Become a tree,' she suggested. 'Roots

deep, trunk long and slender, resilient, able to bow and bend to changing winds.'

Rue stopped her urge to pace again and smiled down at Selena. 'Thanks,' she said. 'That's a good suggestion.'

She moved away, to tuck herself beside a large square column, out of the way, and closed her eyes. She took several deep slow breaths and let herself grow roots down deep into the earth to anchor her.

Rue shook off the thought that soon she would be thousands of meters up in the air, and dug her roots deeper. On another breath, she let herself sway slightly, feeling the flow of sap in her veins, the sinuous strength of her slender wooden body, then, finally, with a release of tension that felt almost like ecstasy, she saw her branches spread wide and leafy above her. She was young, strong, flexible. Her roots were deep and strong, her body resilient, her branches reaching for the sky.

Rue held the sensation for a long moment, breathing slowly, deeply, letting the tension run from her body, letting her breath connect her again with the truth of the world, then she opened her eyes, blinked for a moment, and headed back to where Selena and Clover sat, trying not to think how vulnerable a tree, even though deeply rooted, was to the bite of a coming axe.

'Ebony!' she said, momentarily discombobulated to see her crouched next to Selena's seat. 'You came to see us off.' Her mouth curved in a beaming smile.

Ebony looked up, then stood, and wrapped her arms around Rue, smacked a kiss on her cheek, then grinned at her.

'I'm coming with you,' she said.

Rue's eyes widened. Clover took off her headphones and looked up at her in surprise.

'You're coming with us?' Rue asked, trying to make sense of it.

'Yep. Got Anita to look after the shop, Margie and Tom to organise all the readings and clients, and there we go, Bob's your uncle, here I am.'

Rue was still shaking her head. 'But...'

Ebony looked at her, serious now, face implacable. 'I consulted with Athena,' she said, and thought too of the tarot spread, all the unrest in the world. 'She, in all Her wisdom, said this is a fight I ought to be a part of.'

There was silence after that as everyone thought about the word Ebony had used.

Fight.

Fight?

RUE GOT OUT OF THE DRIVER'S SEAT OF THE RENTAL CAR AND looked up at Hawthorn House, a bubble of gladness rising inside her. It had been a long time.

'Selena!' Morghan strode from the house, Ambrose at her heels, and embraced Selena. It put a smile on Rue's face, and she glanced at Ebony standing beside Clover. She reached out and held her sister's hand.

'And you three,' Morghan said. 'Such a glad sight for my eyes.'

Rue, Clover, and Ebony stepped into Morghan's embrace, and Rue could smell the wind and trees on Morghan — just like always. Morghan never seemed to change.

Except her hair.

'Morghan,' Rue gasped as they stood back. 'Your hair.'

Morghan lifted a hand to touch the thick grey braid and nodded. 'Grief turned it, I think.' She blinked. 'After Grainne.' She smiled. 'I'm used to it now.'

She didn't say whether she meant her hair or the grief.

Rue couldn't take her eyes off the grey hair. It had been dark, almost black, when she'd last seen Morghan. She felt a pang of her own sorrow.

'I still miss her,' Rue said, her throat thickening, and she looked past Morghan at the house. It wouldn't be the same to step inside Hawthorn House and not find Grainne there waiting for them, a wide smile on her lips.

'As do I,' Morghan said, and when Ambrose came to her side, the six of them held each other's hands for a moment, silent in shared acknowledgment for those who were missing.

'I wish I had been able to come for Teresa's passing,' Selena said. They hadn't even been able to come for the funeral, thanks to the travel bans that had come with the virus.

Morghan nodded. 'She would have loved you to be there.'

ERIN HESITATED ON THE STEPS AND WATCHED THE HUDDLE OF five women — not even four as she'd expected, but one more — along with Ambrose, share their grief for people she'd never met. One of whom was her own grandmother. She twisted her fingers into a knot and shifted self-consciously on her feet; she'd spent all day waiting nervously for this moment. Now it was mid-afternoon, and she didn't know what to make of the newcomers yet.

Ambrose turned at last and beckoned her down.

'Selena,' he said. 'This is Teresa's granddaughter, Erin Faith.'

Erin took a quick breath. 'Erin Lovelace Faith,' she corrected and got her hands untangled as Selena reached to take one.

'The resemblance is clear,' Selena said, gazing into eyes and at red hair that could only have come from Teresa. 'How pleased I am that you were finally found. Teresa's heart would be so glad at the sight of you.'

'I wish I'd been able to meet her,' Erin said, and forgot her awkwardness for a moment to look curiously at Selena. She had a calm, placid face, and eyes that gleamed birdlike with bright knowledge. Erin swallowed, nodded self-consciously, then saw the leaves that Selena wore on a long chain around her neck. The oak leaf and acorn. She glanced at the other three women, whose eyes were all sharp upon her, and saw they wore the Wilde Grove leaves too. All three of them, not even just Selena's wards.

It was only she herself who did not. Erin pressed a hand to the crystal egg that hung outside her dress. Why did she not have the leaves also?

Surely she ought to? She was to be the next Lady of Wilde Grove, after all.

So everyone said.

Rue and Clover, and the other, whoever she was, didn't even live in Wellsford.

But Rue and Clover were at least the other ancient priestesses, she thought, and made an effort to look unconcerned and welcoming. They were Bryn and Rhian. She'd met them in her unexpected shifting, and wondered if they'd done the same, slipped backwards to know who she'd been.

Erin stood straighter and tried to smile at them. She wondered if they'd ever become friends, Macha and Bryn and Rhian. They'd been priestesses together, so they must have. Erin felt for Macha's presence at her shoulder, but there was nothing.

Perhaps after all they never had become friends.

She dragged her gaze back to Selena and smiled. 'I'm happy I'm getting to meet you all at last,' she said, pretending that she'd known about them for longer than five minutes.

'And I you,' Selena answered. 'Very glad indeed.' She turned to Rue and Clover.

'Erin, I'd like you to meet my dear daughters,' she said.

Erin frowned slightly. Daughters? They weren't related to Selena, were they? Selena looked old enough to be their grandmother, not their mother. And that wasn't the story Morghan had told.

'Rue,' Selena continued. 'And Clover. And Ebony, who has been a friend to us for so long that she is also family.'

Rue, who looked to Erin's sight to be in her early thirties perhaps, nodded her head and smiled at her. 'We're glad to meet you,' she said.

'Thank you,' Erin said. 'How do you do?'

Rue's brows rose and Erin flushed. She shook her head slightly, then huffed out a breath and turned to the youngest in their cluster of women.

'Hello,' she said. 'You must be Clover.' The younger

woman was almost her sister's opposite, with blue eyes and dark blonde hair.

Clover nodded, but she was looking intently at Erin, studying the colours and impressions that surrounded her. She glanced over at Morghan, then back to Erin. 'You're going to be the next Lady of the Grove?'

Erin opened her mouth then closed it again. She nodded. 'Um, yes. Morghan has taken me on as her apprentice.' She paused. 'I've been here a year now.'

Almost exactly.

Clover looked at her for a minute longer and Erin shifted under her gaze. It was unexpectedly direct, and Erin remembered Morghan saying that Clover was — what had been the term she'd used? — profoundly psychic.

What was Clover seeing when she looked at her?

Feeling suddenly naked, Erin cleared her throat, gazed around awkwardly, and attempted a smile. 'I think I'll go help Mrs Palmer with the afternoon tea,' she said, and turned, almost running up the steps back into the house.

Rue stuck an elbow into Clover. 'That was a bit rude,' she said.

But Clover shook her head. 'Of course I'm going to be curious about the next Lady of the Grove.' Clover thought about the spirits she'd seen: red fox, black and grey raven. And the ancient priestess, Macha, who was very present with Erin, a constant shadow at her shoulder, Clover thought. 'We're going to have to work with her, after all.' She looked over at Morghan. 'But I'm sorry. Rue's probably right; I shouldn't have stared.'

Morghan nodded but looked at the open front door through which Erin had hurried in a flapping of skirts and red hair. 'She belongs here,' she said, glancing at Ambrose, then turning back to the others. 'I'm confident in my choice, even though she has had a late beginning.'

'I wish she'd been found while Teresa was still alive,' Selena said with a sigh. 'But I'm glad your efforts to locate her paid off.'

Morghan nodded again. 'Shall we get you settled in your rooms?' She took Selena's hand. 'You must be exhausted after the long trip to get here.'

ERIN, IN THE KITCHEN, HEARD THE MURMUR OF THEIR VOICES and pressed her lips together, concentrating on putting the correct number of cups and saucers on the tray. From the corner of her eye, she watched Mrs Palmer bustling about with freshly made biscuits.

'It's a big deal, isn't it?' she said after a minute. 'Their coming here.'

Mrs Palmer turned and beamed at Erin. 'It's been such a long time.' She shook her head and her face fell. 'Grainne's funeral. That was the last time they were here.' She looked down at the plate in her hand. 'An awful time.'

Erin paused, thinking about that. They'd known Grainne too. Of course they had.

Everyone knew everything more than she herself did. When she should have. She should have grown up in the Grove.

'But they've come here before that?'

Mrs Palmer perked up. 'Oh yes. Rue first came here as a young teen, when my mother still worked here. Selena brought her here for training. And Clover too, later.' She set the plate of biscuits on the tray and nodded, satisfied.

'What about Ebony? Who is she?'

Mrs Palmer broke into a grin. 'Ebony is here too? Oh, my goodness, that is wonderful. I wasn't expecting her.' She nodded, thinking about where in the house to put her. 'They're all part of the Grove,' she said. 'It wouldn't be the same without them, even if they do live on the other side of the world.'

Erin nodded, asked one more thing. 'Selena called Rue and Clover her daughters.' She looked helplessly at the housekeeper. 'But that's not the story I heard. Morghan didn't say they were related.'

Mrs Palmer laughed and patted Erin on the arm. 'Selena would have meant they were her daughters of the Goddess.' She laughed again and turned back to the tea things.

Erin felt her cheeks burn and, holding herself tightly upright and feeling as though made suddenly of glass, walked off down the corridor back to the main entrance. She stood for a moment looking up the staircase, realising that Morghan and Ambrose were showing everyone to their rooms.

They wouldn't miss her, she decided. The way that Clover had looked at her — as though she could see inside her, could see more of Erin than Erin could herself, unsettled her, and Erin made a swift decision, grabbed her cloak, and let herself out the rear door to quickly cross the terrace.

She skirted around the well, refusing to look down into its confusing depths, and hurried into the woods.

It wasn't until she was deep within their shadows that

she realised that she still hadn't told Morghan about the quarry.

Or the strange Fae lined up along its far side, unsettling and vaguely threatening.

Suddenly, it wasn't Macha's meeting with Bryn and Rhian in her shifting that Erin had echoing in her mind but something she'd not paid any attention to the night before.

Macha's words rang in her ears.

Some faerie do not feel as friendly towards us as they used to.

15

Winsome slipped through the doorway of Haven for Books and blinked as her eyes adjusted to the bright warm light in the shop. She glanced outside where the rain was holding off at least, but everything was grey, close, and there were dark clouds in the distance, over Banwell.

She sighed. They'd probably reach Wellsford before the day was done.

'Winsome! How are you today?'

She turned to see Krista beaming at her. 'I'm good, thanks,' she lied. The truth was that she felt jittery inside her own skin. As though someone were running a mild electric voltage through her nerves. She'd gotten up that morning from a restless night in her bed at the vicarage and even her calm routine of gentle yoga stretches with Veronica hadn't helped.

Not one little bit.

Krista was looking at her, a tiny frown marring her lovely wide forehead. 'Are you sure?' she asked.

Winsome grimaced, sighed. 'You have books,' she said. Then groaned. 'I mean, I know you have books — this is a bookshop.' She rumbled to a stop.

'What are you looking for?' Krista asked, letting herself smile. It was impossible not to love Winsome who so often found herself tripping up on her own earnest devotion to the world.

Winsome smiled at her and let herself relax. 'I'm in safe hands with you,' she said.

'You are,' Krista affirmed.

'Well, then.' Winsome turned her gaze towards the area of Haven where the woo woo books were. It was quite the growing selection.

Krista followed her gaze. 'What would you like to know?' she asked. Something was going on with Winsome. Krista could almost see the shiverings of the Otherworld over her.

'Ceridwen,' Winsome said, the word bursting explosively from her. She closed her eyes a moment, glad the shop wasn't busy right that minute. 'Ceridwen,' she repeated more softly. 'Do you have any books about her?'

Krista had tipped her head to the side. Ceridwen?

'Quite the goddess,' Krista said. 'Have you been seeing her?' She drew Winsome farther into the shop, smiling at old Hugh who was hoping for a spot in the care home, and had a fondness for road trip novels.

'Where's Minnie?' Winsome asked, suddenly remembering that the garrulous girl worked at Haven.

Krista glanced back at her. 'She's at school,' she said.

'Oh.' Winsome all but sagged with relief. 'I'd forgotten she still goes to school.'

'Well,' Krista said, winding around a table and coming to a stop in the part of Haven she thought privately of as the wisdom section. 'She goes when we make her. I have to keep threatening her with losing her job here if she doesn't keep going to school.'

Winsome laughed a little. 'That does sound like Minnie.' She sucked in a deep breath. They were in the woo woo section now, and Winsome gazed around at all the titles, the decks of cards, the small statues.

'Is that her,' Winsome asked, and raised a finger to point. Her hand trembled.

Krista followed her gaze and nodded. 'Yes,' she said. 'That's Ceridwen.'

'She has more animals than the pig.' Winsome was dismayed.

Krista nodded and looked curiously at Winsome. 'How did you recognise her?'

Winsome paused before answering. She could, of course, say that she'd seen a picture somewhere, or that Morghan had described her, or Ambrose. But this was Krista asking, Krista who helped Winsome with all manner of mostly technical, internet things, who came in sometimes and helped teach their computer class for seniors.

It would be unfair to lie to Krista.

'I've been seeing her,' Winsome said, and glanced quickly around the shop. Fortunately, the hour was quiet, the lull after lunch, and there was only old Hugh Jones, who was happily browsing his favourite shelves. Winsome could see the wireless AirPods snugged in his hairy ears, and knew they were a gift from Hugh's grandson, as was probably the phone that would be in Hugh's pocket, and the music playlist on it. Hugh was loved, and Winsome relaxed momentarily, looking at him and knowing that, feeling it in the easy slope of his shoulders.

'Winsome?' Krista touched her gently on the elbow. She'd plucked a book off the shelf and was holding it out.

'Oh, erm, sorry Krista. I'm all at sixes and sevens today.'

She'd been the same yesterday too, if she were being honest. After her vision of the goddess.

Ceridwen.

Winsome took the book from Krista's outstretched hand and looked at it. Her mouth went dry and when she tried to smile at Krista, it felt as though her lips might stretch and crack.

'Celtic Gods and Goddesses,' she read from the cover. 'History, Magical Power, and Healing Energies.'

Strangely, although her mouth was dry, her hands were hot and sweaty.

'You said you've been seeing her, been seeing Ceridwen,' Krista said, watching Winsome with a feeling of great sympathy. Winsome looked as if she were standing on the brink of a high cliff, wondering whether to scuttle back, or learn to fly.

'Yes,' Winsome said, and swallowed, dredged up her courage and determination. She reminded herself that she was the woman who had seen poor Robinson and his parishioners — and helped them.

And lost her job over it. She deflated again slightly.

Winsome sighed and shook her head. 'This has information in it about Ceridwen?' she asked.

Krista nodded. 'A chapter on her,' she said. 'But

Winsome, the best way to learn about her is to enter into a meditation with her.'

'She doesn't speak,' Winsome said.

Krista paused for a moment. 'Winsome,' she said. 'When you say you see her — what exactly do you mean? While in a meditation or a travelling?'

'No,' Winsome said, turning the book over in her hands but finding that her eyes were drawn back to the statue. The goddess on her knees stirring a great cauldron. The pig beside her. And a hen, and another animal Winsome thought might be a cat, or something similar. She couldn't tell from where she stood.

'No,' she repeated. 'She stands on the lawn or between the trees and looks at me — although I did first see her, I think, in a travelling. She told me a story, then, but hasn't spoken otherwise, not when she just appears to me as I'm going along.'

Winsome paused. 'But this last time, she gave me a cauldron.' Winsome held the book against her chest. She already knew she was going to buy it, take it home, and pore over the pages in the hope of finding out what she was supposed to be doing.

She knew, of course, that she could be taking this to Ambrose, but right now, it felt like something she needed to puzzle out on her own.

Krista was holding up a hand. 'Wait,' she said. 'She stands between the trees?'

Winsome nodded. 'By the Church. That when Morghan was having trouble with Blythe — you remember?'

Krista remembered. Of course she remembered.

Morghan might only have come back from her travelling because of the efforts of Erin and Winsome. 'The night Mariah, uh, disappeared.'

Winsome stared at the statue. 'Yes,' she said. 'That night. Also yesterday, at the summer temple.'

'The summer temple?'

'Oh.' She glanced at Krista with a quick smile. 'That's what I call that odd little summerhouse in the woods behind St Bridget's. I go there quite a lot, to pray.'

If you could call what she did there praying.

'I should be used to this by now,' she said, straightening and holding the book out to look at the cover again. 'Seeing things. Goddesses and so on.' She tried a smile for Krista. 'It's very Wilde Grove, isn't it? Sort of par for the course, so to speak.'

Krista nodded. 'Sometimes,' she said. 'Sometimes I think that the whole of Wellsford is within the magic that is Wilde Grove.' She laughed. 'Perhaps those first priestesses of the Deer Mother wove a spell over the whole area, and now we live in a sort of magic zone.'

Winsome looked at the statue and stepped closer to it, picked it up. It was surprisingly light. Not bronze at all as it looked but made from resin or similar.

Good, she thought. *That will be easier on my bank account.*

'That's exactly what this place is,' Winsome said, pressing a thumb over the word *awen* that was written across the cauldron. 'I had some...gifts, shall we say, before I came here, but coming to live in Wellsford was like stepping into the Twilight Zone.'

Krista laughed. 'We're all very glad you're here,

Winsome,' she said. 'Now, is there anything else I can help you with? I think Hugh is ready to make his choice.'

This elicited a deep breath from Winsome. She held out Ceridwen in miniature, and the book. 'I'll take both of these, but do you have a paper bag we can put them in? I didn't think to bring a bag.' She swallowed, her cheeks warming at the thought of trooping down Wellsford's main street with a statue of some ancient goddess tucked under her elbow.

'Of course,' Krista said. 'And let me know what you think of the book, and if you need to go deeper. I can easily source more for you.' She glanced at Winsome as she moved away to the counter.

'Although, of course, I recommend going deeper yourself, and not by book, but through your ability to see.'

Cù LED THE WAY BACK TO THE VICARAGE WITH HIS LONG THIN tail as high in the air as it ever got and a jaunty rhythm to his step.

'You seem pleased,' Winsome said to him, and he turned his head to look back at her, tongue hanging out, a grin on his face. 'Yes,' Winsome said. 'Definitely pleased. You lot won't be happy until I'm well into this morass of pagan woo woo, will you?'

Veronica was clattering about in the kitchen when Winsome closed the front door behind herself and her spirit dog and made quickly for her office, shutting that door too.

Where should she put the statue, she wondered?

Perhaps, she decided, eyeing the big wooden cross on the wall, not in there.

Out of her office she scuttled, sidling past the open kitchen door, then up the stairs and into the safety of her bedroom.

There was a cross on the wall in there as well, and Winsome stared at it, then shook her head, glanced at Cù.

'I'm not moving it,' she said.

He looked back at her, then went and lay down, for all the world as though everything was just fine.

Winsome heaved a breath, clutching the statue in its paper bag. The book was in her handbag.

'Everything is fine,' she huffed. 'It's only me being silly.' She drew in a fortifying breath. 'Right,' she said, striding farther into the room. 'We can do this, Winsome. We really can.' She looked around the room, assessing the flat surfaces for one which might do to put a shapeshifting goddess upon it.

A slightly out of the way corner, she thought. Something not necessarily in direct line of sight.

The paper bag crackled alarmingly as she drew out the statue and Winsome found herself glancing towards the door as though Veronica might come bursting through demanding to know what in God's name was going on.

Winsome rolled her eyes. Oughtn't she be past this, already? Hadn't she done a lot of work with Morghan? Hadn't she entered that ancient cave and gone walkabout in the Wildwood?

She'd done a lot. She helped the dead pass over on almost a weekly basis. For heaven's sake, she was sleeping with a wizard. A spirit dog followed her about wherever she went, silently judging her.

She should, by all rights, be able to do this next thing.

Winsome sat down on her bed, the statue in her lap. That was the trouble, she thought.

'It is the next thing.'

Cù perked his ears up, looking interested all of a sudden.

Winsome looked at him, then at the statue. 'It's not that I haven't done all sorts of things already, and gotten quite used to most of them.' She decided to give herself a break. 'And coped really rather well with it all.'

Cù wrinkled his forehead and Winsome nodded, cleared her throat a little.

'It's that this is like taking the next step.' She stared down at the likeness of Ceridwen. The statue managed to catch a little of that terrifying sense of timelessness and depth and magic that the real goddess possessed. 'I'm opening my arms to it, that's what it feels like,' Winsome told Cù.

That was what it felt like. 'An irrevocable step.' She looked over at the cross on the wall. 'I don't know how to reconcile these things,' she said. 'I don't know where this is all leading me.'

Cù got up and walked over to her, then sat on his skinny haunches and looked at her, head cocked slightly to one side.

'It is serious, isn't it?' Winsome asked him. She held up the statue. 'This. It's a serious business.'

Cù dropped his jaw and grinned at her.

'Well,' Winsome said in mock disgust. 'You're hardly the person to ask. You never take the slightest thing seriously.'

Cù's doggy smile seemed to widen and he got up again, crossed the carpet and flopped back down, stretching out this time, and just like a real dog, going to sleep.

'I guess the discussion is over,' Winsome murmured.

She got up, holding the statue in both hands, and placed it on the windowsill. Then paused, wiped the dust off the painted wood and replaced the statue.

'There,' she murmured. 'Now you can see outside.'

Winsome looked past the statue out over the church lawn towards the trees, half expecting the real Ceridwen to appear in a magic shimmer of the air.

She looked back at the statue, focusing on the cauldron. What did it mean that the goddess had given her a cauldron, she wondered?

That reminded her of the book, and she took it out of her bag and placed it on her bedside table.

Beside her Bible.

16

Erin took the path that would lead down and around to Ash Cottage. Morghan needed to know about the quarry and the Fae. She could barely believe she hadn't told her yet. Other things had got in the way, and everything had happened so swiftly.

Other things being the arrival of Selena with Rue and Clover. And their friend Ebony, too.

Each of them wearing the Wilde Grove leaves. Signs of belonging.

But she belonged too, didn't she?

Erin scrunched her eyes closed then blinked them open. Of course she belonged. She made herself stand taller, pushing her shoulders back.

She was a priestess of the Grove. Everyone knew it. No one could change it. And hadn't she been learning to walk the worlds? Morghan — and Macha — had been teaching her little else the last four months.

'I'll go back to the quarry myself,' Erin said to the trees.

'I'll ask the Fae who they are, what they're doing.' She nodded. After all, the Fae really were most likely part of Queen Alastrina's court.

The sudden decision made, Erin walked faster, and when she got to Ash Cottage, she slipped inside only to get her car keys and purse. Burdock was out with Stephan, so she didn't have to worry about him getting nervous or frightened.

It was cold at the quarry, the wind tugging at Erin's hood, pushing at her shoulders. Erin ignored it. She wasn't like Selena. She couldn't hear the wind speak.

Nor did water sing especially to her.

Perhaps the element of her affinity was earth or fire.

Perhaps, she thought, standing outside the car, and looking over the bleak landscape, it was time to figure that out. She tucked the idea away for later and braced herself to walk across the parking area towards the great hole in the ground.

For a moment, she wasn't sure if she wanted to do this after all. The wind pushed and howled, but it was the only thing Erin could hear. For the rest of it, there was nothing. She tilted her head towards the sky – no birds, just the dark brooding clouds.

Erin shuddered then and pressed back against the Mini. This place reminded her suddenly of Kria's glen, with its remorseless, ungiving land, and the dark steel of the loch. Erin squeezed her eyes shut.

'Shut up, shut up,' she hissed at herself. 'It's not the same place. And you aren't trapped here.'

The wind screamed laughter at her, and Erin's face crumpled. She fisted her hands to her temple, then drew in a shuddering breath.

This wasn't the glen, and anyway, she'd gotten out of there in the end, hadn't she?

Straightening, thrusting back her shoulders, Erin faced the wind, crunched across the gravel, and walked up to the edge of the quarry and took great gulps of air as she looked down at the deep green lake far below.

It was like looking down at the World Pool, she thought, except it had no magic to it, only pain. It was a pool of tears.

Erin looked for the Fae, doing as Morghan had taught her, and letting her spirit flow, her vision widen. She shivered in the cold wind, pressing her face skywards and taking that ever so slight step to the side.

Then screamed in fright.

The Fae stood in a loose circle about her.

Erin turned to look at each of them, her feet scuffing in the dirt at the edge of the drop. She pressed the palms of her hands to her cheeks, startled, eyes wide.

'Well,' one of the Fae said, a wide smile stretching over her face as she spoke, although her eyes were cold, the blue of frozen rivers. 'Who have we here?'

Erin glanced wildly at the group and opened her mouth. No sound came from between her parted lips.

'Do you not know your own name, then?' another asked, sneering.

Erin shook her head, then with an enormous effort, she thought of Morghan and straightened, pulling her hands from her face. 'I am Erin,' she said, and the wind snatched the words from her mouth and scattered them to the four corners.

She tried again, ignoring the weakness in her knees, the fizzing of fear that made her skin clammy cold under her clothes, that made the Fae shimmer in and out of her sight as she struggled to hold onto the change in consciousness.

'I am Erin,' she said. 'Priestess of Wilde Grove.'

The Fae looked at each other and burst into raucous laughter.

'You are no true priestess of your Grove,' the first said.

Erin looked at her in confusion, taking in the fine cut of clothes, the rich cloth, and her face, cruel behind the smile. 'What do you mean?' she asked. Then belatedly. 'Who are you?'

'We are emissaries of the Queen,' the faerie woman said, her mouth still smiling even while her eyes were ice. 'And you are no priestess of the Grove.' She pointed a long finger at Erin's chest. 'Where are your leaves? All you wear is a tiny chunk of quartz on a piece of string – and even that we can see barely belongs to you.'

They laughed again, lifting their chins so that Erin could see their slender throats.

'No one can think much of you if they don't even give you the symbols of a priestess.' The woman stepped closer to Erin, tilting her head lower to look her in the eye.

'I don't think they trust you yet, do they?' Her voice lightened, became musing, thoughtful. 'Your Lady of the Grove – shouldn't she have given the leaves to you long ago?' She tilted her head to the side. 'Haven't you been there – training, supposedly – for a year now.' She paused, cold, calculating gaze never leaving Erin. 'Almost exactly.'

Erin blanched. How had she known to say those words? Did they know everything about her? She pushed out her chest again, standing as straight as she could, trying to remember Morghan's lesson that a strong, straight posture made magic easier.

'There will be reasons,' she said, forcing the words out. 'That the Lady of the Grove has not presented me with them yet.' She paused before those sneering faces. 'I trust to those reasons.'

The Fae threw back their heads and laughed. 'No, you don't,' one of the ones to her side said. 'You've been asking yourself all morning why you haven't got them yet.'

Erin looked at him in shock. 'Stay out of my mind,' she said.

'Why?' This was the one in front again. 'When it's wide open to all, unprotected and desperate to spill your secrets, find some sympathy.'

'Who are you?' Erin stared around at them, took a shuffling step back from their sneering laughter, all the while trying desperately to pull a veil down over her mind.

How did she do that, though? While also keeping her spirit wide enough to see those taunting her?

She licked her lips. 'Who are you?' she demanded. 'You're not Queen Alastrina's people.'

Her question brought only more laughter, as though she was the most amusing person these Fae had ever had the fortune to come upon.

Erin wished she had not come to the quarry. But the way back to the safety of the car was blocked. She could feel the force of the faeries' personalities. It battered at her like a wind, almost physical, although invisible.

'Our kind cannot lie. But would you even know if we were Alastrina's kin?' The woman in the centre said. 'For you've not yet had the pleasure of visiting the Queen's lands yet, have you?'

There was more laughter from the Fae beside her, and Erin shrank back, dropping her shoulders, her head.

The great space of the quarry vibrated behind her.

It was true. Everything the faerie said was true. All of it.

Morghan hadn't given her the Wilde Grove leaves, had she? Erin closed her eyes, swallowed. But she'd given them to everyone else, Erin thought, remembering Rue wearing them, Clover too, the silver leaves on their long chains around their necks. Even Ebony, who was just a friend.

They belonged. They were strangers – didn't even live in Wilde Grove – and yet they belonged more than she did.

Me, Erin thought, clutching her hands together, bent over them. I'm still on the outside. I haven't met the Queen. Morghan hasn't taken me to the Fair Lands. I didn't even know about Rue and Clover until yesterday. She squeezed her eyes shut. Profoundly psychic Clover, who had looked her over like she was checking to see if she was up to the task.

The Fae's laughter surrounded her. Their close presence was a pressure, squeezing the breath from Erin's lungs, the thoughts from her head.

The thoughts she couldn't even protect from them.

How useless she was.

How utterly useless.

She wasn't up to the task, was she? And now she knew even Morghan didn't think so. Not really.

.   .   .

THE FAERIE WOMAN WATCHED ERIN WITH FASCINATION. Humans were so easy to manipulate. Inside them was always so much fear, and within easy reach. And weren't they lucky today to have a priestess of the famed Wilde Grove here.

She shook her head in amusement. The strength of the priestesses had declined with the centuries. Once, she remembered, they had been a force to be reckoned with.

'Oh, you poor thing,' she said, her voice syrupy with mock concern as she twisted the knife. 'No one really thinks you're up to the job, do they?' She straightened, smiling again, and this time her glee was genuine as she repeated Erin's fears. 'You haven't been to see the Queen because the Queen doesn't want to see you – she thinks you're the wrong choice. You don't have it in you to be a priestess. Not a real one. Not one with any power. You couldn't pass the initiation all those lifetimes ago and you haven't improved any since then.'

The words rang in Erin's ears and reverberated around her mind, growing louder with each echo. She shook her head, but crumpled to her knees even as she did, and ground her palms into the dirt.

'Isn't it true?' the faerie woman asked, her voice casual. 'Aren't I telling you the truth?'

Erin tried to rally. 'I passed my initiation this time around,' she said.

That got a hoot of laughter. 'What? That namby pamby thing in the cave? That wasn't an initiation, that was a performance put on to make you feel good.'

Erin stared at her, feeling the woman's words worm deep into her mind, shrill with insistence. They echoed there;

Erin couldn't get them out, and soon, the echoes were in her own voice.

'What did you say?' the faerie asked her. 'I didn't hear you.'

There were tears on Erin's cheeks now, her head bobbing up and down. 'Yes,' she sniffed. 'It's all true.'

'The fact is,' the faerie woman said, eyes gleaming as she drew the pièce de résistance from the puny priestess's own mind. 'No one really trusts you – not when you're apt to wander off into the mists at the drop of a hat.'

Erin squeezed her eyes shut, dropped her elbows to the ground and sobbed. There was no defending herself against the truth.

'You can feel that mist right now, can't you?'

Erin nodded. She could. It was all around her, pressing its greyness against her.

'Ah,' the faerie woman sighed. 'You'd best just do yourself a favour and crawl back into the mist now. You'll never be part of your Grove. Not really. Not truly. You'll never get the leaves, never meet the Queen.' Her smile widened, as she taunted Erin. 'You'll never be anything but the miserable disappointment you are.'

She watched the human girl grovelling on the ground and cast around for what would push her off the edge. For what was the taking of another human life? They were nothing but destroyers of everything they touched.

The world was better off without them.

'The edge is right behind you. It won't hurt, just a fall, and then peace.' The Fae sighed. 'An end to all your worrying. All your suffering. No more failure.' She contemplated the girl on the ground. 'No more struggling just to fail.

Someone more worthy will take your place. Someone who can do much greater magic than any of your puny efforts. Really, if you think about it, you owe it to them to move aside so they can take your place.'

The cluster of Fae laughed.

Erin heard their laughter and knew it was true – all of it. Morghan didn't trust her. That was why – the real reason – Rue and Clover had come all the way from New Zealand. Because Wilde Grove needed a Lady of the Grove to come after Morghan, and Erin wasn't up to the job.

Slowly, in the dirt, mind howling, Erin turned herself around so that her hands scrabbled at the edge of the cliff and the wind pressed against her face, her head hanging over the chasm. The grey mist crowded at the edge of her vision, waiting to swallow her like it always had.

She'd been kidding herself when she thought she'd seen the last of that.

Erin closed her eyes, wondered if she ought to crawl off the edge of the cliff or if she should stand, make her last gesture to the world upright at least. She struggled to her feet, unaware now of the Fae standing about watching her, avid speculation in their eyes. She teetered on the edge, thrust out her arms as though she might fly like a bird.

She would; she would fly, for a few seconds at least.

17

'Erin.'

A quiet voice at Erin's shoulder. She shook her head. 'No,' she said to Macha. 'They're right. I'm useless.'

'They're using your fears against you,' Macha said. 'Why are you listening to them?'

Erin turned her head slightly, her sobs making her voice thick. 'They're inside my head – which makes them right. I'm not strong enough. I'm not worthy; they're telling the truth.'

Macha hissed. 'They're tricking you, trying to destroy you. It's a game to them. Come back from the edge.'

'But...but they're emissaries from the Queen.'

'They are not our allies. Step back from the edge.'

Erin heard Macha's words and red-hot shame flooded through her body. She trembled on the edge of the cliff and almost let herself fall from it so that she wouldn't have to live with how easily she'd been taken in, how easily she'd let herself be convinced.

The Fae moved back, shaking their heads, chagrined to lose the small battle. A blink, and they vanished back into the folds of the worlds.

Erin shuffled backwards a few steps, and tugged in a great breath, raising her head to look around. The Fae were gone.

Macha was gone too. She was alone.

Erin pressed her hands to her cheeks, feeling the wet skin burning under them. She trembled, sickened by what had just happened.

How? How had she allowed it to happen? Why had she listened to their poison? Erin moved her hands to cover her eyes, the tears flooding again, this time hot, ashamed. When she finally dropped her hands, her shoulders still shook with her weeping. She looked out over the quarry, knowing that if it hadn't been for Macha, she would be lying at the bottom of it now, green water engulfing her, bones broken, eyes staring, lifeless.

Erin lurched across the car park, mind full of screaming white static, and she tugged open the car door with numb fingers, then climbed in and leant over the steering wheel to wait until she could remember how to drive.

The clouds let go and rain thundered down upon her.

Rue came into Clover's room, Ebony trailing behind her.

'It's so strange being here without Grainne.' Rue said, sitting down on the bed and plucking at the covers. 'I knew I'd miss her, but it's worse than I thought it could be. Our last visit, for the funeral, was such a blur, such a shock, that it feels like it existed outside everything else.' She shook her head. 'Now we're supposed to be back to normal, and it just doesn't feel that way to me.' She took a breath. 'And Morghan's hair. What must it be like to lose someone to whom you were bonded the way they were?'

'What was their story?' Ebony asked, flinging herself down on the bed and shading her eyes. She was exhausted. Aotearoa really needed to move a whole lot closer to the rest of the world.

'They were together over and over for lifetimes, I think,' Rue said. 'Although for a while, I think there was some sort of rift between them.' She frowned, then yawned. 'I don't know the whole story.' She flopped down beside Ebony. 'Do you, Clover?'

There was silence and Rue realised finally that Clover wasn't paying her the slightest attention. She sat up again. 'What are you doing?'

'Thinking,' Clover said. 'About Erin.'

Ebony spoke, her voice muffled from beneath her arm. 'Why did she leave?' she asked. 'I thought we were going to have afternoon tea together or something.'

'She left because Clover was rude to her,' Rue said, narrowing her eyes at her sister. Then shook her head. 'Teresa's granddaughter.' Rue smiled and sat up on the side of the bed. 'I can hardly believe it. What a shame though that Teresa never got to meet her.' She heaved a heavy sigh. 'I don't know if I'm going to enjoy our visit, you guys. With both Grainne and Teresa gone, it's just not the same.'

Clover turned away from the window. 'We're not here to enjoy ourselves.'

Ebony let her arm fall away and dragged herself to a sitting position. 'Why are we here?'

But Clover shrugged. 'To follow the path,' she said.

Rue sighed. 'I wish the path was signposted.'

There was silence between the three of them for a minute.

'Clarice is still here,' Clover reminded Rue at last, wanting to give her something.

Rue's lips curved in a smile. 'That's true at least. I'll be glad to see her.'

'I didn't mean to be rude to Erin,' Clover said, turning back to the window, from which she could see the spread of lawn and the shimmering ghosts of Erin's footprints where they still lingered. A new skill, seeing them. Clover glanced at her sister and Ebony, then decided she wouldn't mention it. She wanted to talk about Erin, not just her footprints.

'She has Fox spirit with her.'

Ebony laughed. 'Well, that suits her red hair.'

'Fox is good at camouflage and concealment,' Clover said. 'Of moving between the seen and unseen. Fox is a shapeshifter.'

Rue nodded. 'That is not a bad thing. I still wish you hadn't frightened her off. We came here to find our strength together, didn't we?'

'She shouldn't have been so easily scared,' Clover said, but she was regretful too, and she sighed and turned away from the window. 'I wish I could turn it off,' she said.

Rue didn't need to be told what Clover meant. 'I wish you could too.'

'I'm never going to have a normal life, am I?' Clover frowned, then answered her own question, remembering the sight of Rhian, and Blackbird's words. She turned her face away from Rue, so that she wouldn't see her expression. 'I'm not going to have a normal life, and even if I had been able to, the time for it is past now.'

They were quiet for a while, Clover's words hovering like clouds in the room. Ebony stirred finally, shifted the subject slightly.

'What I'd like to know, is what exactly is coming. I feel like we're going into this blind.' She remembered her Tarot spread, but that did nothing to help.

'We are,' Rue said.

Clover pressed her lips together. Outside, the day was clouding over, not spring here but autumn, the days shortening, compressing. Darkening. 'We'll see soon,' she said. Then quoted Blackbird. 'The flow in which the worlds are woven.'

Ebony looked sharply at her. 'What does that mean? What are you talking about?'

Rue nodded. 'Good question. What are you talking about, Clover?'

Shaking her head, Clover didn't know how to answer. Not properly. When they'd gone downstairs earlier and joined Morghan for a cup of tea, Morghan's mind had been on how the Grove was to become a shining light in the times ahead, and Clover hadn't liked to say anything about her last vision. She'd been too tired for starters, and they were catching up, not talking strategy.

They'd moved on quickly from the topic too, to more personal things. What the last six years had been like. Rue's business, Ebony's. Her own, the readings she had been giving. Selena's work helping Rose, their police detective friend, with her missing and murdered.

Morghan's eyes had grown bright and round at that. She'd known, of course, from her intermittent conversations with them all, that Selena had been helping the police in their investigations, but she'd been comically astounded at how deeply involved Selena had gotten.

She'd worked now on several high-profile cases, but always in the background, of course. The police didn't want advertised the fact that they used a psychic as part of their investigative procedures.

Rue interrupted the flow of Clover's thoughts. 'What do you mean?' she repeated.

Clover frowned. 'What did I say?'

Rue shook her head. 'Something about the flow in which the worlds are woven? Sounded just a little ominous.'

'Oh. I don't know,' Clover replied. 'But I think we're about to be caught up in something, that's all.'

Ebony groaned. 'We've got that much. What we want to know is – what is it? What are we about to be caught up in?'

'Something we started thousands of years ago,' Clover said, then sighed. 'I wish Erin hadn't run off.'

'Been scared off,' Rue said.

Clover's mouth flattened. 'She shouldn't scare that easily. She ought to be stronger than that.'

Rue lay down again, yawned and turned on her side. 'I'm so tired. I hate that long flight.'

Ebony checked her watch. 'It's the middle of the night at home.'

'It feels like it.' Rue closed her eyes, then shifted over when Clover came and stretched out beside her.

But Clover's eyes stayed open, even as her vision was turned inward, even as she brooded over Erin, who was supposed to be the next Lady of the Grove.

She wished Erin had stayed with them at Hawthorn House. She had a bad feeling about her.

'IT FEELS ALMOST MIRACULOUS THAT YOU'RE HERE,' MORGHAN said, gazing over at Selena.

Selena heaved a sigh. 'I'm sorry we didn't come over sooner,' she said. 'That we haven't visited since Grainne's funeral.'

They sat in the armchairs by the window, just as they had all the years ago when Selena had been young and Morghan her apprentice. Morghan looked at the third chair around the small tea table and thought of Annwyn.

'The tide always moves on,' she said. Lifespans were short. Often too short.

Selena shook her head. 'Yes,' she said. 'It does, but that's not to say that no detritus is washed up upon the shoreline during the low times.' She leant forward in her chair, pushing her fatigue aside and really looking at Morghan. 'Tell me how you've really been.'

'We've spoken and written to each other,' Morghan pointed out. 'Plenty in the last few years.'

Selena nodded, relented a little. 'True,' she said. 'But it seems different now that you're right in front of me.' She raised her eyebrows. 'Your hair, for instance. You never told me about that.'

Morghan resisted the urge to raise a hand to touch her hair. 'It's only hair,' she said.

'A very outward symptom of your grief.'

'Yes.' Morghan drew a breath, thought about Grainne. 'Grief learns to live with us,' she said.

'Don't you mean we learn to live with it?'

'Do I?' She shook her head and now she did lift her hand to touch the hair that had once been silky and dark, and now was coarser, silver. Grainne had liked to pluck her hair undone at the end of the day, laughing as the great tumble of it fell from its tight bun.

Morghan closed her eyes.

'It seems to me,' she said, looking now out the window at the clouds that bunched up once more above the trees, threatening more rain. 'That grief is a thing that moves into your heart and life and sets up residence, seeking out all the spaces it may fill.'

Selena was silent a minute. She nodded. 'You might be right,' she said. 'It builds whole rooms for itself and lives in them an inside out life, rubbing along with us uninvited.' Her lips twitched. 'It doesn't listen to eviction notices either.'

Morghan smiled. 'The uninvited guest,' she said. 'Whom you get so used to, they seem almost a friend after a while.'

'True,' Selena sighed.

Morghan looked at her. 'Have you decided what to do about Jakub?'

Selena's face broke into a wreathing smile even as she thought about his recent letters, asking her to come to him in Poland. 'Jakub?' she asked and laughed with pleasure. 'There isn't anything to do about Jakub. My situation is little changed from twenty-five years ago when our love was fresh.'

Morghan looked at her for a beat, then nodded. 'I've set up Apple Tree Cottage as a retreat for you while you're here,' she said, knowing how much the tiny cottage had played a part in Selena's love affair with the Polish wood-cutter Jakub, all those years ago when she, Morghan, had first come to Wilde Grove.

Selena flushed with pleasure. 'That was fast,' she said. 'I do thank you, though.'

'It isn't tenanted,' Morghan said. 'And much the same as it always was. Elise freshened it up, had wood and supplies brought in.'

Selena nodded. 'It will be nice to visit it again, but we need, I fear, to be looking forward, not back to the past.' She was regretful even as she said the words. The past, even with its tragedies, was known.

Morghan sighed and tipped her head back. 'Tell me about Clover and Rue's visions.'

'They saw Rhian and Bryn,' Selena said.

Morghan nodded. 'I was shown them too.'

'Rhian was in the cave preparing for some sort of large and ambitious magic, and Bryn was on the lawn of the Forest House, with Ravenna and the others, waiting for something to happen.'

'Something?'

Selena shook her head. 'We don't know what.' She paused, considered, then spoke. 'But it was enough to bring us here. The feeling of it – something beginning that needs to be continued.'

'Yes,' Morghan said, and she gazed out the window again, this time looking at the blue tinge of the wards that she and Ambrose kept up over the grounds of Wilde Grove.

They shimmered slightly in her vision, even in the heavy grey light.

'Ravenna showed me the magic they were weaving.' She shook her head, eyes still fixed on the wards. 'But it was a blessing spell.' Now, she turned to look at Selena, glad again to see her old mentor and teacher. She raised her eyebrows. 'Why a blessing?'

It was a puzzle. 'We were waiting for something to happen, and to spread our magic wide in a net over the land around us. To spread our blessing.' Morghan paused. 'This is what is giving me some trouble. Why a blessing, when for so long now, we have been spreading protective spells over the Grove. Protection, not blessing?' She shook her head. 'It gives me much food for thought.'

Selena nodded, but she had something else she wanted to tell Morghan before she gave in to the jet lag. 'Clover,' she said. 'Her kin have told her that her vision is to widen even further, that she is to wade out into the weave of the worlds. They told her this after her vision of Rhian in the cave.'

Morghan blinked, leant back in her chair. 'To do what?' she asked. 'Wade out into the weave of the worlds – is that even possible? – and to do what?'

'That,' Selena said, keeping her voice steady. 'That is what we don't know.'

18

CLOVER SHIFTED ON THE BED AND SAT UP. SHE LET GO A SLOW breath; Rue and Ebony were both asleep, sprawled against each other, exhausted from the long flight.

Clover felt the jet lag pinching at her too. But she couldn't sleep. Not until...

She eased herself from the bed and bent to pick her shoes and her jacket up, creeping about the room on the balls of her feet. She didn't want to wake Rue up, didn't want to tell her she was going outside to look at ghostly footprints.

Rue had been her saviour, keeper, protector, all these years, and at the expense of her own personal life. She'd rarely dated, had concentrated on Clover and her business.

Clover felt bad about it, that she took up so much of her sister's energy.

She made it to the door and turned back briefly to look at Rue. Still asleep. Good. Sometimes, Rue had a second sense about Clover, always seeming to know when something was going on with her.

This, Clover suspected, went back to their early days, when it was just the two of them, and only Rue's ingenuity keeping them alive.

She let out another breath, that shuddered in her chest, and slipped out the door, closing it behind her as quietly as possible.

Perhaps, she thought, stealing down the hallway towards the stairs, perhaps it was time for Rue to stop feeling responsible for her. Maybe, Clover considered, it was time she herself grew up and stopped needing her sister.

She was glad of her jacket when she stepped outside. Emerging suddenly into a bleak and damp autumn, with winds that knifed through the trees, was a shock after the growing warmth of spring back home, fickle as it often was.

Clover moved to the edge of the terrace and squinted towards the tree line, looking for Erin's footsteps. She couldn't see them from this vantage point, of course, but still – she felt that she could almost see something, a shimmering of energy, perhaps. This thought made Clover frown, for shouldn't it have dissipated by now?

How long had it been since Erin had taken off across the lawn and into the woods. Clover checked her watch, which she wore on a leather strap around her wrist. She'd discovered years before that if she wore a watch that touched her skin, it stopped working after a matter of days.

And she didn't like to carry her phone everywhere. Her phone, with its addictive YouTube app was only for when she wanted to learn something, or block the world out by opening up the window to the virtual one.

She didn't even need to use it to call Rue, although she generally did.

She huffed out a breath. Whatever, she thought. She was stalling and made herself step off the terrace and walk across the lawn where it sloped down to the trees. Erin had been gone an hour, two at the most. Definitely her energy should have dispersed by now – or so Clover would have thought, if anyone had asked her to think about it.

But was that true? She thought now of tracker dogs. Couldn't they find scents from someone who had passed by even a week ago?

'Great,' she muttered. 'Now I'm a psychic dog.'

'Clover!'

She turned, saw Morghan striding across the lawn towards her.

'Can I join you?' Morghan asked when she was close enough.

Clover nodded, glad it was Morghan. She could tell Morghan about the footprints.

'Are you all right?' Morghan asked, looking at her.

'Tired,' Clover said. Her brow wrinkled. 'And puzzled about something.'

Morghan could see that. It was in Clover's aura, nothing that Morghan could have pinpointed if asked, but more of a sensation within it.

'What are you puzzled about?' she asked.

Clover paused, then turned and pointed to the footprints. 'These,' she said, and glanced back at Morghan, hoping helplessly that Morghan would be able to spy them also.

Morghan looked. She didn't see anything. 'What are they?' she asked.

'You don't see them?' Clover asked, then sighed and shook her head. 'I hoped you would. I'd like someone else to see the things I do.'

Morghan touched Clover gently on the elbow, and energy flared for a moment between them. 'Open my eyes,' she said. 'Tell me what you see.'

Clover looked at her in sudden hopefulness. She'd felt the sizzle of energy between them, and she touched her elbow at the spot where Morghan had. 'How did you do that?' she asked.

Morghan held up her hand for Clover to see and Clover narrowed her eyes a moment, then widened them in surprise.

'It's gleaming like it's gold,' she said. 'I didn't see that before.'

Morghan looked at it, turning her hand this way, then that. 'The Queen did it,' she said. 'A few months back.' She checked herself. 'Almost a year ago now, I suppose.'

'What did she do?' Clover couldn't take her eyes off Morghan's hand. 'It's like what, King Midas's hand?'

Morghan laughed. 'You know that old story?'

'Tara read me all the fairytales from her childhood. For a while they were all I wanted to hear at bedtime.' But Clover shook her head again and reached out her hand towards Morghan's, fascinated. She withdrew it again and looked at Morghan.

'May I?'

Morghan nodded and held out her arm. The gold reached about an inch up her wrist.

'She cut off my hand,' she said. 'The Queen. I went to visit her one day, and she took me to a temple and before I had a moment to know what was going on, she grabbed my arm, laid it on the altar, and lopped off my hand.' Morghan paused, bemused by it still. 'She threw my own hand to her hounds and gave me this one instead.'

Clover was astonished and lifted her gaze from the golden hand to Morghan's face. 'And I thought I had weird stuff happen to me,' she said, wonder in her voice.

Morghan laughed. 'No,' she said. 'Weird stuff doesn't just happen to you.'

Shaking her head, Clover marvelled over the story Morghan had just told her. 'I'm glad I came here after all,' she said impulsively. 'I finally don't feel like the only freak.'

She heard the words come out of her mouth and reared back, her hand flying to cover her lips. 'I'm sorry, Morghan – I'm sorry; I shouldn't have said that.'

But Morghan just laughed, and the wind settled in the trees nearby. 'Don't worry,' she said. 'I can understand the sentiment.'

Relieved, Clover nodded. 'I still want to touch it,' she said.

Morghan held out her arm again.

'Feels just like skin,' Clover said, wonder tinging her voice. She flattened her palm over the back of Morghan's hand. The world swirled suddenly around her.

She gasped, tried to focus on Morghan. 'Is this what happens,' she said, her lips numb, tongue thick, 'when you touch someone?'

Morghan took a slow deep breath and shook her head. 'Not usually like this.'

Not to this extent.

It was dizzying, the way the world swung suddenly around her, the trees, receding then moving forward as though their roots no longer anchored them. The ground under her feet seemed to grow farther away as though she herself stretched then came back to size. Clover's fingers went to slip from her own.

'No,' Morghan forced herself to say from between numb lips. 'Don't let go. I want to see what happens.'

A feeling had wormed its way inside her. A whisper of a voice that told her to hold on, to look.

To see what could be seen.

And then, just like that, like an elastic band snapping, her vision flicked into place and the world steadied. Clover's hand gripped hers.

'This is it,' Clover said, and her voice was full of wonder, a trill of sound that Morghan saw float on the air for a moment, coloured shapes that fluttered then dispersed as though on a breeze.

Morghan licked her lips. 'This is what?' she asked.

Clover shook her head but answered anyway. 'This is what's always really here.'

'Ah.'

'There, look,' Clover said, and she pointed to Erin's footprints. 'Those are what brought me out here. I could see them.'

Morghan looked. The footprints shimmered upon the ground, and she knew that's what they were, although they weren't really the shape of a footprint. More like...Morghan tried to think of a way to describe them to herself. More like a signature, she decided.

'They're everywhere,' she said, surprise swelling her voice, making her words round like bubbles on the air before they burst and vanished. 'Look.'

Clover turned and gazed back over the lawn. There were tracks crisscrossing the grass everywhere. She glanced wide-eyed at Morghan, then back at the ground.

'There are mine,' she said, and she traced them across the grass, around the well, and back towards the terrace. 'And yours. I can see yours.'

Morghan nodded, but she was curious. 'How do you know they're mine?'

Clover considered the question. 'I don't know. I guess, they just feel like you.' She pointed to another set. 'Those are from an animal,' she said, lips curling in a smile. 'A cat.' She shook her head in amazement. 'This would make tracking easy, don't you think?' She laughed, bewildered and excited.

Clover turned back to look at Erin's prints. 'Do you see Erin's?' she asked Morghan.

Morghan nodded. To her expanded vision, there was no mistaking them as Erin's.

'She was upset,' Clover said. 'I knew it anyway, but I can see it in her prints.' She glanced at Morghan who nodded. 'I upset her.'

'It's hard feeling on the outside,' Morghan said, and squeezed Clover's fingers. 'That was what really upset her.'

'I stared at her. I couldn't help it – she's one of us, one of the Forest House priestesses.' Clover gave a tight shrug. 'I wanted to see, you know? If we'd liked her.'

Morghan thought of Erin's own vision from the evening before. Macha's arrival at the Forest House, the less than warm welcome she'd gotten from the other priestesses. It wouldn't have helped matters, from Erin's perspective.

'We shall find our way together,' she said now. 'That's what is important; that we negotiate the coming weeks, months, and years in alignment.'

She looked up at the sky then, and gasped.

'What?' Clover asked. 'What is it?' She followed Morghan's gaze upwards.

'Oh,' she said.

Morghan tightened her grip on Clover's hand, unwilling to let go, for her vision to return to normal until she'd had a chance to take the sight in properly.

'What are they?' Clover asked.

Morghan lifted her other hand, traced the bands of colour that shimmered in the sky. 'The dark blue,' she said, then glanced at Clover. 'Do you see it as colours?'

It didn't pay to take anything for granted.

But Clover nodded, so Morghan continued. 'The dark blue weavings – they are the wards that Ambrose and I place over the Grove twice every year.'

Clover recognised them. 'But why?' she asked. 'Why do you put them there?'

Morghan paused, because that was a good question, wasn't it?

'For privacy, mostly,' she said after a minute. 'Because for so long, most of our practices have had to be in private.' She considered it. 'There was a need for concealment.'

But had that ever worked? Was not it almost a game for village teenagers to creep up on solstice nights and watch the dancing, to see if they could see the faeries that came to dance with them?

Many of them could.

Morghan thought then of Mariah. Winsome had told her the village's story, about Mariah doing just that, as a girl of eighteen.

She forced her mind back to the matter of the wards that covered the sky overhead in a shimmering translucent spell. 'They keep unmoored spirits out, also, so that I am not constantly hounded by them.'

But what of the weaving behind it, so ancient that it was only the merest glimmer in her vision? She thought she probably would have missed it altogether if she hadn't, only the other day, seen it being spun.

'Do you see the one behind it?' she asked Clover. 'Pale silver blue. Just the barest hint of it left.'

Clover looked, searching through the layers of energy so that she almost grew dizzy and held Morghan's hand tighter to steady herself. Then she nodded. 'Yes,' she said. 'I see it.'

She examined it, searching for the meaning to it, the purpose imbued within the weaving.

'What is it?' she asked. 'It's not a ward. It's something else.' She blinked, shook her head. 'And old.' But familiar. Almost. 'The Forest House,' Clover said. 'I can almost feel Rue's energy in it.' She glanced at Morghan. 'And yours.'

It was true. The faint magic had strands in it from them both.

It was fascinating.

'What is it?' Clover asked.

'A blessing,' Morghan answered, gazing at the ancient magic. 'Not a ward over the Grove, but a blessing. And I cannot figure out why.'

Clover turned her attention to Morghan. 'But surely a

blessing would, like, make sense, I guess? This is kind of a sacred place, after all.'

Morghan nodded. 'Yes,' she said. 'In that context, certainly. But from our visions, this was a major undertaking. A piece of magic that was prepared for and had a meaning bigger than I'm able to see.' She pursed her lips a moment, puzzling away at it.

Clover turned and looked again, nodding slowly. 'This is what you all were doing while I was in the cave.' She gazed at the pale, almost forgotten weaving. 'But why?' she asked.

'Why would a blessing be such a big deal?'

She left her next question silent in her mind.

What was she doing then, in the cave?

19

Erin's phone buzzed with an incoming call. She sniffed, swallowed, looked to see who was calling her, even as she knew it would be Stephan.

He would be able to feel her upset.

She answered the call, spoke straight away. 'I'm all right, Stephan,' she said, trying to make her voice lighter. 'Everything's okay.'

She listened to him for a moment, not really hearing what he said. 'I'm all right,' she repeated. 'I'll tell you what happened when you get home. But it's no big deal, I promise.'

She ended the call and stared out of the window, realising finally that she was still at the quarry, and suddenly, she wanted to be a million miles away from it.

Shuddering, the tears still wet upon her cheeks, Erin started the Mini and pulled away down the road from the quarry. She didn't know if she could ever make herself go back there. The last half an hour hung blackly in her mind; she could feel it there, a stain upon her.

She hesitated at the turnoff to Wellsford, her hands tight around the steering wheel. She thought of turning the car in the opposite direction, away from the village and Grove, away from Morghan and Stephan and everyone else she felt she would never be able to look in the eye again.

She considered, idling at the turnoff, pulled slightly off the road, where she should go instead. There was the flat in the city — she could go there. There was even her old home; her father still lived there, his girlfriend moved in with him now, or at least spending more nights there with Vincent than not.

Erin closed her eyes, drooping against the steering wheel again.

A rapping against the driver's window made her jump. She stared at the face bent down to look at her, not recognising it at first, her mind going blank, filling with the white static again.

Then recognition came, and she pressed the button to lower the window, her hand shaking.

'Are you all right, Erin?'

She drew in a great shuddering breath, then to her consternation, burst into tears.

Jameel walked around the car, opened the passenger door and slipped into the seat. 'Erin?' he said, shaking his head. 'What's happened?'

But Erin couldn't stop the flood of tears. She covered her face with her hands and shook her head.

Nodding, Jameel made his voice soothing. 'Never mind,'

he said. 'Seems like you need a good strong cup of tea or coffee and a friend to talk to.'

Erin moaned softly and bent forward in the driver's seat as though she would curl up into a ball. The Mini jerked forward slightly, and Jameel moved the gear to neutral.

'Come on,' he said. 'Let's pull your car off the road, and you can come back to mine for a bit. Until you feel better.'

Erin lowered her hands and eyed him.

He put his hands in the air. 'You don't even have to tell me what's wrong. You can just take a minute.'

Erin squeezed her eyes shut for a moment. They were raw from crying. 'What about Henry?' she asked. 'I don't really want to see anyone.'

Jameel smiled. 'Henry is at work for hours longer yet. It'll just be you and me and Arooj.'

'Arooj?'

'Our new kitten. She's the cutest button you've ever have laid eyes on.' Jameel looked at her. 'Say yes. I can't leave you here like this.'

Erin sniffed. Nodded finally. 'Okay.'

Jameel's face broke into a wide smile. He pointed out the windshield. 'Park over there. It'll be safe enough. I can bring you back when you've had enough of petting Arooj, although that might be never, come to think of it. She's very sweet.'

Erin nodded, only hearing half of what Jameel, Henry Block's husband, was saying, but she understood his tone of voice. It was soothing; she clung to it and followed Jameel's instructions to pull the Mini off the road.

. . .

'YOU WANT TO TALK ABOUT IT?' JAMEEL ASKED, SETTING A HOT tea in front of Erin and sliding onto a stool at the breakfast bar next to her. He'd turned the lights on in the kitchen, since it had grown grey outside with the rain. 'I promise I'm a good listener. No judgements.' He pushed the cup a nudge closer and nodded. 'I can imagine you're under a lot of pressure right now.'

Erin looked up from the kitten in her lap. Arooj was just as lovely as Jameel had said, and he was right – it was calming to stroke the small and purring animal. Erin still felt pale, and as though she'd been sucker-punched, but at least the tears had subsided to a slow leaking.

'Pressure?' Her thoughts were jumbled. She didn't understand.

'With Morghan teaching you,' Jameel said. 'Expecting you to take things over one day.' He leant back and shook his head. 'Not sure it's a job I'd want, with the world the way it's heading.'

'Heading?'

Jameel sighed. He was probably taking the conversation in the wrong direction, only it was always on his mind these days. The weather had always been a topic of conversation in Britain, but now there was so much more to say about it.

He gave an elegant shrug. 'The world's going crazy, with the weather, with the people. I've never seen so much acrimony between people; throw climate change in there – things will only get worse.' He paused. 'With Morghan asking what we will be doing to help, how we can open up the Grove, well, it's bound to be a weight on your shoulders especially.'

Erin stared at him, then frowned, dropping her gaze

back to the cat. 'I hadn't really thought about it like that,' she said, her voice barely more than a whisper. 'I don't know if I'm even the right person for the job.'

The taunting voice of the faerie woman echoed in her mind.

'Morghan seems to think you are,' Jameel said, wondering if they were sidling up to the real issue. He felt perhaps they were. 'We all know she's training you up to be the next Lady of the Grove.'

Erin nodded. She looked down at the small cat in her lap, and its purring seemed unbearably sweet, and Erin was afraid that she was going to cry again. What she really wanted to do now, she thought, was go home and go to bed, pull the covers over her head and sleep for the next hundred years.

'Erin,' Jameel said, giving her a fatherly look and reaching out a hand to touch her gently on the wrist, pull her back from wherever she'd done inside her head. 'Let me help?'

Lifting her tear-stained face to him, Erin shook her head. 'There's nothing you can do.' She sniffed and managed a sad smile. 'But thank you. Your caring is lovely.'

'I do care,' Jameel said. 'We all do – you're part of the Grove now, Erin. One of us, and we look out for each other. To me, that's the biggest part of what the Grove is. Humans who care about each other and the world.'

Erin's face crumpled and she squeezed her eyes shut tight in an effort not to let the tears fall. She seemed to have a deeper reservoir of them than she ever knew.

'What's happened?' Jameel asked. 'Something's happened. I can tell.'

Erin concentrated on the kitten's tiny purring body, feeling it vibrate with every breath under her hand. She took a great shuddering breath of her own.

'I saw some Fae over at Brunton Bank Quarry,' she said.

Jameel frowned. 'Brunton Bank? But hasn't that place closed?'

A nod from Erin. 'Stephan and I, the other day, we heard on the radio that there has been a spate of suicides there, so we went to have a look, in case there was something about the place that made it a hotspot.' She blinked, cleared her throat. 'Something...other, you know?'

The frown on Jameel's face deepened but he didn't interrupt, feeling that Erin was on the verge of telling him why the tears hadn't stopped tracking down her pale cheeks since he'd first seen her in her car on the side of the road.

Erin sniffed, took another shuddering breath. 'We saw some Fae there, and meant to tell Morghan about it, but she's been really busy with Selena and Rue and Clover, and we never got to.' Erin paused, hung her head. 'I decided to go back on my own this afternoon.'

Jameel raised an eyebrow but opted still not to say anything. He was glad suddenly to be in the gleaming kitchen in the flat he shared with Henry, all their favourite things around them, the thick walls and double glazing keeping the world out.

'They were there, the Fae,' Erin said. It was something of a relief to tell Jameel. 'I did the spirit flexing thing so I could see them, and they were there again.'

She wound down, unwilling to say much more. Wondering if she should have kept her mouth shut. But no, Stephan knew about the Fae, so soon everyone would.

They'd never know what they'd tried to do to Erin, though. She'd never tell anyone. Not that they'd almost convinced her to throw herself off the edge.

'They were from our Queen's court?' Jameel asked at last when it became clear Erin wasn't continuing the story.

Erin paused, shook her head. 'I don't know.'

'What happened?' Jameel asked, the implications of Erin's revelation reeling in his mind. He leant forward over the breakfast bar and ducked his head to see Erin's face. She was so young, he thought, and so upset. Something had happened.

'Something happened,' he told her.

Erin took a great shuddering breath. 'They frightened me,' she said and lifted watery eyes to meet Jameel's then flicked her gaze back down to the cat.

Jameel straightened. This was a lot more serious than anything he could have thought of on his own. 'Are you hurt?' He looked her over again, but there were no rips or tears in her clothes. There was dirt on the fine fabric of her skirt – he'd already seen that, but nothing more.

'I'm not hurt,' Erin said, but even as she said it, she knew it wasn't true. They had wounded her. She could feel it, in her heart, a great gaping hole there where they had torn away her dignity, her sense of safety, and her gladness in her path.

She didn't know if it would ever heal. Or even if it ever could.

Shame reddened her cheeks.

Perhaps she'd would be like this from now on, walking around with a hole inside her while horrified and embarrassed that she'd ever let happen that which had.

She should never have let the Fae get to her the way they had done so.

She'd almost jumped. She'd almost thrown herself over the edge.

That was something she couldn't tell anyone. Ever.

'I need to go home,' she said, a shaky smile on her face. 'Stephan will be getting home soon.'

She didn't know how she was going to face him. Stephan would know straight away that there was a hole inside her now, a quarry-like chasm inside her into which she felt she could still fall.

Was falling.

Jameel gazed at her in consternation. 'You'll tell him what you saw?' He paused. 'And Morghan?'

Erin nodded, looking down again at the kitten curled up asleep in her lap. She wished she could be like the little cat, comfortable, trusting, at peace.

But her composure had been shattered, perhaps forever. She lifted her head and gazed around Jameel and Henry's beautiful kitchen. It was sleek and modern, very different to Ash Cottage, and Erin found herself wanting the scent of woodsmoke, the small cosy rooms of her home closed protectively around her. She pasted on a smile again.

'I should get going. Thank you for the tea, and the listening ear.' She nodded. 'It's helped.'

But Jameel was still looking at her in consternation. 'These Fae,' he said. 'Do you know what they were doing there?'

Erin stood up, the kitten in her arms stretching, blinking up at her with big blue eyes. She shook her head.

'I think they were there to make anyone who came along...' She paused. Shrugged and turned her face away.

'Kill themselves?' Jameel shook his head slowly. 'That's what you said, wasn't it – what you and Stephan heard on the radio?' Shock ran through him, turning his blood cold. 'Erin,' he said. 'What on earth were you doing going back there on your own?'

20

'Everyone's coming,' Veronica said when Winsome had made it down to the kitchen. She glanced at her and stopped, holding a plate of biscuits over the table. 'What's the matter?'

Winsome flicked a glance around the room. 'What do you mean?'

'Your cheeks are all pink.'

Winsome pressed the palms of her hands against the offending cheeks. 'I'm warm, that's all,' she said, then dexterously changed the subject. 'Who's coming?'

'Everyone. Remember the meeting you missed? It was decided we'd continue the conversation this afternoon.'

'Oh.' Winsome nodded. 'What's it about, again?'

Veronica put the plate down. 'Where's your head, Winsome?' she asked. 'You know what's on the agenda.'

'Right,' Winsome said, trying her best to dial back into the happenings within Wellsford and not just think about spirits who appeared from nowhere to give you gifts of magic cauldrons. 'Right,' she repeated, then, more brightly, 'what can I do to help?'

'You can take these biscuits through,' Veronica said, frowning at the woman she considered a friend as well as mentor. It had been a tough few months, feeling like the world was not after all the place she'd forced it to be, but Winsome had counselled her through it, with common sense and good humour. She'd also given her a place to stay and work to do.

And surprisingly, Veronica thought, she was enjoying being in charge of the charity shop, and it was actually making her look more broadly at the issue of surplus clothing and there being far too much of it, while simultaneously striking deals to bring better stock into the shop in the first place. Wellsford was a pretty nice place, but they couldn't stock the shop themselves, and just wear each other's clothes in a never-ending circle.

Anyway. Veronica was fitting surprisingly well into Wellsford, aided by the fact that right from the beginning Winsome had told her she would feel better if she did something that would benefit more than just herself. Surprisingly, and perhaps alarmingly, considering her background, it was proving true.

Veronica thought about the photograph she kept upstairs in a frame, the one of her as a kiddie, with her grandparents – and the seaside monkey, of course. She thought of it, then smiled, and looked at Winsome.

'I'm excited by the ideas we've been throwing around,' she said. 'I'll be glad to make some decisions.'

'Are we ready to make decisions?' Winsome asked.

Veronica narrowed her eyes at her. 'Are you feeling all right, Winsome?'

'I saw her again,' Winsome blurted, not knowing she was going to do so. Not, in fact, having come downstairs with any determination except to do the opposite and keep quiet.

Now Veronica stood with the kettle in hand. 'Saw who?'

'The mysterious goddess or spirit or whoever, who appears to me every now and then,' Winsome said, sitting down and hanging her head. 'She gave me a cauldron. What am I supposed to do with a cauldron?'

Veronica opened her mouth, then closed it again. She frowned. Of course she knew that Winsome saw spirits. Claimed to see spirits anyway.

'A cauldron?' she asked.

'Yes,' Winsome said. 'Me, a vicar, or retired vicar, at least, got given a cauldron by an ancient goddess.'

To Winsome's surprise, Veronica laughed, throwing back her head and cackling like this was the funniest thing she'd heard all year.

'Why are you laughing?' Winsome said, scowling at her.

'Oh god,' Veronica said. 'Just go with the flow, will you? You're shagging a wizard, I'd have thought you'd have to expect an ancient goddess would take a bit of an interest in you. Just be glad it's not the devil or something.'

Winsome shuddered. 'The Dean – of the Church, that is – wants me to retire away from Wellsford into a Church community.'

Gosh, Winsome thought. She hadn't meant to say that, either.

Veronica stared at her, then very quietly turned and filled the kettle, switched it on. She'd already gathered the cups and saucers and so on, ready to take through to the big room at the front of the house where they'd have their meeting.

She checked her watch. Everyone would be arriving in a few minutes. Julia was always early, slinking in the door to claim a corner in which to stand like a wallflower.

She sat down opposite Winsome while the kettle began its steaming.

'Tell me,' she said.

Winsome took a deep breath. 'It's what I just said.'

'Yes,' said Veronica, who sometimes marvelled that a woman so obviously wise when it came to other people's issues, could be so unsettled by her own. How did that even work?

'Yes,' she repeated. 'But I don't understand what you mean by it. Retire away from Wellsford?'

'Yes.' Winsome shifted on her bottom. 'I am still, technically, a vicar, just a retired one. And while I've been given this house for a year, the Dean has decided, in his wisdom, that it would be better for me...'

'Better for you?' Veronica interrupted.

'Better for everyone, were his exact words,' Winsome said, Dean Morton's email seared on her brain.

'Okay.' Veronica ignored the boiling kettle, which switched itself off anyway. 'Carry on.'

Winsome nodded, cleared her throat. 'So, erm, better for everyone if I retired somewhere else.'

'Somewhere else?'

'Yes. Exactly.'

'Away from Wellsford?'

'He says the county team are concerned by my demeanour.'

Veronica's eyes widened. 'You have a demeanour?'

'That causes concern, apparently.'

'I want to hear more about that,' Veronica said. 'But tell me first, since we've only about thirty seconds, where it is exactly that they want to farm you out to?'

'A place in Yorkshire,' Winsome answered faintly.

Veronica stared at her. 'And they can do this?'

'Yes,' Winsome said, even more quietly.

'I think we need to put Wellsford on the map,' Cynthia said, then looked around the circle. 'We've a lot of marvellous people here, doing quite wonderful things, but no one can do anything except over the internet, which is very useful, I admit, but wouldn't it be nice if we could have people actually come to us?'

There were a lot of nods, Winsome saw. 'What are you suggesting?' she asked, feeling a bit breathless inside. She hadn't meant to tell Veronica, who was even now shooting her surreptitious glances, anything, and yet she'd gone and blurted out everything. Winsome looked around for Cù, but he'd made himself scarce, as he always did when there were meetings like this.

Cynthia was leaning forward now, her face glowing. 'Here it is, or a piece of it, anyway. We broached this in the last meeting, but I've been giving it a lot more consideration. I'm thinking we start having regular market days. Advertise them across the county.'

'Market days?' Winsome asked.

'It's a great idea,' Melanie enthused, having been the one to suggest it in the first place. 'We've got a lot of people doing handicraft things here – like you, Lynsey. You and Marshall, you ought to be famous throughout the district for your knitting and weaving.' She shifted to look at the others. 'Nan, you too. Goodness, we have so much going on here, and there was that article and documentary, remember. We should be building on that. Bringing people, and their money, to Wellsford.'

Cynthia was nodding. 'We can also, of course, take advantage of Wellsford's rather...unique...flavour.'

'You mean Wilde Grove,' Winsome asked, feeling the blood drain from her face.

'I do, actually,' Cynthia said, and there were more nods around. 'Wilde Grove exists.' She smiled at Krista. 'I mean, it even has a website now. We should take advantage.'

'Become a pagan stomping ground?' Winsome asked. 'So to speak.'

Cynthia was surprised at Winsome's choice of words. 'Only in the manner that Krista here will find another outlet for the beautiful work she does, with her amulets and the books she makes.' She looked at Krista. 'What do you call them?'

'Grimoires,' Krista said. 'But really, they're just journals. You can write whatever you want in them.'

'There you go,' Cynthia said, and she looked around for Erin and Clarice but didn't see either. No matter. 'Erin can sell her artwork – it could make a real name for Wellsford. And Clarice could put on dance classes during the market, give people something to do.'

'Goodness,' Winsome said. 'You'll be popping a fortune teller on the street corner next.'

Cynthia frowned at her. 'Winsome,' she said. 'I didn't think you'd be so resistant to this. You know we've been trying to grow opportunities for all of us here in Wellsford.'

'I didn't realise we were going to bring the Grove quite so far into things,' Winsome said. 'It's like you want us to be the new Glastonbury.'

There was silence for a minute.

'Oh my god,' Winsome said. 'You want us to be the new Glastonbury.'

'Well,' Linda said. 'Why not? It works for them, doesn't it? With St Bridget's gone now, we might as well embrace what the village does have.' She shrugged. 'And that's Wilde Grove.'

Cynthia broke in. 'I think we're talking about presenting an interesting slant to Wellsford.' She spread her arms. 'Come to Wellsford – wonderful food, beautiful handcrafts, and a slightly mysterious aura. Mysterious auras are sexy. People will come.'

'Not to mention we can highlight all the good things we've got going on here,' Stephan said.

Winsome looked at him in surprise. She hadn't realised he was there too.

'I can sell my teas and blends,' Stephan said, and he looked over at Julia. 'You have roses and services to sell too, right?'

Julia nodded.

Stephan grinned at Winsome, his earlier weird feeling about Erin forgotten. 'As far as I'm concerned, the only question is when should we start? The weather's not on our side right now, and we're going into winter, so perhaps we should be talking about how to manage what we're planning around that.' He paused, thinking about it, head bent, dark hair falling over his face. 'The road into Wellsford is good for travelling, so that's a point in our favour. We've got some good trails through the woods here – not the Wilde Grove ones, but up into the hills, and we're rewilding everywhere, so it would be nice, when the weather's better, to run some walking groups around those and do a bit of education at the same time.' He wrinkled his nose. 'I'd like to see that sort of thing, personally. A bit of education mixed in, so you could have classes in veg growing or whatever each market day too, so there's plenty for visitors to do.' He wound down. 'Like I said, there's only really the weather to hold us back.'

'Listen,' Emily Bright said, her eyes lit up. 'We need a theme to it all – especially if we're going to start now and have winter markets. Something that can draw the village together with the Grove influence, and in which we can sort of line up all our offerings.' She smiled at the word, excitement fluttering in her belly. 'I know what it could be, and all.' She looked around at everyone. 'Let's make Wellsford folklore central.' She grinned at Winsome. 'You could get Ambrose to do some storytelling – I hear he's a fair shake at that.'

Winsome's eyes widened.

There were murmurings all around. 'I love it,' Cynthia said. 'Folklore central. It's practically perfect.' She gave an elegant shrug. 'I mean, with the Grove here, and all its history, mythology and folklore are almost living things here. We can even capitalise on the fact that we once had a witch living here.' She shrugged. 'A historical one, I mean, who was persecuted. We could make that part of our known history.'

Winsome groaned inwardly. The trouble with this, was that it was a good idea. It would bring even more prosperity to the village, while actually offering something of value to the public.

Only, it wouldn't go down well with Dean Morton. He'd be dragging her off to the convent even quicker now.

'Krista,' Emily said. 'And you Stephan, Charlie – do you know any other local legends? Folklore that seems based in the land around here?' She considered it. 'Wait – don't we have some natural springs here? I mean, accessible ones, not ones on private property like yours, Charlie?' She nodded. 'People like things like that. It catches the imagination. There are lots of fantastic stories about wells and so on.'

Stephan scratched his head. 'Well,' he said, then grinned before growing serious again. 'There's an ancient one behind Apple Tree Cottage, and that place doesn't get used anymore.' His eyes widened. 'Wow,' he said. 'I've just had a brilliant idea.' He looked over at Krista. 'We could make Apple Tree Cottage like a cafe and bookshop, or something. People go make offerings at the spring, bring back that tradition, then have a scone and buy a book. It's perfect.'

Winsome sat with her eyes closed. It was perfect. Even the idea of bringing Blythe back to life as part of Wellsford's history.

All of it. Perfect. Brilliant, even.

Only, she wouldn't be able to be around for any of it.

Not if she wanted to stay a vicar.

Or even part of the church.

21

'I CAN'T BELIEVE YOU WENT BACK THERE!'

'I can go wherever I want!' Erin shook her head at Stephan, tears springing back to her eyes, scalding. She turned her face away 'I'm not a child. I don't have to ask for permission.'

It was easier to yell at Stephan than to look at his worried face and tell him the truth of what had happened.

Burdock whined. Why were his people shouting at each other?

Stephan screwed his eyes shut and blew out a breath. 'Of course you're not,' he said, and looked at Erin, holding his hands out. 'I'm sorry — I just freaked out when you told me because...' He tapered unhappily off. Something had happened though – he could feel it in Erin's energy. Usually when they were together, their energy intertwined, strong and sinuous, but right now, something was wrong with Erin's.

For some reason, she was holding herself back from him, and what he could feel was brittle, all sharp edges.

Erin looked away. 'I'm tired,' she said, the fight going out of her. 'The day did not go how I wanted it to.'

Stephan looked at her. 'But you saw the Fae there again, just like we both did the other day?'

Erin nodded, knowing she was lying. It hadn't been just like the other day. 'They were still there, or there again, or whatever,' she said.

Stephan pulled her into an embrace. Perhaps he could feel what was wrong with her if Erin was inside the circle of his arms.

But Erin shook her head and stepped away. She wouldn't look at him. 'I need to go and lie down. I'm tired. I think I might be coming down with something. I have a headache.'

The last bit was true. Her head was pounding, probably from all the crying she'd done. Her tears had returned once she'd opened the door to Ash Cottage and a minute later she'd found herself on the sitting room floor in front of the woodstove, bent over her knees, face in her hands, sobbing as though her heart would break.

Or as if it were already broken.

Burdock whined again and thrust his cold nose in her hand.

She'd managed to pull herself together in time for Stephan's return, splashing cold water on her swollen eyes and throwing off her skirt that was covered in dirt from the quarry's edge, putting on something clean. She hid the dirt-smeared one at the bottom of the hamper.

She'd been sitting in front of her altar, dry-eyed and

hollow when she'd heard Stephan's hand upon the door and Burdock had come bounding inside, finding her straight away.

Erin glanced at Stephan now. 'Perhaps you ought to spend the night at home,' she said. They hadn't officially moved in together, although Erin could count upon one hand the number of nights they'd spent apart.

Stephan's eyes widened. 'You want me to go?'

Erin hugged herself. 'I'm not going to be very good company tonight.'

But Stephan stood still and frowned at her. 'What's wrong?' he said. 'Something happened, didn't it? Something you're not telling me.' He paused, probing the air between them. 'What did they do? The Fae? What did they do to you?'

Erin closed her eyes. This was the problem with her and Stephan. There was no keeping secrets from each other. She shouldn't have come back here. She should have gone to the flat in London or something. It was still there, available for her use. Veronica, who had moved into the vicarage, sharing the big house with Winsome, had secured it for her own use, and Erin's.

Stephan reached for Erin and drew her around to look at him. 'Tell me,' he said, his voice hoarse with horror at the thought that anyone could have hurt her. 'Tell me what they did?'

Erin gave him a tight smile then closed her eyes and let herself step back into his arms and rest her head on his chest. She tried to relax her energy a little, make it seem more normal, but she was still too jittery, and she really did have a headache. Behind her eyes flashed the scene with the

Fae again, herself in the dirt on the edge of the quarry wondering if she should just crawl over the edge or if she should get up and jump.

If Macha hadn't turned up just then...

Erin whimpered and Stephan's arms gathered her closer still. He could feel her short breaths, her pounding heart. Something had happened.

'What did they do?' he repeated.

Erin shook her head. 'They frightened me, is all.' She closed her eyes tighter, swallowed. She wouldn't start crying again. She wouldn't. If she did, then the whole story would come tumbling out and she'd never be able to look Stephan in the eye again.

He'd know how weak and pathetic she really was.

'How did they frighten you?' Stephan demanded, keeping his voice as calm as possible, but firm too.

Erin shook her head against his chest, then looked up at him. 'You were right,' she said. 'I should never have gone out there on my own. The way the Fae looked at me...' She ducked her head down again. 'It was really scary. They're not friends, or allies, or anything like that.' She paused. 'I think they're our enemies.'

'Our?'

Erin pressed a palm against Stephan's muscular chest. He had filled out a lot since working on the rewilding scheme. She knew she was lying to Stephan in a way, even though she was telling him what she did actually think – she was still directing his thoughts away from his concerns about her.

But she was all right with that, she thought. Because there was no way she could admit to what the Fae had almost talked her into.

'Our enemies,' she repeated. 'Humans' enemies. That's what I think.'

Stephan squinted, thinking, gazing around unseeing at the plants that Teresa had hung from every beam, put in every nook and cranny. He also didn't see the new pictures on the walls that Erin had done, even though his eyes grazed over them.

'We need to tell Morghan and Ambrose about this,' he said after a minute. 'I can't believe that we haven't already.' He pressed his lips to Erin's temple. 'You didn't get the chance today, did you?'

Erin shook her head, stepped away from Stephan's arms and sat down on the sofa by the woodstove. She was cold suddenly, even though the room was toasty. Burdock came over and she put an arm around his shoulders, rested her head on his hairy neck.

'I didn't,' she said. 'She was busy with her family,' Erin said.

Stephan's brows folded down in a frown. 'They're not family.'

'Yeah,' Erin said on a pained sigh. 'They are. They act like one, and they have all this shared history.' The Fae might have been plucking her fears right out of her head, but at least this one was grounded in fact. She gave Burdock a pat and stood up, gazing around the cottage. This was an impossible conversation to have sitting down, vulnerable to Stephan's too perceptive gaze. She needed something to keep her occupied until she could go upstairs and get into bed. She didn't know if Stephan was going to go or stay.

Probably he would stay. She knew Stephan. He was too

like Bear, protective. He wouldn't want to leave her if he thought she'd been hurt somehow.

And she had been hurt. She knew he could feel that. There was no way she could hide it from him well enough to convince him otherwise.

Stephan, she knew, would only leave if she made it absolutely clear that she didn't want him around.

Was that the case? She didn't know. Erin's eyes fell on the teapot and she made for it. Making a hot drink would give her something to do. Would keep her hands busy so she could ignore the fact that she wanted to cry again.

'You don't like them?' Stephan asked, watching Erin's hunched back. 'You met them today, right?'

Erin, still with her back to him, had to think a moment before she remembered what they'd been talking about. She nodded and put the kettle on the cooker to boil and sighed, turning finally to look at Stephan. 'I'm sure they're all really nice.' She blinked. 'Selena has the same sort of look in her eyes as Morghan has.' She rubbed at her arms. 'You know? That calm, clear, unperturbable expression.'

Stephan nodded. Bear Fellow had the same look. He hoped he'd have it one day himself. Erin would, he knew. Sometimes she already did. It was just a matter of knowing that the world was a really big place, and that you fit in it, and were really big too.

He didn't have any better words for it.

'What about the others?' he asked. 'Rue and Clover.' He still wondered how they both had come to be named for plants. Maybe their parents had been keen gardeners.

Or witches, he thought, remembering Teresa with a pang. Then gazed at her granddaughter and smiled again.

Erin was looking broodingly at the kettle, at the thread of steam rising from it. Meeting them that morning seemed so long ago, and yet the discomfort was still bright in her mind. 'It was a bit unsettling, meeting them,' she said at last. 'And Ebony. Their friend came with them, so there were three of them, not counting Selena.'

'Unsettling?'

She nodded. 'The way Clover looked at me, it was like she was seeing stuff, or worse, looking for stuff, but she didn't say what she saw, which made it...awkward.' She plucked up the steaming kettle. 'I didn't like it,' she said. 'It was rude.'

'And that was when you ducked out and decided to go to the quarry without me?'

Erin didn't look at him and poured the water into the teapot instead, wishing she could take her cup of tea and crawl into bed. She would do just that, she decided, in a minute. As soon as it had steeped.

'They were all wearing the Wilde Grove leaves,' she said, and she leant her hands on the kitchen bench.

'Who?' Stephan frowned, wanting to turn Erin around to face him but going and sitting down at the table instead, sensing she needed a little bit of space. 'The Fae?'

Erin shook her head. 'No. Selena and the other three.'

'Rue and Clover?'

'Yeah. And this Ebony woman.' Erin turned around finally and looked at Stephan, knowing a small amount of the pain she felt was showing in her face. 'They all wear them — but how come Morghan hasn't given them to me?' She touched Teresa's crystal egg. Tightened her fist around it.

Stephan frowned. He wanted to take Erin back into his arms. She looked exhausted, her face drawn. He still suspected she hadn't told him everything, but perhaps she was doing that right now. 'The leaves?'

Perhaps this was why she felt so small and brittle.

Erin nodded. 'The Wilde Grove leaves,' she said. 'The silver leaf and acorn that she wears?'

Stephan nodded. 'Right. Those. What about them?'

'Rue and Clover are wearing them too. Morghan gave them to them. And even Ebony. As a symbol of belonging to the Grove.' Erin tipped her head back and closed her stinging eyes. 'Selena has them. Morghan has them. Rue and Clover and Ebony have them.'

She picked up the teapot and brought it across to the table where Stephan had sat down.

'I don't have them,' she said.

'Maybe Morghan just hasn't given them to you yet,' Stephan said.

'Well, obviously she hasn't,' Erin said, then winced. 'Sorry.' She took a deep breath and sat down. 'I shouldn't speak like that.'

Stephan snaked out a hand and placed it on top of Erin's. 'I'm absolutely positive Morghan will give you the leaves too. She's probably just waiting for some particular time she's decided on.'

Erin nodded and sighed. 'Yeah,' she said, not knowing if she believed it. 'You're probably right.'

'I'm definitely right.'

'You're probably right.' Erin put her head in her hands. 'I'm going to go to bed,' she said. 'I have a headache.'

Burdock heard the distress in her voice and pushed his head under her arm.

Stephan looked at her. His question was careful. 'Do you still want me to go?'

Erin lifted her face and looked at him. 'You would if I said yes?'

Stephan frowned. 'Of course.'

'And you wouldn't hold it against me? Wouldn't think I was shutting you out?'

She was shutting him out. It was an unfair question to ask him, and she knew it even before it was properly out of her mouth. Erin shook her head before he could answer.

'No,' she sighed. 'I don't want you to go,' she said, and stood up, picking up her cup of tea. 'But I'm taking this to bed. I wasn't lying about the headache.'

She made herself bend down and kiss Stephan on the forehead. 'I love you.'

The words brought tears to her eyes again and she turned quickly away, made for the stairs.

22

IT TOOK PERHAPS HALF AN HOUR OF PACING THE WELL-
appointed — and quite large — kitchen for Jameel to decide
what to do with the information he'd gleaned from Erin. He
knew she hadn't told him everything.

They'd frightened her, she'd said.

Quite obviously too. She'd been as distressed as anyone
he'd ever seen. The tears had not ceased rolling down her
cheeks the whole time she'd sat with him at the breakfast
bar, Arooj in her lap.

He held his phone now, wondering if he ought to call
Henry first, but shook his head and scrolled through his
contact list for Ambrose's number.

They spoke for five minutes then Jameel ended the call
and picked up his car keys.

In the kitchen at Blackthorn House, Winsome looked at
Ambrose with raised eyebrows. 'That sounded serious.'

Ambrose nodded, his phone still in his hand. 'Jameel

came across a very upset Erin today, on the road to Wellsford.'

Winsome's eyes widened, and she put down the knife, the pile of vegetables forgotten. She'd come up to see Ambrose, hoping to get her nerve up to tell him everything.

So far, she hadn't managed even to make tentative inroads into the matter. Fortunately, he'd been full of news of Selena's arrival, and if she'd been a tiny bit preoccupied, he hadn't noticed.

'Erin?' Winsome asked, turning around. 'Is she all right?'

'On the surface, yes, Jameel says.'

'But?'

'She'd been to Brunton Bank Quarry.'

Winsome frowned at this cryptic information. 'I don't understand,' she said. 'Why would she go to a quarry and why would that upset her?' She dried her hands on a tea towel.

Ambrose shook his head, absorbed in trying to make sense of the call he'd just received. 'He's on his way over to explain properly.'

'Jameel?'

Ambrose nodded, flicked his wrist over to look at his watch then brought his phone back to life. 'I'm going to call Morghan to come over.' He considered it briefly. 'I think she should hear this too.'

'Morghan?' Winsome asked and her heart quickened. Something serious must have happened to Erin. What on earth could it have been, though? At a quarry?

But Ambrose was already making his call. He spoke quickly to Morghan, explaining the little he knew, nodding as he listened to Morghan's reply, then pressing end and standing there silent, frowning.

Winsome knew this knotted look and decided she'd put the kettle on. Ambrose disappeared into the house, and she looked at the chopped peppers and salad she'd begun on and wrinkled her nose. She should probably put them in the fridge. This – whatever it was – sounded like it could take a while. What had gotten Erin upset about a quarry? She huffed a breath, making herself admit that she was a little bit pleased their evening had been disturbed. Now she had an excuse not to tell Ambrose about Dean Morton's proposition.

Although, it was less of a proposition, and more of a demand.

She needed more time to think about it herself. It, and this goddess business with her cauldron. Winsome remembered the statue of Ceridwen on her bedroom windowsill, and flushed, drew herself back to the kitchen with an effort.

'Shall I put this lot in the fridge, then?' she called to Ambrose.

He came back into the kitchen, his thick journal tucked under his arm, pen in hand, and looked blankly at her. 'What was that?'

'This,' Winsome said, gesturing at the half-prepared vegetables. 'Shall I put it in the fridge?' She raised her eyebrows. 'It sounds like this might be a while?' Then she paused, frowned. 'If this is Grove business, though, perhaps I ought to head home?'

It would be perfectly okay if she had to head home.

Ambrose blinked at her, then shook his head. 'You're part of the Grove, Winsome.'

Her heart somersaulted in her chest, and she shook her head ever so slightly.

No. She wasn't part of the Grove. Not really. It wasn't that easy.

'Well, I think you ought to stay,' Ambrose said.

Winsome nodded and got out a bowl to put the beginnings of their meal in. When she turned around, Ambrose was gone again.

He was in his study, standing at his desk tapping a finger on his journal.

'What's happening?' she asked, leaning against the doorway.

Ambrose shook his head. 'I don't know.' He frowned. 'I don't know why Erin and Stephan haven't told us about this already.'

'About what?' Winsome thought about seeing Stephan that afternoon. He'd seemed fine.

'The quarry.'

Winsome came in the room and sat down beside his desk. 'What about this quarry?' she asked gently. 'I don't know about it, remember?'

Ambrose gazed at her, thinking hard, then pulled himself up abruptly and really looked at Winsome. She was tired, and her hands were knotted together in her lap. 'I'm sorry about dinner,' he said. 'When we're done here, I'll finish making it for us.'

Tears sprang to Winsome's eyes, and she blinked them away with a sniff. 'You're a lovely man, Ambrose,' she said.

Ambrose swivelled his chair around and took Winsome's hands in his own. They were cold, despite the fire rumbling away quietly in the grate. 'And you are the light of my heart, Winsome Clark.' He lifted her fingers to his lips to lay kisses upon them, then noticed her expression. 'Is something wrong, darling? Hopefully this won't take too long, and we can pick up where we left off.' He smiled. 'Except I shall cook for you.'

Winsome cleared her throat and hurriedly shook her head. 'I'm all right,' she said, not quite answering his question.

There was a knock at the door and Ambrose looked up. 'That was fast.'

Winsome nodded, scooting quickly out of the room. 'I'll get it.'

'Morghan,' she said with real pleasure when she'd opened the door.

'Hello Winsome. Sorry to be descending upon you like this.' She smiled. 'Which reminds me that you must come over soon – tomorrow, perhaps – and meet Selena and the girls.' It was hard not to keep calling Rue, Clover, and Ebony "the girls", although all were grown now.

'I'd like that,' Winsome said, then looked past Morghan's shoulder and the early evening, gloomy with clouds and settling darkness. She shivered and hunkered down in her jumper, remembering that something was going on with Erin.

'Do we know what's happened?'

Morghan shook her head. 'Ambrose will tell us,' she said, 'and I believe we're waiting for Jameel as well.' She looked at Winsome. 'Shall we go in?'

'Oh, yes, of course.' Winsome realised she was blocking the doorway and stood back, letting Morghan into the house. 'I'll put the kettle on, make some tea.'

Morghan had already gone into Ambrose's study, which was the largest room in the house. It had been the sitting room at one stage, Winsome suspected, but was much better served as his study – it was where he spent most of his time when he wasn't outside. She walked back through to the kitchen and stood for a moment in front of the fireplace, holding her hands out to warm her fingers, frowning as she did so. Ambrose and Morghan might call her the bridge between Grove and village, but she didn't entirely know what that meant yet.

And with Morton's decision, it would all have to change.

Winsome let out the breath she'd been holding and felt the tension knot at her muscles.

Was Ambrose right that she was part of the Grove?

'Aargh,' she said to herself. 'Always fretting. Stop fretting.'

'Are you talking to yourself?' Morghan asked, appearing around the corner.

Winsome grimaced. 'Bad habit, I'm afraid. Can't seem to get rid of it.'

'What are you fretting about?' Morghan drew away and went to make the tea, looking back over her shoulder. 'You can tell me.'

Winsome knew she could. She'd gotten rather in the habit of telling Morghan whatever was on her mind. And there was usually something on her mind.

Although, she hadn't told Morghan this yet, about the Community of the Sacred Name. She'd been planning to, after telling Ambrose.

'I try to walk calmly through life,' she said now. 'I wish I had your poise, your unflappability.'

Morghan laughed. 'I wish I had your warmth.'

'My warmth?' Winsome frowned, looking at her friend. 'You wish you had my warmth?'

'Yes,' Morghan said, switching the kettle on to reheat and getting cups down enough for them all.

'You don't think you're a warm person?' Winsome asked the question with genuine curiosity.

Morghan paused, raised her eyebrows. 'Is that how you'd ever describe me?'

Suddenly, Winsome was flustered. 'Erm. I don't know. Deep, perhaps. Attentive.' She straightened. 'Calm and welcoming – isn't that warmth?'

'I don't know,' Morghan said, coming to lean against the wall, looking at Winsome. She'd said what she had because Winsome's natural warmth was one of the things she admired most about her friend, but she gave this new question her attention. 'I feel like you effortlessly bridge the gap between yourself and other people, meeting them right where they are.'

'And you don't?'

'My nature is more reserved,' Morghan said, then surprised herself with her next words. 'Loneliness has had an effect too.'

Winsome gaped at Morghan, then sprang forward to grasp Morghan's hand. 'You're lonely?' she asked, amazed.

'Sometimes,' Morghan admitted. 'I still miss Grainne.' She paused. 'Oddly enough, it's seeing Selena and Rue and Clover and Ebony that have made the loss feel more immediate.' She looked down at her hand clasped in Winsome's. 'They were last here for Grainne's funeral.'

'I'm so sorry,' Winsome said, her heart hurting for her friend. 'I never thought —'

'Of course not,' Morghan answered. 'I wish you'd met Grainne. She'd have loved you as much as I do.'

Morghan's words made Winsome's cheeks blush with pleasure. 'I wish I'd had a chance to know her as well.' She squeezed Morghan's fingers, still trapped in her own.

Nodding, Morghan sighed. 'I think we'd best get these tea things ready. I've a feeling Jameel will be here any moment.'

There was a knocking at the front door and Winsome raised her eyebrows at Morghan and laughed. 'Tell me that you didn't know that was about to happen?'

Morghan smiled, but she said nothing. She'd felt Jameel's presence on the path through the woods. Her gifts, she thought, cultivated through hard work and effort, were growing.

Since the day in the cave that she'd had her first vision of the churning sea, the refugees to the Summer Lands, and the dark stain spreading across the world. Since then, things had changed.

She was changing.

Rising, she hoped, to meet the coming challenges.

Drawing her attention back to Winsome, she slid her hands gently from Winsome's grasp and swung back to the kitchen and the tea things.

'I'll get those,' Winsome said. 'You go in and see what's going on.'

. . .

'THERE ARE FAE HANGING ABOUT THIS QUARRY?' MORGHAN'S voice was sharp, her forehead creased.

Jameel nodded. 'That's what Erin said, and whatever reason they're there, it isn't a good one. She was upset. I mean, really upset.'

'What had they done to her?' Winsome asked, glancing over at Ambrose, who she could see was equally disturbed by the news.

'I don't know,' Jameel admitted. He wanted to get up and stride about the room, running his frustration through his legs, but there wasn't the space. His call had drawn a concerned audience. 'She said they'd frightened her.' He paused, took a sip of tea and shook his head. 'I warred with myself over coming here. I feel like Erin should be telling you this, but I decided that she was in no state to do so when I saw her. They'd wounded her somehow.'

Morghan stood up, dipping her hand into the pocket of the jacket she wore and bringing out her mobile phone, staring at it as though surprised to find it actually there.

'I'm going to call her,' she said. 'Erin. I'm going to call her.'

'She said she and Stephan went there in the first place after hearing on the radio about a bunch of suicides at the quarry,' Jameel added. He winced. 'I kind of got the impression that's what they might have tried with Erin.'

Winsome's eyes widened. 'You think these Fae, whoever they are -'

'They're not any we're allied with,' Morghan said.

Winsome shook her head. 'But you think they tried to make Erin...' She couldn't bring herself to say the rest.

Jameel put his cup down and ran his fingers through his dark hair. 'It's just a guess.'

Morghan heard his answer, then walked out of the room, paused in the hallway, then pushed open the front door and stepped out into the dusk.

Why hadn't she picked up on Erin's distress? She should have known. Should have felt it.

Morghan stood in the middle of the clearing that was Ambrose's front yard and closed her eyes. The fact was, she had known Erin was upset, hadn't she? She'd picked up on it that morning, as they were greeting Selena and Rue and Clover and Ebony. Something had happened then, and Erin had become upset.

It was the leaves, Morghan thought at the time. The fact that they were all wearing the Wilde Grove leaves, and she hadn't given them to Erin yet.

That and the way that Clover had looked at Erin so intently.

Seeing Erin's kin, assessing strength of her spirit.

Morghan turned around in a slow circle, eyes still closed, until she faced roughly the direction of Ash Cottage. She'd been planning to take the leaves down to Erin the next morning. There was no reason to save them until the Samhain celebrations now.

She lifted her phone and pressed the numbers for Erin's mobile. Listened to the call go through, the phone ring.

'Morghan.'

She recognised Stephan's voice at once. 'Is Erin there, Stephan?' she asked.

He cleared his throat. 'Ah, she's gone to bed with a headache.'

Morghan nodded, even though he couldn't see her. 'Did she tell you what happened today?'

'About going back to the quarry?'

'Mmm.' Morghan thought quickly. 'Stephan,' she said. 'I'm going to come down now and see her.'

'She's asleep.'

'Even so. Is that all right?'

There was only the briefest of hesitations. 'Shall I wake her up and tell her?'

'No need, I think. I'll wake her, if necessary,' Morghan decided. 'I'll see you shortly.' She pressed end before Stephan could respond, and she stood there still for a moment more, staring out at her beloved trees. The sun had sunk already below the hills and dusk lay upon the land in a shadowy rose and gold blanket.

Winsome crept out behind her. 'Is she all right?' she asked.

'I'm going to go and see her. Will you come with me?' Morghan replied.

'Me?' Winsome was startled. 'Wouldn't Ambrose be a better choice?'

Morghan turned and looked at her, eyes dark in the gathering night. 'I'd prefer you this time, if you'll come?'

Winsome nodded. 'Of course,' she said. These were, at least right now, still her people. Her friends.

'Of course I'll come.'

23

THEY PASSED THE SHORT TRACK THAT LED DOWN TO THE garden behind the vicarage garden. Morghan glanced down it, saw a smudge of light between the trees.

'How are you getting along sharing the house with Veronica?' she asked.

'Oh,' Winsome said. 'Very well, to tell the truth. You know how big it is – we each have our own little sitting room, plus a communal one, and we spend a lot of time planning and chatting in the kitchen. She's settling in surprisingly well – seems to have found a bit of a calling with the charity shop, finding stock, making deals.' She paused. 'And for myself, I spend a lot of nights with Ambrose now.' Winsome winced. 'I'm trying not to feel guilty about that.'

Morghan looked at her in surprise. 'Guilty? Why?'

'Well.' Winsome turned her face away and frowned. They were passing the church below them, still sitting empty and unused. It would be coming up for sale shortly, and then there would be some decisions, that was for sure. More decisions. Would she end up having any part in them? Love for the old building welled up suddenly inside Winsome and she pressed a hand to her heart as though to hold it all in.

'Well?' Morghan was still waiting.

'Well, I don't know. We've very different backgrounds. Sometimes I have trouble with that. Or all of it really. I always thought if I met someone, we'd eventually get married – that sort of thing. But...' She paused. 'Veronica calls Ambrose my wizard, but the truth is, I don't quite know what to do with a wizard. I'm not sure I know how to... reconcile our religious differences. On the face of things, you know. The village still thinks of me as Christian.' She stumbled on a tree root. Actually, she wasn't sure the village did think of her anymore as a Christian, although many of the older folk still called her Vicar, even though she tried correcting them. 'It's all so very new and different. I'm still finding my way.'

Winsome flushed, looked down at Cu, who walked beside her in the dimness of the woods. He turned his head as though he felt her gaze on him and seemed to stare reproachfully at her. She narrowed her eyes at him.

'Oh.' Morghan shook her head in understanding. She took a moment to think about it, since she'd brought the subject up, or at least the subject that led to it. 'In Ambrose's tradition too, making a commitment is important.'

Winsome hesitated. 'Is that what you and Grainne did? I know you speak of her as your wife.'

'We didn't. We didn't have a formal, public ceremony, at least.' Morghan turned her gaze away, remembering with a shiver the night they bonded themselves to each other, not just in this lifetime, but inside and outside of time. She knew it hadn't been just herself making the whispered commitment, but all aspects of her soul. Morghan turned her mind back to Winsome's predicament. 'It's good for humans to have ceremonies to mark their milestones, I think. Especially if those ceremonies bring the community together.'

'I don't know if marrying Ambrose – which it's much too soon to think about, by the way – is necessary to bring our communities together.' She paused. 'We had a meeting today about a village market.' She paused, eyed Morghan in the waning light. 'There were some interesting ideas put forward.'

Morghan nodded. 'Yes,' she said. 'Charlie called. She and Krista are going to tell me all about it after our full moon ritual.'

Winsome nodded. That was good, then. 'May I come?' she asked.

'To our full moon ritual? Winsome, you would be most welcome.'

'Oh, erm, I meant to the meeting afterwards.'

Morghan laughed. 'That too, if you like.'

They were getting closer to Ash Cottage and Morghan lapsed into silence, her mind turning again toward Erin, towards her own recent visions, the returning of Rue, Clover and Ebony, to help her turn the Grove into the beacon it needed to be. The vision also of herself standing upon the tor, watching the lights coming towards her, borne by those she knew and those also whom yet she didn't.

'What is it?' Winsome asked, for Morghan had stopped walking suddenly.

In Morghan's vision, it hadn't been just Ravenna standing beside her. Morghan thought about this, remembered it, lifted her face to the coming night and felt the shock of remembering make her limbs tremble.

'I had forgotten something,' she said, and made herself start walking again.

'What was it?'

It was Catrin, standing on her other side on the tor. Ravenna on one side, Catrin on the other. What did it mean? Morghan wondered, then shook her head briefly. She knew what it meant, and now, heading toward Ash Cottage to speak to Erin about an unknown group of Fae, she realised that the coming years might be more than a trial.

In some ways, they might be a battle.

She shook her head at Winsome's question. 'Something I need to think upon more,' she said apologetically.

'She's in bed,' Stephan said, as Morghan and Winsome stood in the small, warm sitting room. 'Asleep. I hoped you wouldn't have to wake her. She was pretty upset earlier.'

'Do you know why?'

Stephan shifted slightly on the rug and Burdock, sitting beside him, gazed up at his face. 'She went back to the quarry – I was mad at her for that.' His mouth turned down at the memory.

Morghan nodded. 'This quarry,' she said.

'The Brunton Bank Quarry,' Stephan told her. 'The

company's gone bankrupt and just left it this great hole in the ground.' He looked at Winsome. 'They're supposed to give it back to nature, make it a reserve or something. Do something so that it becomes a healthy part of nature again.' He shook his head. 'They sure haven't done that.'

Morghan had her head tilted toward the ceiling, thinking about Erin. She dropped her chin and looked at Stephan. 'The Fae there?' she asked.

Stephan winced and shifted uncomfortably again. Burdock whined quietly, and Stephan stroked him. 'We wanted to tell you the other day, at Ambrose's place, but with all the other news, we didn't get the chance.'

Morghan nodded. 'Still,' she said. 'I wish you had.'

Stephan did too. 'We didn't recognise them, the Fae, I mean.' He glanced at Winsome. 'But we wouldn't though, would we? Neither Erin nor I have been to the Fair Lands.' He shifted again. 'We thought they were probably the Fae who are our allies – I mean, why would there be any others around here?'

Stephan grimaced. He wasn't sure he was telling the truth there. Had they thought, that first time, that the Fae there weren't strangers to the Grove? He thought they really hadn't known one way or the other.

But they had wondered if the Fae there had anything to do with the suicides.

Morghan ignored the comment about not having gone to the Fair Lands yet. She had been busy teaching Erin other things. Nothing could be done all at once. And the Queen had made no request yet to see her.

Perhaps though, a visit was in order.

Because, Morghan suspected, this other faction, for she

felt definitely that they were another faction, changed everything.

'I'm going to go upstairs and see Erin,' Morghan said. 'Please wait for me down here.'

Stephan looked at Morghan in dismay. 'Something really happened there, didn't it? I knew Erin was hiding something.'

But Morghan didn't answer. She simply nodded and climbed the stairs to the bedrooms.

Stephan drooped, shoulders falling as he shook his head. 'Erin has been so happy lately,' he said. 'Why did this have to happen?'

Winsome scooped an arm around him and herded him toward the kitchen. 'Shall we make a cup of tea?' she asked. 'Things do happen, I'm afraid, that's pretty much a guarantee in this life.'

Morghan eased the door to the main bedroom open, and stepped inside the room. A single lamp was burning, its electric light dim and yellow, soothing.

There was still a chair next to the bed and Morghan pulled it closer – just as she had the last time she was in this room, when it had been Teresa lying under the blankets – and sat down upon it. She touched Erin on the shoulder.

Erin shook her head. 'I don't want to do anything but sleep, Stephan.'

'It's Morghan, Erin.'

Erin opened her eyes, brain muzzy, and stared at Morghan sitting at the side of the bed. 'Wha?' She squeezed her eyes shut but when she peeled them open again, Morghan was still there, her grey hair framing a face that gazed seriously upon her.

'Morghan?' Erin lifted her head off the pillow, hitched herself up slightly in the bed and gazed at Morghan in shock.

Morghan nodded. 'The thing we have to know beyond any doubt about the Fae, Erin, is that they are very dissimilar to us.'

Erin gaped at her, then looked wildly about the room. Was she dreaming, she wondered? Why was Morghan in her bedroom, talking about the Fae?

'Who told you?' she whispered.

'Jameel. He was worried.'

Erin sank back against the pillow, dismayed but unsurprised. 'I guess I would have done the same, if I were him. I was pretty upset.'

Morghan nodded slightly. 'They are not like us, and sometimes this makes them unkind.'

Erin snorted, turned her head to look at Morghan. 'They weren't being unkind, Morghan. They wanted to hurt me.' Her voice cracked and she paused for a moment, feeling the heft and weight of that hurt inside herself, behind her ribs. She pressed her lips together. There was nothing more she wanted to say about it.

Morghan saw this. Thought about reaching out and taking Erin's hand, using that to forge a connection between them, the better to read what the Fae had done to her.

But she didn't. Erin was hurt and vulnerable — that much was obvious in her energy, which felt sunken, drawn in, diminished. To explore more, without Erin's explicit consent, would be an intrusion the young woman didn't deserve.

'They most often keep their motives to themselves,'

Morghan said instead. 'Why they do what they do. Even those with whom we are allied seldom tell us why they ask us to do the things they do.'

Erin shook her head. She scooted up until she was in a sitting position, glad she had put on a nightdress before getting into bed. It was weird enough waking up to find Morghan sitting beside her, let alone if she'd been nude between the sheets.

She crossed her arms over her breasts.

'I don't think these Fae were part of Queen Alastrina's court,' she said, her voice rough with the effort not to start crying again. 'I've been thinking about it, and they can't be. They simply can't be. It's impossible.' She stared at the lamp on the dressing table opposite. It had been her grandmother's, she thought, as had all the furniture in this room. It was her room now. She was safe there. Even with Morghan sitting beside her. She turned to look at her.

'This is serious, isn't it?' she asked. 'The world — things are getting serious.' She dropped her gaze to the blankets and then closed her eyes. 'Those Fae I saw today, they were there to do harm. At least to any people who were unlucky enough to cross their path.' She looked at Morghan. 'Why would they do that?'

It was exactly the question Morghan wanted answered. Particularly since Erin was so convinced these were different Fae than those who came to dance with them — something Morghan agreed with. 'I don't know,' she said. 'But we need to find out.'

Erin turned away. 'I don't think I should go back there.'

'No,' Morghan said, watching her closely. 'Not yet, anyway. I think though, that we should go elsewhere.'

Erin turned her head slightly, listening. She wet her lips. 'Where?'

'To see the Queen. She will hopefully know more about these Fae than either you or I can speculate.'

Erin was silent.

'It's time you met her anyway,' Morghan said. 'I've had much else to teach you, but now this becomes important.'

Erin was looking at her now. 'Why?' she asked. 'Why does this become important now?'

Straightening, Morghan took a breath. 'All the last year, I have had visions of the coming darkness.' She got up and went to the window, parting the curtains and gazing out into the evening, picking out the shadow and form of Teresa's well in the centre of the garden, the beds radiating off it like spokes of a wheel.

'The coming darkness?' Erin repeated.

'Yes,' Morghan said, watching the waxing moon rise in the eastern sky, its plumpening form reflecting light over the hills behind Ash Cottage.

'I don't know what you mean,' Erin said, drawing her knees up under the bedcovers and hugging them. 'I mean, you've mentioned it in the context of us needing to be keepers of the light, as the priestesses of the Grove always were, but I'm not sure what you mean, otherwise.'

Morghan turned around, leant against the windowsill. 'You have done wonders this last year, taking care of your personal business.'

Erin considered this. 'You mean, Kria,' she said. 'And Wayne?'

'And your mothers,' Morghan added. 'Our first responsibility is to heal ourselves and our bloodlines. Our ancestors.'

In the bed, Erin paused, then nodded. 'What comes after that?' she asked, almost too afraid to utter the words, for she was sure suddenly, that she wouldn't be able to do any of it. There would be others better at all of this, she thought, the wound inside herself opening up again and weeping once more.

'Every generation,' Morghan mused, 'is sure that the end is upon them, the end of the world as they know it, that things will change beyond their recognition.' She lifted a palm and through the open curtain, moonlight spilled upon it as though she cupped gleaming water in her golden hand.

Erin waited, tears dribbling once more down her cheeks.

'Our generation however, and those to come, are facing more than ever before.' Morghan tightened her hand into a fist and dropped it to her side. 'There are times coming such as we have not seen before within memory.'

She walked back to the chair beside the bed and looked at it. 'The last time I was in this room was the day your grandmother died.'

Erin stared at Morghan in consternation.

Morghan sat down and looked seriously at Erin, taking in the wet eyes and the radiating pain.

'Whatever they did to you, Erin,' she said, 'remember this. You were born to be part of this Grove. You were lost to us for a while, but we searched for you — your grandmother searched for you and in this very room, sitting upon this very chair — I promised to continue looking until you were found.'

Morghan's mouth curved upwards slightly. 'And we did

find you, and now you are here where you belong, one of our number to help us keep and spread the light in the world in the coming years.'

Erin stared at her, mouth open in astonishment.

Now, Morghan did reach for Erin's hand and take it in hers, holding it.

'We all have been wounded,' she said, feeling the fresh sharpness of Erin's pain. 'We all carry the scars of these wounds. And yet somehow we must learn how not to let them fester, and how instead, to be strengthened from them, to carry on, hearts open, mind and spirit strong.'

Morghan looked at Erin. 'Close your eyes,' she said.

Erin widened them instead, then after a beat, let her eyelids drop, her hand still in Morghan's.

Morghan reached over with her other hand, the one that gleamed now in the low light of the room, golden and bright, and placed her palm upon Erin's chest, and she let her spirit soar.

24

SHE TOOK ERIN WITH HER WHEN SHE SHIFTED.

'Where are we?' Erin asked, then fell to her knees as she took in the view around them. An ocean spread out around her, vast and glittering although there was no moon that she could see in the night sky. Erin clutched at the grass, fistfuls between her fingers lest she tumble from the high tor into the waves far below.

For a moment, her grovelling reminded her of kneeling in the dirt on the quarry's edge, and pain swept through her, making her cry out.

Morghan's hand was on her back then, and warmth flooded through Erin. It did not brighten her however, only made her dip her forehead to the grass and sob.

'Hush,' Morghan said and drew in a deep breath of the night air. 'I brought you here to see something.' She looked down at Erin bent upon the ground. 'Come out of your pain and look at mine,' she said. 'Look at my joy.'

Erin raised her wet face, puzzled by Morghan's words. 'Look at your pain and joy?' she asked.

'Yes,' Morghan said. 'Stand next to me and see.'

Straightening, Erin shied away from the view. 'It's too much,' she said. 'It's like the first time I saw the World Pool.'

'I am next to you,' Morghan said. 'Lean on me.'

Erin glanced at her, saw that Morghan stood straight, feet planted firmly upon the ground of this high tower of land, her hair loose down her back, eyes bright with both terror and love. She struggled to her feet, and Morghan put an arm around her back, steadying her.

At last she was standing, and Erin, drawing in a breath, let herself look about them.

'Where are we?' she whispered.

They stood on a high finger of land, and below them to the left, the ocean churned and heaved. To the right, Erin could make out land, much of it covered in the lights of camps and settlements and civilisation, the brightness of souls living in flesh upon the earth.

Erin gazed upon it, then clutched Morghan's arm. 'What is that?' she asked, and if she'd been wearing her own flesh, it would have broken out in a rash of goosebumps.

It was darkness, coming across the land like a great black wave, putting out the lights.

Putting out most of the lights, for some still shone, wavering and weak in the shadows.

'What is it?' she asked again, but did not wait for an answer, instead watching open-mouthed and horrified.

'Listen,' Morghan said, and to Erin's ears her voice was placid, unperturbed at the sights spread out all around them.

'Listen and look.'

Erin strained her ears and eyes, and in a moment she heard something.

Singing.

Below them, upon a path that wound up the great tor of land upon which they stood, came a procession of lights.

People.

Erin blinked at them, strained her gaze to make them out. Listened hard to the song.

'Who are they?' she whispered.

Morghan did not answer.

The singing swelled over the crashing of the ocean, and Erin closed her eyes for a moment, listening to it.

'I recognise it,' she said. 'It's the song of the trees.'

'The ones who stand strong against the darkness,' Morghan said.

Erin opened her eyes, the song swollen between her ears, and she looked down at the procession of people winding their way up the hill, bright torches in their hands.

She swayed against Morghan. 'It's me,' she said. 'I'm there.'

'Lights against the darkness,' Morghan said. 'Beacons of hope and love.'

Erin peered at the coming procession. At herself, holding a torch, singing the song taught to her by trees. Then she closed her eyes and the vision swirled away.

'She's sleeping,' Morghan said, touching Stephan on the arm, knowing her touch would leave tingles of energy upon his skin. 'Let her rest. I will see her tomorrow.'

'Is she all right?' Stephan asked, pressing his fingers to the spot where Morghan's fingers had briefly rested. 'Do you know what happened?'

'Enough of it,' Morghan said and nodded. 'Enough of it.'

Stephan looked at her. 'It was those Fae, wasn't it? They did something to her.' He squeezed his eyes shut and let his hand drop to touch Burdock's warm head. 'I should have done something. Made sure she didn't go there. Not on her own.' He gazed at Morghan. 'I should have made sure we told you about it.'

'Perhaps,' Morghan said. 'But things are playing out and each of us finds our way.' She looked at Winsome. 'Time to go, I think.'

Outside, Morghan and Winsome walked up the lane to the vicarage.

The sky shivered with wind and Winsome drew her coat closer around her. It had been cosy warm in Ash Cottage. Her knuckles were white where she clutched her coat together.

'What's going on, Morghan?' she asked at last, and looked up at the sky, where the stars were hidden on the other side of the clouds. 'I mean, I know that we have a lot happening in the world at the moment what with the virus still giving us trouble, all the political awfulness, and the coming climate crisis.'

'The climate crisis is upon us already,' Morghan said.

Winsome felt anxiety settle uneasily in the pit of her stomach. It was hard to believe that the world was on the brink of changing so drastically. She couldn't have imagined this in a hundred years — growing up, she hadn't had an inkling of it.

'But,' she said, her voice a half-whisper. 'How do we keep going when everything is going to become so chaotic?' She paused, frowning, then stopped walking and turned to face Morghan in the moonlight.

'I mean — what's the point? How do we live our lives with this looming? I don't understand.' Winsome drew a breath, shifted on the edge of the paved lane. 'I'd hate to be a young person just starting out. How do you start out in this world when you don't know what it's going to look like in twenty or fifty years?' She coughed out a laugh. 'I guess I am starting out, though, aren't I? A mid-life change, of course. But how do we live in these times? They're frankly terrifying.'

Winsome thought of the Dean's insistence that she leave Wellsford. What purpose for her life would she find there? There was an attached small hospital and a care home, so there would be good work she could still do - even her end-of-life care.

But still.

There was a lot she would have to leave behind in Wellsford, and would that even be possible?

Wellsford had made the world different. It had made her different.

Winsome shook her head. If she stayed in Wellsford, was she really up for the job, though? Of continuing onwards, despite the stress and the struggle of the coming times? Wouldn't it be a relief, in some ways, to go back to a quiet life of prayer and routine, and each day prescribed and safe?

Or as safe as it was probably possible to be.

'I feel very insecure,' she said, her cheeks heating with

embarrassment at the admission. 'I thought I'd worked everything out, but now I find that I haven't. Not at all.'

Morghan lifted her face to the sky, then settled her gaze back on the worried features of her friend.

'I don't have all these answers,' she said at last. 'I have been asking myself the same questions, and always come back to what I have been telling myself for years.'

Winsome straightened, looked expectantly at her.

'That we begin where we are, with what we have, and our vision for love in the world,' Morghan said, and reached out her hands to place them gently on Winsome's shoulders. 'And my dear, we have much.'

Winsome nodded. 'I have you,' she said.

Morghan laughed and dropped her hands, turning to resume their walk. 'Yes,' she said. 'You have me, and all of us in the Grove and village. You have Ambrose.'

Winsome nodded again, folding her arms over her chest and hunching down into herself. 'Yes,' she said. She expected that she ought to be going back to Blackthorn House, but she'd called Ambrose and said she'd decided to stay at the Vicarage, since it was closer and she was tired.

It hadn't been a lie. Both those things were true.

Only so was it also true that everything was a jumble in her head. She felt as though she had come to a great crossroads, with no idea about which direction to take. She didn't know where any of the branching paths led, and she wasn't good at not knowing where she was going.

Start where you are, Morghan said. That was very well, Winsome considered. She wasn't sure she even knew where she was. Also, at some point didn't you have to stop starting and actually get going? What then? Where were you supposed to go if you hadn't mapped it out already?

'I don't know who to pray to anymore,' Winsome said, then slapped a hand over her mouth. 'I didn't mean to say that. I can't believe I said it out loud.'

Morghan looked at her. 'I can well imagine that the events of the last year would bring you to this place. Everything has shifted around you and grown. Your world is so very much larger.'

Winsome swallowed down the lump in her throat and nodded. She should have known that Morghan would understand immediately.

'All my life, Jesus and a nice omnipresent God have been a constant,' she said, the words tentative, as though she was feeling her way along the string of them. 'But now there are...others.' Winsome shivered, unable to help herself. 'The pair in the Otherworld forest — the one who told me the story, who I saw on the lawn of the church.' She bowed her head, staying quiet about Ceridwen's latest appearance. 'What do I do about her? Them?'

'Perhaps you can explore relationships with them both,' Morghan said, her voice mild as though the suggestion was natural and obvious. Then she smiled widely, mischievous. 'It sounds as though another trip to the cave is called for.'

Winsome laughed, but it was pitched a little too high and sounded slightly hysterical even to her own ears. She shook her head, took a moment to calm herself, reminding herself of everything she had done and seen over the last year.

'Yes,' she said, still surprising herself with the answer. 'All right. You're on.'

After all, perhaps she needed all the allies she could get, if what Morghan said was coming was true.

If she was to stay, of course. And since staying would mean a final letting go of everything she'd always held onto, she'd need something more to fill the space.

Even if that something else terrified her.

Morghan ducked her head into the sitting room at Hawthorn House, found it empty, and climbed the stairs instead. There was a light on in Selena's room, and Morghan knocked lightly on the door, then stepped inside when Selena answered.

'I'm sorry I've left you all alone,' she said, seeing that Rue, Clover, and Ebony were also in the room, making use of the small sitting area.

'You've been really busy,' Clover said. 'What made you rush away this afternoon?'

Morghan leant down over Selena's chair and kissed Selena on the cheek, before taking her hand and seating herself on the footstool at her feet.

'I apologise for being gone all evening,' Morghan said, smiling up at Selena who reached out and stroked her hair. Tendrils of it had come loose from the braid she had it in, and Selena let these drift through her fingers. Her touch was warm.

'Will you take me to the stone circle tomorrow?' Selena asked. 'I would like to walk some of the old paths.' She closed her eyes. 'I would like to see Apple Tree Cottage again too.' She smiled slightly. 'Somehow, being back this time makes me nostalgic.'

Morghan nodded. 'Of course,' she said, and caught Selena's fingers to drop a kiss upon them. 'How are you feeling?'

'Not as vigorous as I would like,' Selena laughed. 'The flight was an ordeal.'

Morghan nodded, then looked over at the other three. 'How about you?' she asked. 'I imagine you're jet lagged.'

'No more than past times,' Rue said. 'But it is a very long flight.' As if to prove the point, she gave a wide yawn. 'But tell us what's happened here.'

'We know something has.' Clover said, a statement rather than a question. 'I can feel it in the air — there are patterns of disturbance all around.'

Ebony nodded in agreement.

Morghan's eyebrows rose. 'All around?'

But Clover shrugged. 'All around,' she said. 'I don't know how to be more specific than that.' Checking herself, she widened her gaze for a moment, and the world spun out, vast and deep. Clover nodded. 'It is like the air spins in mini hurricanes in some places. I don't know how else to describe it, but I can feel the patterns of disturbance almost everywhere.'

Morghan considered this. 'We all know why we're here,' she said at last, sighing as she did so.

'We're not staying,' Rue said, glancing at Ebony. 'Not more than a week or two. Ebony and I have businesses that need us.' She looked across at Selena, and tried to smile. 'Are we?'

Selena shook her head. 'I am staying,' she said. 'But I think you know that.'

Rue looked down at her lap, her feelings conflicted.

When she looked up again, her eyes were wet but clear. 'Yes, I know. This is your home.'

'Where I began this life,' Selena nodded. 'Where I wish to be when it ends.' She smiled at Rue. 'Despite the most wonderful adventure I had in a far land.'

There was a minute's quiet.

'We all know why we're here,' Clover said finally, and repeating Morghan's earlier words. 'Selena to come home.' She looked at Rue and Ebony then turned to Morghan. 'But not just that. There is something beginning — or something returning, that must be dealt with.' She frowned. 'What happened this afternoon? Rue's right — something did.'

'Yes,' Morghan said, and leant against Selena's chair. 'I think you'll be very interested to hear this. Near Banwell, there's a quarry, which is no longer in use, but has not been restored yet to nature. Erin encountered a group of Fae there this afternoon.'

'The Queen's?' Selena asked.

Morghan shook her head. 'We think not. They were not...kind...in their greeting to Erin. In fact, they tried actively to harm her.' Morghan thought of the deep woundedness she had felt within Erin and her own heart hurt in response.

'Who were they, then?' Ebony asked. 'Why did they do that?'

'We don't know,' Morghan said. 'But there have been a spate of suicides at the quarry, and I cannot help but think that these Fae have something to do with it.'

'But it's been a long time since the Fae have bothered with us,' Rue asked. 'Hasn't it? — I mean, except in alliances like the one we have with the Queen and her people. Isn't that right?'

'I don't know,' Ebony said. 'There's an interesting theory these days that the alien encounter and abductions are actually Fae related. That we see them as aliens now, due to cultural and time reasons.'

'Aliens?' Morghan was shocked.

Ebony shrugged. 'There are remarkable similarities. Although I think that's pretty much outside of our scope."

Morghan nodded, baffled at Ebony's suggestion, not knowing what to make of it at all. Finally, she decided that right now, the idea that aliens were Fae was definitely just going to cloud the matters at hand. She decided to try answering Clover's question instead.

'The world is a changing place,' she said. 'The veil thins, and it is the Fae forcing that. I can only believe that there are some courts who wish to take a less delicate approach than we are used to in returning the world to a more openly inspirited place.'

Morghan paused before continuing. 'And perhaps there are those who harbour grudges and no longer wish to remain hidden or unseen.' She pursed her lips. 'I don't know how this all relates to the visions that have brought us here together, but there must be a connection. Centuries ago, during the Great Turning, we made magic, a great spell of blessing over the Grove.' She shook her head, for this,was the part where she always came undone.

Now she tried again.

'A blessing to keep the land sacred?' she asked, feeling her way around the question. 'A blessing that would be a promise?'

'A promise to who?' Ebony asked.

Morghan shook her head.

'It was the Fae who brought the veil down,' Selena reminded them. 'Perhaps a promise to our Queen.'

'What for, though?' Rue asked. 'And how is a blessing a promise?'

'If the blessing keeps the land sacred and in honour to all the worlds, then that would be a sort of promise,' Ebony countered. She looked around at their group. 'Wouldn't it?'

They were silent then, and troubled, for it seemed to each that they only had part of the puzzle yet.

25

WINSOME SLIPPED INTO THE VICARAGE AND NABBED HER laptop from her office and climbed the stairs with it. There was the sound of a television coming from the room Veronica used as a private sitting room and Winsome was glad. She enjoyed sharing the big house with Veronica, but right now, she needed some time to figure things out.

Cù waited for her in her bedroom and she shook her head slightly at him.

'Must be handy, to just teleport up the stairs. You ought to teach me sometime. Save my hips.'

Cù just looked at her in that way he had, as though she amused him very much, and lay down under the window where the statue of Ceridwen stared out into the night.

Winsome glanced at the small resin statue, then at the cross on the wall, and stood still on the carpet in the middle of the room for several breaths before going to the bed and putting the laptop computer on the covers. She rummaged in her drawers, got out her pyjamas and changed into them.

'Might as well be comfy, when we're contemplating radical life changes,' Winsome said to Cù.

Cù yawned.

'I don't know why I talk to you,' Winsome said, doing up the buttons on her shirt. 'You know, I've heard tell that some spirit animals actually do the talking. Couldn't you be more like one of those and dispense your wisdom in aphorisms and commandments? Rather than yawns and looks of mild amusement at my human foibles?'

Cù stared at her and said nothing, then closed his eyes, for all the world like he needed some beauty sleep.

Winsome rolled her eyes, whether at the spirit dog or herself she wasn't quite sure. Then she checked her door was closed and doused the overhead light so only the lamp on her bedside table glowed, and the one by the window next to her small armchair.

Right, she thought, clambering onto the bed and reaching for the book Krista had given her on Celtic goddesses and gods to set beside her laptop.

'Right.' She sat cross-legged, contemplating things. 'What I've got to remember,' she said in a low voice, speaking perhaps to herself, perhaps to Cù, 'is how much I've done already.' She nodded, glanced over at Cù. 'There's Julia, remember.'

Cù twitched, opened his eyes, gazed at her.

Winsome nodded again. 'That's right. There was Julia. I helped her come to terms with suddenly being able to see spirits and colours, the auras around her roses.' She breathed deeply. 'That was me,' she said. 'I did that.'

What else had she done? Another look at Cù. 'I helped

Robinson and the others. They were stuck here, and I helped them find peace.' Winsome nodded, drew in a deep, slow breath, felt calmer. 'That was me too,' she said. 'I did that.'

It was true. But there was more still. 'I went with Erin to find Morghan in the...' She struggled for a moment. 'Well, I guess it was some sort of past times. When Morghan helped Blythe.'

Winsome cleared her throat. 'That was also me. I did that too.'

Rain hit the window like pellets, startling her, and she glanced over at it. The curtain was open, and she could see only darkness behind the rectangle of glass. The sight made her shiver, recalling Morghan's words about the creeping darkness that she'd seen moving over the land with her Otherworldly vision.

Cu was sitting up, looking at her.

Awkwardly, Winsome got off the bed, and walked over to the window. She put her palms on the wide windowsill, the left one almost touching the statue of Ceridwen and her cauldron and animals.

But Winsome was gazing outside, although in her mind, she wasn't looking out over the dark churchyard, the trees behind St Bridget's whipping in the wind. In her mind she was seeing the echo of Morghan's words. And she wasn't in her bedroom in the vicarage anymore, either. The sound of the rain was hypnotic, and Winsome had a vivid imagination.

She was in a tower, a high finger of stone that looked out over the darkness. She could feel it around her, a circle of stone blocks, and she, gazing down from it.

Was it ivory, her tower? Keeping her safe, or hiding her away?

Winsome shook her head and felt Cu's warmth against her leg. Still though, she looked down from the window and saw the world spread out beneath her. The wind sounded like the ocean and all around her, lights were going out, being extinguished in a great wave.

Winsome blinked, tried to get her mind under control again. Corral her imagination.

Something moved way down on the ground, far beneath her tower. Someone stood there, she was sure of it, and dazed, Winsome pressed her forehead against the glass, trying better to see.

Yes. She was sure of it. While she stood up here in the tower, someone was down there, standing her ground. Facing the darkness.

Her?

Winsome squinted, her movement sluggish, and nodded to herself. Yes, she thought to herself. It was the ancient goddess, of course. Winsome could see the pig at her feet, although how she could make them out, she didn't know. The tower was high, and it was dark out there.

So very dark.

There was a rapping at the door, and Winsome swung back from the window, startled out of her dream.

She yelped. 'What?'

'Winsome?' It was Veronica, of course. 'I'm making a cup of tea, do you want one?'

Winsome staggered slightly. She'd been asleep on her feet or something. That was it. She'd been sleepwalking.

'Winsome?'

'Oh.' She blinked, shook her head. 'Erm, yes please, that would be nice.' She staggered over to the door and opened it; she'd remembered Morghan saying it was important to eat or drink after jaunting elsewhere. It grounded you, she said.

'Tea would be lovely,' she said.

Veronica frowned at her. 'What were you doing?' she asked. 'You look a bit odd.'

'I'm fine,' Winsome said. 'I was just caught up in my reading. I think I fell asleep.'

Veronica nodded. That she could relate to. 'I fall asleep every time I try to read a book,' she said. 'A novel, that is,' she corrected, since she'd just ordered quite the sturdy pile of coffee table books on fashion and style.

Winsome found herself trailing behind Veronica as she went downstairs, barely hearing Veronica's chattering, and still feeling a little discombobulated. Honestly, she thought. There was something about this place, about Wellsford. It was like it sat half in a dreamworld.

The Otherworld, she thought. It sat half in the Otherworld.

Thanks to Wilde Grove.

'What do you think about this plan to market Wellsford as woo woo central?' she asked.

Veronica turned around and looked at her in surprise. 'What?'

That hadn't been what they'd been talking about.

'You know,' Winsome insisted, sitting down at the table and resting her elbows on the sturdy wood. 'Taking advantage of the history of Wilde Grove to put Wellsford's market on the map.'

'I think it's brilliant,' Veronica said. 'I mean, it makes sense, doesn't it? There are a lot of people doing some pretty interesting things here, and quite a lot of artists and so on. Why shouldn't we put on a market?'

'Oh,' Winsome said. 'I agree with that. Only, do we need to put that sort of slant on it?'

Veronica laughed. 'What's gotten into you, Winsome? Where's this coming from — you're not a vicar anymore.' She paused. 'You're not even really a Christian anymore, are you?'

She'd never been any such thing, herself. Never been religious at all, although she'd used to go to church with her grandparents the few times she'd stayed with them.

Winsome's eyes widened. 'Not a Christian?'

Veronica lifted her shoulders in a shrug. 'Well, are you? You spend more time with Morghan and Ambrose than with Jesus, I'll bet.'

'I still go to church,' Winsome said. 'In Banwell. I'm even still a clergywoman. I'm just retired.'

'Winsome, they forced you out. Because you were participating in pagan rituals.'

Winsome closed her eyes. What, she wondered would Jesus do? She groaned silently. Asking what Jesus would do used to be a constant question for her — one she'd lived her life by.

Now, she had to admit, she was more likely to ask what Morghan would do.

And that was a bit of a problem, wasn't it?

'I'm going to go see the Community of the Sacred Name,' she said, and straightened.

'What community of what name?'

Winsome took the cup of tea Veronica passed her. 'Community of the Sacred Name,' she said. 'It's the place in Yorkshire, for nuns, basically.'

'You can't seriously be considering moving there, can you?' Veronica was stunned. 'What about everything you're doing here? What about all your friends? And Ambrose? Even me? What about me?'

Winsome placed her palms down on the table and looked at her hands. They weren't old hands yet, she knew that. There was a lot of good work they could still do. 'Dean Morton has strongly suggested this place for me.' She paused. 'It has a small hospital and nursing home attached. I would be busy. I could continue my end-of-life care.'

Veronica sank down onto a chair as though the bones in her legs had melted way. She shook her head. 'Tell me you're not serious. You can't be serious. Wellsford is your home.'

'I've lived here a year,' Winsome said, and wondered why she was arguing so strenuously for leaving.

Except she knew why.

'I'm frightened, Veronica,' she said. 'I'm frightened of staying here.'

Veronica regarded her with astonishment. 'What? Why?'

Winsome examined her nails, then closed her eyes. 'If I stay here, things will...continue.'

'What on earth does that mean?'

'It means I'll still see the dead. I'll walk in the woods and strange goddesses will come up to me and want goodness knows what from me.'

This was a bit more than Veronica had been expecting. She shifted slightly in her seat and grimaced. 'Perhaps you ought to be talking to Ambrose about this. Or Morghan.' Or even Erin, for that matter.

'I know I should be talking to Ambrose,' Winsome said miserably. 'But there are feelings involved there, and I wouldn't be able to make a clear-headed decision.'

'Feelings are involved even when he isn't in front of you, I should hope!'

'Of course they are,' Winsome said.

'Then why are you talking to me, instead of him?'

Winsome didn't know that. 'I think because I just couldn't keep it inside anymore, and you're here right now.' She frowned. 'Also, you're at a sort of crossroads yourself. Learning how to begin a new life, trying to decide what that new life might look like.'

Veronica gazed at her. 'Well,' she said after a minute. 'I suppose you're right.' She shook her head. 'And it's not easy, is it?' She waved a hand at the room they stood in. 'I mean, if you were to tell me six months ago that I would be living in a drafty old vicarage and spending my days up to my elbows in people's cast-off old clothes, I would have looked at you like you were bonkers.'

She shrugged. 'And yet, here I am.'

'Here we are,' Winsome agreed. She looked across the table. 'Will you come with me?'

'With you?'

'To visit the community.'

'Wouldn't that, I don't know, cramp your style? Or put them off you?'

'No,' Winsome said, reaching for her cup to stare down into the amber liquid. 'And I think I could do with the company.'

26

'You'll join us?' Selena asked the next morning as Morghan appeared on the terrace. The sun was reaching over the horizon with its first streaks of light. It was getting easier to rise with the dawn now that the sun stayed abed later.

Morghan paused, looked with love at the four people standing on the lawn ready to greet the day. 'I am so glad to see you all,' she said, and pressed a palm to her heart. 'Thank you again for coming, for returning here in this time of need.'

'It's a pivot point,' Clover said. 'Like we said last night, we all need to be here right now.' She paused, looking out into the growing day and seeing something else entirely. 'I think more of us may come and go from here over the next years. This is a hub of sorts.' She frowned while they all watched her. 'A hub on the Wheel.' Clover's eyes fluttered closed for a moment. 'May the way open before us.'

She was right, Morghan thought, and echoed Clover's

prayer, lifting her face to the sun and straightening, baring her heart to the world.

'May the way open before us; may we follow the path of our destiny.'

She held the pose for a moment longer, then relaxed, feeling the trees of the Wildwood around her, as she stood in both worlds.

Morghan nodded to the others, seeing their beautiful and strong auras, their spirits shining.

'Things are being rearranged into a pattern larger than that which I can discern,' she said. 'From where we stand.' A small smile lit her face. 'There are many working to make this happen, and we will need to remember that we walk with them.'

Which was also why she couldn't stay to greet the day.

'I'll be back to have breakfast with you,' she said. 'But I'm afraid I need to see Erin this morning.' She smiled at the other Grove priestesses — how they shone, she thought. How bright they were. 'And I would like to bring her back here as soon as possible to be included in our planning.'

Rue and Clover exchanged glances with Ebony, then nodded.

Selena beamed. 'I for one would like very much to get to know her better.'

MORGHAN TOOK THE PATH THROUGH THE WOODS WITH SURE strides and a mind as clear and receptive as she could make it. Thoughts swam around the edges, brightly coloured little fish, trying to make their way in, but she swept them away. There would be plenty of time later for focused thought on the matters at hand. Now, she needed to walk peacefully through the lightening woods, all the way to Ash Cottage.

She slipped through the gate into the walled garden. Burdock lifted his head and thumped his tail at her. He liked Morghan, even if she did walk with a wolf always at her side.

'Morghan!' Erin lowered her arms from her dance in surprise. Tears sprang suddenly to her eyes, and she pressed her hands to her face.

'Good morning, Morghan,' Stephan said, and bowed in greeting. He was wide open from his morning devotions, and in his gaze Morghan glowed silver and green.

Morghan returned the bow and smiled at the pair. How close they'd grown — they weren't living together yet, not officially, but Morghan could see how their energy, when near each other, swirled around them both in a figure eight.

It was how it had been with herself and Grainne, all those years ago now.

'Good morning,' she said. 'I'm sorry to disturb you, but what I want to give you can wait no longer.' She was looking at Erin, whose energy was still weaker than usual, as the pain she had suffered still radiated from her.

But, thought Morghan, she was out here with Stephan greeting the day, and that was a fine thing. She hadn't been entirely sure that Erin would get up again so quickly.

'Give me?' Erin flushed, folded her arms tightly over her chest and cast an uncertain glance at Stephan.

'I'll leave,' Stephan said.

But Morghan shook her head. 'No,' she said. 'I'd be pleased if you would stay.' She turned to Erin, and drew a small box out of her pocket. 'I had these made to give to you at Samhain, but it seems to me that you ought to have them now.'

Erin looked at the slim square box in Morghan's hand and shook her head, perilously close to tears again. 'No,' she said. 'You can't. Not now.' Her throat was thick, and her breath shuddered in her chest.

Morghan looked gently at her. 'Yes,' she said. 'I think so. Perhaps even I should have had them to give them to you months ago, after your initiation.'

She couldn't think now why she had not.

'I am sorry that I didn't.'

Erin dropped her gaze and shook her head. She'd been struggling all morning, and the only reason she'd come out with Stephan to greet the day in their usual devotions was because of the vision Morghan had shown her the night before.

If it hadn't been for that, she thought she'd still be curled up in a ball in the bed, Burdock wondering why she wasn't getting up.

She cleared her throat, shook her head again. 'I don't think you should give them to me,' she said, her voice low and rough. Sniffing, she unhooked an arm and mopped away the tears that had escaped to roll down her cheeks.

'Why is that?' Morghan asked, her voice as peaceful as her gaze.

Erin shook her head. 'I'm not ready.'

That hadn't been what she'd meant to say. She'd meant to tell Morghan she wasn't worthy.

'I let them get to me,' she said, and looked away, unable to meet Morghan's eyes. 'I should have been stronger.'

Morghan held a hand up to stop Stephan's rush to put his arms around Erin, comfort her.

'Here is the truth,' Morghan said. 'You are young. Your journey and task this lifetime is only beginning. You are only at the very start of learning to tap into the wisdom of the worlds and who you really are.'

Erin squeezed her eyes shut, head turned away, chin almost on her shoulder.

'Here is also the truth,' Morghan continued. 'What you have achieved already is astonishing. You have reached and you have not fallen short.'

Morghan turned Erin's head so that Erin would look at her once more, and smiled at her. She pried one of Erin's hands loose and held it.

'While this is not the ceremony with which I wished you to have them, I'm going to give the leaf and acorn of Wilde Grove to you now. Because Erin Lovelace Faith, you are a priestess of Wilde Grove, one day to be Lady of the Grove, Lady of the Forest, of life and death and love of the worlds.'

She squeezed Erin's hand then let it go and took the lid off the small box, taking out the silver leaf and acorn on their chain and passing the box to Stephan who took it from her with alacrity.

'Erin,' Morghan said, lifting the chain and slipping it over Erin's head. 'Welcome to the Grove. Your place here is certain, in the Grove, and in my own heart.'

Morghan's words pierced Erin, and she cried out, the tears running freely down her cheeks now, and she sagged where she stood, until Morghan caught her up in her arms.

'Don't make yourself small in this world, Erin,' Morghan said, and held her until Erin's legs steadied and Erin was looking into her eyes. 'You are the one who learns the song of the trees, who carries the torch, who holds back the darkness.'

Erin gazed at her, hand going to touch the silver leaf and acorn that hung now around her neck. She managed a nod, closing her eyes, seeing in the darkness behind them the vision of herself winding in procession up the tor, bright torch in her hand.

'Thank you,' she whispered.

Morghan nodded, smiled, their faces close enough to share breath. 'We have a task, you and I,' she whispered. 'As does everyone now on this earth, but we remember it and strive towards it, and we will not fail even when we falter.'

She looked up then, one hand still on Erin's arm, and gestured for Stephan to come closer, and she drew him into their circle.

'Here we are,' she said, 'letting the song of love for the worlds flow through us, just as we have lifetime after lifetime. This is our way, to sing always, to walk the paths of the worlds, to be and shine as brightly as we can, for spirit is the truth of the world, and with that knowledge certain upon us, we stand against all those who would have the world forget this, who would have the world suffer instead.'

She rested a hand on Stephan's shoulder. 'We are the beacons lit across the land. You and I and so many others, shining the light of our souls in even the most difficult of times. We can do nothing else but this, because this is our path. We are neither special nor chosen, but we shine because it is our nature and we have not forgotten but have held onto the ancient knowledge of it.'

Morghan fell silent. Closed her eyes and listened to the

sound of their combined breaths, the sighing of the wind, and letting her spirit flow until she could feel every part of the land in which she stood, the garden, the stone cottage, the lane, the village, the hills. And within it all, the fierce bright lights of the souls who lived there.

Finally, she came back to herself and dropped her hands from the two young people, whom she had known for lifetimes, and stood looking at them.

'Now,' she said. 'The true work begins.' Her smile beamed at them.

Erin gazed down at the leaves of Wilde Grove around her neck. She was dazed, light-headed. She thought that Morghan might just have spoken a spell over their heads, committing them — or perhaps dedicating them — to the path she'd shown her in the vision the night before.

She glanced at Stephan, who stood with eyes shining, excited and strong, ready and willing for everything that was to come.

Erin cleared her throat. Was she ready for it? To pick up the torch and carry it no matter what? She clasped her hand around the leaf and acorn, feeling the edges of the silver leaf bite into her hand.

Morghan broke the silence. 'I must get back,' she said, then looked swiftly at Erin. Her energy was stronger, she saw, but still not back to its usual bright swirl of colour.

Ah well, she thought. All things take their own time. All life is a process, and Erin will grow and learn from this latest challenge. But still, she decided, she would keep a close watch on her young priestess. She nodded at Erin.

'This afternoon,' she said, deciding as she spoke. 'This afternoon I am going to this quarry to see for myself. I will take Selena, Rue, Clover, Ebony, and Ambrose with me.' She looked at Erin. 'Do you wish to come also?'

'I will,' Stephan said. 'For sure.'

But Erin paled and backed away a step. 'No,' she said, shaking her head, horror and terror blooming inside her again. 'I can't. I can't go back there.'

Morghan had not expected anything else. The wound was too raw yet. It needed time to heal. 'That is well,' she said. 'Will you meet us at the stone circle after you have finished work, then?'

Erin, still clasping the leaves, nodded. 'I'll go straight there.' She glanced over at Burdock, who had kept his distance while the magic was strong around them, and looked back at Morghan. 'I can leave Burdock with Mum.'

'As you wish,' Morghan said, then looked around, realising the sun had crawled higher into the morning sky. 'I must get back and leave you to finish your devotions.' She bowed slightly to Stephan and Erin, then turned and let herself out of the garden.

Erin stood still where she was, looking down at the leaf and acorn in her hand. Now, she thought, she wore exactly what Morghan did. Leaf, acorn, and egg. The others had not worn the egg. She closed her eyes.

'What do you think?' Stephan asked. 'How does it feel to have them now — and to know she meant to give them to you all along?' He drew Erin into his arms and kissed her wrinkled forehead. 'I knew she did.'

'She only gave them to me today to stop me from feeling left out, like a silly child.'

Stephan laughed. 'Is there a better reason? You heard

her — she was going to give them to you at Samhain. Now that you've been here a year. Almost exactly.'

Erin squirmed out of his arms. 'Don't say that.'

'Say what?'

'Almost exactly.' She shuddered. 'That's what they said.'

'Who?'

'Them. The Fae. At the quarry.'

Stephan shook his head. 'You didn't tell me that yesterday. What else did they say?'

Erin hugged herself, the Wilde Grove leaves still in one hand. 'I don't want to talk about it,' she said. 'I can't talk about it. They were cruel — and knew things they shouldn't have.' She looked at Stephan. 'I can't go back there.'

'I don't think you should,' Stephan said.

Erin gazed off around the garden, seeing none of it. 'They'll think I'm weak.'

'Who will?'

'Rue and Clover.' Erin's throat convulsed as she swallowed. 'They probably already think I'm an idiot.'

Stephan made to take her in his arms, but she sidestepped him and shook her head, turning for the house.

'I have to get ready for work.'

27

Morghan shook her head, shivered slightly in the cold wind.

'I don't like this place,' she said in a low voice to Ambrose and Clover beside her.

Rue overheard. 'It's hurt,' she said. 'The land. You can feel how wounded it is.' She looked out over the deep gouge in the hillside that the quarry had left and echoed Morghan's shiver.

'They shouldn't be allowed to leave it like this,' Stephan said, folding his arms over his chest and wondering if this was where Erin had been standing the day before when the Fae had — what exactly?

Launched their vicious attack on her? He hadn't been able to get any real answers out of Erin. She hadn't told him exactly what had happened, but they'd spoken to her, these Fae, and they'd hurt her badly.

He knew that much.

Stephan pulled himself back to the present with an effort. Erin would be at work by now, and that would keep her busy at least, and maybe seeing Wayne would cheer her up.

'They're — the people who made this mess — they're supposed to clean it up, turn it into a nature reserve.' Stephan looked over at Ambrose. 'We should get in touch with them, and the Banwell council and see what's going on.' He paused, gingerly touching the atmosphere with his senses. 'Light a fire under their arses.'

He shifted on his feet. The quarry felt bleak and sour, and the wind whistling down and blowing about the high stone cliffs wasn't helping. The sooner this place could be rewilded the better, because right now it felt abused and horribly empty, as though the spirit of the place had given up and moved on.

Or been killed. Death by bulldozer and digger. Trampled by lorry.

Stephan shifted again, frowning as he looked over the far side of the ravaged hill and caught a glimpse of something.

Movement perhaps.

A flash of colour. Or perhaps just a ripple in the air.

He pointed, then hastily tucked his finger back into his fist and made a gesture in the direction inside. 'Ah, do you guys see something over there?'

Morghan looked and nodded. She scanned the line of Fae.

'Yes,' she murmured. 'I see them.'

Rue shared a wide-eyed glance with Ebony, her skin prickling. 'Why are they here?' She drew herself straighter, unwilling to let the strangers think she cowered at the sight of them.

'They've been here all along,' Clover said. And looked at Morghan. 'You saw them, right?'

Clover could not only see them, but she could feel them as well, a pressure, pushing against her. She could feel their gazes on her, their interest in her brightness.

It made her very uncomfortable. She had felt similar pressure before, growing up, but never had it had this conscious intention behind it.

Once, when she'd been perhaps thirteen or fourteen, she had crossed the road into the Botanic Garden and wandered there for a happy hour before realising someone was following her. A man, head down, hoodie shadowing his face. Clover remembered the shock of realising he was there, made worse that it came with the knowledge of what had almost happened to Rue in the same place. She'd felt the tainted touch of his spirit. It had been somehow slimy, greasy in a way that alarmed her more than anything. She could see the tumble of his thoughts, saw that they were disfigured, distorted, ugly, and she had cringed away from him, her breath hitching in her throat, heart thumping, and for a minute, she hadn't known what to do.

At the quarry, Clover shook the memory away. In the end, she'd pulled her phone out of her pocket and called Rue, talking to her loudly, telling her that she'd meet her at the end of the path in just a moment.

The man had slunk away, taking his diseased spirit with him.

These Fae though, didn't feel to Clover as the guy had, even if they did remind her of him.

There was none of the distortion around them. She could not feel their minds, but their energy was clear of that awful greasy sensation.

But it was also bleak, uncaring, ungiving. Whatever these Fae wanted, they wanted it with the cold certainty of steel.

And, she thought, they would happily cut and wound to get it.

She was not surprised they had attacked Erin. They would do the same to anyone who wandered this way. And most who did would not have the defences such as Erin had.

Morghan heard Clover's question and nodded. She'd seen them as soon as she'd stepped out of the car, and now she watched them as brazenly as they watched her.

'They spoke to Erin,' Stephan said. 'Will they approach us, do you think?'

Selena shook her head. 'We are too many for them. I'm sure they prefer their victims here on their own and defenceless.'

'Erin wasn't defenceless, at least,' Clover said. She looked at Stephan, seeing the warm swirl of his energy, the hare at his feet, and behind him, in the shadows of the Otherworld, Bear, and a man whose face was creased with laughter lines. It was a good, clear energy, and she felt drawn to it.

Stephan turned and frowned at her. 'What do you mean?'

The question was asked sharply, and Clover returned his frown. Morghan had not given many details of what had happened during Erin's encounter with these Fae, but she'd said enough to let them know it had been wounding.

'I mean what I said,' Clover told him. 'Her kin are strong, and if she is a priestess of the Grove, then so is she strong too.'

'She is a priestess of the Grove.'

Clover nodded, realising that whatever had happened, it had been severe, to judge by Stephan's defensiveness. She directed her sight back to the far side of the quarry where the line of Fae stood, facing them off.

She was not surprised that it had been.

It hurt her senses to look at the strange Fae, for whoever they were, they were not their friends.

'I feel like we're in one of those face-offs in an old Western, or something,' Ebony said. She shook her head, glanced at Selena. 'They're not our allies, are they?'

'No,' Selena said. She'd been thinking the exact same thing. 'They are not.'

'What do they want?' Ambrose said, then spread his gaze, taking the temperature of the whole quarry. 'And why are they here? This place is cursed,' he said.

Stephan narrowed his eyes, letting out a long slow breath as he sought the vision that would show the Fae more sharply.

It also had the effect of heightening his perception of the land around him, and he felt its hurt once more, now a sharp physical pain in his side.

Cursed, he thought, was a good word for it.

'There are so many of them,' he said, and found himself swallowing a nervous mouthful of saliva. 'The Fae. That's a bit many who hate us in one place.'

Rue agreed; the hostility coloured the air, made it almost hard to breathe when she looked at them. She wrenched her gaze away from the Fae lined up over the other side of the quarry, their clothes and hair untouched by the wind that was trying to fling her own across her face and over her eyes, and looked at Morghan.

'Do you know why they're here?' she whispered, wondering suddenly if the strange Fae could hear them.

'I do not,' Morghan said, and she kept her gaze steadily on the row of Fae, counting twelve of them ranged along the sharp edge of the quarry cut.

'We will not greet them as ordinarily I would insist upon,' she said at last to her people on their side of the deep quarry. 'I think Ebony is right — we are facing off with them.'

Ebony grimaced. She didn't want to be right. She would have preferred it if they had bowed to each other and declared friendship. But she knew, looking at the lineup of Fae, that these would sneer at such an idea.

'What do we do, then?' she asked.

Morghan drew breath. 'This,' she said, and closed her eyes to weave a blessing that would waft out over the wounded land, silvery and fine. It would not be enough on its own, but it would be a good beginning.

Stephan watched and saw the blessing expand as it settled over the riven rock and dark lake. He closed his eyes and added a prayer of his own, sending it spinning over the edge to soothe the wounded land.

Selena nodded. 'They're leaving,' she said, watching the Fae turn and vanish into folds of the world and out of sight.

'Perhaps they didn't like Morghan's blessing,' Rue said.

She withdrew from her expanded vision and hugged herself as the wind was suddenly colder, buffeting against her.

'We will come back,' Morghan decided. She spread an arm out to gesture at the broken landscape. 'We will do a proper healing ceremony for this land. The spirits here need it, both those of the land and the people who died here.'

'What about the Fae?' Clover asked, still able to see shimmers of energy where they had disappeared. She wondered if Selena and Morghan could also — because they could follow that energy, if they wanted.

Clover glanced at Selena, saw how tired and pale she was, underneath her determination. The flight had taken a toll on her.

'We should leave now,' she said. 'It's cold here, and there's nothing more to see.'

WAYNE LOOKED AT ERIN AND WISHED SHE'D TELL HIM WHAT was wrong. She'd been dragging all day, had hardly heard a word anyone said to her, and looked to him as though she was carrying the weight of the world on her shoulders.

'Are you sure you don't want to tell me what's wrong?' he asked, trying one more time before she left for the day. She had two weeks off, and he wouldn't see her except when she popped in to visit.

He himself was quite a bit improved, and there was talk of finding him another place to live. Wayne wasn't sure he wanted this, although of course they'd probably need his bed for someone else — but he wouldn't see Erin near so often if he didn't live somewhere she worked.

Erin shook her head and dredged up the strength to smile.

'I'm just a bit off my game today,' she said, then paused, frowning, her bag in hand. 'Wayne?'

'Yeah, honey?'

'Can I ask you something?'

Relief washed through Wayne, and he nodded. Of course he nodded. 'Anything,' he said.

Erin backed up and sat down, glancing towards the door. They were in the lounge, and she hoped no one would come in wanting to watch the telly in the next minute.

Wayne picked up the remote and muted the TV. It was only the news on, and when he glanced at it, at the report of yet more fighting somewhere, he thought that perhaps if the news had celebrated more good stuff — there was plenty of good stuff that went on, he was sure of it — then the world wouldn't be in half the pickle it was.

'What is it?' Wayne said, putting the remote down and leaning forward in his own chair.

Erin stared at the carpet.

'What is it, pet?' Wayne asked. 'What happened? Something has happened, hasn't it? You're not yourself at all.' A thought sliced into him. 'It's not your fella, is it? Stephan — he's not gone and hurt you in some way?'

Erin looked at him, startled, and he relaxed a fraction. That was good. Not Stephan, then, which would be right; the young man worshiped the ground Erin walked on.

Erin cleared her throat. 'Wayne. I don't feel good enough to take over from Morghan one day.'

Sitting immediately straighter, Wayne was shaking his head even before he answered. 'That's bollocks, that is, pardon my language. Of course you are — she chose you, remember?'

Erin nodded, but reluctantly. She'd been thinking about this all day. 'But she only chose me because of Macha, because of who I've been in the past.' She leant forward in the chair, hugging her bag with its change of clothes tightly against her.

'That was lifetimes ago, Wayne. I'm not Macha anymore. I'm just stupid little Erin, who keeps losing her way, who has always lost her way.'

Wayne was silent for a minute, looking closely at her. She was like a daughter to him — he wasn't afraid of admitting it. If things had been different — much different — she would have been. Maybe not his kid biologically, but still.

She was so pale. There were bruises under her eyes that he'd never seen before.

'What happened, love?' he asked, and this time his voice was low, entreating.

Erin took a deep, shuddering breath. She wouldn't cry again, absolutely she wouldn't. So she sniffed again, rocked a little in the chair and clasped her hands together.

'If I tell you, will you promise to keep it to yourself?'

'That depends on what it is,' Wayne said, feeling pale now himself. 'What if you need more help than I can give you?'

Erin was shaking her head. 'I don't want anyone else to know.' She closed her eyes. 'Just promise, or I'll go home, and we can forget about it.' She looked at him. 'You're the only one who might understand, even a little.'

What? Wayne didn't know what to make of that. After all, he had a pretty poor record with his life choices. He looked at Erin in bewilderment. He couldn't imagine her falling into some problem with drinking or drugging, not Erin, not now.

'I promise,' he said, his voice coming out a croak.

Erin nodded, sniffed again, looked down at her knotted hands.

'I let some people talk me into...something,' she said, not prepared to tell him it was suicide. Then Wayne would really freak out. She cleared her throat. 'Almost talk me into it,' she corrected, glancing at Wayne who stared at her, eyes round.

'And now...' She drew in a shuddering breath, bracing herself. 'And now I hate myself for it. I feel hot and panicky every time I think of it, and I don't know how to face anyone, because it was so stupid — I should have known better.'

Wayne waited for her to continue, but it seemed she was done. 'Is this why you're suddenly thinking you're not worthy of being the next Lady of the Grove?'

Erin had explained the Grove stuff, and while he still wasn't entirely sure what it was all about, he knew good people when he met them, and Morghan was good people.

Erin nodded, a stiff, jerky little movement.

His hands clenching into fists, Wayne decided he wanted to hurt these people Erin was talking about. Who were they? Where were they?

He uncurled his fingers with an effort, tamped down his temper, and tried to be what Erin needed him to be right then and there.

Even better, he thought he understood.

'That's shame talking,' he said. It was an emotion he was intimately acquainted with. 'That's what that is, and it's inside you working away on you like corrosive acid. I ought to know — I can recognise it when I see it.'

Erin nodded. She knew it was shame she felt. 'I don't know how to get past it, though.'

Wayne looked at her, at her wan face, usually so bright and expressive, and he wanted suddenly to cry. Shame crushed the spirit, he knew that. And Erin's spirit was so bright and precious.

'You gotta tell someone other than me,' he said. 'You gotta let the poison out, and heal where it's been.' He scowled. 'You gotta do one of them healings, like your Morghan and Winsome did on me.'

He nodded and looked urgently at her, holding her gaze when she lifted her head. 'That's what you all have taught me.'

He pressed the point home.

'You gotta forgive yourself.'

28

'WHAT WAS THAT ABOUT, DO YOU THINK?' AMBROSE STIRRED embers to flame in his kitchen grate, shaking his head. 'I don't think I've ever seen them like that.' He paused, log in hand, a frown on his face, then shook his head. 'No, never away from the Grove like that, as though they had trouble on their minds.' He dropped the log on the fire and got up, dusting his knees and putting the guard back in front of the fireplace before turning to fetch the cups.

Morghan was pouring water into the teapot. She'd taken one look at Selena when they'd got back from the quarry and insisted that the girls take her to go and lie down.

What she was planning required Selena to be rested and alert. At least, though, she was in good health. Morghan hugged that knowledge to her heart. It was lovely to have her back in Wilde Grove. And for Rue, Clover, and Ebony to be there too, of course, even if it was all only for a short while.

But she had to curb her impatience. Selena had travelled far and needed to take care of herself. She was remarkably spry for her age, but even so, the journey had tired her.

'Have you?' Ambrose asked, bringing her back from her thoughts. 'Seen them away from the Grove like that?'

Morghan took the pot to the table and sat down, grateful for the warmth from the growing fire.

'No, not like that,' she said at last. 'But I'm rarely away from the Grove, particularly now that Winsome has taken over half of my death care work.' She gave a wry smile. 'Those were not Queen Alastrina's people however. I'm certain of that, at least, if nothing else.'

'I agree,' Ambrose said, coming over and sitting down. He tapped the table with restless fingers while he thought on it.

'What I'm wondering,' Morghan said. 'Is why there?'

'Why there?'

'They had the air of making a statement with their presence.' Morghan considered it. 'Today, at least.'

'They didn't try anything on with us,' Ambrose said.

Morghan gave a humourless laugh. 'They knew it would be foolish — too many magic weavers lined up in a row on the other side.'

'Magic weavers?' Ambrose considered Morghan and the phrase she'd used. 'I don't think I've ever heard you call yourself that.' Ambrose shook his head.

But Morghan was thinking on her vision. Ravenna on one side of her, and Catrin on the other. If anyone had woven magic from the elements, from the great web that connected everything, it was those two.

'Perhaps,' she said slowly, 'it is time to do more magic.'

Ambrose squinted at Morghan. 'I'm not entirely sure

what you mean.'

Morghan shook her head and poured the tea. 'Ambrose,' she said. 'Nor am I.'

She slid the teacup over to Ambrose and they sat in silence for a moment, the fire crackling away in the grate now. Morghan lowered her hand and touched Wolf's fur. Around her gathered the trees of the Wildwood, and as always seemed to be the case now, part of her stood in the Wildwood, the worlds spinning, the wheel turning, the web gleaming, and above her always, the bright, guiding light of the North Star.

'Is it too late?' she asked and turned her gaze to Ambrose. She saw him with eyes wide with the vision of the Otherworld and watched as his aura shimmered and flexed around him, as blue and clear as a summer's sky.

Ambrose frowned at her. 'Too late for what?'

'To save the world.'

Her words sent a shiver of shock through Ambrose, and he straightened in his chair to gaze at her, consternation on his features.

Morghan looked at him. 'I think I'm serious,' she said.

He shook his head. 'I never would have expected that question from you.'

Morghan laughed, but it was a rather hollow sound. 'We've passed the point of no return, though, haven't we? There will be consequences now, from climate change. The world will change. This, in certainty, lies ahead of us.'

Ambrose nodded slowly in agreement. 'All the more reason to step up our work,' he said, looking levelly at Morghan. 'There are some uncomfortable years ahead for humanity — for everyone, thanks to us humans.'

Morghan turned her head and gazed out the window. She looked at the trees of Wilde Grove, her friends, those who had taught her all the songs she knew how to sing.

'So,' she said after a moment. 'We are in agreement, then?' A pause. 'About the need to do more? To also protect as many as we can against the likes of those whom we saw at the quarry today?'

'More magic?' Ambrose shifted in his chair, trying to divine what that would mean. He looked inside himself at the pattern of the world — this was how he thought, in terms of patterns — and searched for how all the pieces might fit together.

'Isn't that what the Goddess and Queen have been showing us for the last year, now?' he asked at last.

'For even longer than that,' Morghan replied. 'I remember the first time she showed us, Selena and I, a vision of beacons, and darkness.' She was still for a moment, then sipped at her tea. 'That was right before Selena left to find Rue and Clover.'

'A long time ago.'

'This mess has been an age in the making, and I'm sure our Otherworldly allies would have been concerned right from the beginning.' Morghan put her cup down. 'Their instructions have been clear,' she said. 'In the middle a pear tree, for the immortal soul. To one side a church, on the other, a school.'

'And if we don't?' Ambrose asked. It was the question that had been unspoken between them for some time.

This day's events, however, made Ambrose feel it was impossible to ignore for any longer.

Morghan gazed at him. 'I think we know, don't we?' she

said.

'We see more of what we did today.' Ambrose wasn't sure whether it was question or statement.

'And worse. Not only the impatient amongst the Fae,' Morghan said. 'But all the other faeries, among them the entities whose sport it is to prey on the weaknesses of humans.' She thought of her vision of Ravenna at the Forest House, of Clover's recited vision, and knew they'd had to consider this before.

Ambrose nodded, feeling more of the pieces slot into place in his internal pattern. 'Yes,' he said. 'Since most have forgotten their connection with spirit and with the land we live on — and should serve.'

Their conversation made him feel cold, even with the fire spitting out its flames and heat a short distance from him. He shook his head, looked again at Morghan.

'What do we do?' he asked. 'In practical terms?' He paused. 'This "more magic" of yours.'

'The church and the school,' Morghan reminded him, although truthfully, she felt still as though she were groping around for the answers. 'Build the church and the school, let the beacons light across the land.'

Ambrose tucked his chin down and considered Morghan's words, the meaning behind them.

'We have to move further into the world,' he said.

Morghan nodded. 'And deeper into spirit.'

'That's.... not going to be easy.'

Morghan laughed, shook her head. 'No,' she said. 'It's not. But haven't we already made a start?' She paused, pursed her lips. 'When does Molly Wainwright return? Is she still keen to work on some sort of book with you?'

'She is,' Ambrose said. 'Her sister has just been diagnosed with cancer, however, and Molly wants to spend time with her.'

Morghan nodded but remained silent.

'Do you want to follow the lead of the other Druid Groves?' Ambrose asked. 'With their training courses?'

This was a good question and Morghan had already been thinking of her answer. She and Ambrose had had several meetings lately, with the other Groves, and their conversations had been productive.

'I do not want to repeat what they are already doing so well,' Morghan said.

'We would do it differently,' Ambrose told her.

'Yes, but I want our efforts to overlap, not repeat, even with a twist.'

Ambrose nodded. That was reasonable. 'School and church,' he said.

'And the pear tree,' said Morghan. 'The symbol of the immortal life of the spirit.'

They drank their tea in silence.

'Tell me,' Morghan said at last. 'How is Winsome?'

'Winsome?' Ambrose was surprised by the question, and he frowned at Morghan. 'Did you not see her yourself yesterday?'

'I did,' Morghan agreed. 'She seems troubled by something. I wondered if you knew what it was.'

Ambrose was taken aback. 'You know I would not repeat conversations she and I have had in private.'

'I do not expect you to,' Morghan said with a gentle smile, and gazed past Ambrose at their surroundings. She was very fond of this small kitchen — had spent many hours here, debating with Ambrose, and before that, of course, she'd lived here herself.

Morghan turned away from that memory, of Grainne laughing in this very room.

Ambrose looked at Morghan. 'Winsome's good. Of course.'

'Why of course?'

Ambrose stared at her. 'You want to talk about Winsome?'

'Perhaps,' Morghan said. 'She is my friend.'

That got a nod from Ambrose. She was, he thought, perhaps Morghan's closest friend, now that Teresa was gone. There was Lucy, and Charlie, of course, but Winsome and Morghan had bonded in a way that had surprised him at first, and now pleased him enormously. The two most important people in his life.

Morghan added to her statement. 'The church building will be up for sale soon. If it is bought by someone who wishes it to be for the use of the village, Winsome will most likely have a hand in deciding what that usage will look like.'

This got a nod from Ambrose. He'd already thought about it, knew it was also on Winsome's mind. He knew the changes of the last year were still hitting her hard.

'You are thinking of purchasing St Bridget's?'

'It is no longer St Bridget's,' Morghan said. 'Although I could not think of a better goddess for it to be dedicated to.'

'No, I suppose it lost that name with the deconsecration.' That had been a hard day for Winsome. She'd gotten through the ceremony brilliantly — heroically, Ambrose thought — then collapsed afterwards in floods of tears and recriminations towards herself.

He repeated his question, for it wasn't something Morghan had mentioned to him before this minute.

'You are thinking of purchasing it?'

'It has to stay in village hands,' Morghan said. 'I feel that strongly.'

Ambrose nodded. 'As does Winsome. I think she's hoping that Veronica will buy it.'

'And will she?'

'I don't know. Her divorce settlement is far from sorted. From listening to Winsome, I'm not sure that Veronica will have the funds available in time, and of course, this is a transitional time for Veronica. Winsome is aware that she may choose to move on once her divorce is final and she has a firm vision of what she wants for her future.'

Morghan nodded. 'I'm taking Winsome back to the cave sometime soon.'

Ambrose's eyes widened, and then he smiled. 'She's said she wants to go?'

'She has agreed to.'

Ambrose laughed. 'That's not quite the same thing.'

But Morghan ignored his comment. 'I'd ask you to drum for us, but Winsome's energy still goes haywire when she's in the same room as you. It would probably be distracting for her to have you there.'

'You've travelled before with Clarice doing the drumming, haven't you? Ask her again.' Ambrose made the suggestion even as he was flooded with warmth from Morghan's comment. He had been afraid — although he kept the fear to himself — that once Winsome knew him better, that she would grow impatient with his ways and idiosyncrasies. For he was, he knew, a creature of habit and his studies and enthusiasms could possibly, he thought, be quite boring to live with.

He had promised himself that he would make an effort to become more active in his practices, yet still he spent hours a day in study. His was a nature suited to it.

Ambrose cleared his throat and gathered up the empty teapot. 'We still haven't decided upon our next steps,' he said.

Morghan gazed out the window at the trees again.

'These are them,' she said at last.

Ambrose turned back to listen.

'Selena, Erin, and I will visit the Queen.'

Ambrose nodded. He thought that was a good idea.

'Perhaps you could speak to Maxen,' Morghan said, the thought just coming to her. 'He always has his ear to the ground.' She let herself smile slightly at the thought of Maxen, whose interest in human business had taken root centuries ago when she had first come to him to ask for help with Blythe. Since then, he had become a firm friend — particularly with Ambrose.

'I will do so, if he is about.'

Morghan nodded. 'I would like it if you, and perhaps Stephan, although he is much busier now with his studies, could contact the Banwell council about the quarry. We need to deal with that on a practical level.'

'I will do so first thing in the morning,' Ambrose said.

'Ask them about the plans in place for returning it to beauty, and also tell them we wish to perform a public healing service there, for the land.'

Ambrose's brows rose. He had not expected this. 'Public?'

'Yes,' Morghan said feeling out her decision. She touched her hand to Wolf at her side and nodded. 'A public one. We're going to have to move out into the public sphere.' She smiled slightly. 'Molly's work has begun that, fortunately.'

'And if the council disagrees?' Ambrose asked. 'They likely will.'

'Then I will speak to them myself, so if that's the case, make me an appointment with someone who has the capacity to make decisions on the matter.'

Ambrose stared at Morghan. 'You'll talk to them yourself?'

With a laugh, Morghan nodded. She rose from her seat. 'Times are changing, Ambrose. I must change with them.'

'And after the quarry is taken care of?'

Morghan shook her head. 'Let me speak to the Queen. After that, we will see.'

She gathered up her few things. Patted her pocket to check her phone was there — she was making a concerted effort to remember to take it everywhere with her, no matter how much she disliked doing so.

'We are making this up as we go along, Ambrose,' she said. Then shook her head. 'No, that's not quite right, is it? We follow the path, wherever it goes.'

'Even when we don't know where it will lead us?' Ambrose asked. 'Or through what trials?'

Morghan smiled as she moved to the door.

'Even then,' she said.

29

Clover stared out the window at the trees, most of whom were shedding their leaves and thrusting bare knuckled branches at the grey sky. She was watching the fine spell of protection that shrouded the grounds of Hawthorn House and spread out over a great swathe of the woods. It shimmered and wafted occasionally in an unseen breeze, and yet held strong. It was something that she'd never given a thought to, in any of her visits to Wilde Grove, and yet this time, she could barely keep her gaze from seeking it out.

'What are you thinking about?' Rue asked, putting aside the magazine she'd been flipping through. Morghan wasn't back yet from Blackthorn House, and Selena was upstairs, resting. Ebony paced the room like a caged tiger, a look of complete preoccupation on her face.

Rue was also feeling restless. The hour they'd spent at the quarry had distressed her on a level she wasn't expecting. There had been energy there that had been unpleasant to touch. Almost, she thought, malevolent. Whoever those Fae were, they did not like humans.

She sighed and looked over at her sister.

'The wards that surround Wilde Grove,' Clover said, answering Rue's question.

'Wards?' Ebony perked up and went over to Clover's window to look out. 'Where are they?' She couldn't see anything. 'What do they look like?'

Clover shrugged. 'To me, they're like a fishing net, I suppose. Except one made of energy. And they cover the whole property that I can see.'

Ebony lifted an eyebrow. 'You can really just see them? You don't have to shift or anything?'

'When I look, I see them,' Clover said, who needed to make little effort to do so.

Ebony straightened. 'What about when you don't look?'

'Then I don't see them, I only feel them there.'

'You're aware of them, even when you're not paying attention to them?' Ebony thought this was fascinating.

'Of course,' Clover said, frowning and turning back to the view. 'Like you're always aware of the sea not far away, even when you're not thinking about it. It's the same thing.'

'Except I'm not aware of the sea nearby unless I turn my attention to it.'

Clover looked dubiously back at Ebony. 'Really?' she asked. 'You don't feel the land, the hills, the ocean, the sky? Unless you're looking at them, or thinking about them?'

Ebony considered the question. 'I don't know,' she admitted finally. 'I don't think I've ever considered it.'

Rue uncrossed her legs, leant forward in her seat. 'Morghan and Selena taught us this sort of attention, didn't they? To be able to turn it on and off.'

'Turn it on and off, yeah,' Ebony said. 'But not feel it as a matter of course.' She turned back to Clover. 'You can always feel the land and so on?'

'Of course,' Clover said, who didn't know any other way of being. 'We're part of it. Oughtn't we be able to feel it as it feels us?'

Ebony reared back and held out her hands. 'Whoa,' she said. 'Hang on in there, cowboy. The land can feel us in return?'

Clover nodded, but her attention was snagged again on the wards outside. She was wondering about them. Why did Wilde Grove need wards in the first place? How long had they been there?

And the ancient magic that lay behind them. The blessing. Why had a blessing been woven?

That was probably the real question. Ravenna and Bryn and the others had made it, after all. Morghan had seen that — Rue had seen that.

And all the while Rhian had been in the cave, preparing to wade out into that whiteness. The fog that shrouded everything.

The flow of the worlds, Blackbird had said.

But still, she felt that if she worked backwards from the wards to the blessing, she might get somewhere.

It was something to start with, anyway.

'What do we feel like, to the land?' Ebony asked, wonder in her voice as she considered the question. 'I mean, do we feel like something that belongs, or like, I don't know — trespassers or something?'

'We are part of the pattern,' Clover said absently. 'For the most part we belong and are sensed as such.'

'For the most part?' This time it was Rue who asked the question, her interest piqued. She glanced at Ebony, widened her eyes.

Clover shrugged. 'Some people's energy grates upon the land, like that person is a predator, careless. Others are more in harmony. Do you think Selena used to put wards up around the Grove when she was Lady here?'

'Put up wards?' Rue was confused by the sudden jump in topic.

'I would guess so,' Clover said in response to her own question. She couldn't remember if Morghan had said how long the tradition had been going for. 'I know Morghan does it now. Maybe Ambrose too.'

'Both of them, probably,' Ebony said, planting herself next to Clover at the window and squinting out at the view. She wanted to see the threads of these wards Clover was talking about.

'Sink into your second sight and look for them,' Clover said, feeling automatically what Ebony was trying to do. 'The looking will likely let you find them.'

'Huh.' Ebony made herself breathe deeply for several breaths, and let herself sink, then float, as she exhaled, putting herself into the expanded state she used when doing house clearings and moving lingering spirits of the dead onwards.

'Crikey,' she said, twisting her head to gaze upwards out the window, her vision paradoxically blurred and sharper.

'It works; I can see it. I think. Is it that, I dunno, sort of blue shimmer over everything?'

Clover nodded. 'Yes, that's it.' She twisted around in her seat to look at Rue. 'Maybe Selena could tell us about them. They might be similar to those we put around Windswitch.'

'Probably,' Rue said, getting up finally to come and crowd around the window to have a look.

'WHY ARE YOU SO INTERESTED IN THE WARDS ALL OF A sudden?' Rue asked, watching with a frown as Clover knocked on Selena's door. They should be letting Selena rest, not barging in on her with weird questions.

Clover didn't know if she was ready to put her reasons into words. Right now, her need to know felt like a piece of a puzzle she was trying to do. She was afraid of trying to force it into the space she suspected it belonged and would prefer that it simply slipped into place.

'Come in,' Selena called.

Clover pushed the door open enough to stick her head through. 'Do you mind if I ask you a few questions?' She'd known from the bottom of the stairs that Selena was awake, and sure enough, she was sitting by the window reading.

'Of course,' Selena said. 'In fact, why don't I come downstairs, and we can have some tea while we discuss what's on your mind.'

Clover smiled. That would be perfect.

'WELL,' SELENA SAID, GIVING THE QUESTION SOME consideration, while her fingers warmed on her teacup. The fire was crackling merrily in the grate and Selena felt deeply at home, in a way that she realised she never had in New Zealand, no matter how she'd enjoyed living there. She must, she reminded herself, go for a walk around the grounds soon. 'Well, Annwyn taught me when I was pretty young,' she said. 'I think making sure the wards are strong is something that's been a habit here for a long time.'

Clover nodded. She was getting a feeling for the shape of the puzzle piece now, she thought. 'But who started it, and why?'

Selena took a sip of tea and thought about it. 'Who? I don't know. They've been in place for my entire lifetime, and probably for long before that.' She paused. 'Why?' Another sip of tea while she considered the question.

'Perhaps because of what we saw today?' Clover asked. 'At the quarry?'

'The Fae?' Selena wrinkled her brow. 'I'm not sure I understand your meaning?'

'Could it have been to keep faerie like them away?'

Selena thought about it. 'I always thought it was more to keep humans at bay, actually.'

Ebony was frowning. 'Can I ask something? About the Fae at the quarry today?' She was looking at Clover, who nodded. 'Only what you said earlier — about the land being able to feel us, does that go for them today? For any faerie, for starters?'

'Of course,' Clover said. 'In fact, they're more in relation-ship to the land, so they both sense each other all the time.'

'Fuck,' Ebony said, then winced. 'Sorry Selena. But that's really interesting.' She looked back at Clover. 'Even ones like those we saw today, who seem like nothing but trouble?'

'Nothing but trouble to us,' Clover said. 'To the land? To Gaia? No, probably not.'

'So they'd have the same sort of relationship to the land that all faeries likely do — much closer than our own?'

Clover nodded, thought about it. 'I learnt this word a while ago — symbiotic. Faeries have a symbiotic relationship to the land in our world as well as their own, as they're really aspects of the same.' She sighed. 'We're supposed to, as well.'

'But we don't,' Ebony said. 'We rape and pillage it instead.' She shook her head. 'Sometimes I hate humans.'

'Those Fae we saw today agree with you,' Rue said with a shudder.

Clover turned to Selena again, and wished that Morghan was about as well. 'How much do we really know about what happened at the Great Turning?'

'Almost nothing,' Selena said. 'The little we know about it is from glimpsed rememberings.'

'UPG,' Ebony said.

Rue frowned at her. 'What's that?'

'Unverified Personal Gnosis,' Ebony said, and flung her arm along the back of the chair she sat in. 'A person knows stuff through their private experience, but has no material proof of it.'

Selena thought about that. 'Many of the things we do – the rituals and so on, the stories we tell – have been picked up along the tides of time, a lot of it, such as the titles for the seasons, from within the last hundred years. We call our path the Ancient Way, but little but the core of it is actually ancient.' She smiled. 'Of course, what really matters is that core, the heart of it all, that we are soul as well as flesh and blood, that we have a relationship with the world that is meant to be respectful and reciprocal, and that everything has spirit and the world is vast and meaningful.' She shrugged. 'The rest has evolved as the years have gone by — format of the rituals we do, the mythology, even the language. Some of it is very old, some of it is more recent.'

Selena laughed, getting up to go and meet Morghan at the cave for their travelling. 'Humans are naturally creative, and so are our practices. We also follow fashions, reinvent things.'

Clover listened, but somewhat impatiently. It was clear to her that Selena didn't know enough about the wards around the property, and none of them had any idea about that ancient blessing that preceded it. The assumption that the wards were to keep out hostile villagers was reasonable, and made sense within that context, but what, she nodded to herself, about the blessing? How did that figure into everything?

She pursed her lips and considered the view out the window again. What she needed, she thought, was another of her seizures. Another quick jaunt into the past, to see exactly what was going on way back when with that blessing.

And to find out what she was up to in the cave.

The idea made her tap her fingers nervously on the windowsill, the vision of Rhian rising in front of her, sight-less, blind to the everyday, her vision instead turned relent-lessly towards things of spirit.

'Are you all right?' It was Rue, worried.

Clover nodded. 'I'm fine,' she said. But she kept her eyes, wide open and seeing perfectly — for now — focused on the view outside the window and the sight of the shimmering blue wards that draped over the property.

Perhaps, she thought, there was a way to induce a shifting, a seizure. Perhaps there was a way to go back and see exactly what had happened.

And why.

30

Erin found herself walking slowly, climbing the hill through the woods with feet made of lead. She didn't want to go ahead with this, she thought. That was the problem.

She didn't feel up to standing across from Rue and Clover and Ebony, feeling Clover's gaze on her again, knowing she was seeing things, but not being told what.

And the Queen. Meeting the Queen. It had been something Erin was looking forward to, but not anymore. She thought that if she went through with this, and stood before the Queen, the faerie woman would see immediately there was something wrong.

Erin nodded to herself. The huge stain that was on her spirit.

She stopped walking. Looked around herself at the trees, their leaves no longer green, but changed, beginning their great letting go, to turn to mulch upon the woodland floor. She touched the Wilde Grove leaves that hung against her breast with her grandmother's crystal egg, then closed her fist around them and took them off.

Erin's heart pounded as she stood there in the shadow and shade of the autumn woods and looked at the glint of silver between her fingers. She took a breath, held it, then took another.

And turned on her heel, back down the path the way she'd come.

MORGHAN PACED IN FRONT OF THE CAVE. 'SHE SHOULD BE here by now.'

'Perhaps something has happened to hold her up,' Selena said. 'Do you have your phone? You could call Ash Cottage, or the care home if she was working there today.'

But Morghan shook her head. 'I left the damned thing back at the house.' She looked over hopefully at Clarice.

'No,' Clarice said. 'I didn't bring mine either.'

Morghan stopped her pacing and blew out a breath. Shook her head. Touched her solar plexus. 'I don't have a good feeling about this. Something is wrong.' She moved her hands, held her head. Looked out into the trees, searching for Erin.

'She said she would meet us,' Selena said. 'She's only what, 10 or 15 minutes late?' But even as she asked the question, she was standing up, peering into the woods beside Morghan.

'Something has kept her even while she knows this is important,' Selena said. She looked at Morghan, a frown gathering on her brow. 'Are you sure she's the one?'

Morghan turned and stared at Selena in surprise. 'The one what?'

'The right one to take your place,' Selena said, almost apologetically, giving Clarice a swift glance also. 'Yes, I know you've told me that Erin is one of the original members of the Grove — but she also spent 21 years away from your influence when she should have grown up here.' Selena paused. 'Perhaps this other influence was too much. She left abruptly yesterday, for no reason, and now hasn't turned up today, even though she knows this is vital.'

Morghan shook her head, emphatic. 'She's the right one.' She looked over at Clarice. 'Wouldn't you agree?'

Clarice was frowning at the turn of the conversation — and why, she wondered, had Erin not joined them? She definitely knew it was important.

'I agree,' she said. 'Erin's been working hard.'

'Rue...' Selena said, and faltered a moment under Morghan's gaze, then tried again. 'Rue has been a priestess of this Grove since she was 16. Under your tutelage and mine. She is more than qualified to take on the leadership when it is time.'

Morghan opened her mouth to speak, then was silent. She turned back to the trees, to the path that led around the hill from the cave where she waited.

Selena watched her. But Morghan's face was set, her mouth tight.

'Perhaps we were wrong,' Selena said, gentling her voice. 'Perhaps Rue and Clover are here because they are supposed to stay.' Selena closed her eyes, considered it, then opened them to look at Morghan again. 'The Priestess and the Oracle. You must admit, it makes a certain amount of sense.'

Morghan turned to face Selena. 'Erin is late, that is all.'

'Do you feel her anywhere in this forest?' Selena asked.

Morghan sighed. Shook her head. 'No.'

'Then where is she? Perhaps what happened to her at the quarry was too much for her.' Selena stepped forward and put a hand on Morghan's arm. 'I do not mean to sound harsh,' she said. 'I just want you to be flexible in your considerations. Not everything works out the way we hope — or even how our kin plans.'

Morghan stared at Selena.

'Tell me,' Morghan said finally. 'What did Clover see when she met Erin? She saw something, did she not?'

Selena returned Morghan's gaze. 'She saw Macha — isn't that what she was called?'

Morghan nodded, not taking her eyes from Selena.

'She saw Macha, she saw her Fox and Raven kin,' Selena repeated. 'That is all.'

'That is all?'

Selena considered it. 'I believe there was an amount of distrust between the women. That Macha had ways about her that were wild and unpredictable.'

Morghan heard the words Selena spoke to her, and let them sink in. Then she turned back towards the trees and laughed.

'We are not going to let a centuries old disinclination towards immediate friendship stop us from our task now.'

'Not a disinclination towards friendship, Morghan,' Selena said. 'A hesitation to trust.'

'I trust Erin,' Morghan said, tilting her face towards the

sky. 'And as for wild and unpredictable magic — you knew Grainne, you're aware of Catrin. Which means you know I've experience enough of it.' She paused. 'Erin has only just begun to touch her magic. Yes, it would have been better had she begun her training younger — but that is no barrier to learning now, and she is still young, and full of promise.'

Morghan paused. 'After all,' she said, looking now at Selena. 'That is what we will be asking of everyone — inside and outside of this Grove — to learn their magic no matter age or circumstance.'

Morghan lifted a brow at Selena, then turned back to the path. 'I stand by my choice.'

Selena nodded, stood beside her. 'Then I shall also,' she said. 'But what will we do this minute? Do you wish still to visit the Queen?'

Clarice broke in, finally, having followed the conversation with growing consternation. She'd become used to Erin. They'd become friends. 'I'll go look for her,' she said. 'You don't need me to drum for you — you can travel without it.'

ERIN CROSSED THE LAWN TO HER FRONT DOOR, FUMBLED IT open and pushed her way inside to stand in the quiet of the cottage looking around in dismay.

She loved this place. Loved the house, loved everything inside it. Loved Burdock, and Stephan.

'It's just for a little while,' she said, and looked down at the silver leaf and acorn in her hand. 'Just until...' She didn't know how that sentence ended, so instead, Erin took a breath and went up the stairs.

At least it was good timing, she decided as she hauled her suitcase out of the wardrobe in the spare bedroom. She was on two week's holiday from the care home.

Erin told herself that two weeks ought to be enough, as she took the suitcase through to her bedroom and laid it open on the bed then stared at it in dismay.

It was still full of many of her old clothes, she realised, sifting through them, pulling some out. The ones she'd worn before coming to Wellsford a year ago.

'Almost exactly,' she murmured, then turned to her drawers and wardrobe, and added a few things to the top of the pile and zipped the suitcase back up.

She'd put the Wilde Grove leaves on her dressing table, and now, suitcase in hand, ready to go, she stopped and stared at them for a moment, before scooping them up and tucking them in her pocket.

She wasn't leaving Ash Cottage to forget how to be a priestess of Wilde Grove.

She was leaving so that she could remember.

In the kitchen, she wrote a note to Stephan, left it on the table. He would look after Burdock, she knew — Burdock was already with him, since she had been going to the cave to travel with Morghan and Selena. Her hand hesitated over the note, wondering if she ought to write another, for Morghan.

Erin shook her head, opened the door, and dragged her suitcase across to her car. She walked as if in a dream, part of her unable to believe she was actually doing this.

Leaving Ash Cottage, Wilde Grove? How could she?

'It's only for a few days,' she said to the wind and the trees and the raven that watched her. 'A week, maybe.'

· · ·

MORGHAN SHOOK HER HEAD. 'No,' SHE SAID. 'WE WILL WAIT until Erin is with us.'

'I don't think she's coming,' Selena told her. 'Something has delayed her. Do we really want to delay asking the Queen our questions about the Fae at the quarry?'

Morghan stood still, her thoughts in conflict. Finally, on a sigh, she turned. 'You're right. It shouldn't wait.' She looked over at Clarice. 'I'd be glad if you could go and find her. She had a shock the other day. I am concerned about her.'

Clarice nodded, passed her drum to Morghan. 'Look after this for me. I'll go see where she is.'

She strode off into the trees, graceful as a gazelle, determined to find Erin before there was too much more dissent in the Grove.

That was the last thing they needed.

Morghan stood watching her until Clarice turned a corner and disappeared from view. She was thinking much the same thing.

'Selena,' she said, turning and taking Selena's hand. 'Do you remember teaching me that when a path is chosen, a disruptive force will come along in an attempt to derail one from the path determined?' She thought a moment. 'Particularly if the path is the right one?'

Selena gazed at her. 'You think that's what this is? That this is why Erin hasn't turned up?'

But Morghan shook her head and stroked Selena's hand in her own. 'No,' she said. 'I think your questioning of what has already been decided and settled might be.'

Selena heard this in silence and didn't reply straight away. In truth, she was shocked at Morghan's words. She drew her hand back.

'We have one goal,' she said clearly to Morghan. 'And that is to preserve and spread the teachings of the Ancient Way, so that a path of grace and love might be followed by all who will it through the upheaval to come.' She took a measured breath.

'I do not seek to disrupt that goal with my questions. I am not the instrument of disruption.'

Morghan was silent.

'I am asking these questions,' Selena said, 'because it is logical and prudent to ask them. We do not know all the details of our destinies, and things do go wrong.'

She pursed her lips. 'I think we'd best leave this travelling until another day. No matter the urgency. I fear the harmony of will necessary for us to travel together has been broken.'

CLARICE DROPPED HER HANDS FROM THE YOUNG BIRCH SHE'D leant against to listen to Morghan and Selena's conversation, and ducked back onto the path, her brow furrowed into a deep frown.

Which one was right? Morghan or Selena? Clarice didn't know, but it made her uneasy that they were arguing in the first place.

She shook her head and hurried her pace. First, she decided, she'd find Erin, and then she'd drag her over to Krista's and there they could talk about it. Decide what to do, if anything needed to be done at all.

When she broke out of the woods and walked the last distance to Ash Cottage, Clarice noticed straight away that Erin's little Mini was gone from its customary spot in front of the garage. Still, she tried the front door, found it locked, frowned, and made her way around the building to the gate into the back garden.

'Erin?'

Clarice paused a minute, then went to the door that led to the utility room and into the house.

The door was closed, but not locked. Clarice, the frown still on her face, slipped inside, walked through into the kitchen.

'Erin!'

The cottage was silent except for the gentle ticking of embers in the cooker's firebox. Clarice bounded up the stairs.

'Erin.'

Clarice stood in the doorway to the room she knew was Erin's, then stepped slowly forward.

There was a small pile of clothes on the bed and Clarice picked up the sparkly top in one hand and looked at it, before dropping it and moving around the open wardrobe door and taking in the sight of four empty coat hangers dangling from the rail.

'Oh, Erin.'

31

RUE FINALLY JOINED CLOVER WHERE SHE WAS BACK AT THE window yet again, concerned over Clover's single-minded preoccupation with wards and weavings. 'We're missing spring,' she said casually, looking out at the cold day, not seeing the wards Clover had been frowning over, but believing entirely that they were there just as she said.

'Perhaps we'll be back for summer,' Clover answered. But her mind wasn't on her words. Instead, she'd turned inward, to search the whiteness, searching for a way to see what she wanted. She'd been looking and looking, girding herself to wade out into it, determined that she could induce the state that so often took her by stealth. Finally, she took a breath and stepped out into the whiteness, letting it surround her.

'Let's go into the village,' Rue said. She looked at Clover, thinking Clover would be pleased with the idea, but Clover was staring off into space. Rue touched her gently on the shoulder, but Clover was gone already.

Another seizure.

'Help,' Rue called to Ebony, as Clover swayed where she stood. 'Help me lie her down.' Rue put her hands on Clover, sure that Clover wasn't going to manage to stay standing this time as she usually did, and she drew her down to the floor, going with her, until Clover's pale face rested in her lap.

'They seem to be getting more frequent,' Ebony said, coming to crouch beside them.

Rue just shook her head even though she agreed. 'Where's she gone now?'

CLOVER DIDN'T HEAR HER SISTER'S QUESTION. SHE WAS NO longer with her body, but walked outside it, her spirit glowing fiercely. She walked and walked through the whiteness, blinded in the nothingness and then, quite suddenly, it cleared.

At first, she thought she was on the streets of the City of Lost Souls, and she gathered her brightness to herself, dousing its light. Blackbird came and rested on her shoulder, and at her side, a big yellow lion appeared and swung her head cautiously, looking about.

The wind blew a crumpled paper cup against her ankles, and Clover kicked it quietly away, looking around.

Why would she be in the City of Lost Souls? She'd wanted to step into the past. To be Rhian, to see what magic Bryn, Ravenna, and the others were doing. The reasons behind the blessing that Morghan had shown her the day before.

Not this.

She drew in a breath and the wind was tasteless against her throat and there was a buzzing in her ears and the vision around her blurred and she caught sight of shadows, the world spinning fast around her, so that she stumbled a step to the side, dizzy.

Then it slowed, came back into focus, and it was not the City of Lost Souls, Clover saw. It was somewhere else.

Somewhere else entirely.

For a moment, she longed for home, to reach out and grasp Rue's hand.

Because now, she was somewhere far, far away.

Clover touched her fingers to the cat at her side and looked around, straightening her shoulders and knowing she needed to pay attention.

Where was she?

Clover blinked. *When* was she?

There was a rushing in her ears and with it came sound, and all around her, the chatter of voices, shouts, yells. Crying. Clover walked tentatively along the street and looked about her.

There was a thread of people in front of a chain link fence. They were lining up for something and Clover squinted at them, seeing their dirty faces, their shabby clothing. Shadows clustered around and between them. She peered down the line behind the fence, wondering what they were queuing for.

Food. Now Clover was behind the fence, watching some sort of soup or broth being ladled into bowls, handed out with a piece of bread.

Now she was back on the street, watching a couple of

girls her own age. Younger perhaps. One of them held something in her hand.

There were shadows clustered around these two as well. Clover shied away from them, then came back to listen.

'There's no reason not to do it,' the girl said. She thrust the phone at her friend. 'Look, you just download the Last Breath app, and we do it together. All of us. Why not? There's nothing here anymore. I wish I'd never been born.'

Clover reeled backwards, looking around the street scene in horror even as it faded from her vision, even as she felt herself returning to her body, to her own time, to Hawthorn House.

'Clover?' Rue touched her fingers to Clover's cheeks as her sister's eyelashes fluttered.

Clover wet her lips with her tongue, blinked several times, then stared up at her sister.

'You're back now,' Rue said. 'It's all right.'

Clover just stared at her, at Ebony's concerned face, her vision ratcheting around inside her head. The filthy street. The hungry people lined up for soup and a crust of bread. Somehow Clover knew that was their only meal of the day.

And the app. Last Breath. A suicide app. She closed her eyes, struggled to sit up, then turned her face away from Rue.

'Clover?' Rue turned her back, cupped her palms around Clover's cheeks, wiped away the tears with her thumbs. 'Where did you go?'

Clover shook her head, moving Rue's hands with her. She swallowed and her throat made a dry clicking sound. 'They were killing themselves,' she said.

Rue started back in surprise.

Ebony frowned. 'What?'

'The teenagers.' Clover turned her head again, gazed out the window. The trees were too far away to see at this angle. There was only the sky, grey and brooding with clouds. 'They had an app on their phones. Helping them do it. Connecting them to others so they could all do it together.'

She shrugged off Rue's hands and rubbed her dazed face. 'I'm thirsty,' she said.

Rue nodded, got to her feet, looked around for some water, but she'd been drinking coffee. She held out a hand for Clover. 'Come on. We'll go to the kitchen. You can have a drink and something to eat.'

It would steady Clover. She shot Ebony a look of consternation.

A suicide app?

She helped Clover down to the kitchen, put her in a chair at the table, ran a glass under the tap, gave Clover the water. Ebony rummaged in a cupboard for the biscuit tin she knew would be there.

'Here,' Ebony said. 'Eat these.'

Clover nodded at the saucer with two biscuits on it. Picked one up. Held it between her fingers.

Her hands were shaking.

'A suicide app?' Rue said, sitting down opposite her, pushing the saucer closer to Clover.

Clover nodded, broke the biscuit between her fingers. Chocolate crumbs fell onto the table.

'They wished they'd never been born,' she said. Crumbled the biscuit some more.

Rue shook her head. 'Eat it.'

Clover looked down at the biscuit between her fingers. 'I feel sick,' she said, her stomach suddenly heaving. She pushed back her chair and got up, wobbled a moment, then dashed off to the downstairs bathroom, leant over the toilet, and vomited up a thin stream of bile.

'Are you okay?' Rue asked at the door. 'Do you need to lie down?'

Clover nodded dumbly at her. 'I feel like I've had a big shock,' she said, and shivered. For a moment, she was a kiddie again, seeing what had happened to her best friend's mother. She'd been murdered, Jack's mum, but these girls she'd just seen were doing it themselves.

Killing themselves.

'Thousands of them,' she whispered as Rue wiped her face and led her upstairs to the bedroom she was staying in.

'Thousands of them doing it,' she said. 'A suicide plague.' She put her head on the pillow and closed her eyes. 'And the rest starving.'

Rue drew the blankets up over Clover and stood looking down at her. Clover's face was so pale her eyelids looked almost translucent, and there were dark shadows staining the thin skin under her eyes. Rue shook her head.

Always before, Clover had gone back to the past – their shared past, usually. Brought back stories that were sometimes hard, but that they'd already lived through, didn't have to repeat.

But this, Rue thought. This was different. This wasn't the past. There were no mobile phones and apps in the past. She tipped her head back and closed her own eyes.

This was the future. She swallowed.

Starving people and suicide plagues.

What sort of future was that? Were things really going to get that bad before they got better?

When she looked back down at Clover, she saw Clover was sleeping, and was relieved. The rest would be healing, she knew.

Rue tucked the blankets more closely around Clover, then let herself quietly out of the room and stood uncertainly in the hallway looking into Ebony's wide eyes.

'Come on,' Ebony said. 'Let's get a little bit of air.'

RUE STEPPED OFF ONTO THE LAWN, EBONY TRAILING BEHIND her, and walked over to the well, staring down at the deep swirling colours in the water and letting her mind empty.

'What are we really doing?' she asked and looked over at Ebony. 'I'm not sure I understand any of this, not really.'

'We came here because something's turning,' Ebony said. 'Something that, I dunno, echoes something that has happened here before.'

'I want to go home,' Rue said, wrapping her arms around herself. 'I'm worried about Clover — I don't think being here is the best thing for her.'

Ebony was silent. Part of her agreed, but she didn't know if there was any getting out of whatever was going on.

Rue shook her head, staring at the water. 'The well through the worlds,' she murmured, remembering Morghan's teachings. The sacred water flowed through all the worlds, and where it sickened in one, where it was poisoned and polluted, it would affect all the other worlds also. World to world to world. She bent her head, closed her eyes. Once, she had thought — after Morghan had told her about her own experiences — that she would be a well maiden too, keeping the purity and clarity of the water that flowed in her world as well as she could.

But, she had to admit, it was an easier task to keep to the prayers and the devotions, when they were in times of peace.

'Rue?' Ebony touched her on the arm.

Rue nodded. 'I'm okay.' She looked back at the circle of water that reflected the grey sky and added its own mysterious swirls of colour to it.

'We've polluted the well, haven't we?' she asked with a sigh.

Ebony stepped closer to the well and gazed with Rue down into its shadowed depths. She searched for something to say, but Rue continued before she'd found anything.

'Clover — you heard her. She didn't travel back into a past lifetime. She went into the future,' Rue said, not taking her gaze from the water. 'It sounded terrible.' Finally, Rue looked up and into Ebony's eyes. 'I don't want that future. It terrifies me.' Rue looked away, closed her eyes, rubbed at them with tired hands.

'She saw terrible things, Ebony. Hungry people, kids with no hope.' Rue couldn't bring herself to talk about the suicide app. 'It's too late, isn't it? To do anything now?' She shook her head. 'We're still living like nothing has changed. There are still wars. Children are still going hungry.'

Ebony nodded.

Rue sighed. 'What if it's too late?'

Ebony considered this. She was shaken by what Clover had seen, felt as though the ground was unsteady under her feet. But really, hadn't they known? Hadn't they known that this was a future they could be heading towards?

'No,' she said finally. 'No, it can't be too late, or we wouldn't be here trying to figure out what to do.' She shook her head.

'It's not too late. Only more urgent.'

32

'WHAT DO YOU MEAN, SHE'S GONE?'

Krista stared at Clarice in consternation, then gestured to follow her into Haven's back room.

'What do you mean Erin's gone?' she repeated once they had some privacy.

'Just what it sounds like,' Clarice said. She shook her head and drooped over Krista's high table for a moment, then pushed herself back upright. 'She's taken clothes and stuff and gone somewhere.'

'Stuff?' Krista was having a hard time processing this.

Erin gone?

Clarice dragged her fingers down her cheeks, momentarily bringing a blush to her pale skin.

'Toothbrush. Hairbrush. Stuff.'

Krista hooked a stool and sank down onto it. 'Have you spoken to Stephan yet?'

Clarice shook her head. 'I don't have my phone. Left it

behind because I didn't want it going off when everyone was travelling.' She paused. 'Another thing.'

Krista looked at her. 'There's more?'

Clarice glanced back through the doorway into the main shop. Minnie was casting curious glances, but she wouldn't barge in. Clarice scooted a stool closer to Krista's and perched on it, even though she wanted to pace back and forth while she spoke.

'Morghan and Selena had an argument,' she said.

'An argument?' Krista shook her head. 'That doesn't sound like them. What about?'

'Selena suggested that Rue would be better suited to being the next Lady of the Grove.'

Krista stared at Clarice. 'I don't understand.'

'Nor do I,' Clarice said, her voice hard. 'But that's what Selena suggested. She said that Macha was too wild to be trusted.' Clarice huffed out a breath. 'I'm paraphrasing, but that's it in a nutshell.'

Krista was silent. She could barely believe what she was hearing. 'And Morghan,' she said. 'How did Morghan answer that?'

Now Clarice did slide off her stool, unable to stay still a minute longer.

Minnie sidled up to the doorway. 'Is everything all right, guys?'

Krista looked at her. 'Have you seen Erin today?' she asked.

Minnie thought about it. 'Yeah, I saw her for a minute after she finished work. She was walking up towards where the track starts behind the vicarage.' Minnie paused, looked at the other two. 'What's going on?'

'How did she look?' Krista asked. 'Did she seem okay?'

'She looked real preoccupied, actually,' Minnie said. 'I called out to her, but I don't think she heard me. She was like, deep in thought or something.' Minnie moved farther into the room. 'Has something happened to her?'

Krista shook her head. 'I don't think so.'

Clarice stared at her, then looked at Minnie. 'She's left,' she said.

'What?' Minnie's face folded into a frown. 'What do you mean, she's left?'

'Packed a suitcase and gone,' Clarice said, then felt Krista's eyes on her and turned back to look at her. 'What?' she said. 'We don't keep secrets. Minnie's part of the Grove.'

Krista sighed. She wanted to know more about the argument between Morghan and Selena — she was still finding it hard to fathom there'd been an argument at all — but while Minnie was indeed a Grove member, she was apt to go off half-cocked and do things others might regret. She was still only sixteen, after all. Impulse control was not fully developed.

'But Erin would never leave us,' Minnie said. 'I don't believe it. Why would anyone ever leave?'

'I don't know,' Clarice said. 'I'm going upstairs to get my phone. Call Stephan.'

'Here,' Krista said, picking hers up off the table and holding it out. 'Use mine.' She looked at Minnie. 'Can you help Mrs Kingley, please? She's ready to buy her magazines.'

Minnie glanced back into the shop, grimaced, but made her way to the cash register.

Clarice was already waiting for Stephan to pick up.

'Krista?'

'It's Clarice. Have you seen Erin today?'

'Not since this morning, why?'

Clarice paused.

'Why?' Stephan repeated. 'Is something wrong?'

'We think she's left,' Clarice said, and tugged rough fingers through her pale hair.

There was silence on the other end of the phone.

'Morghan asked me to look for her when she didn't turn up for the travelling,' Clarice said finally. 'I went inside the cottage, and there were signs upstairs that she'd packed up and left.' She cleared her throat. 'There's a note on the table with your name on it.'

'What does it say?'

Clarice shook her head, even though Stephan couldn't see her. 'I didn't read it.'

She waited.

'I'll be right there,' Stephan said. 'Are you still at Ash Cottage?'

'No.'

Clarice told him she was at Haven, then ended the call and looked at Krista.

'He and Burdock are coming back right now.'

'Is he coming here, or to the cottage?'

'Cottage,' Clarice said. 'To see what the note says.'

Krista nodded, drumming her fingers against the table. 'We'll meet him there?'

'I CAN'T BELIEVE SHE ACTUALLY LEFT,' STEPHAN SAID, standing at the kitchen table, his shoulders drooping, the note dangling from a hand.

Burdock whined.

'At least we know where she's gone,' Krista said, putting an arm around Stephan.

'Yeah, but what do we do about it?' Clarice asked. She was still pacing, four long steps one way across the tiny kitchen, turn, four long steps back the other way.

Burdock whined again. Stephan sank onto a chair and patted the dog.

'Can we do anything about it?' Clarice asked. 'She's a grown woman. If she says she needs a few days to herself, then don't we have to respect that?'

Krista wasn't so sure. 'Stephan, you said something happened to her?'

He nodded. 'At the quarry, yeah.' He put the note on the table and stared at it. 'Fuck,' he said. 'How did everything get to be such a mess so fast?'

No one answered him.

'The argument,' Krista said at last. 'You didn't finish telling me about it.'

'We didn't argue,' Stephan said. 'Well, I was mad at her for going back to the quarry on her own, but the mad didn't last.'

Krista put a hand on his shoulder. 'Morghan and Selena argued. At the cave while they were waiting for Erin.'

Stephan looked up, confused. 'They were arguing? I've barely ever heard Morghan raise her voice. They were arguing? Are you sure?'

Clarice's face was grim. 'Well, it was short and there were no actual raised voices, but there was a definite difference of opinion going on.'

'What about?' Stephan asked. 'About Erin?'

Clarice nodded reluctantly. 'I'm only going to repeat it because it seems important. I shouldn't have been listening to it at all.' She flushed, thinking how she'd hidden behind the trees to eavesdrop. She'd not done anything like that before.

'Selena was saying that Rue would make a better Lady of the Grove than Erin.'

Stephan stared at her. 'What?'

Clarice threw up her hands. 'I don't know! She said something about Macha, about Macha being too wild to be trusted by the others, way back when.'

'But that's crazy,' Krista said.

Clarice lifted her shoulders in a shrug, glanced out the window where the day was beginning its slow slide toward dusk.

'What did Morghan say?' Stephan's voice was little more than a croak. 'She came around yesterday and gave Erin the Wilde Grove leaves. I can't believe she wouldn't want to continue training Erin.'

'She disagreed with Selena, of course,' Clarice said. 'She told her that wild magic was nothing new, that she'd had plenty of experience of it with...' Clarice paused. 'My mother.' Another pause. 'And Catrin.' She stopped pacing and looked flatly at the others. 'Morghan stands by Erin.' She raised her eyebrows. 'I do too. As much as I love Rue and Clover.'

'I don't even know them,' Stephan said.

'I don't either,' Krista said.

Clarice nodded. 'I don't know if Selena has talked this over with Rue, or if it's just something she came up with right then.'

'It's not the sort of thing you'd say spur of the moment, surely?' Krista asked.

'I'll ask Rue,' Clarice said. 'Then we'll know the answer to that one, at least.'

Stephan was looking miserably down at the note again. It was just a couple lines.

'Maybe Erin has changed her mind,' he said. 'Maybe she doesn't want to be here anymore.'

'That's rubbish,' Clarice said. 'She was fine —right up until whatever happened, when? Yesterday at the quarry? Last time I saw her, she was brilliant, relishing what Morghan and Macha were teaching her.'

Krista was nodding. 'She is really keen on the oracle cards we are making. I don't think she holds doubts about any of this. Not unless they were deep deep down, anyway, and which of us doesn't have those?'

Burdock whined again, and licked Stephan's cheek. Everyone was unhappy, he thought, and where was Erin? Was that why they were unhappy? He was unhappy that she wasn't there to smile at him and scratch behind his ears just the way he liked it.

'It's all right, boy,' Stephan said. 'She'll be back.'

Clarice came to a decision. 'You should try calling her again,' she said to Stephan.

Stephan nodded, picked up his phone, called.

Erin's voicemail picked up.

Stephan shook his head, left a message begging Erin to call him. Pressed end.

'What now?' he asked.

Krista patted his shoulder. 'We give her some space, I guess.'

But Clarice was shaking her head. 'I'm going to talk to Rue. And maybe we'll give Erin some space — but only for a couple days. Then I'm going down to see her.'

'To London?' Krista was wide-eyed.

'You're coming with me,' Clarice said.

'I'll come too,' said Stephan.

But Clarice shook her head. 'No. I think you should let us handle this.'

Stephan frowned at her. 'Why?' he asked. 'She's my girlfriend.'

'Exactly. You speak to her, and everything else gets wrapped up in it. Your relationship now, all the ones you've had together in the past.' She put her hands on her slim hips. 'Better just Krista and me. Cleaner.' She lifted her gaze to Krista. 'Besides, if anyone knows the Fae, it's me, right?' She paused. 'I know what they're like. What they can do.'

A thought occurred to her, and she stilled, considering it.

Perhaps, she mused.

'What have you thought of?' Krista asked, seeing the look on Clarice's face.

'Maybe I should go there,' Clarice said. 'Ask what they're doing.'

'Go where?' Stephan said. 'To London, you mean? I don't understand.'

But Krista did, and she shook her head. 'Oh no you don't,' she said. 'You're not going to the quarry on your own. Stephan's told us they did something to Erin when she went there. Something severe. Why would it be any different if you faced off with them?'

'Because I know what they're like,' Clarice said. 'I know how the Fae think.'

'Maybe,' Krista said even while she was still shaking her head. 'But what would you hope to achieve anyway? It's not like you can get them to take it back, the hurt they did to Erin.'

'I could find out what they're doing,' Clarice said. 'Why they're there at the damned quarry in the first place.'

It was Stephan who answered her. 'No,' he said. 'We know why they're there — they're taking advantage of the place.'

Krista turned to him. 'What do you mean?'

'I've been thinking about it all day. The spirit of the place was killed when they started digging great chunks out of the hill. The Fae are there to punish us for doing it.' He shrugged. 'And because they can, I guess.' He sniffed.

He looked at the others. 'I reckon this sort of thing will happen more and more as things go to shit over the next fifty or a hundred years or whatever.' He dug his fingers into Burdock's fur. 'I bet it won't be just the Fae doing it either. I think, if we continue on the path we're on, it will get to be a free for all.' He sighed. 'It probably already is, to some extent. I mean, it's ideal for them, isn't it?'

He picked up his phone and called Erin again, listened to it go through to voicemail once more.

'You can't fight what you don't believe in, after all.'

33

CLARICE WASN'T SURE WHO SHE'D MEET FIRST WHEN SHE walked up to Hawthorne House, crossing the lawn under the evening sky and stopping briefly at the well. She'd been up to see everyone when they'd first arrived of course, and it had been lovely to meet all of them again after so long.

This time, she felt more apprehensive.

'Blessed Goddess,' she murmured. 'You give me the strength I need in these wild times.'

She took a calming breath, inhaling the cold tang of water that seeped up from deep within the earth, then bent down and touched a fingertip to the surface and wet the skin of her forehead in a benediction.

Clarice took a breath, looked to the house where she still had a room, but where she barely ever stayed anymore, preferring instead to share Krista's bed over the shop in the village.

'Clarice?'

Clarice spun around and there was no helping the smile

that blossomed on her face. 'Rue,' she said. 'I was just coming to look for you.'

They folded each other into an embrace.

Rue stepped back, held Clarice at arm's length. Ebony stood grinning at them.

'It's really been a long time, little sprite,' she said, using the old nickname.

'I still can't believe how well you're looking, Clarice,' Rue said. 'Or how much you've grown. You look so much more like your mum.'

'I was just a teenager last time you were here,' Clarice said. 'A lot's happened since then.'

Rue nodded, looked up at the house. 'It's weird, being here without Grainne. I keep finding myself looking for her, you know?'

Clarice did know. 'It's a hard habit to get out of.' She shook her head. 'Mum still turns up in my dreams every now and then — tells me what she thinks of things.'

'Yeah?' Rue said. 'I'm glad.' For a moment, she thought about her own mother, but that was an old wound now, and life — and Grainne — had gone a long way to healing it. She looked at Clarice.

'Hey,' she said. 'Did you say you were looking for me?'

Clarice nodded, glancing over at the women she had always thought of as her friends. Ebony looked as sharp as always, but Rue was looking pale, and there were dark shadows under her eyes. Clarice wondered at them, but there was something more pressing on her mind, the reason why she'd trekked up to the house.

'Is it true you want to be the next Lady of the Grove here?'

Rue stared at Clarice in shock. She glanced at Ebony, then shook her head. 'What?'

'That's what I heard,' Clarice said with a lift of her shoulders.

'From who? Ebony asked, as startled as Rue.

'Why?' Rue rocked back on her heels, shaking her head, frowning. 'Why would someone say that? Where did you hear it?'

'It's not true, then?'

Rue didn't even have to consider it. 'No,' she said. 'I've never even thought of it. Isn't Erin training for that?'

Clarice relaxed a fraction. So, Selena had just been speaking off the cuff. She nodded at Rue and Ebony, both of whom looked rocked by the suggestion.

'I don't even live here,' Rue was saying. 'I mean — I have a life back home, and yeah, we're here right now for Grove business, but the plan is to go back home. Certainly for Clover and Ebony and me, anyway.' She looked at Ebony. 'Isn't that right?'

Ebony nodded. 'Definitely.'

'Selena isn't going back with you?' Clarice didn't know how she felt about that idea. She loved Selena — after all, she'd been, for years, like a grandmother to her.

But that had been a long time ago. Time had moved things on, the way it always did. Selena had been gone a long time now. Sixteen years. A lot changed in sixteen years.

'I don't know her plans for sure,' Rue said, watching the emotions flicker over Clarice's face. 'But where did you hear this rubbish about me wanting to be the next Lady of the Grove?' She shook her head. It was mind-boggling that someone would be suggesting it.

'I overheard Selena telling Morghan that you're the logical choice for the next Lady of the Grove.'

Rue leant back, gazed unseeing at the trees at the edge of the lawn. Her thoughts tumbled. She shook her head.

'No,' she said. 'Selena has never mentioned such a thing to me.' Rue turned and looked at the house, started towards it.

'Where are you going?' Clarice asked, alarmed.

'I'm going to ask Selena what she was thinking, of course,' Rue said back, her voice clipped.

Clarice stared after her in dismay, but had she really expected something else to happen? She — and Rue — had been brought up to play their game of life with the cards face upwards. Things were not to be kept hidden, because then they had a mighty habit of festering.

Misunderstandings needed to be respectfully aired, resolved.

'Come on,' Ebony said. 'I think we need to hear this.'

They hurried after Rue. Clarice grimaced. She would have to admit to eavesdropping, and she would be sorry for that, but it seemed the lesser of things going on.

Selena was in the drawing room with Clover, who sat by the fire, staring into the flames.

'Are you okay?' Rue asked her.

Clover turned at the pain in Rue's voice and nodded. 'I'm fine,' she said. 'Or as fine as it's possible to be.' She turned back to the fire. 'The magic of this place is so strong. I'd forgotten it was like this.' She glanced toward the window and shivered, despite the fire's heat. 'I feel permanently wide open here. We need to get to business as soon as possible.'

'What does that mean?'

It was Selena who asked the question, but Rue nodded. She wanted to know as well. Ebony sidled up behind her to hear.

But Clover stopped short, frowning. What was their business? She closed her eyes, looked inwards at the great spread of white nothingness, felt herself — felt Rhian — walking the mists, sightless and seeing more than ever before, then shook her head.

Then shied away from what she'd seen that afternoon. That was their business, she thought. Avoiding that. But it was too soon to talk about it. Right now, it hurt too much.

'I'm going to go and lie down,' she said, ignoring the question. 'I'm tired.'

Rue watched her walk from the room, then looked at Selena.

'Has something else happened to her?' she asked. 'While we were outside?' She looked around but everything seemed normal.

Selena shook her head. 'I don't think anything else has happened, thank the Goddess. I think Clover's just so deeply connected to this place, and the veil between the worlds, between lives — even apparently between time-lines — is so thin here that she's just constantly plugged into it.'

Rue warred with herself for a moment, over whether to go to Clover or stay, but she wanted an answer to her question.

She looked piercingly at Selena. 'Did you suggest to Morghan that I be the next Lady of this Grove?'

There was movement at the door and Clover came back

in, stood beside Clarice and Ebony, listening. Rue glanced at her, then stared back at Selena.

'Well?' she demanded.

Selena's glance flicked to Clarice. 'You heard us, of course.'

Clarice nodded.

'Well.' Selena looked back at Rue. 'I did,' she said.

A rush of shock flooded through Rue at Selena's admission. It threatened to turn to anger, and she reminded herself of who she was speaking to. Rue closed her eyes for a moment, tamping down her emotions so she could pause before responding.

'But why?' she asked through gritted teeth. 'Why would you suggest a thing — especially without asking me?'

Selena looked back at her, gaze direct. 'I thought perhaps it was some of what we came here for. The next few decades are going to require much from us — from you, since I shall not be around for them. You are well trained.'

'I'm sure Morghan is training Erin perfectly,' Rue said. 'And Erin is younger. There's only twenty years difference between Morghan and me.'

Selena nodded. 'It was a spur of the moment suggestion.'

'That you argued for, apparently,' Rue said, not looking back at Clarice.

'I did. All things deserve consideration.' Selena took a breath, sighed. 'I'm sorry Rue. I shouldn't have made such a suggestion without consulting you.'

Rue answered swiftly. 'You shouldn't have made such a suggestion at all. Erin has been here, how long?' Now, she did look at Clarice.

'A year,' Clarice said.

'There we go — a year.' Rue dragged in a breath, shook her head again.

'We didn't come here for Rue to take over this Grove.' It was Clover who spoke, and she moved farther forward into the room, looking at Selena, then at her sister, peering at them through the whiteness that had come to shroud her vision.

Selena stilled, watching Clover closely. 'Why, then?'

'To light the fire,' Clover said, wading knee-deep in the ripples all around her again. She smiled. 'And then to take the embers back home, and fan them to life there.'

She lifted her head, tracing the threads of the web. 'The fire must blaze so that all who come to it may take the embers back across all the seas with them, fan them to life, be the great light of the beacons across the darkening land.'

The weave in her mind brightened until her vision filled with nothing but light, and then it winked out with a snap that was almost audible to Clover's ears. When she blinked, Morghan's drawing room was back in focus, reassuringly solid, the people in it their usual forms, auras glowing softly.

'What did I say?' she asked, noticing that everyone was staring at her.

'You don't remember?' Ebony asked, and Rue came over to Clover, holding her shoulders and peering at her, into her eyes.

Clover shook her head and put her hands on Rue's. 'I'm okay,' she said. 'It wasn't a seizure.'

Clarice glanced at Morghan, who had come silently to

the door moments before Clover had spoken her...what? Clarice wondered. What did you call that? A prophecy?

'It seems,' Morghan said, walking over to the middle of the room and looking at everyone. 'It seems that we have our task, then, in no uncertain terms.' She looked at Clover and smiled.

Rue shook her head and moved to one of the armchairs and sat abruptly down.

'Things are never going to be the same again, are they?' she said, and looked at her hands as they lay in her lap. The business she'd worked so hard to grow — would she still get to do that when they returned home? Rue didn't know.

She didn't feel as though she knew anything. So, she looked over at Morghan. 'What does it mean though — in practical terms?'

Morghan nodded. 'This is the question I've been considering for most of the year. Since it became obvious through my travellings that we are required to do something — specific, that is.'

Clarice broke in. 'It is the Queen who commands us,' she said carefully, considering as she spoke.

'And the Goddess Elen, she of the paths and ways,' Morghan said.

Clarice nodded. 'But the Fae.' She couldn't believe she was about to suggest this, but she was still banned from the Queen's realm in the Fair Lands, and it had been months now since she had last been there.

'What about them?' Selena asked. She had sat down too and seemed to feel the weight of the worlds upon her tired shoulders.

Looking around their small group, Clarice hesitated.

Morghan touched her arm. 'You may say whatever it is that is on your mind. You are among friends.'

'Can we trust them?' Clarice asked. She shook her head. 'I can't believe I'm saying this, but in light of everything — can we trust them?'

The room was quiet for a minute, everyone looking toward Morghan for an answer.

She took her time, giving Clarice the consideration she deserved.

'There are different factions of Fae,' she said at last. 'Different Courts. Not all of them will be in agreement as to the best way forward through these coming times.'

Clarice nodded. 'They're bringing the veil down, though, all of them, aren't they? Bringing themselves closer to us?'

It was something that Clarice had been giving a lot of thought to over the last months. Why the Fae would want the separation between their world and that of humans to be removed, or at least made less.

'Yes,' Morghan said. 'And we are grateful that they are doing it slowly. Although it has always been permeable, this separation between us. They had always been able to appear to us, just as some of us have always been able to make our way to their lands, either accidentally or on purpose.'

'It's not just them we have to worry about,' Clover said, turning her head to gaze out the window. 'The Fae, I mean — they're not the only entities out there.'

She went and sat near Rue, who reached for her. Clover clasped her hand.

'When I saw the future — the possible future — there was one thing I didn't tell you when I came back.'

'What was it, dear?' Selena asked.

Clover shook her head and didn't answer straight away. When she did, it was with a sigh, and she hunched over on the couch.

'I saw the people – humans.' She looked around, checking that everyone understood. 'But I also saw others. Entities. Invisible to the humans, I think, but attached to them.' She looked at Selena, then Morghan. 'Do you know what I mean?'

Selena nodded. 'Attaching spirits,' she said.

'We'll see a lot more of those,' Morghan said. 'They're already everywhere, I'm sure.'

'I don't know if I'm following properly,' Clarice said, shivering slightly. She hated the idea of attaching spirits, was familiar enough with that. 'Why will we see more of them?'

'Why are we already seeing more of them?' Rue asked.

'When the power imbalance among humanity becomes as skewed as it is,' Morghan said, trying to explain, 'we become easily corrupted, and our thoughts and actions are affected, as there are certain entities who are fulfilled through this, and find those corrupted people and attach to them, feeding on the warped energy, and helping more be created.'

Selena nodded. 'This is why deep foundations in truth and light are necessary. Where we are weak, there we leave ourselves open to these creatures. They ride our backs like invisible jockeys.'

Rue turned away from the image. 'Sounds horrible,' she said.

'It is,' Morghan said.

'And the veil thinning or falling will let more of these things into our world?' Clarice asked.

But Morghan shook her head. 'No. They already move around in complete comfort in our world. What the falling veil means is that more of the world of spirit will be visible to humans — and humans have forgotten that this aspect of the world exists, and I rather fear that seeing such strange sights will...'

'Send them around the bend,' Clover said.

34

Erin pressed the number into the keypad and pushed the door open. And there was the London flat, just the same as it always was.

Erin stood in the doorway, one hand clutching the handle of her suitcase, the same suitcase she'd dragged out of this same flat a year ago.

Almost exactly.

Erin screwed her eyes closed at the phrase that wouldn't leave the inside of her head, and stepped gingerly into the flat, looking around, seeing that everything was just the same as usual.

It was only her that was different.

She closed the door behind her, listened to the quiet snick of the lock, then stood there in the middle of the big living room, not quite knowing what she was doing.

Or even why she was there.

Why was she there?

Erin thought of Ash Cottage, the cosy kitchen, her

grandmother's plants hanging everywhere, the art on the wall — not just Teresa's now, but some of her own too — and she shook her head miserably.

She'd much rather be back there.

Then why wasn't she? Why had she thrown some clothes in the suitcase, left a note on the table for Stephan, and driven all the way back here?

Erin shook her head. Because the weight upon her heart was too heavy, that was why.

Because she couldn't hold her head up around the people she loved. Couldn't face them when she felt like this.

And how did she feel? She huffed out a sigh and wheeled the suitcase into the master bedroom. One of its wheels squeaked.

She left it there for a minute, and prowled around the flat, reacquainting herself with a part of her life that she thought she'd discarded like an old snakeskin.

Everything was as it always had been. She knew someone had been there since she'd wheeled out the door all those months before, because it was clean, the bed made, no crumbs in the kitchen, the pile of mail she'd left there tidied away.

But of course it was. There was a woman who came in and cleaned it before and after the family's visits.

Erin sat down on the couch, picked up the TV remote and stared at it a moment before aiming it at the big flat screen attached to the wall opposite.

It switched on in a blare of noise that had Erin scrambling to turn the volume down. On the screen, a vivid forest scene, rich reds, browns, greens, and then a big white stag walked into the picture, turned his head and gazed at the camera. Erin stared at it, fought back tears, then aimed the remote again, changed channels and got up, going into the bedroom for her phone.

Four missed calls.

She chewed on her lip. They were all from Stephan.

She didn't listen to the voice messages but put the phone down and heaved the suitcase onto the bed, unzipped it. Each movement she made sent off strange echoes inside her. Hadn't she put the suitcase on the bed like this a year ago?

Almost exactly. Erin straightened. The faerie woman had repeated those words to her, voice full of sneering laughter that Erin couldn't banish from her mind, no matter how she tried.

Perhaps she just hadn't tried the right thing yet, she thought. Perhaps she needed a drink. To go out, get lost in a crowd, listen to music so loud you couldn't hear anyone speak, not even the voices in your head.

Erin stared down at the clothes in the suitcase, then at what she wore. One of Lynsey's handwoven skirts. Teresa's jumper, knitted by Marshall. Sensible, low-heeled boots.

Suitable for tramping the tracks through Wilde Grove.

Erin untied them, kicked them off.

She nodded to herself, and dug around in the suitcase, pushing aside the things she'd taken of her grandmother's, and the clothes she'd bought in the last (almost exactly) year.

Instead, she dug out a pair of jeans and a silky, spaghetti-strapped top. Autumn had laid claim to the year, but it would be hot in the club, especially if she was dancing.

Her phone, on the bed beside the pile of clothing, rang again, and Stephan's picture popped up on the screen. Erin sat down and picked it up, holding it close to her face, staring down at his photo.

How blue his eyes were, she thought. How much she loved his mouth, nose, dark eyelashes, curling hair. How much she loved everything about him.

She closed her eyes, let the call go to voice mail.

When it went quiet, she put the phone down and went to run a shower.

ERIN HOOKED THE SPIKED HEEL OF HER SANDAL ON THE STOOL and the bartender slid her a drink. She nodded her thanks, sipped at it, and looked around the club.

This place was where she used to come with Jeremy. It seemed a lifetime ago, and she squirmed slightly on her stool, avoiding the mirrors behind the bar, and squinting instead into the crowd of dancers on the floor, wondering if she knew anybody there. The music was as loud as she'd wanted it to be, the bass beating in time to her heart.

She didn't recognise anyone. That was a good thing; she could imagine what everyone thought of her disappearance a year ago. She'd only come to this place because she knew it. Clubbing hadn't been her number one occupation.

That had been disappearing into the mists.

Erin gulped at her drink, waved at the bartender for another. Perhaps in a minute, after this drink or the next, she'd get up and dance. She could feel the alcohol hitting her system, spreading warmth through her, undoing some of the knots, dulling the voice of the faerie woman. Erin swallowed another mouthful, watched the people on the dance floor.

She'd always loved dancing. It was like losing yourself and finding yourself over and over. Erin blinked at the thought, not sure that she knew what she'd meant by it.

These days, when she danced, she went places. Not just into a mist, but to actual places.

That wouldn't happen here, she thought, swallowing the last mouthful of sweet alcohol and putting her empty glass down on the bar. Here, she would just lose herself in the pulse of the movement, the thrum of bass and heart.

The bartender came over and took her glass, held it up in a question. Erin shook her head, her blood humming. She'd have another later, perhaps.

She entered the crush of bodies on the dance floor and let the music flood through her in a wave of sound. Soon, she was conscious of nothing but the beat, her body, her breath.

Then, she was standing on a hillside, the ground wet underfoot, the moon riding high in the night sky, a silver eye staring down at her.

When she looked down, Erin saw that she was no longer herself, but Macha instead. She flexed her fingers, felt around inside the mind that was not hers yet still felt familiar.

She was confused, not even sure that Macha was aware of her presence inside her head, but then curiosity made her peer out through Macha's vision, watching as she strode down the hillside and entered a great garden, where flowered bowers and rooms opened out before her.

A figure approached and Erin stared, for the woman, to

her first glance, appeared spun out of the glow of the moon, gleaming with otherworldly light.

Macha fell onto a knee, bent her head, and Erin was staring at the grass. When she looked up again, the figure was closer, and Erin realised who she was looking at.

'My Queen,' Macha said.

The woman looked back at her. 'Am I?'

Erin felt Macha's sudden confusion. 'Your Majesty?'

'Your Queen. Am I your Queen?'

Macha rose slowly and Erin could sense her sudden wariness and understood that Macha did not entirely trust the Fae — not this woman, not any of them.

'We are in alliance,' Macha said. 'Therefore, do I give you my deference.'

Erin, riding inside Macha, nodded her head.

Queen Alastrina turned slightly, as though mollified. 'Why then have I found you trespassing upon my land?'

Macha was indignant, and Erin felt her tamp the emotion down so that she could answer without causing further offense.

'I know not,' Macha said. 'It is my dreaming that has led me here. For which purpose, I cannot say.'

There was a slight smile on the Queen's lips at the answer, but it was a private amusement, and she did not share the cause with Macha. Instead, she sat down upon a bench under a spray of pink roses.

'Sit next to me,' she said.

Macha shook her head. 'I prefer to stand.'

'Sit.'

Macha sat.

'It is customary for all priestesses of the Forest House to

be brought, eventually, to my presence and introduced formally — and yet, here you are, unaccompanied, wandering across the borders in your dreaming.'

Macha sat silently. What the Queen said was true, but she had no answer for why she was there. Only that she had rested her head upon her bedlinen, and now she was in this foreign land. Macha looked about her. Where all was forever summer.

For what need of seasons did those have whose lifespans lasted millennia?

'Perhaps you are among the chosen,' Queen Alastrina said, and her voice spun out upon the fair night as clear as the sound of a silver bell.

'Chosen?' Macha frowned, and Erin did also. 'We are none of us chosen,' she said. 'But all equal in the eyes of the Goddess.'

The Queen laughed. 'The Goddess calls each of us,' she said. 'Thus, then are each of us chosen, it is true.'

'Why make your remark, then?'

'To see when you would say.'

Macha suppressed her grunt of displeasure. 'I do not like to be tested,' she said.

Erin shrank back, inside Macha.

'Without testing, how may we know our strength?' The Queen's voice was placid, her hands folded upon her lap, her gaze turned outward over the meadow in front of them.

Macha did not have an answer. Nor did Erin.

'In these and coming times,' the Queen added, as though an afterthought.

'Times coming?' Macha asked, and her voice was sharp.

'Your people have turned from the deep life of the spirit,' the Queen said. 'You know this to be the truth.'

Macha was silent. It was true, she thought, Erin listening in. They kept much of the old worship alive, but now its purpose was to beg for strength and victory against enemies, for wealth and power even over friends.

It was why she had followed Ravenna across the sea to come to this house of priestesses who pledged to live in the fertility of spirit and the Goddess for all their days.

All their lives.

If that made her a chosen one, then it was she herself who had done the choosing.

As was right. All, she thought, must one day come to their own choosing.

As she had. As she had bound herself to the choice. For all her days, for all her lives.

'May the Goddess bless and lead me,' she whispered. 'May the bindings of my choosing never weaken.'

There was a touch, rough and grabbing upon Macha's arm. Except, Erin realised, it was not upon Macha's arm, but her own, and she was wrenched back to her body.

'Erin? What the fuck are you doing here?'

She blinked, looked around herself, realising she stood once more not on a moonlit hillside, but on a crowded dance floor.

'I thought you were still living in that tiny village way out in nowheresville.'

Finally, Erin focused her bleary gaze on the person in front of her.

'Jeremy?' The name was thick in her mouth, clogging her throat. She tried to lick her lips, but her tongue was dry.

The hand tightened around her upper arm again and she stumbled after Jeremy off the dance floor and over to the bar.

'You want a drink?' he asked, letting go of her so that she subsided against a stool. Jeremy looked her over. 'You look like you've had a few already.' He nodded. 'Fit though. You look fit.'

Erin slapped her hand down on the bar and steadied herself. One moment she'd been dancing, the next she'd been Macha.

Now she was back again, and Jeremy stood beside her, his mouth opening and closing and opening and closing. She had no idea what he was saying. The room spun in lazy circles around her.

'Jeremy?' she repeated.

'I asked if you wanted a drink?'

She heard him this time, the words sounding as though they came from far away. She moved her own lips experimentally.

'Ah. Water, please.'

'Water?'

Erin nodded. She looked around, dislocated both from the travelling and the booze. Then back at Jeremy, frowning at him. 'What are you doing here?'

Horror at his sudden appearance flooded through her.

He pushed a glass in front of her. 'I asked you first. Have you left that place?'

Erin stared at him. Reached for the glass, took a big gulp, spluttered, coughing. 'That's not water.'

He shrugged. 'So,' he said. 'Have you?' He grinned,

baring his teeth at Erin. 'Didn't work out in the sticks with the witches and the voodoo, then?'

'They don't do voodoo,' Erin said. It came out sounding slightly mushy and she pressed her lips together.

'Yeah,' Jeremy said. 'If you say so. Tell me, you still wandering off in your head?' he shook his own, his hair thick and expensively cut.

Erin stared at him, blinked, trying to make him just a figment of her imagination. He wavered in her vision, then solidified again. He was real. He was really sitting in front of her.

She shivered, glanced around at the club. What was she doing here? What had she been thinking?

Jeremy was shrugging. 'You always were a bit weird, weren't you? Probably why your mum was so keen to offload you onto me.'

Erin stood straighter. She was dizzy from the sudden return, as well as the drink.

This had been a terrifically bad idea. She shook her head at Jeremy.

She didn't know what she'd ever seen in him. He was like some toothy shark dressed up in smart clothes. Erin looked down at her own outfit and felt a sudden dismay.

'Hey,' Jeremy said, grabbing her arm. 'Where are you going?'

Erin twisted out of his grip and aimed herself at the exit. She didn't bother replying.

It was raining outside, and Erin stood there on the footpath staring out at the rain that was made golden by the streetlamps. She wiped at her mouth with the back of her hand and flinched back when a car sprayed water up onto the footpath. Someone shoved at her to get past, and she turned, stumbling and unused to her high heels, to find a taxi.

'Where are we going, then?'

She gave the driver her address and hunched back in the seat, watching the blur of streets and people. There was too much of all of it, Erin thought. She'd gotten used to the quiet pace of life in Wellsford, where the only crowds were those of trees. They stopped at a red traffic light.

'Fuck,' the driver said, as something thumped against the windscreen. 'What the fuck?'

Erin peered between the front seats and looked at the dark thing now sitting on the bonnet of the car.

'What is it?'

'It's a crow,' the driver said, staring at it. 'Or a raven or something.' He shook his head. 'We're near the Tower, must be one of their ravens.' But he'd never seen anything like it before, the bird just perched there on the car.

He wound down his window, shouted out at the bird in the rain.

'Go on, git!'

The raven flapped its wings and lifted into the air, flew away into the rain and the light. Erin watched it.

The traffic light turned green, and the car moved forward.

35

Morghan slipped from the house, thinking she'd risen before anyone else. She pulled her cloak around her, for the air had a sharp nip to it, despite the clear sky in which the night's stars still glittered.

There was a dark shape standing beside the well, and Morghan knew at once it was Clover. She held still her desire to be alone and walked over.

'I want to go with you,' Clover said.

Morghan looked at her in surprise. 'I am only going to the stream, to do my usual morning devotions.'

But Clover nodded, trembling, then lifted her face to Morghan. 'Will you bless and cleanse me?' she asked, her voice barely above a whisper. 'I cannot get my vision out of my head — it haunts me.' She paused. 'It hurts me. I don't want our future to be like that.'

Morghan unclasped her cloak from around her neck and draped it over Clover's shoulders, tugging it closer around her to warm her.

'Yes,' she said. 'Of course I will.'

Clover nodded, then tucked her chin down. 'I see all these things,' she said. 'But I don't really know why.'

Morghan put a gentle hand on Clover's shoulder, and drew her away from the well, towards the trail that led through the woodland.

'That is what we're all here to decide,' Morghan said. 'You yourself have told us the reason.'

But Clover shook her head. 'When I was a kid,' she said. 'It was fun for a little while. I could help Rue, I knew things about people without even thinking about it, and when Selena found us — well, that was the best thing ever. I remember how excited and relieved I was. I was only little, but I remember.'

Morghan touched her fingers fleetingly to the trunk of a tree.

Lend me your strength, she prayed. Let me be upright, looking to the light.

'Then I had lots of people around who loved me,' Clover said. 'Rue and Selena — and Tara and Damien and Natalie and Rose and Kiri, and so many others. Rue's friends. Ebony. It was brilliant. I wasn't lonely.'

Morghan listened without comment.

Clover glanced at her. 'A few years ago, I started to get this...itchy feeling, I guess.' She frowned down at the ground, watched her feet for a few steps. 'It was like something inside me was hatching or growing, or something, I don't know.'

'Something new?'

Clover nodded. 'That's when the seizures started. Rue

freaked out. I don't think even Selena knew what was happening.'

'The seizures sent you travelling?' Morghan asked. She remembered her conversation with Selena, when it had begun happening, but this was the first time she'd heard from Clover on the subject.

'Yeah. Sometimes into a past life, sometimes just to some place somewhere I didn't recognise.' She shook her head. 'But here's what I want to know.'

Clover stopped walking and looked up at Morghan. They'd walked not to the stream, but followed Morghan's impulse to go to the stone circle, and now they stood in the middle of it, the sky lightening around the edges, the stars' light fading.

'What do you want to know?' Morghan asked. She swayed slightly, her body beginning a humming she was becoming increasingly familiar with.

Wolf sat down at her side, staring expectantly at Clover, who glowed in the light of Morghan's vision.

Clover hung her head for a moment, and her aura dimmed and tightened in Morghan's vision.

'Am I a glitch?' Clover asked, raising her head to look at Morghan.

'A glitch?' The strands of the web crisscrossed above them, brightening in Morghan's sight.

Clover nodded. 'That's what I feel like. Like I'm something that went a bit wrong when I was being made. Like someone didn't wire me up right, or soldered the connections to the wrong terminals, or something.' Her voice petered out and she shrugged her shoulders, hunched deeper into Morghan's woollen cloak, grateful for its shrouding folds.

Morghan's hand gleamed golden in the dawning light when she reached out and touched Clover's arm.

'You are not a glitch, but a gift,' she said.

Clover looked at her. 'It's a hard gift,' she said, barely more than a whisper.

'These are hard times,' Morghan said, feeling the worlds in their slow spin around them.

Clover stared at her. 'Sometimes,' she said. 'I just want to be normal.' She hugged herself. 'Have friends. A boyfriend, maybe. Go out, have a laugh.' She paused, then told her greatest secret. 'I don't want to see all this. I don't want to see the warp and weave of everything I look at.'

Morghan nodded. 'It's so big, isn't it?'

Clover stared at her. 'You see it too?'

'Perhaps not as you do, but I see it. My vision has grown since I stood on top of a mountain and watched the worlds at war, watched the darkening of a million souls.'

They stood in silence for a minute, then Clover shook her head. 'It's all very well to see it all — but what do we do about it?'

'We light the beacons,' Morghan said. 'Just as you saw that we must.'

Clover tipped her head back, stared at the lightening sky. 'But what does that mean? In practical terms?'

Morghan surprised them both by laughing. 'That is the question, isn't it? I've been wrestling with it for a year now.'

Since the first vision she'd had of Ravenna. Back only days before Teresa had passed on to the Summerlands.

'Will you bless me?' Clover asked abruptly. 'I feel like it would help me.'

'Of course,' Morghan said. 'Of course I will.'

Clover grew larger in Morghan's vision, her spirit flowing and swirling around her, and Morghan marvelled at the sight of it. Seldom, she thought, did she see someone's spirit so bright. This, she decided, was what they were all supposed to look like. Connected, flowing, filled with life.

'Your brightness is a gladness in the world,' she said. 'Your light shines against all that would bring sorrow to the world. While today you stand in a place that threatens darkness, your heart will forever know love for the world, and compassion for all who walk in it, yourself included. You are the blessing upon the world. Your spirit shines and my heart is lifted just from being near you.'

Morghan paused, laid her golden hand on Clover. 'May the Lady bless and keep you in her peace. May she show you the path you are meant to walk, and may she gift you with her own peace, so that you may always know that you walk in love and wholeness.'

Clover nodded, lifted her face to Morghan, and smiled. 'Thank you,' she said. 'Your blessing brings peace to my heart when it sorely needs it.' She nodded, growing serious again, glancing off into the trees.

'What is it?' Morghan asked, seeing the change once more in Clover's aura.

'Did...' Clover made herself look at Morghan. 'Did Selena tell you...about Rhian? About what we saw — about what's going to happen to me?'

Morghan paused. 'She said she had seen Rhian in a dreaming. And that Rhian's vision had turned...inwards.'

Clover looked up at the fading stars. 'I think that's what's going to happen to me, too.'

There. She had said it. 'Rhian went blind,' she said, swallowing, taking a breath. 'Blind to everything except her visions.' Clover glanced at Morghan again. 'I think that's what's in store for me.' She paused. 'The seizures — that's what Rue calls them, even though we know that's not what they are — I think they might get more frequent.'

Another pause, and Morghan let her gather herself. 'And things like last night. Saying stuff without knowing that's what I'm doing.'

Clover blew out a breath. 'I think...' She faltered, tried again. 'I think this is my reason. For being alive.' Finally, in a rush, the last truth. 'But I'm afraid, Morghan. I'm scared.'

Morghan drew Clover into her embrace, held her there, feeling the girl's breath, the heaving of her chest as she wrestled with the knowledge of the task given to her.

'We could rail against this,' Morghan said, her voice soft but clear upon the growing morning. 'We could wish it were all otherwise, that we could have normal lives, go about our days getting up, going to work, coming home, loving, looking around, losing, loving anyway.'

She fell silent for a long minute. Remembering her own vows. Her own relinquishing to the needs of the path she had chosen.

'But that life isn't for us, is it?' Clover said, pulling back and swiping at the tears on her cheeks.

'Truly,' Morghan said slowly, 'I don't think that life is for anyone, anymore. A matter of degrees, perhaps, but we must all take up the light of the soul, become beacons.'

Clover nodded. This had the ring of truth to her ears.

She tucked her chin down, thinking hard. When she looked up at Morghan again, the sight of Morghan's calm, clear eyes made her feel more steady.

More ready.

'What do you think is happening, though?' she asked. 'I mean, back in the past, what happened then? And now — it's related to something happening now, I'm sure of it.'

Morghan herself had been thinking of little other than this. 'We really need to visit the Queen,' she said. 'Alastrina was around before, during Rhian's and Ravenna's time. She will know what is repeating.' A measure of impatience flooded through Morghan's body, giving her an itchy feeling. Really, they should have done this already.

They should have done it when the strange Fae were first sighted at the quarry.

She sighed, thinking of Erin. What was she to do about that, as well?

'We should go see her now,' Clover said. 'You and I — you're right, it can't wait anymore.' She shrugged, abashed suddenly. 'I mean, we could, if you wanted to. If it might be a good idea.'

Morghan looked down at the petite 20-year-old, with her shining hair and clear but troubled blue eyes. Perhaps, she thought, Clover had a point. Things were in disarray. Action needed to be taken.

There were things she needed to know, she thought. And this — visiting the Queen's court — was the easiest way to find them out.

She nodded. 'All right. I think you might have a point.' She paused. 'Are you certain you want to accompany me?'

'Yes,' Clover said after only the slightest hesitation. She pushed her shoulders back, nodded again.

'Yes,' she repeated.

36

Clover balked at the entrance to the cave. She looked at the darkness between the rocks, then at Morghan.

'This is the same cave, isn't it?'

'The same?'

Clover nodded, heaved a sigh, and blew it out between pursed lips. 'The same one Rhian would have had her visions in.'

Morghan understood at once. 'Yes,' she said. 'Most likely. There are two caves, the other is much smaller. It is more likely that she used this one. Particularly if she didn't go into it alone.'

Had Rhian pursued her visions alone in the cave? Clover looked inside for the answer to that and saw only the whiteness.

'But we are going inside together,' Morghan said, touching Clover's arm with gentle fingers. 'We will also be travelling together.'

'Are you sure?' Clover asked. Then shook her head. Of

course Morghan was sure. She'd been doing this for practically her whole life.

'I'm sure,' Morghan said kindly. 'As much as it is possible to be.'

Clover's lips twitched. That was the thing, wasn't it? Sometimes spirit had a way of imposing its own will upon things.

'Okay,' she said on another outdrawn breath. 'Let's go, then.'

Morghan nodded, and drew Clover into the cave with her, walking the short distance to the back wall in the darkness, knowing the way through long familiarity. She put her hand unerringly on the lantern that stood on its shelf and reached into her bag for a match with which to light it.

'There,' she said. 'That's better. And at least it is always dry in here.' She set the light back on the shelf.

'It's cold, though,' Clover said, even though she was still wrapped in Morghan's cloak.

That was remedied in only a matter of minutes. The fire crackled, caught, bit into the logs of dried wood. Morghan dipped her hand back into the bag she wore at her waist, and sprinkled herbs upon the flames.

'May we be blessed in our endeavours this dawning day,' Morghan said, and glanced across the fire at Clover. Her face was pale but composed.

Clover nodded. 'May the path lead us where we need to go. May our allies welcome and guide us.'

Morghan closed her eyes, feeling Wolf press against her side. When she opened them again, a large female lion sat next to Clover, strong and regal. She smiled slightly.

There was a disturbance in the air, and Morghan turned her attention to it, frowning. Clover followed her gaze.

'Maxen?'

The faerie man bowed slightly, visible in the half-light, in the space they occupied between the worlds. 'I thought I might accompany you, if that is favourable to you.'

Morghan, surprised, didn't answer for a minute. 'Of course,' she said, bemused at the turn of events. 'Your presence is unexpected but welcome indeed.'

Maxen bowed slightly to her, then lowered himself easily to the floor of the cave and turned his attention to Clover, examining her with interest.

'We have not met,' he said, and flashed her a brilliant and charming smile.

'Maxen,' Morghan said. 'This is Clover. Clover, Maxen, a friend of ours.'

Maxen nodded, his smile widening as he let Clover look at him as frankly as he had her. 'Clover,' he said. 'I believe I have heard a great deal about you, over the years. You are Selena's ward, are you not?'

Clover nodded, but the word he used to describe her touched a nerve and she looked over the reddish light of the fire at Morghan. 'Ward,' she said. 'I've been meaning to ask you something.' She looked quickly at Maxen. 'Perhaps, if you have been an ally to us for a long time...'

Maxen smiled with high amusement. 'A very long time,' he agreed.

Clover shifted uncomfortably. 'Then what I want to know, is why are there wards all over the Wilde Grove property?' She glanced at Morghan, then elaborated. 'I mean, specifically, why were they put there in the first place?'

It was Morghan who answered first. 'I can't say as to why they were woven in the first instance,' she said. 'But for the last generations, they have been in place — and renewed half-yearly — to provide a measure of protection and invisibility to the Lady of the Grove.'

'Protection from who?' Clover asked. She glanced at the Fae sitting cross-legged next to her then back to Morghan.

'From the world that doesn't believe in her,' Morghan answered. But her brow was creased as she considered Clover's question. It was of course, the one she had been asking herself, in light of seeing Ravenna's weaving of a blessing. There were also implications to it now. If the Grove was to be opened to the world, then were the wards still necessary in their present form?

She would have to think on that one. Talk it over with Ambrose. The idea of living unprotected made her shiver and then sigh inwardly. These were difficult times, she realised yet again.

Clover however, had turned back to Maxen. 'And the first time they were put in place — was that for the same reason?'

Maxen acknowledged the question with a tilt of his head. 'Indeed. During the time of the witch hunts in your world.'

Clover considered this. 'But before that?'

'Before that there were no wards over the land. But is this not part of the reason you seek the Queen's presence today?'

Clover nodded, thoughtful. 'Yes,' she said. 'I think so.' She looked over at Morghan. 'The wards,' she said. 'And the blessing.' A breath. 'And whatever magic I was doing in this very cave.'

Maxen smiled at her. 'Then let us go to her, for she is waiting.'

Morghan raised her eyebrows at that, but there was no real surprise inside her. The threads of the web covered everything, and what were the threads but information? The warp and weft of the world. If you knew how to tap into those, then there was little limit to what you could foretell or glimpse.

MORGHAN SIGHED, LOOKING DOWN AT THE WAY BEFORE THEM, the spiral staircase that twisted around the wall of the deep hole in the ground. 'This way?' she said to Maxen. 'Must we?'

Maxen gave an easy shrug and peered down into the darkness.

'I thought you'd take us one of the quicker ways.' Morghan tamped down on the vexation, acknowledging under it the sudden nervousness that thrummed through her.

'There are many ways to the Fair Lands,' Maxen said, tipping a wink at Clover, who stood grim but composed beside Morghan. 'Whichever way opens to us is the way we must go.'

Morghan couldn't argue with that, unfortunately. She knew it to be unequivocally true. When one travelled with purpose, the way opened according to it. Unfortunately, she wasn't currently the only one holding the purpose.

She was only one small part of the whole.

'Right then,' she said. 'We'd best get on with it.' With that, she stepped onto the staircase and began the twisting descent.

'It's dark,' Clover said, feeling the dampness of the earth close to her face.

Maxen laughed. 'Allow me,' he said, and flicked his fingers together to spark a light that floated down into the darkness ahead of them, illuminating the way.

Clover grimaced, able now to see the rich loam of the earth, the things crawling within it. 'I don't know if that's any better, honestly,' she said, then clamped her lips shut and followed Morghan's strong back down and down and down.

At the bottom, finally, Morghan looked around, taking in the dark tunnels. They were jammed with spirits, and she frowned.

'The last time I came this way,' she said to Maxen, Clover listening quietly, 'these tunnels were full with spirits. More than I'd ever seen before.' She shook her head, gazing about them. 'Now there are even more.'

'They gather here,' Maxen said. 'Like sheep, waiting for their shepherd to herd them onwards.'

Morghan was silent for a moment, aware of Clover's gaze upon her. 'They think this is safety?' she asked at last.

'They do,' Maxen said easily, and slipped to the front of their little entourage to lead the way.

'Who is their shepherd, then?' Clover asked, wincing at the cool touch of a spirit as they squeezed by.

'Who indeed?' Maxen asked. 'Who will gather the lost and take them onwards?'

Clover was silent, and when she glanced at Morghan,

she thought she saw her own disquiet reflected in Morghan's expression.

They walked the tunnels once more in silence, until the roar of a river filled the space with its noise.

'Almost there,' Maxen said cheerily.

Morghan looked with interest at the great black river that wound its way through this part of the worlds.

There was no sign of the small faerie people she'd seen last time splashing and boating and enjoying themselves in the river's generous current.

She shook her head. Things, it seemed, were changing everywhere.

The thought disquieted her.

'Thank the Goddess,' Clover burst out when they were out of the darkness at last, standing at the rose-covered gates to the Fair Lands. 'I will be glad to see the sun.'

Morghan was in perfect agreement.

Maxen said nothing, merely pushed open the gate and beckoned them on. They followed him through, blinking in the light, feeling it silky and warm upon their skin.

'The land of perpetual summer,' Morghan said, bemused.

'And grateful we are for it,' Maxen said.

'Indeed,' Queen Alastrina said, stepping forward from a bower to welcome her guests. She looked them over, her face calm, belying her emotions.

Morghan sank to a knee, head bent, and after a beat in which she gazed at the Fae Queen, dazzled, Clover followed suit.

'Although,' the Queen said. 'Lately ill winds have blown even here in this land, and some of our blooms are dying upon their trees.' She paused. 'You may rise,' she said.

Morghan and Clover regained their feet.

'Your land is suffering?' Morghan asked, horrified at the thought. She gazed quickly around, but all that she could see was as it had always been.

'Yes.' Alastrina was looking at Clover. She smiled slightly. 'Clover Wilde. It has been some time since we have had the pleasure of your company in our Fair Lands.'

Clover gulped, then risked her voice. 'I am honoured to be in your presence once more, Your Majesty.' She paused. 'I have many questions, that I think you could help us with.'

The Queen looked at her, finely arched eyebrows raised in amusement. 'Many questions?'

Morghan interrupted. 'We do,' she said. 'It is time you gave us some more to work with.'

Alastrina's gaze was still fixed on Clover. 'You will not follow blindly?'

Clover flinched, and was glad of Morghan's sudden, steadying hand on her shoulder.

'We follow our paths,' Morghan said. 'But would prefer not to do so blindly, when the answers are available to us.'

Alastrina shifted her stare to Morghan. 'They are, as they always have been, available to you. Have already been given.'

Morghan paused, then sighed. 'Clarification, then.'

Alastrina threw back her head and laughed, the sound like a hundred silver bells on the wind. 'Very well,' she said. 'Although why you ask what you already know, I cannot discern. Let us walk and talk.'

Clover looked uncertainly at Morghan, who gave her an

encouraging smile as they followed, Maxen falling in by her side.

'What are your questions?' Alastrina asked, coming to her favourite garden seat and lowering herself to it.

'We have several,' Morghan warned, letting herself sit beside the Fae Queen, with whom she'd been acquainted for lifetimes.

'Ask, then,' Alastrina said, then looked off into the distance and sighed. 'For we've little enough time for your understanding to be clear.'

'Little time?' Clover asked. She stood with Maxen, brow knotted together.

Alastrina waved a hand at her garden. 'Although it looks as though we inhabit different worlds, it is only by a matter of degrees. As your world is in trouble, so does ours suffer.' She paused. 'On a scale not seen before.'

'Is that why some of your kind have come out to roam our world and torment us?' Morghan asked, her voice sharp.

Alastrina turned eyes the colour of the sky to her. 'Yes,' she said. 'What is there to lose? What have you humans become but the cause of strife that will ruin all our lives?'

Morghan rocked back on her seat, closing her eyes. 'You condone their behaviour?'

'I understand it,' Alastrina said. 'But I am not part of it. Many centuries ago, you and I formed an alliance and I have honoured it since.'

Morghan opened her eyes and nodded.

'What made you?' Clover said.

The Queen turned her gaze to Clover.

'What made you do that?' Clover asked, quaking even as

she became more determined to get the answers she needed. 'Why the alliance? What happened then?'

'You were there,' Alastrina said mildly. 'Why do you not ask yourself, particularly as you have the gift of vision.'

Clover frowned. 'It would be easier — and quicker — if you were to just tell us.'

At that, the Queen seemed to sag a little. 'This is not the way it is,' she said. 'I cannot just tell you. These are things that you must experience, or re-experience, as the case may be.'

'Why not?' Clover felt her stubbornness rise up. 'A lot is being asked of us.' She touched her chest. 'I feel that, here. But we stumble around, not knowing what's really going on.'

Alastrina stood, and for a moment, Clover cowered back, but the Queen merely shook her head. 'Listen well,' she said. 'Experience is the greatest teacher. What you have seen you will see again. What you have done, you will do again. That is why you have returned, because you have done this before. You know how.'

She paused, shook her head. 'Here is what you need to know, for all our sakes. Your world is in upheaval. It threatens our world too, and some of us — some of the Fae — will take advantage of that, take revenge for it, try to move back into the sphere they once claimed as their own, with the reasoning that they are justified, because what have you managed but destruction?'

Alastrina took a breath. 'Others of us wish a different path.'

Morghan nodded. This, she was well aware of.

'Others of us — and not merely the Fae, as you know —

wish the evolution of your species so that we may once
more live in peace together, sharing the bounty of the
world.'

'Evolution?' Clover frowned.

'Yes,' Alastrina said, and she repeated it once more.

'Evolution or destruction. It is your choice.'

37

CLOVER GAZED TOWARD THE ENTRANCE OF THE CAVE, AT THE rain falling outside. It had, she thought inconsequently, rained almost constantly since she and the others had arrived.

'Evolution?' she said to Morghan finally. 'That seems a pretty big ask, doesn't it?'

Morghan nodded, reaching into the bag around her waist and drawing out a chocolate bar. She broke it in half and handed some over to Clover.

She wished she could quiz Maxen about Alastrina's idea of evolution, but he had stayed behind in the Fair Lands. They were currently on their own with it.

'I mean,' Clover said, leaning forward slightly and letting the sweetness of the chocolate flood her mouth. 'Evolution takes centuries or more, doesn't it?'

'Depends on whether the Queen was speaking of spiritual or physical evolution, perhaps,' Morghan said, also perplexed by the use of the word. She tucked the chocolate wrapper away and sifted sand over the fire to put it out. 'Let's go back to the house,' she said. 'I could do with a hot cup of tea.'

Clover nodded, but she was still frowning. 'And then what?' she asked. 'Then what do we do?'

That, Morghan thought, was a question there was no avoiding. She stood and stretched, managed a smile for Clover. 'We begin, I think, with practical matters. And let things unfold from there.'

'Practical matters?' Clover asked as they slipped out into the cold drizzle. She was still wearing Morghan's cloak, and felt guilty about it as the rain darkened the fabric of Morghan's shirt. She hurried toward the shelter of the trees.

'The church and school,' Morghan said.

'What about the Fae at the quarry?' Clover chewed on a lip. 'And my vision of the future?'

'The only thing we can do about the future,' Morghan said, 'is to change things today.' She mused on the other half of Clover's question as they hurried along the track to the house.

'As for the Fae at the quarry, I think we tackle that first by healing and blessing the land there.'

Clover looked askance at her. 'How will that get rid of them?'

'Their issue is with the harm done to the land. If we right that...' Morghan considered it. 'Well. It is a place to start anyway.' She tapped long fingers against her thigh as they walked, a plan formulating in her mind. Ambrose, she decided. She needed to speak to Ambrose about it. He was her sounding board; they made an excellent team.

They would have to approach this issue on several fronts, she realised.

Play to each of their strengths.

'WHERE HAVE YOU BEEN?' RUE ASKED. SHE STOOD ON THE terrace, where she'd come after finding Clover's bed empty. 'I've been worried about you.'

Clover shook her head. 'You don't have to worry about me. We're at Wilde Grove.' She glanced at Morghan, slipped the cloak from her shoulders, and handed it to Morghan. 'Thank you,' she said.

Morghan took it and smiled. 'You were very welcome,' she said, then looked at Rue's haunted face. 'She's been with me the whole time.'

Rue shuddered a breath. 'I'm sorry,' she said. 'Clover's seizures...'

'They're not seizures, Rue,' Clover said, straightening to her full height and pulling in a breath. 'They're visions. That's what they are. I think we shouldn't hide them behind some medical term anymore.'

Rue stared at her for a long minute. 'I don't know that calling them that makes me any less worried.'

Clover surprised them all by laughing. 'It's supposed to be a gift,' she said, and looked at Morghan, expression growing serious. 'I think it's time we put it to work.'

'Whoa,' Rue interrupted. 'What do you mean?'

Ebony came out onto the terrace. 'There you are. Bloody hell it's cold out here.'

Morghan nodded. 'Ebony is correct. Let's get inside and warm up. Clover and I have had a busy morning.'

There were nods and everyone disappeared inside the house. Morghan hesitated a moment, then, wrapping her damp cloak around her shoulders, stepped back to the edge of the terrace, and cast her gaze wide over the lawn and the trees.

There it was; the criss-crossing bindings of the wards. How long had they protected Wilde Grove?

Her entire lifetime, and for generations beforehand. Every six months, she and Ambrose went quietly around the boundaries of the estate, reworking and strengthening the wards, weaving them strong and clear with words and gestures and energy.

She could not imagine the property without these borders that were invisible to most eyes. They made her feel protected, stronger. Which had been their purpose, Maxen had said, since Blythe, Lady of the Grove, was hanged for witchcraft.

'What are you doing?'

Morghan turned at Selena's voice. 'It's cold out here,' she warned. 'And growing chillier.'

'I bundled up,' Selena said. 'Everyone else is around the fire, having tea. Why are you still out here?'

'The wards,' Morghan said. 'I was looking at them.'

Selena nodded, lifting her gaze to the haze in the air that was the protective spell. 'What about them?'

'I have considered for a long time only that they are to shroud the house...' Morghan winced slightly. 'And its occupant, meaning myself and you before me, from the gaze of society.'

Selena turned her attention to Morghan, listening.

'Which, in light of Blythe's fate, was a reasonable

precaution.'

'Yes,' Selena agreed. 'It was.'

Morghan drew breath, looked at the magic that arched across the grounds.

'It is one still needed?' she asked. 'Since our purpose now is to open the Grove to outside eyes?'

Selena shook her head. 'It may be,' she said, 'that we must spread our teachings as we can – but with the internet, we can do that online.' She turned to look at Morghan. 'You do not have plans to open Hawthorn House to the public, do you?'

'No,' Morghan said. 'Of course not.' She paused, sighed. 'But I don't know that this explains what we've been seeing – about the weaving of a blessing rather than these wards.'

They stood silently a minute.

'Perhaps it has yet to become clear,' Selena said on a sigh of her own.

'Hmm.' Morghan shook her head, reached out and took Selena's hand. 'Everything has implications, does it not?' Selena's fingers were warm. 'The world is an intricate weaving.'

'One that more need to come to see,' Selena finished.

'That is the truth.' Morghan squeezed Selena's hand and let it go, turning to face her instead. 'Clover and I visited the Queen this morning. She told us little that we could not already surmise, but it was an important visit nonetheless.' Morghan paused, considering their next moves. 'I feel that we're going to have a busy Samhain season,' she said. 'In ways different to previous years.'

Selena frowned. 'Why? What are you planning?'

Morghan laughed a little. 'That, I will let you know as soon as I do. It is little more than a feeling at this stage.'

'Well,' Veronica said, getting out of the driver's seat and gazing over the array of buildings. 'This is a lot nicer than I expected, I have to say.'

Winsome was looking around with wide eyes at the neat parking area, the manicured and fragrant gardens, the mullioned windows in the stone building that sat serenely in the middle of it all.

'It's lovely,' she said. 'Very calm. It feels very calm.'

Veronica narrowed her eyes at Winsome over the roof of the car. 'That's because it's old. Don't make up your mind just yet.'

'I'm not,' Winsome said, closing the car door and huffing out a breath.

'Because this isn't your place,' Veronica said, pushing.

'So you keep saying,' Winsome told her as she smoothed down her skirt, then poked a finger at the clerical collar she'd stared at for several minutes that morning before putting on.

It was the first time she'd worn it since the deconsecration of St Bridget's.

The car beeped as Veronica locked it. 'What do we do now?' she asked, staring around. 'There's no one about.'

Winsome wiped her palms on her skirt, pretending to smooth the fabric again. She tamped down the impulse to tug at the car door until Veronica unlocked it so that she could dive back into its upholstered luxury and hide all the way back to Wellsford.

'Shall we go home?' Veronica asked, seeing Winsome's nervousness.

Winsome shook her head. 'No,' she said, with all the conviction she could muster. 'No. I said I'd come and look.' She gazed around. 'It doesn't mean I have to go ahead, but I have to look, don't you see?'

She was convincing herself as much as Veronica.

But Veronica just sighed. She wasn't entirely sure she did see, but it wasn't her call. She was here for moral support, she reminded herself, and that was all.

Although Winsome was looking a bit faint, actually, so Veronica moved around the car and pressed a hand to Winsome's elbow. Physical support could be in the purview too, if necessary.

'Where do we go?' she asked.

Winsome pointed. 'That door there, I'm guessing,' and she nodded, stepped away to steady herself, standing as straight as she could manage and marching forward.

AN HOUR LATER, A DAZED WINSOME AND VERONICA WERE expelled into the garden, pointed in the direction of the carpark, and left finally to their own devices.

'Well,' Veronica said, and didn't know what ought to come after that.

'Well,' Winsome said, clearing her throat.

'That was sadder than I expected.' Veronica tipped her face towards the sun, which peeped through the clouds like a saviour.

'I thought I'd enjoy looking around more,' Winsome said. 'That there'd be more on offer.'

'The rundown of their history was awful,' Veronica said. 'It seemed like everything they did was eventually closed down.' She turned and gazed at the building, realising now, that only part of it was inhabited by the nuns. 'Sister Lavinia would start talking about something exciting they were doing, and then say it had closed in 2010, or 2019.'

'Or 1980, or 1954.' Winsome sighed. 'I wouldn't even be surprised if they gave up this one building left and moved out to live separately in the community.' She shook her head. 'I'm confused, frankly,' she said. 'Perhaps Dean Morton gave me the name of the wrong place.'

'They were expecting you,' Veronica reminded her.

'Yes. I mean, I called them to say we were coming today, but the Dean had been in touch.'

'So, it's the right place.'

Winsome nodded and looked around the garden. 'Except it isn't, is it?'

'They do pastoral care at the hospice — isn't that what you were interested in?'

'And they do still have a life of prayer and service. They're similar enough, I suppose, to my last community that the Dean might have thought it would suit.' She wrinkled her nose. 'But I'm afraid I've become spoiled by Simon's biscuits.'

Veronica stared blankly at her for a minute, then burst out laughing. 'True,' she said. 'Even the good old custard creme doesn't compare after a while, does it?' She stepped down one of the little garden paths and turned to look at Winsome.

'You can't come here,' she said. 'Seriously — you do far more good at home that you'd ever be able to do here.' She paused, trying to read Winsome's expression. 'I mean, even disregarding Ambrose for a hot minute, and your friendship with Morghan, which I also happen to know is important to you — even forgetting about those for five minutes, there's so much more going on in Wellsford than there is here.'

'Perhaps I could breathe new life into things here?' Winsome said, but her lips were pursed, dubious.

Veronica's answer was a caw of disbelief. 'This house of sisters is on the way out, Winsome.' She shook her head. 'I don't even know why we came.'

'Because it's the last step,' Winsome said. She was still standing on the lowest step, and she twisted around now to look back at the door they'd come through. It was closed.

'It's the last step I have to take,' she repeated. 'And I wanted to make sure.'

Veronica frowned at her. 'What do you mean, the last step?'

Winsome's hand went to her collar. 'If I don't move away from Wellsford,' she said at last, 'then I'll have to leave the Church.'

Veronica was startled. 'Why's that?'

'There are rules for vicars, even those forced into early retirement.'

'Ah.' Veronica nodded sagely. 'Can't be seen to throw shade onto the church. Heaven forbid.' She lifted her hands. 'Winsome — Wellsford is the future. It's a tiny place, sure, but exciting things are happening there. Things which, for the most part, you helped start.'

'That's not entirely true.'

'It's practically true.'

Winsome took the last step and moved past Veronica on the path into the garden.

'Oh,' she said, coming to a stop. Veronica came to stand beside her.

'What is it?' Veronica asked. 'What's the matter?'

But Winsome just shook her head, staring at the small, perfectly round pond with a tiny water feature fountaining a tinkling stream of water into it from an artful array of rocks at one side.

'It's a well,' she said.

'It's a pond,' Veronica corrected.

But Winsome shook her head and breathed in deeply. She could smell the water, cool and damp.

'Remember,' she said. 'At the meeting? Stephan and Krista were talking about the wells? The sacred spring, rather — Emily, I think it was, wanted to bring that sort of thing into the practice of the village, to share with tourists.'

'I remember,' Veronica said, and shrugged. 'But what's that got to do with this?'

Winsome's mouth flattened to a line, and she closed her eyes for a moment, wishing, absurdly perhaps, that Cù were with her.

She'd not seen him since she'd left the vicarage that morning.

'I don't know,' she sighed, opening her eyes again to gaze at the well.

Yes, she realised it was a pond, just a common garden feature, really, although a pretty one, but seeing it shifted something inside her.

It made her long for home.

And home, she knew now, was Wellsford.

And Wilde Grove.

She was the bridge. The one who crossed from one world to the other, who belonged in both.

And also, she was the proud owner of a cauldron.

Whatever that meant.

'Come on,' she said, turning for the carpark. 'Let's go home.'

38

WINSOME BOOTED UP HER LAPTOP, HOLDING HER BREATH while the screen came to life, and she navigated the mouse to her email programme.

It was time.

Cù came and sat beside her, his ears twitching as he looked for all the world as though he was reading through the Dean's email with Winsome.

Required to leave Wellsford. Vicarage going on the market.

Yada, yada, yada, as Krista would say.

The thought of Krista made Winsome smile. Everyone in Wellsford made Winsome smile, she thought, and glanced over at Cù, who had been waiting for her on her return, determined to be seen, as though he'd been making a point with his absence on her little jaunt.

'I get the message,' she said, and took a breath, sank down into herself, and placed a tentative hand on Cù's neck.

Yes, she thought. She could feel him. In this sort of half state, she could feel his fur, the warmth of his skin under it.

Just as though he were real.

Winsome laughed, shook her head, then forced herself to look back at the email from Dean Morton. She skimmed over its contents, even though she could have recited it from heart had she wished.

'I'm going to do it,' she said to Cù. 'I'm going to hit reply.'

Cù looked at her, his amber eyes glowing.

She clicked reply.

Her mouth was dry. She reached for her glass of water and took a sip.

Then began typing.

'Winsome.' Ambrose's smile was wide and warm. 'I wasn't expecting you tonight.'

Winsome looked up at him standing in the doorway, then turned her head and glanced at the seat under the tree. 'Remember ages ago, when I came running up here all upset, and we sat under that tree?'

Ambrose didn't look at the tree. He didn't need to. 'I remember,' he said, keeping his gaze on Winsome. She looked different.

More radiant than usual. As though something had lit her up from the inside.

'What's happened?' he asked.

Winsome turned back to look at him, and breathed in the sight of him, his broad, strong chest, the fair hair that always seemed to flop over his eyes.

And his eyes. Green like pools of water she wanted to swim in. She giggled.

His eyebrows rose. 'What's funny?'

Winsome shook her head, but another giggle escaped her lips. 'You'd better let me in, Ambrose,' she said. 'I've gone and done something.'

Startled, Ambrose stepped back from the doorstep and gestured for her to come inside. He was frowning, seeking to sense what was going on. Judging by Winsome's energy, whatever she'd done, it hadn't been that bad. She seemed a little fired up, but he could feel something suspiciously like peace and gladness in her as well.

He made to lead her down to the kitchen but Winsome shook her head. 'No,' she said. 'How about the sitting room? I want to sit close to you, because we need to talk. I need to tell you something.'

'Do you want a cup of tea?' Ambrose tamped down any impatience to hear what she had to say, even while his body suddenly buzzed with anxiety. But no, he told himself. Her demeanour would be completely different if she'd come to break things off with him.

And hadn't they been getting along almost perfectly?

It was the almost that bothered him.

'I might need something stronger in about ten minutes,' Winsome said. 'But right now, I'd rather just get to telling you what I need to.'

Ambrose nodded blankly and turned into the small room he used as a sitting room, and that only occasionally, although more often now that there was Winsome. He turned on the electric heater.

Winsome sat on the couch and patted the cushion at the

other end. 'Sit down, Ambrose.' She nodded at him. 'Please?'

Ambrose sat. 'I don't understand,' he said. 'What's going on?'

On a huffed breath, Winsome tried to centre herself. Even she could feel her energy was all over the place, practically jangling about her body. 'I'd best start from the beginning,' she said.

Ambrose stared at her. 'I'm baffled,' he said. 'You feel... excited, but I'm worried.' His fear overtook his rational mind. 'You're not going to...'

'Break up with you?' Winsome reached over and took Ambrose's hand in hers, scooted a little closer and held his hand to her heart. 'You live in here,' she said, and tears sprang suddenly to her eyes. 'You are my heart.' She sniffed. 'Isn't there a poem like that? I'm sure I've heard one somewhere.'

'I carry your heart,' Ambrose quoted. 'I carry it in my heart. William Carlos Williams.'

'Of course you know it,' Winsome said and squeezed her eyes shut a moment so that the tears wouldn't fall. 'You are so glorious.'

The fear drained from Ambrose, and he clasped Winsome's hands and dropped a kiss on her knuckles. His voice was gentle with relief when he spoke.

'Tell me.'

Winsome nodded. 'I got an email from Dean Morton a week or two ago.'

'A week or two?'

She grimaced. 'Two. Two weeks ago, but in my defence, I did do my best to ignore it for a week.'

Ambrose nodded, shifted slightly on the couch, so that he faced her more fully. He didn't let go of her hand.

'What did he want?' he asked, guessing it hadn't been something easy.

'He informed me that I was — am — required to leave Wellsford.'

Ambrose stared at her. 'But...'

'I know. It was too good to be true, really, to think that I'd be able to stay on in the vicarage. I think he was just using the last several months to think of something to do with me.'

'And now he's decided?' Ambrose felt suddenly cold despite the heater. He glanced over at the window, expecting to see ice against it. But there was nothing. The chill was inside him, making its way to his bones.

'He found a community for me.' Winsome shook her head slightly. 'Not my previous one, but another. In Yorkshire.'

Ambrose's eyes widened and he cleared his throat.

'Yorkshire?'

'Veronica and I went there today to look around.'

Ambrose let go of Winsome's hand and leant back. His mind was blank with shock.

Winsome touched the back of his hand. 'I went to make sure,' she said. 'I had to make sure. You understand that, don't you?'

Ambrose didn't answer. His head was full of static. He felt turned to ice, a sculpture, set any moment to shatter.

'I know, I probably should have told you all of this as it was happening,' Winsome said.

'Why didn't you?' Ambrose's voice was barely a croak.

Now it was Winsome's turn to sit back. She gazed at her lap, frowning, searching for the best way to explain things.

Because Ambrose was right, of course. She should really have told him.

So why hadn't she?

'If I don't leave Wellsford,' she said. 'I have to leave the church.'

'But you're not part of it anymore, anyway.' Ambrose shook his head. It creaked on his neck.

'In practical terms, perhaps,' Winsome said. 'But I have my status and responsibilities as a retired vicar, and I've never formally left the Church.' She paused. 'So, there's that.'

Ambrose swallowed and his throat clicked dryly. 'There's more?'

'I've never wanted anything but to live a religious life, Ambrose,' Winsome said, reaching for his hand again and hoping he would let her hold it.

His hand was limp, but he didn't withdraw it. She squeezed his fingers, willing him to understand her.

'And that's always been a life of service, to God, and to my community, wherever that has been.' She closed her eyes briefly. 'Giving the last of that up is no small thing for me.'

'But you still have your community,' Ambrose said. He didn't understand. 'You're still just as busy ministering to the people of Wellsford as ever you were when you were actually vicar.'

It was true. Winsome didn't think she was explaining this very well. 'Yes,' she said. 'I do still have Wellsford, and I'm humbled and glad for it.' She shook her head. This wasn't going well. She hadn't thought it would go terribly well.

But she had hoped she wouldn't make such a colossal mess of it, either.

'Here's how it is,' she said on a sigh. 'The Church has been precious to me since I was a child. I found my place in it and relished it. Then I came here and everything changed, and I've been off-kilter ever since, trying to adjust, trying to find a new way to live.'

She paused. 'Seeing Ceridwen everywhere I go doesn't help either. Especially when she gives me a cauldron.'

Winsome tipped her head back and screwed her eyes shut. A gust of wind rattled the window behind her, and she imagined the ancient goddess out there in the falling dusk, standing between the trees, golden cauldron in her hands, her white sow nosing about at her feet.

'Things aren't normal here,' she said. 'It's like a world of its own, like Alice in Wonderland. Except it's Winsome in the Wildwood, and I'm definitely still learning my way about. Still coming to terms with it at all, really.' She looked at Ambrose finally, who gazed back at her, his green eyes chill with shock.

'You've been here for a long time now,' she said to him. 'It's all old hat to you. Normal. You've probably forgotten how very strange it all actually is.' She shook her head. 'Wilde Grove — even Wellsford — is not like the rest of the country.'

It was true, Ambrose thought. And yes, he'd been there almost twenty years.

'I'm so new to it all,' Winsome said, twisting around towards him again and looking earnestly at him, willing him to understand. 'And embracing this place means giving up something that has been precious to me for my whole life.'

Ambrose cleared his throat, stared down at her hands covering his. Her skin was warm. 'Which is why I don't understand you keeping this to yourself.'

'Because I was afraid that if I told you, you would persuade me I had to stay. Which you'd be able to do, because of how it is when we're together sometimes.' She shook her head. 'I don't know how to explain it properly. I can't think straight when I'm around you. You get inside me like wine in my bloodstream. You're intoxicating.' She gave snorting giggle. 'And I had to be sure, don't you see? On my own terms?'

Ambrose nodded. He thought he did perhaps see a glimmer of understanding.

The heater glowed in the dim room, sending out shimmering waves of heat.

'You've decided to stay?' Ambrose asked at last.

Winsome nodded. 'It became very obvious that was my only choice. By going to see that community today, I was able to feel for certain my bonds to the one here. Spirits and goddesses included. Wellsford is part of me now.' She bowed her head then looked at Ambrose. 'I think Wilde Grove might be too. I think part of me is learning to walk in the Wildwood.'

Ambrose couldn't help the smile that curved his lips. 'Ceridwen?' He shook his head. 'She's really been appearing to you?'

'I went to Haven,' Winsome said, letting him focus on the details, the way he did with everything, and giving him more. 'And bought a statue of her.'

Ambrose's eyebrows disappeared under his fair hair. 'A statue?'

Winsome hunched her shoulders about her ears and grinned sheepishly. 'Yes. But what's this cauldron business? Why would she give me a cauldron?'

'She gave you a cauldron?' Ambrose sat up a tiny bit straighter.

'I was praying at the summer temple...'

'Wait.' Ambrose held up a hand. The ice had melted from his bones now. The heater warmed the room. 'The summer temple?'

'It's what I call the little summerhouse in the woods behind St Bridget's.'

'Ah.' Ambrose digested that titbit of information and gazed at Winsome. She really had had a tough time of it, the past year, he thought. Her vision of the world torn right open. She was right, he realised. She had lost what was precious to her and been left with the herculean task of learning to navigate a whole new world.

Really, she was doing admirably.

'You saw Ceridwen at the temple?'

'She just appeared there. Winked, and offered me a cauldron.' Winsome held her hands apart. 'About this big. She set it on the grass for me and disappeared, her and her pig.'

A smile twitched at Ambrose's lips. He couldn't help it. 'So now you have no church, but you have a cauldron.'

Winsome stared at him for a moment. 'That's right,' she said. 'And it's official. I emailed Morton this afternoon, telling him I will be leaving the church and any responsibilities I might still have to it.' She huffed out a breath. 'I have indeed swapped the church for a cauldron.' She closed her eyes. 'Whatever that means.'

There was movement, and then Ambrose's arms were around her, and she was breathing in the scent of him. Wood fire and wind. Ink and books. She sank against him.

'Welcome to the Wildwood, Winsome,' Ambrose murmured. 'May your cauldron ever be filled with magic, may your path open under your feet, may your kin rejoice in you as I do.'

Winsome looked up at him, blinking tears away. 'You do?' she asked. 'You understand? You're not mad?'

He tipped her chin up and pressed his lips to hers, feeling the immediate flare of energy between them, the twining rising that meant something incredibly precious to him.

'I understand,' he said. 'I'm not mad.'

Winsome felt the rising energy too, and in one fluid movement, she hooked a leg over him and sat in his lap, her hands pressed against his chest. A scholar he might be, she thought, but he was strong and fit, from the qigong, from his wanderings about the woods.

She kissed him again, and he tasted of magic.

39

THE MORNING WAS THICK WITH MIST, SEEPING BETWEEN THE trees like white wraiths. Morghan tucked her cloak around her and was glad for her warmest boots. The cold seemed like its own presence in the world that morning, and she bowed her head before it, hoping the physical exercise of the walk up to the hill overlooking the sea would go some way in warming her.

She stopped briefly to greet the stones of the circle, and Grandmother Oak, reminding herself that it had been a little while since she'd visited Grandfather Oak in the Wildwood, then drew breath and continued onwards.

It took an effort for Morghan to clear her mind of all the concerns of the day, and to walk with spirit streaming, vision open. But there was a rhythm to walking like this, she knew, and she sought and found it, and hummed then as she strode up the path, muscles warming, heart beating.

She thought of her vision and picked up her pace,

hoping that the fog would be clear from the view at the top of the hill.

It was. Finally it thinned around her, scraps of white instead of a blanket, which reminded her of Clover's ongoing experience of the white fog when she looked inwards. The weaving of the worlds, her Blackbird had called it, and Morghan shook her head.

Something was coming, she thought. Something precipitous.

Above the fog the sky was a startling blue and Morghan lifted her face to it, welcoming the light on her skin, for it felt as though they'd been under grey clouds for months now. She stood at the end of the path and spread her arms, letting her cloak fall aside and she soaked up the light, feeling the world swing around her as it always did.

She'd brought her staff with her, and leant now on it, clasping it in both hands, the hawk feathers tied to it fluttering in the cool breeze.

This was the closest she could find to the spot in which she'd stood in her vision. Far beneath her, under the fog, which was clearing even as she watched, was the sea, blue, reflecting the sky. Below her, the path she'd just taken wound around the hillside.

This was what she liked to do as often as practical – bring her travellings into the waking world. Sometimes it was simply a matter of finding a thing equivalent to that which she'd seen, or been given in the Otherworld, and so having a mirroring version in each world. She considered this now, knowing that in the bag at her waist was a sliver of wood to match that which the Fae Queen had given her many years before. Likewise, under the soft fabric of her shirt she wore a ruby heart, to echo the one also given to her by the Queen.

And now, she stood here, at the place in the waking world that most closely resembled the landscape of her vision. Morghan breathed deeply, letting herself settle as she leant on her staff. Letting herself breathe and drift and be, part of the landscape, part of this world, part of all the worlds.

She looked to one side, and remembered Ravenna in her vision, standing there with her also. Turning her head, Morghan looked on her other side, and remembered Catrin. A small measure of disquiet shivered through her, for she always felt slightly conflicted at Catrin's presence, even while knowing that they were, deep within herself, the same person.

Just as she and Ravenna also were.

She blinked as she stared at the grass beside her, thinking, considering. Ravenna on one side, Catrin on the other. It did make sense, Morghan decided. Her two most prominent lives — she smiled at the sky then. Three, if she would count herself.

They all had a part to play in this. Perhaps Ravenna and Catrin had already played theirs, but as soon as Morghan had this thought, she knew it wasn't quite true. In one sense of the word, Ravenna and Catrin still lived, still lived in herself, their experience and strengths still available to her.

Perhaps that was also what the vision was telling her. That while both earlier incarnations had laid the foundations for where Morghan found herself now, they were not now irrelevant.

Morghan closed her eyes, took another breath, felt for a

fleeting moment Ravenna's solid determination and depth of experience within herself.

And Catrin? Morghan searched for her also, and encountered a block, for it had been a long time since she had allowed herself to feel true kinship with the woman she had once been, many hundreds of years ago.

Opening her eyes, Morghan gazed at the sky, at the far sea, at the green hill under her.

'May my way open before me,' she said, and her voice floated out upon the breeze.

'May my resolve be strong, my heart true.' Morghan bent her head over her hands on her staff.

'May I find the wisdom necessary for the tasks ahead. May compassion guide me in all I need to do.

'May my allies not forsake me. May wind bring me clarity, water bring me depth. May the earth grant me steadiness, may fire kindle my resolve.'

She lifted her head.

'May my spirit touch always the truth of the heart.

'World to world to world.'

Morghan gazed down at the path, saw in her memory the lights of the beacons as they wound their way around the hillside, and she heard again their chanted song, the song of the trees.

She frowned slightly, for at the head of the procession had been Erin.

Yet Erin was not in the Grove.

The thought wound a sudden consternation through her, and her breath faltered. She let herself step out of the half-trance and back into full presence on the hillside under the sky that was already clouding over again.

Erin, she thought, and nodded. It was time for Erin to return to Wellsford and Wilde Grove.

She was needed.

Morghan took the path back down from the hilltop as swiftly as was practical, formulating a plan as she walked, until she was satisfied. Once back in the comforting company of the trees of her Grove, Morghan let her senses expand again, in gratitude for their presence, even as they wound down into the season, their consciousness beginning to drift and dream as they let go their last leaves. She touched her fingers to the rough bark of the tree nearest her, a whispered blessing upon her lips.

'Dream well, my friend. Let us hold each other and the world in our hearts.'

For the next several minutes she walked in their calm atmosphere, letting it soothe and strengthen her. At last, however, she dipped into her pocket, feeling for her phone.

Of course, it was not there, and Morghan flattened her lips in brief irritation. Of course, she was not carrying it – she preferred not to during her morning devotions – but now it would have come in handy. With a slight sigh that turned to a smile at the predicament her mobile phone – not even a very smart version – always seemed to provide her, she changed course and took the next path to Blackthorn House.

'Morghan,' Ambrose backed away from the door, holding it open. 'Winsome's just put the kettle on. Do you have time for a cup of tea?'

Desire for a hot drink warred with the need to keep moving, then won out. 'That would be lovely,' she said. 'But I'll not sit and dawdle.'

Ambrose's eyes crinkled in a smile. 'On a mission?'

'You could say that,' Morghan told him, walking down the hallway to the kitchen at the back of the house, her stomach rumbling suddenly as it realised she hadn't had breakfast. 'I'm going to Haven.'

'It won't be open yet,' Ambrose said, smile widening to a grin.

Morghan glanced back at him, rolled her eyes. 'I'm not going for the books,' she said. 'As you well know.'

'What do we well know?' Winsome said, standing in the kitchen, kettle in hand. 'Good morning, Morghan.'

'We well know that I don't read as much as some people think I ought,' Morghan said, smile wide in greeting.

'Ah. Ambrose is teasing you then,' Winsome said. 'Tea?'

'A quick one, please,' Morghan said.

Winsome nodded and turned, put the kettle down and reached for an extra cup.

'What do you want with Krista and Clarice?' Ambrose said, popping an arm around Winsome and kissing her on the cheek.

Morghan watched them, seeing the way their auras merged as they stood together. Blended and rose around them, entwined.

Something, she thought, had happened between them. They'd always had an...attraction, but now it seemed more than that.

She looked away, knowing she was seeing something private. A joining, a bonding.

'We need Erin,' Morghan said, turning her mind back to her own business, pouring tea into the cup Winsome passed her and wrapping her chilled fingers around it. Blackthorn

House's kitchen was nice and warm, and she took the opportunity to stand by the fire and thaw out.

Winsome nodded, a slight frown marring her forehead. 'I hope she's doing all right there on her own. Veronica has called and she says she's fine.' Winsome sank onto a chair at the table. 'Do you think she is, though? Should I tell Veronica to go down to London to see her?' She paused, thinking about the night Jameel told them what he thought had happened. 'It was bad, wasn't it? Whatever they did? The Fae.'

'Worse than I thought at the time,' Morghan said. 'I knew she was deeply hurt, but I miscalculated it.'

'You're going to go get her?' Ambrose asked.

Morghan had considered this, but she shook her head. 'In this instance, I think it might be better if our young people go to her. Clarice has already told me she wants to.'

Winsome nodded. 'I can see that. They've become strong friends. Their own support system.'

'Yes,' Morghan agreed. 'My relationship with Erin always carries the weight of expectation with it, which in these circumstances may not be helpful.'

'She'll need your blessing and your forgiveness when she gets back, though,' Winsome said, and she glanced over at Ambrose, who smiled softly down at her.

Morghan nodded. That was a given. She looked toward Ambrose too. 'The real reason I'm here,' she said. 'Have you spoken to the council about the quarry?'

Ambrose tipped his head back and groaned. 'I have tried,' he said. 'They're fobbing me off at every turn.'

Morghan shook her head, drained the rest of her tea, and straightened. 'Get us an appointment with someone with some clout on the council. We will be doing a land healing ceremony whether they like it or not. I would prefer to be able to go there legitimately.'

Ambrose raised his brow dubiously. 'I'm not sure we'll be able to convince them of any sort of legitimacy.'

But Morghan was already disagreeing as Winsome looked from one of them to the other. 'Times,' Morghan said, taking her cup to the sink and rinsing it, 'are changing. We will be doing things our way now, and they are going to have to fall into step with us.'

'Goodness,' Winsome said.

Morghan smiled at her. 'You can come to the appointment with us,' she said, then paused. 'You're still clergy, correct?'

Winsome stared at her, startled.

'Technically, I mean?' Morghan was untroubled by her question.

'Well,' Winsome shrank back in her chair, glanced at Ambrose, then looked at Morghan again and cleared her throat. 'Not for much longer.'

'Not for much longer?'

'No. Not for much longer.'

Morghan frowned, looking at Winsome, glancing at Ambrose. There was an undercurrent there that she couldn't decipher. 'You're being defrocked?' She shook her head. 'Do the Anglicans do that?'

'Only if the priest has committed some sort of crime.' Winsome drew herself straighter. 'Which I did not.'

'So, why for not much longer, then?'

Winsome shook her head. 'The rules around it all are quite complicated, you see,' she said. 'For instance, properly,

I oughtn't be having anything to do with former parishioners, and certainly not giving them pastoral care of any sort.' She drew breath. 'So, the things I'm doing, I'm doing as an independent person. Not affiliated with the church in any way.' She winced. 'I've been hiding my activities from them, to tell the truth.' She shook her head, aware that while she might have been doing that, the Dean knew all about it anyway.

It was, after all, up there for all to see on her website.

Morghan nodded slowly. There was still something Winsome wasn't telling her, she was sure of it. 'I'd still be glad if you came with us to the meeting that Ambrose is going to arrange.' She glanced at Ambrose. 'The three of us to see whomever on the council you can convince to sit down with us?'

Ambrose nodded slowly, still bemused that Morghan would be coming along.

40

W<small>INSOME</small> <small>HURRIED</small> <small>ALONG</small> <small>THE</small> <small>PATH</small> <small>THROUGH</small> <small>THE</small> <small>TREES</small>, tugging on the tie belt of her coat. 'It's cold today,' she said. 'Has it ever been so wet at this time of the year?'

Morghan shook her head. 'Not to my memory,' she said, and slowed her pace.

'Thank you,' Winsome said, taking a welcome breath. 'Not everyone has your long legs.'

Morghan nodded, but her mind was still rolling along previous tracks. She glanced at Winsome. 'You're leaving the Church? That's a big step for you.'

Winsome took a breath. 'Yes,' she said. 'I am, and yes, it is. I've had quite a bit of contact with Dean Morton lately. He sent me several emails reminding me of my responsibilities.' She paused, knowing she needed to tell Morghan the rest.

'You still had responsibilities?' Morghan was genuinely curious.

Winsome laughed and was glad she felt able to. Talking

to Ambrose, telling him everything, had made it all a little less of a burden.

That, and finally making the decision to stay in Wellsford, she thought. Even with, well, with the consequences that came from that.

'Let me list them,' she said, and held up a hand. 'Nothing more to do with the parish website.'

'Didn't you change that already?'

'It was my own website, so that was the first thing I did, months ago,' Winsome answered, shaking her head. 'Which I told him was the case, although he is still very unhappy.' She considered. 'Also, nothing to do with my former parishioners or church endeavours.' She paused, then ploughed ahead. 'To the point that Morton decided I must move from Wellsford. He even suggested a community for me.' She stopped walking and forced Morghan to do the same.

'Veronica and I went to look at it.'

Morghan looked at her, Winsome's words sinking in. The Dean had been very serious about it. 'What sort of community?'

'It used to be a convent, back when those were still able to flourish.'

'Ah.' Morghan glanced away into the trees, trying to imagine no Winsome in Wellsford. She found she couldn't. 'And what is it now?'

'Not much,' Winsome said, and she shook her head. 'Not enough.' She thought of the well in the Sacred Name garden, the effect that seeing it had had on her.

'It became obvious that I have to formally leave the church to continue doing what I'm called to.'

Morghan nodded, spoke around the lump in her throat. 'A big step.'

'Yes,' Winsome answered. 'I had to force myself to deal with making a decision – which I've only just done.' She frowned and looked at Morghan. 'I'm sorry I didn't talk to you about it,' she said. 'Our friendship deserved that.'

Morghan bent her head. 'Thank you,' she said. 'Why didn't you?'

'I didn't talk to Ambrose either,' Winsome said, and stared off into the woods for a breath. 'It's the last step,' she said finally. 'The irrevocable one. I had to do it in the quiet of my own heart.'

Morghan nodded, understanding immediately, and she smiled at Winsome. 'You're staying?' she asked, just to be sure.

'I am.'

'I'm glad,' Morghan said. 'I'm so very glad.'

Winsome smiled at her, feeling another weight fall from her shoulders. 'To tell the truth,' she said. 'I think it's been a while since I've really been able to call myself a Christian.' She thought of some of the prayers she said now. 'And we're supposed to ask what would Jesus do – and instead, I find myself asking what would Morghan do?'

She giggled.

Morghan stared at her a moment, then threw back her head and laughed. 'Winsome,' she said. 'I'm so glad you're not leaving us.' She looked at her for a minute. 'You've reminded me,' she said. 'We still have that trip to the cave to make. That might give you someone better to ask for examples of behaviour than me.' There was the glimmer of a figure behind Winsome.

A goddess, Morghan thought. Winsome's ancient goddess.

Winsome shifted on her feet, thinking about Ceridwen. 'Ambrose has suggested the same thing. Heaven help me. What am I getting myself in for?'

She gave a rueful shake of the head and changed the subject slightly. 'St Bridget's is up for sale next week.' She paused. 'They've decided to sell the vicarage soon after.'

'Even though you're supposed to be able to live in it for a year?'

'Yes,' Winsome said grimly. 'Well. I wouldn't need it if I were mouldering away in a community in Yorkshire, would I?' She sighed. 'The Dean is very serious about me leaving Wellsford. Or the church. Only one or the other will do.'

Winsome's mouth turned down. 'Make no mistake, I've nothing against Yorkshire. It's beautiful there.' She shook her head. 'The Dean told me it would give me the opportunity to live a quiet and Christly life in these turbulent times. He suggested it as just what my soul needs.' She shook her head.

'I emailed him yesterday and said that I have decided formally to leave the Church.'

Morghan contemplated her friend. Her closest friend. 'You're doing good work here,' she said gently. 'Important work.'

Winsome nodded, lifted her head and smiled. 'I will be staying here,' she said, and looked squarely at Morghan. 'In Wellsford.' Her heart lifted and her smile widened. 'It's where I belong, and there's so much to do. We're only just getting started, after all.'

Morghan closed her eyes, surprised at the depths of her

relief. 'I am so glad to hear that.' She pressed a hand to her heart. 'You've become my friend, Winsome. I would miss your company, and your wisdom, if ever you were to leave.'

Tears sprang to Winsome's eyes, and she wanted to cry out at Morghan's words. 'Oh, Morghan,' she said. 'Thank you. I feel the same way about you.'

She managed another laugh, a little teary this time. 'I don't know how much wisdom you gain from me, though. I think it's mostly the other way around.'

But Morghan shook her head. 'You underestimate yourself, Winsome. You really must stop doing that.' She considered Winsome thoughtfully.

'What?'

Morghan turned for the path again, that led down to the vicarage. 'Ambrose said something to me the other day, that I haven't been able to forget.'

'Oh?' Winsome warmed at the thought of Ambrose. She felt they'd made a real turn in their burgeoning relationship. 'What did he say?'

Morghan looked at her. 'He said you were the future of the Grove.'

'What?'

'The way you relate to others.'

'Oh. That makes a bit more sense,' Winsome said, still shocked. 'I suppose.'

'Hmm.' Morghan nodded. 'I wonder...'

Winsome waited. 'Wonder what?' she asked at last around a sudden lump in her throat.

'I wonder if next year, you might help me with Erin.'

Winsome stopped walking. 'What do you mean, help you with Erin?'

'When I was 18 or so, I spent a lot of time with Teresa — Erin's grandmother. She passed away not long before you arrived.'

Winsome nodded. 'You've spoken of her many times.'

'Yes.'

They reached the path that branched off down to the vicarage, and Morghan hesitated. There were other things she had to do this morning, as much as she would have liked to step into the vicarage kitchen and quiz Winsome over this convent — community — and everything else that she'd been dealing with. On her own, apparently.

While Morghan had been otherwise occupied. Understandably, with Selena and the girls' arrival, but still. Morghan didn't want to lose sight of Winsome in everything that was going on.

Relief flooded through her. The thought that Winsome might have decided to leave Wellsford!

Morghan shook it away. 'Teresa taught me about plants, about their spirits, about singing with them.'

Winsome looked at her quizzically. She had no idea where Morghan could be going with this. Winsome did not have a green thumb. She couldn't even reliably keep a houseplant alive and flourishing. The ones she didn't manage to over water or forget to water at all still looked all sort of limp and sad.

Maybe she needed to talk to them more.

'She taught me about gardening,' Morghan said, then reached out and touched her fingertips to a tree. 'Not so much about physical gardening, but about the necessity to plant and prune and weed in all aspects of life.'

Winsome frowned.

Morghan caught the expression and smiled. 'Teresa was a good teacher. She had a pragmatic streak a mile wide, but it was tempered with this understanding that we must be careful with ourselves. We are a garden, she used to tell me. We must tend to ourselves remembering this.' Morghan flattened her hand on the damp tree trunk and felt the energy humming under her hand.

'I like that,' Winsome said, still wondering what any of this could possibly have to do with her. 'A garden.' She nodded as the idea sank deeper into her. 'Our minds and hearts are a garden. Yes. I like that a lot.'

'It's a very beautiful and fertile way of thinking about it,' Morghan agreed. 'Particularly as with the idea of a garden must come the need to tend it. And our hearts and minds require loving tending.'

Winsome was delighted by the notion but she looked at Morghan and found she had a question. 'Did you do any physical gardening when you were learning from Teresa?' She giggled. 'I find I just can't imagine that. It somehow seems beneath your dignity, bent over a garden, soil under your fingernails.'

Morghan laughed. 'I did plenty of physical gardening, I'll have you know. Teresa's garden didn't look then as it does now — she did that when Stephan came along — but there was plenty to do. I spent a full round of seasons with her, learning the rhythm and song of the land.' She looked seriously at Winsome.

'I would like Erin to spend a similar amount of time with you.'

Winsome was taken aback. 'What?' She pressed a hand

to her chest. 'Me? What would I teach Erin that you couldn't possibly do a million times better?'

'Community,' Morghan answered promptly. 'Relating from the heart. Compassionate and practical aid to those who need it.'

Morghan's reply had Winsome staring at her. 'But...'

'Let's just think on it, shall we?' Morghan smiled, then looked down the path. 'I'd best get on. Will Veronica be in this morning, do you think? Clarice and Krista will need the London address.'

41

MORGHAN WAS SURPRISED TO FIND THE DOORS OF HAVEN FOR Books wide open under their awning. Was it that late already?

'It has been quite the day so far,' she murmured, and stepped up inside the shop. Only to immediately come to a halt.

'Morghan,' Clarice said, surprise bringing her also to a standstill. She'd been on her way across the road to grab two of Lucy's coffees. 'Is everything all right?'

Morghan shook her head slowly, but her thoughts were focused on the silver talismans hanging from their display near the door. She lifted a hand and sent one of the evil eye talismans spinning. 'I'd forgotten that Krista makes these,' she said at last.

Clarice nodded. 'She's only ever sold a few over the counter. They're not the sort of thing people here tend to buy.'

'They're beautiful,' Morghan mused. 'She sells them online?'

'Yup. We've been building up the esoteric side of the online shop. It's sort of separate to the bricks and mortar bit.' She leant against one of tables covered in books and folded her arms. What she was about to say was probably a little pre-emptive, but the conversation had made an opening for it and that couldn't be ignored.

'Although,' she said. 'That might not be the case for too much longer.'

Morghan raised her eyebrows. 'How so?'

Clarice shifted a little. 'You know the village market collective?'

It took a moment for Morghan to remember what Clarice was referring to. 'Oh yes,' she said. 'They're thinking about ways to bring people to the village – a market, like a farmers; or craft market, am I right?'

Winsome had mentioned it a while ago.

Clarice nodded. 'Yeah, that's the one. Krista and I have been going to the meetings. Well, Krista more than me, but Stephan too. He's been going along. And Erin, of course, since we all do things that would have a place at a market like that, you know?'

Morghan nodded. The sun, weak as it was, glanced off the silver talismans, and caught her eye again. They really were exquisitely made, although Krista, a bit of a renaissance woman, was more involved in her bookbinding these days, Morghan thought. She wondered if Ambrose was still working with her in any way. He hadn't spoken of it.

She thought he was busier now with the prospect of writing a book with Molly Wainwright.

'Well,' Clarice said. 'It's pretty much been decided that we will definitely have some sort of ongoing market here.' She nodded and pushed her white hair back from her face.

'That's excellent news,' Morghan said. 'Really good news for everyone.'

'There's more to it,' Clarice said.

'More to what?' Krista asked, coming out of the back room and seeing them talking almost in the doorway.

'Clarice was just telling me about the plans for a regular village market,' Morghan said.

Krista looked at Clarice. 'She was?'

Clarice cleared her throat. 'I hadn't got to the details, yet.'

'I'll be glad to hear them later,' Morghan said. 'But right now, I want to talk to you about Erin.' She glanced one last time at the symbols finely wrought in metal, then turned her attention fully to Krista and her stepdaughter. 'I need your help,' she said. 'It's time. It's time for you to go and get her.'

'What do you mean, you need her back?' Veronica looked in astonishment at Morghan. The morning had been going well until Morghan Wilde stepped through the door.

Winsome winced in the background, grimacing an apology at both of them. Veronica had yet to come to terms with Morghan, she thought. Fright lingered, and Morghan had spooked Veronica terribly when she'd spoken to her in Veronica's grandmother's voice.

'She's in London,' Clarice said.

Veronica shook her head. 'I know that,' she snapped.

'I've spoken to her. Where's my phone?' She looked around the kitchen for it. Had she left it in here, or was it still in her room? She hardly ever used it anymore, and the damn thing was never where it ought to be when she wanted it.

It wasn't in sight, so she glared at Morghan instead. 'This is on you,' she said. 'Something you did sent her running.' She shook her head.

Winsome put a hand on her arm. 'It's not because of Morghan, Veronica,' she said. 'Something upset Erin, yes, but it wasn't Morghan.'

'That would be a first,' Veronica said, pressing her lips into a thin line.

Morghan rested her hands on the back of a chair. 'I do take some responsibility,' she said. 'I should have realised Erin was more deeply hurt than I'd seen.'

'Listen,' Clarice said. 'We can play the blame game all you like another day.' She turned to Veronica and made an effort to be gracious. 'Will you give us the London address? We'd like to go and talk to Erin. Make sure she really is okay.'

'You're saying she's not? That she lied to me on the phone?'

Winsome interrupted again. 'Not that she lied to you,' she said. 'That's not what Clarice is saying at all. Only that they'd like to check on her, see if she's ready to come home.'

Veronica shook her head. 'I'll go to London and get her,' she said, mind racing. 'Talk to her. See what's really wrong.' She frowned at Morghan. 'What is wrong with her? I thought you two were getting along perfectly.' She shook her head. 'Erin takes so many pains to stress to me how wonderful you are, after all.'

'It was something else,' Clarice said, breaking into the conversation again, impatience rising in her. She was aware from Erin that Veronica was still ambivalent about Morghan. Well, she thought. There wasn't time for that. 'Something else happened.'

Veronica dragged her gaze away from Morghan. She'd come to a wary sort of truce with her daughter's mentor but couldn't help reliving a little of the fright she'd felt the day Morghan had spoken to her in her grandmother's voice.

And feeling frightened always made her angry.

Veronica backed away from asking exactly what had happened. The mere fact that Morghan was in the room was enough to let her know she didn't want to know.

She was still easing herself into that part of Erin's life.

'I'll go to her,' she said. 'It sounds like she needs me.'

'I'm going,' Clarice said, leaning forward, looking very clearly at Veronica. 'I'm going to go get her. I just need the address for where to find her.'

Veronica turned to her. 'I will go. She's my daughter. I should be the one.'

Clarice sighed. She'd wanted to be away already. The morning was getting on and the drive would take a couple hours. Krista was getting the car ready.

'I know the Fae better than anyone,' she said, deliberately making her voice gentle, letting herself feel compassion for Veronica. If she had a daughter, she'd probably want to rush to help as well. 'I think it would be best if I were the one to talk to Erin about this.'

Veronica's eyes widened. So, she was right. It was some awful fairy stuff. Things she didn't want to really know about. Not at this stage of things.

She turned to Winsome. 'What do you think?' she asked her.

'I think Clarice is probably right,' Winsome said apologetically. 'She will know more than we do.'

Veronica tamped down her fear, but it still made her harsh. She would call Erin, she decided. As soon as these people left. She would call her straight away. They could talk on the phone. Veronica's face crumpled. She could call Erin, she knew, but if it was something about fairy people that was going on, then how much use would she be?

'It's not hard to know more than we do,' she said finally. 'Not around here. I know I'm a convert to your ways, so to speak. But some of them are still very weird.'

Winsome laughed and put an arm around Veronica. 'I have to agree with you. But Erin will be all right – Clarice will make sure of it.'

Veronica nodded reluctantly. 'Are you going too?' she asked Morghan.

'No,' Morghan said. 'In this case, I am convinced that Erin's friends – her peers – will be the best ones to go to her.'

Veronica nodded and gazed out the window. 'I should have known something more was wrong,' she said. 'She's my daughter. I'm supposed to know.'

Morghan, who had had similar thoughts about how she should also should have known better, pushed away from the chair she'd been leaning on.

'All will be well,' she said.

Veronica looked dubiously at her. 'How do you know that?'

It was a good question. Morghan blinked, turning her gaze to the web around them, to the memory of her vision.

'Erin is integral to the Grove,' she said. 'She has a place in the weaving and will return to it.'

Veronica's lips flattened together. 'That is no answer at all. What if she doesn't want to return to her place in your weaving?'

'She belongs here,' Clarice said. 'You're here. Her friends are here.'

'Then what's keeping her away?' Veronica retorted.

'That's what I'm going to find out,' Clarice said. 'If you'll give me the address.'

'WE'RE PREPARED TO STAY A COUPLE NIGHTS,' CLARICE SAID, stuffing down her apprehension at being away from Wellsford. Which was something she'd never done before. She'd never been farther than Banwell since the day she and her mother had arrived. She glanced at Krista, who gave her a reassuring smile.

Morghan nodded. 'I cannot thank you enough for doing this,' she said.

'Erin is our friend, our sister priestess,' Clarice said. 'I hate the thought of those Fae hurting her. Just when she was really finding her way.'

'Yes,' Morghan agreed. 'I can only imagine the things they said to her. They do not make good enemies.' She walked with Clarice and Krista over to the car. 'Where's Stephan?'

Clarice shook her head. 'At the community garden, I

think, burying his fears in soil. It was all we could do to stop him from racing down to London as well.'

Morghan could well envision it. 'Drive safely,' she said, then paused. 'I've a feeling that things are moving according to their own course.'

'What do you mean?' Clarice suppressed a shiver.

'That something will come of this,' Morghan said, feeling the largeness of the world around her. She shook her head. 'Perhaps.' A sigh. 'I feel as though lines are being drawn.' Morghan frowned. 'As though pieces are falling into their places, as though great cogs and wheels are turning.'

She thought of the Queen's words and shook her head slightly.

'That sounds ominous,' Clarice said. 'I don't like it.'

'And yet,' Morghan said. 'We are not alone, and we are still blessed even within these times.' She drew breath. 'We follow the North Star, and we walk the path, and we shine the light of spirit.'

Krista nodded, came around the car, reached out a hand, which Morghan took. She clasped Clarice's hand, and in a moment they stood in a circle of three.

'The Goddess blesses you,' Morghan murmured. 'Take her blessings to Erin. May you ease the sting of her wounds; may you show her the greatest compassion she can have in this world is for herself. May you go in peace, with the blessings of the world upon you.'

42

The buzzer rang, a burring that wound its way into Erin's dreams, then pulled her from them, thick lipped and muzzy headed. She sat up in bed, frowning, disoriented — where was she?

Then the buzzer went again, and she threw back the covers, glanced at her phone, saw with a shock that it was almost lunch time and that she'd missed a call from her mother, and stumbled through to the intercom by the front door.

'Two ladies to see you, Miss Faith,' the doorman told her, his voice made tinny.

Erin cleared her throat. 'You must be mistaken.'

There was a pause, and Erin squeezed her eyes together, opened them again, and yawned.

'No, Miss Faith. They say they're here to see you.' Another pause, shorter this time. 'Ah, Clarice Wilde and Krista...'

Erin didn't wait to hear the rest. She goggled at the

intercom then pressed it with numb fingers.

'Let them up,' she said.

'I CAN'T BELIEVE YOU'RE HERE,' ERIN SAID. SHE CLOSED THE door behind them and shook her head.

'I can't believe you are,' Clarice said, ignoring the warning look Krista sent her.

'Well, ah...'

'You ran away,' Clarice insisted.

'Clarice,' Krista hissed. 'That's rude.'

'It's true, you mean,' Clarice said, and turned back to Erin. 'What were you thinking?'

Erin stared back at her, eyes burning. She plucked at her sleeves. She was still wearing her pyjamas.

'You weren't there,' she said. 'You don't know the things they said to me.'

Clarice considered her. Took a breath and sighed. 'Let's make some coffee,' she said. 'I need some after that drive.'

'You didn't drive,' Krista said lightly, trying to dissipate some of the thickness in the atmosphere, but she looked around for the kitchen. The flat was beautiful, she thought, big and immaculately appointed.

'I was in the car,' Clarice said relaxing, and with a smile at Krista. 'That's practically the same thing.' She raised her eyebrows at Erin. 'I like the PJ's.'

Erin looked down at herself, then turned on her heel and went back to the bedroom.

She closed the door, leant against it for a minute. Then opened it again.

'Is Stephan with you?' she asked.

Krista shook her head. 'He wanted to come,' she said.

'We didn't let him,' Clarice finished.

Erin looked at them, confused, then went back to her room and gazed at the jumble of clothes still in her suitcase on the floor. She sat down on the edge of the bed where she'd spent most of the last two days, hidden under the covers, or on the couch numbing herself by watching television and ignoring – studiously – the cawing of ravens.

Which she shouldn't have been able to hear at all.

She got up again. Went to the bathroom, came back. Sat down again. She could hear the murmur of Krista and Clarice's voices as they fussed with the espresso machine in the kitchen.

She was dreaming, she decided a minute later. Obviously, she was dreaming. That was the only explanation for Clarice and Krista being here. They weren't. They were still in Wellsford where they belonged. Krista was at her workbench in the room off the bookshop, bent over one of her hand bound journals, and Clarice – where would Clarice be?

Walking the woods, perhaps. Prowling back and forth along the boundaries of the Fair Lands.

Erin shivered at her mind's mention of the land of the Fae. They were the whole reason she was here, in London, sleeping practically all day, and not where she belonged.

Where did she belong? Erin's mouth turned down and she drooped over her lap. She ought to be in the garden, dancing, or walking the paths with Morghan, or sitting in her cosy cottage sketching. She should be working on her oracle cards in Haven, with Krista. She should be laughing in the kitchen of the vicarage with her mum and Winsome.

She should be in Wellsford.

She stared at the suitcase, feeling the turmoil inside her like a physical thing. If only she could put her hands on it, wrench it straight and strong. Untie everything that was knotted.

A knock at the door startled her.

'Are you all right in there?' It was Krista, and the sound of her familiar voice brought the sudden prickling of tears to Erin's eyes. She stood up and opened the bedroom door.

'I can't decide what to wear,' she said.

Krista looked at her for a long moment, taking in the bloated face, the sleep-stained eyes, then nodded. 'That's all right. You probably need coffee right now. You can decide what to put on in a few minutes.' She stood aside so that Erin could follow her out of the bedroom.

Clarice passed her a mug of strong coffee, and Erin perched on a chair at the dining table. 'I can't believe you came all this way,' she said.

Clarice glanced out the window, shook her head. They must be on the sixth or seventh floor at least. 'Nor can I.'

Erin's heart was immediately stirred. 'Are you all right?' she asked. 'It must be so strange, so disorienting, being away from Wellsford.'

Clarice turned from the window. 'As long as I don't look out there,' she said. 'How high up are we?'

'This is the 8th floor,' Erin answered.

Clarice shuddered. 'I'll pretend I'm a bird in a very well-appointed nest.' She picked up her mug and clasped it.

For the next several minutes, no one said anything. They sipped at their drinks in silence, Erin with her eyes closed, letting the coffee's warmth spread through her.

She thought of Macha, of the shifting back to Macha's life her first night in London. *May the bindings of my choosing never weaken.* That's what Macha had said, inside her mind where Erin was listening in.

How disappointed Macha must be right now.

Erin squeezed her eyes shut tighter.

There was a light touch on her hand and Erin opened her eyes. Clarice was looking at her.

'Tell us,' Clarice said.

Erin shook her head, throat tight with words she couldn't bring herself to spill.

'When I was a kid,' Clarice said. 'Selena taught me something. I haven't always used the technique like I should.' She glanced at Krista, then looked back at Erin. 'But it works.'

Erin pressed her lips together, then reluctantly asked the question. 'What is it?' she said. 'What did she teach you?'

'She told me that if I expressed my emotions in words, they became easier to deal with.' Clarice pointedly raised an eyebrow.

Erin was silent. Shook her head.

'Some things are too big for words,' she said.

'That's not true,' Clarice told her. 'There are words for everything.' She saw how Erin was holding her mug protectively in front of her. 'Embarrassment, uncertainty, hurt.'

Erin pressed her lips together. Then forced herself to speak. 'How about humiliation?' she said. 'Shame.'

The three women looked at each other, and Krista nodded. 'Those are potent ones.'

Erin swallowed. Her throat was dry, and she took a sip of

coffee. 'That's what they did,' she said, and the words tumbled from her mouth.

The others were quiet, waiting for more.

'She humiliated me,' Erin said, staring down into her mug. 'The one who did most of the talking. It was like she knew all about me, and she told me how worthless I am, how anyone else would make a better Lady of the Grove than me.' Erin closed her eyes.

It had been how Rue or Clover would make better leaders than she would, but Erin got as close as she could.

'She told me I got to the Grove too late. That I was supposed to have been born there, but since I wasn't, I didn't belong. Not truly.'

Tears welled under Erin's lids, dribbled down her cheeks.

She snorted a laugh, but there was no humour in it. 'She said there was no point continuing to try. She said that Stephan only loved me because of who I used to be.'

Erin took a steadying breath, eyes still closed, unable to look at the two women sitting with her. She thought of Macha.

How disappointed she must be.

She hadn't been around, that's for sure. Not hide nor hair since that first night.

'I can't do it,' she said, and opened her eyes to look at Clarice and Krista. 'I don't have it in me. I'm the weak link.' She sniffed, wiped her tears with the back of a hand. 'Macha – she bound herself, in all her lives, to the purpose of keeping the Way, but I'm letting her down.'

'Has Macha said that?' Krista asked.

Erin shook her head.

'Has anyone said that?' Clarice asked.

Erin shook her head again. 'I'm saying it.' Her voice wobbled.

Clarice leant back in her chair. 'The faerie woman, she took your fears from your head and said them back to you.'

'There's no truth in any of it,' Krista added.

'She did it to hurt you. Deliberately to hurt you. Twisted everything so that it would.' Clarice again.

Erin shook her head, but it wasn't in disagreement. 'She wanted me to throw myself off the cliff.' Erin looked away, shocked that she'd said the words, wondered if she dared say the next.

She took a breath, made herself look at her friends. The two of them who had come all this way to make sure she was all right. Clarice, who had never gone farther than Banwell since she was a child. Krista, who had probably had to shut the shop to come all this way.

'I almost did,' Erin said, and heard the sound of the words as if from far away. She forced herself to sit up, to stay with that she'd said. 'I almost did,' she repeated. 'I believed what she was telling me, and I almost jumped from the cliff.'

Tears tumbled down her cheeks.

'So, you see, even if she was just using my fears against me – she was right. No one that easily led ought to think she could possibly take Morghan's place.'

Erin made herself finish. 'I'm only alive right now because Macha stopped me. She pulled me back from the edge.'

Erin put her cup down, heaved a great, gulping sigh.

'There,' Krista said. 'I bet that feels better. For having told us, for saying it out loud.'

But Erin stared at her in teary disbelief. 'It doesn't make me feel better,' she said. 'Now I've just humiliated myself in front of two of the people I admire the most.' She sank down in her seat, shaking her head. 'I'm such a loser.'

'No,' Clarice said. 'You're not. You're just human, like the rest of us. And someone preyed on you. Someone who wanted to hurt you.'

'But I let them,' Erin said.

'Of course you did,' Krista told her. 'You weren't prepared for it. You didn't go there expecting to have to fight for your life. You were taken by surprise.'

Clarice nodded. 'I'll tell you what, though,' she said. 'I bet you're never taken by surprise like that again. I bet you can take this and make yourself stronger.'

Erin looked at her. 'What doesn't kill me makes me stronger?'

'Sometimes,' Krista said. 'Not harder, though. Don't let it make you harder.'

'Just more prepared, perhaps,' Clarice said and glanced at Krista. They made a good team.

'I don't know,' Erin said. 'I don't know how to keep going from this. I've let everyone down. Macha. I've let her down.'

'But she's you,' Clarice said. 'You realise that, don't you?'

'She's nothing like me,' Erin said.

Krista laughed. 'I've a feeling that's not even close to being true.'

Erin shook her head, but she didn't say anything. Was she like Macha? Could she ever be that strong, that stubborn?

That dedicated?

'Think of all you've done already,' Krista said, her voice gentle. 'How you dealt with Kria, with Wayne.'

Erin turned her head and looked out the window at the London skyline. 'I did,' she said. 'I did deal with them.' She wiped her cheeks again. 'And I've been learning from Morghan. Every day. She teaches me every day.' Erin managed a shaky laugh. 'I even helped my own mother. Veronica, I mean.' She paused.

'Maybe I'm not completely rubbish.'

'Hmm,' Clarice agreed. 'Maybe not.'

'But,' Erin said. 'But this. This undid it all, don't you see?'

'No,' Krista said. 'I don't see that at all. You don't think you're allowed a set-back or two?'

'Of course you are,' Clarice said. 'As long as you get up from it.'

'What if I can't get up from it?' Erin whispered.

'Then we help you,' Clarice said. 'We hold you until you can stand.'

43

'Are you ready?' Ambrose asked, standing in the hallway looking at Winsome, his lips curving into a wholly unconscious smile.

They'd had little more than a cup of tea on rising, and the sun was yet to show over the hills, and Winsome, he thought, had that still sleep-tousled look that he loved best on her. It made her eyes shine with honey warmth, and her cheeks were lightly pink.

Winsome shook her head, hair swinging about her shoulders, which she hunched about her ears.

'I don't believe so, actually,' she said.

Ambrose couldn't help laughing.

'You're laughing at me,' Winsome said, but her lips twitched, and she broke into a smile of her own. 'Oh, come on then. Let's go see what I'm supposed to cook up in this new pot of mine.'

Ambrose took the two steps to her, placed his palms on her cheeks, and kissed Winsome on the lips.

He liked her lips too. They were soft and warm.

'What was that for?' Winsome asked when he'd let her go again. 'Not that I minded it at all, of course.'

'It was because you are utterly delightful,' Ambrose said. 'And I am in love with you.'

'The real me,' Winsome said, and she cleared her throat slightly. 'The one who's wobbly and uncertain.'

'And yet who does a superb job of tending to what she believes in.'

'The one who can't make a decision without a month of agonising over it.'

'And yet the one who will see another's need and approach them with a giving heart.'

Winsome wrinkled her nose. They'd parried back and forth like this already, and each time, Ambrose was determined to point out her strengths.

'You,' she said. 'You do love me.'

Ambrose was tempted to kiss her again, perhaps even lead her back to the bedroom. 'I do,' he said, 'and just as much as that, Winsome, I see you.' He paused to make his point. 'All of you.'

Winsome flushed. 'Oh go on, then,' she said and shook her head. 'Maybe you do, at that.'

Ambrose's smile widened. 'Shall we get on, then?' He picked up his drum in its carry bag and swung it easily onto his back.

Winsome grumbled under her breath but followed him out into the pre-dawn morning.

'Are we going to the cave?' she asked. She reached out and snagged a hand in Ambrose's, glad of his warm touch in the darkness. 'How can you even see where we're going?'

'I've walked this way so often,' Ambrose said. 'I could do it blindfolded.'

'We practically are blindfolded,' Winsome said. 'Is there any reason we couldn't have waited for the sun to rise?'

'It is rising.'

Winsome glanced up at the sky just visible between the trees. 'It's still dark.'

Ambrose squeezed her fingers in his. 'Nervous?' he asked.

'There's a whole barrel of butterflies in my stomach,' she said. 'Actually, they may be squirrels. Butterflies doesn't really do it justice.'

Ambrose let go of her hand and threaded an arm around her shoulders instead, pulling her close for a moment on the narrow path. He kissed her temple.

'We're going at this time of the day because it's a dreaming time, with the sun still rising. It's neither here nor there, but everywhere at once.'

'Morghan took me to the cave in broad daylight.'

Another kiss. 'Yes, but we're also trying to fit this in before you have to get back to the village and all you have to do there today.' He gestured at the sky and this time when Winsome looked up at it, she thought it seemed the tiniest bit lighter.

'Red sky in the morning,' she said. 'Shepherd's warning. More rain later perhaps.' She disentangled herself from Ambrose's arm and grasped his hand instead, tugging him along the path.

'Come on, then. Let's do this mad thing.'

. . .

'IT'S WEIRD BEING HERE WITHOUT MORGHAN,' WINSOME SAID, sitting cross-legged on the ground in front of the fire Ambrose had lit. 'She won't, erm, mind, will she?'

'This cave is available for the use of us all,' Ambrose said placidly.

'Couldn't I just meditate on the image of the cauldron instead of this?' Winsome asked, shifting uncomfortably. She thought she might be sitting on a twig. 'Or read the book again, the one I got from Haven, which suggests just that thing? Wouldn't that do?'

'Either of those things would be very good,' Ambrose said, reaching into his bag for a herb bundle. He touched it to a flame from the fire and after a moment waved it in the air to start it smoking.

'We should do that, then,' Winsome said. 'I don't know how to do this without Morghan kick-starting things.' She cleared her throat. 'If you know what I mean.'

'I know what you mean,' Ambrose said, watching the fragrant smoke rise, before setting it on a stone with a dip in it that made it a natural bowl.

He looked across at Winsome, and smiled. 'That's all you have to do here, this morning,' he said. 'Relax, meditate upon the cauldron. See what happens.'

'That's all?'

He nodded. 'I'm going to drum softly, just to help you relax. You don't have to go travelling, although don't fight it if you find that's what happens. Otherwise, hold the image of Ceridwen's cauldron in your mind, and here.' He touched a fist to his chest. 'In your heart as well. Then let come what will.'

Winsome nodded. Perhaps that wasn't too bad. She

looked at Ambrose. It wasn't that she didn't trust him to keep her safe or to take her travelling; it was just that she was used to being with Morghan for it, that was all.

Really, it was still herself that she didn't trust.

'Believe in yourself,' Ambrose said quietly. 'Borrow some of my belief, if you must.'

She blinked at him.

'Borrow my gaze with which to see yourself,' Ambrose said with a smile. 'It is a very favourable gaze.'

Winsome nodded, her throat too thick for speech.

Finally, she forced some words out. 'Will you...say a prayer to begin?' she asked.

Ambrose nodded, smiled again at her. He picked up his drum, and began a slow, quiet beat. Winsome closed her eyes, let the fire warm her, smelling the sweet scent of Ambrose's herbs in the air. The drum beat in time to her heart, slowly, surely.

Her chest rose and fell with her breath.

'Here we walk the path of the Pole Star,' Ambrose said, his voice low, in time with the beat.

'Here we walk the path of all worlds, our kin to guide us.'

Winsome put out a hand and touched Cù's wiry fur. She paused a beat before breathing in.

'Here we seek the vision that shows us the way, the light, the path.'

Winsome set a cauldron on the fire in front of her. And held another against her chest.

'We seek the peace of the worlds.'

There was a shadow at the back of the cave that Winsome had never noticed before and she got up to look at it, surprised to find that it was not a shadow, but a hole, steps cut into the earth, leading downwards.

Ambrose's drumbeat followed her down into the ground.

Winsome went down into the earth, one hand against the packed soil of the wall, blinking in the dimness. How she could see at all, she didn't know, didn't think about; she only went down and down the steps, and when the steps ended she threaded her way along the tunnel path, until it opened out into a room, an underground womb.

A burrow, she thought, her lips lifting in a smile. A birthing chamber.

In the middle of the room was a fire, and upon the fire, a great golden cauldron.

Of course, Winsome thought, and edged nearer.

And there was Ceridwen, walking around the side of the great cauldron to come look at her.

'You have come to accept my gift?' she asked.

Winsome's knees quaked at the sight of the goddess. She shook her head. 'Who are you?' she asked, her voice thin as the autumn wind.

'I am the mother,' Ceridwen said. 'And I am the enchantress. I am the shapeshifter, the devourer and the saviour.' She touched a hand to the side of her cauldron.

'How can you be all those things?'

'You have read my legend?'

Winsome remembered the book from Haven. She nodded. 'You brewed a potion for a year and a day, to make your son handsome.'

'To give him wisdom.'

'And, erm,' Winsome hesitated, dazed. 'You were a bit pissed when the other guy tasted it instead.'

'Yes,' Ceridwen said. 'That is the story.'

'Isn't it the truth?'

'Stories continue. Truth manifests over and over.' The goddess tilted her head. 'I am more interested today in you.'

Winsome shook her head. 'Why, though?'

But Ceridwen did not answer. Instead, she picked up a spoon and filled a cup from the cauldron. Held it out to Winsome.

'Drink,' she said.

Winsome looked at the outstretched hand holding the cup. 'Where did you get that cup from?' she asked.

It was the same as the one she had used for communion.

Ceridwen held it up and examined it, as though she had not before paid it any attention.

Then she offered it again.

'Drink,' she said. 'For this is the brew of life. The fertile liquid from which all else spills forth.'

Winsome, helpless suddenly, found the cup in her hands. She looked inside at the liquid, a bubbling golden water, that smelt of herbs, she thought. And sunlight.

'Drink,' Ceridwen said. 'Drink and tell me what you will gestate inside yourself. What life will you bring forth into your world?' She smiled. 'What shapes will you shift into? What dreams will run through you? What paths will you follow under sun and moon?'

Winsome found the rim of the cup against her lip, her mouth filled with sweetness, and she drank, swallowed, lowered the cup.

Ceridwen smiled at her.

'Is it poison?' Winsome whispered.

'Do you wish to grow something foul and deformed?'

Winsome shook her head.

'It is the brew of life,' Ceridwen told her. 'Only you can know what you will bring forth.'

'What about you?' Winsome asked. 'Do you know what I will do?' She shook her head slightly. 'And if you don't, then aren't you taking such a chance on me?'

Ceridwen threw back her head and laughed and laughed, as though Winsome had said the funniest thing. Finally, still laughing, she waved a hand, and Winsome knew she was dismissed.

She looked down at the cup, found that it was empty, and clasping it to herself, she backed out of the womb-like room and retraced her steps, up and around and upwards, back to the cave.

'Winsome?' Ambrose touched her gently on the shoulder, waiting for her gaze to focus on him. He had seen her return to her body.

Winsome worked her lips. 'Am I back?'

'You are.' Ambrose sat lightly upon the ground opposite her, smiled at her over the flames, then reached for the thermos of tea they'd brought with them.

Winsome held her hands out in front of her, looking for the cup, but of course, her hands were empty.

'She gave me something to drink,' she said feeling the worlds revolve slowly, dizzyingly around her. 'In the communion cup.'

'She?'

'Ceridwen.' Winsome stared at her hands, then accepted the mug of tea gratefully, sipped at it, expected for a moment for that same sweetness to flood her mouth, then gulped at the tea, which steadied her.

She sighed, feeling more present in her body.

'Well?' Ambrose asked. 'You met her then?'

Winsome pointed over to a spot near the back wall of the cave. 'There was a hole there,' she said. 'With steps leading down into the ground, to a room where Ceridwen was tending her cauldron.'

'And you drank of her potion?'

Winsome nodded. Stared at Ambrose with wide eyes.

'She asked me what I would bring to life now.'

44

'I'm going to seek another vision,' Clover said.

Rue looked at her in consternation. Breakfast was barely over. 'What?' she said. 'No way — you've pretty much only just come back from a travelling with Morghan.' She wished that Morghan was sitting at the breakfast table with them, to talk some sense into Clover, but she had left early to tend to one of the dying at the hospice in Banwell.

'That's exactly why,' Clover said, her mouth turned down. She'd been thinking of little else since she'd got back from the cave. How there was no point being afraid — and in fact, if she took her destiny and purpose in her own grasp, well, that was better than being jumped and pummelled by it.

'I don't know what you're talking about,' Rue said.

'You mean, you don't want to know what I'm talking about,' Clover said. She put down her knife and fork and pushed her plate away. She'd finished eating anyway, her appetite secondary to everything else going on.

'Now kids,' Ebony said. 'No bickering at the table.'

'Or anywhere,' Selena added, then looked narrowly at Clover. 'Tell us what you want to do, so that we can help you decide the wisdom of it.'

Rue pressed her lips together. She was finding that rather than wanting to dig deeper into her life as a priestess, she wanted solely to turn around and go home. That wasn't going to wash, however — one look at Clover's face told her it would never happen. She looked down at her hands on the table and frowned. If she wasn't going to get her true wish, to go home, what had she better do, then?

What she came here for, she told herself. Whatever that might actually be. But something. It was probably time to be that priestess she actually was, the one she had worked hard to be when she was young.

She sighed, nodded. 'What are you planning, Clover?'

Clover gave Rue a quick glance. She had sounded neutral, not in opposition as she had only minutes before. Clover gathered her thoughts quickly.

'I want to know what happened here with Bryn and Rhian. They — along with Macha and Ravenna, I'm sure — wove a blessing over the Grove.' She nodded. 'Not wards, as there are now — those came later. It was a blessing, and I want to know why. It seems an odd thing, don't you reckon? When the land would already have been sacred.'

Selena frowned down at her plate. 'That's a good question,' she said. 'And you're right — the land would have been sacred then as it is now. Wards, protective spells, I could understand, but why weave a great blessing over land that, we would assume, was already blessed every day?' She nodded at Clover's surprised face. 'Yes, I agree with you that it's interesting.' She pushed her plate away. 'And how does it mesh with what is going on now? The faction of the Fae that wishes us harm. The growing disruption in the world.'

'Why do you think it has to mesh with that?' Rue asked. She glanced at Ebony who shrugged.

'Because,' Selena said. 'I can't think why else we should suddenly be reliving that particular time.' She relaxed slightly. 'Not reliving it perhaps but seeing glimpses of it. We are always shown that which is timely. That's how it works, generally speaking.'

'There,' Rue said, gazing over at Clover. 'So, can't we just talk it over, or something? You don't need to go back searching.'

Clover didn't say anything. But she didn't drop her gaze from Rue's until her sister sighed and threw up her hands.

'Fine,' Rue said. 'I give in. I can't beat you.'

'So you'll join us, then?' Ebony asked, her face serious.

Rue narrowed her eyes at her. 'Join you? What do you mean?'

Ebony shifted her position, leant forward over the table. 'Rue, we're here for reasons that we all know are serious. You've been wanting to go home since the moment you got here. You've been real resistant.' Her face finally cracked into a smile. 'Remember what one of Morghan's biggest lessons was? Measure your resistance.'

Rue shook her head even though she knew Ebony was right. 'Sure,' she said. 'I remember.' She dropped her elbows on the table and lowered her head to her hands, closing her eyes and thinking about it.

Everyone waited without speaking.

Finally, Rue looked up, gazed around the table at the

people in her life she loved most. 'I don't want things to change, that's the truth of it.'

Clover opened her mouth to speak, but Rue held up a hand and shook her head.

'I know they're changing,' Rue said. 'No matter what, everything is going to slowly, inexorably change.' She screwed up her face for a moment, then relaxed. 'That's what I was trying to do with my business, after all. Show a different way to do something.'

Ebony nodded, reached out and patted Rue's hand. 'We know,' she said.

Rue looked at her. 'But now there's this, isn't there?' She smiled sadly over at Clover, nodded, took a breath. 'All right. I commit. I fully commit. I will walk this path wherever it takes us.' Tears stung at her eyes, and she squeezed them closed for a moment.

But Clover was nodding. 'Good,' she said. 'You're Bryn, after all. We've always stuck together.'

Rue nodded. It was true. She was Bryn, and Bryn had vowed for both of them to take care of Rhian, no matter what. She sat straighter, bracing herself. 'So,' she said. 'What's your plan, then?'

'I'm going to seek Rhian,' Clover said promptly. 'I'm going to seek the past.' She looked over at Selena. 'Do you think you all might be able to come with me, the way that we can travel together?'

'We have never travelled together into our different lifestreams,' Selena said.

But Clover shook her head. 'They might be individual lifestreams, but they're the same, time-wise. We were all there together.'

'Well,' Selena smiled apologetically. 'Not quite, I was gone to the Summer Lands by the time Ravenna and Macha arrived.'

'And as far as I know,' Ebony said, 'I wasn't there at all.'

'Perhaps it would be better to have Ravenna and Macha with us when we try,' Rue suggested.

Clover digested this, frowning. 'I don't know why,' she said.

'Strong bonds,' Selena told her. 'If you want to do it together, the most effective way of doing it would be to have each of us in the same room. We would be touchstones.'

Clover nodded slowly. 'That makes sense, I guess,' she said.

'It does,' Rue agreed, relieved at the thought that they'd at least be getting Morghan in on this harebrained scheme.

'Okay,' Clover said, relenting. 'We'll do it later then. With Morghan.'

'And Erin,' Ebony reminded them. 'She is Macha, after all.'

Clover nodded, thinking of Erin's fox and raven. 'Yes,' she said, then pushed away from the table. 'In that case, I think I'm going to go to my room for a while.'

'To do what?' Rue asked, eyeing her suspiciously.

'Pray,' Clover said and looked at Rue steadily.

Rue shook her head. 'Okay.' She glanced over at the other two. 'Either of you fancy a walk to the village?'

'I do,' Ebony said promptly. 'I want to visit the bookshop and see its setup.'

'The bookshop?' Rue asked. 'Why?'

'I'm thinking of expanding Beacon,' Ebony said with a

shrug. 'Books are a big thing amongst us witches and radical rebels.'

Rue nodded and looked over at Selena. 'Would you like to come?' she asked.

Selena considered it, then shook her head. 'I think I'll go visit Apple Tree Cottage for a while. It was an important place for me when I lived here.' She smiled and looked away. 'Morghan says she's furnished it for me to spend some time there if I wish, and I think I do. I may stay there the night — sort of a small retreat.' She smiled at them. 'Definitely a treat.'

Selena waved off Rue and Ebony on their trek to the village, then checked on Clover, poking her head around the bedroom door.

Clover however, had fallen asleep and Selena nodded to herself, knowing full well how tired travelling and very hard thinking could make one. She eased out of the room and closed the door gently behind her. In her own room — which was not the one she'd kept when she had lived in Hawthorn House, but one of the guest bedrooms — she sat down and pulled on her walking boots.

She felt a quiver of nostalgic excitement at the thought of seeing Apple Tree Cottage again and shook her head.

'You're getting sentimental in your old age,' she told herself, but kept on lacing her boots anyway, then went over to pick up her journal from the small table by the window and shuffled through the pages, drawing an envelope out, holding it for a moment, then tucking it delicately into her jacket pocket.

There was no one about as Selena let herself out of the house, and she was glad for it. Company, especially of those she loved, was most usually a welcome thing, but right now, all she wanted were the trees and sky and the destination she had in mind.

A walk down memory lane.

Apple Tree Cottage looked very much as it always had. Selena stood on the long driveway staring at it with a lump in her throat. She pressed a hand to the pocket that held the letter, took a deep breath, and walked towards the front door.

She leant against it for a moment when she reached it. Morghan had been true to her word, then, Selena thought, for the tiny cottage looked in good repair, even if no one lived there any longer.

From another pocket, she withdrew a key, shiny with age, and slipped it into the lock, then paused before twisting it to take a deep breath. The door creaked slightly as she opened it and Selena smiled. It always had been a bit sticky.

A moment later, Selena stood in the middle of the main room — there were only four — gazing around in astonishment. She shook her head, a smile coming to her lips and the sheen of tears to her eyes.

Morghan, she thought. Morghan must have done this.

Selena moved slowly around the living area, putting a hand to the furniture, the sofa and armchair, the table and chairs. None of it was the same as had been there last time she'd stepped foot in the place, but still, it was furnished, and cosy. Her hand moved to the letter in her pocket again, hesitated, then fell away.

There was wood by the fireplace, a neat stack of logs

just the right size. Morghan had organised this too. Selena knelt down and laid the fire, picking up one of the small logs and inhaling its fragrance. Apple wood, she thought. Of course.

The fire caught, blazed, talked to her in its crackling wheezing voice, and Selena smiled back at it, then got to her feet and went to the small kitchen, having a good idea what she would find there.

A kettle, just as she'd expected. When had Morghan found the time to make all this happen? There'd been less than forty-eight hours between announcing they were coming and arriving.

Selena stood in the kitchen for a long, bleary-eyed moment, then stirred herself and made a cup of tea, took it back into the living room and sat down at the small table.

How often she'd sat here with Jakub! In this very spot, drinking tea together, or sharing a meal. Selena twisted around and glanced through the doorway to the tiny bedroom. Yes, she saw. Even that was furnished.

Now, she fished out the letter, laid it on the table and smoothed her hands over the thin airmail paper, looking at her address on the front, written in a hand she still recognised, even after all this time.

Jakub, she thought, was well into his 80s also. How time had crept up on them! The days and months and years just slipping along one after the other while one was busy.

And then, she thought, the next thing she knew, here she was.

The paper crinkled in her hand as she unfolded it. Onion skin, that's what the paper was. It had been such a long while since she'd received any sort of letter — snail mail, wasn't it called these days — that wasn't a bill or account of some kind.

Never a love letter.

Her lips curved upwards into a wholly unconscious but sweet smile as she read over the words that were so familiar now that she could have recited them if she'd pleased. But if she'd recited them, then she wouldn't have had the pleasure of looking at Jakub's swooping letters written in a blue ink as vivid as his eyes had been.

They'd been lovers. The priestess and her woodcutter, Jakub had called them. Selena smiled. She'd been only in her 40s then, Morghan newly come to Wilde Grove.

Doomed lovers, she supposed. Destined to part when Jakub was needed back in Poland and she unable to go with him. Both of them with responsibilities that took them away from each other. Selena turned her hand over and gazed at the ring she wore. Jakub had given it to her, made her keep it even when she'd turned his marriage proposal down. Gold, and amber from his precious forest where he lived. Selena rubbed it, sighed, then got up and slipped out the back door. There was one more thing she wanted to see before tucking up by the fire to dream a while.

Dream and ponder.

The small gate into the orchard was just as it always had been, although more lichen grew upon it now. Its hinges had been recently oiled, however, and it swung open easily. Morghan and Elise, Selena smiled, thought of everything.

There was the well. A small, natural spring, ancient rocks set about it in protection by hands long unremembered by history. Selena knelt down before the little dip in the earth filled with fresh cold water and put her fingertips in it. A blessing, both on her and the water.

'I remember you,' she murmured. 'I'm glad Morghan kept her promise to you, to tend you all this time.'

It was neatly kept, grass and plants not allowed to clog the small pool of water.

Selena sighed, withdrew from yet another pocket a small flat stone, pitted with tiny holes. 'From another land,' she said. 'Where I've made my home for these last sixteen years.' She dropped the volcanic pebble into the water. 'All the parts of myself reunited.'

Selena contemplated her words for a while, then nodded at the sacred spring, regained her feet and went back to the cottage. She would spend the day there, she thought.

And consider Jakub's second proposal.

45

CLOVER HEARD THE SNICK OF A DOOR CLOSING, SOMEWHERE deep in the recesses of her mind, and turned over on the bed. She didn't want to wake up, wanted to stay there in the place between sleeping and waking, another sort of travelling.

The white mists surrounded her, and she forced herself to wade through them, determined that she would, that they would eventually recede, and she would see what she needed to see.

But the white mists didn't clear, and she wandered around in them for a good while before giving up and opening her eyes.

She sat up on the bed and glanced at the clock. It had only been forty minutes since she'd lain down – Ebony and Rue had probably only just left for Wellsford. Clover swung her legs off the bed and sat there for a moment, checking that she really wanted to do what she was contemplating.

At last, she nodded. Yes, she decided. She really did

want to do it. She wouldn't have to worry about Selena – Apple Tree Cottage was down near Teresa's house.

All she had to do was find her way back to the cave.

And she remembered the way perfectly well.

Five minutes later she was dressed – warmly this time – and creeping through the house, keeping an eye out for Selena, in case she hadn't left yet.

It was Mrs Palmer she ran into, literally, at the bottom of the stairs.

'Goodness,' Mrs Palmer said, planting a hand against her chest. 'You did give me a scare. Why are you creeping about?'

Clover grimaced. 'I didn't want to disturb anybody.'

'Ah, well.' Elise looked about. 'I don't think there's anyone here, actually.'

'I'm going for a walk,' Clover said, then made her voice confiding. 'I feel a bit restless.'

It was the truth, after all.

Elise nodded knowingly. 'I can imagine. It feels like something is in the air, doesn't it?'

Clover paused and looked at the housekeeper more closely. She took in the vibrant swirl of colour around her and smiled. Of course Mrs Palmer was going to be sensitive to things. She lived and worked closely with Morghan, after all.

'Yes,' she agreed with a sigh.

'It's the times,' Elise said. 'Everything's a bit disturbed.' She nodded. 'Don't get caught out.'

Clover's eyes widened. 'Caught out?'

'Forecast says the rain will get that much heavier later.'

'Oh.' The weather. Of course. She smiled. 'I don't think I'll be too long,' she said. 'But thank you for the warning.'

CLOVER MADE IT TO THE CAVE WITHOUT SIGHTING SELENA OR the others anywhere. She looked at the entrance to the cave, knowing she had been there recently, but still, taking another good look at it.

It wouldn't have changed much, she thought. Since Rhian's time. It would be much the same, even thousands of years later.

A quivering overcame her, as though she vibrated within her skin and her vision blurred. She closed her eyes, nodding softly to herself. Yes, she thought. She had been right to do this. Go to the source, she thought. Go to where it all happened.

At least for her.

Rhian.

With that, Clover hesitated no longer and instead ducked into the cave, squinting in the dimness around the fire pit, and stepped over to the ledge where the lantern was kept. She fumbled in the pouch she wore at her own waist – made with Grainne when visiting Wilde Grove years ago — and found her matches.

A moment later and the cave flared with gleaming, flickering light.

And a shadow in the entranceway. Or perhaps only in Clover's gaze.

'May I enter?' Maxen asked.

Clover blinked at him. 'Why are you here?'

He ventured into the cave's craggy interior and looked at

the young priestess. He bowed his head to her. 'I thought you might like me to sing you on your way.'

'How do you know where I am going?'

Maxen gave an easy shrug and grinned at her. 'I saw you sneaking here. For what other reason but to go travelling along the river of time to seek the answers to your questions?'

'Hmm.' Clover tried to frown at Maxen's handsome face, but she couldn't manage it for more than a moment. 'Okay,' she said, and a little part of her was relieved that someone would know what she was doing, and where she was going.

Even if that someone wasn't human.

'I will use my voice to sing your way, if that suits you?' Maxen said beside the fire, crossing his legs gracefully.

Clover watched him, barely aware of his question. She was marvelling at how real, how solid he seemed to her. Wilde Grove, she thought, was a very magical place. Everything – even for her – was doubled in strength.

'If I were to touch you,' she said, then blushed. 'Your hand, I mean. Would you feel solid to me? You look like you are?'

Maxen beamed at her, held out his hand. 'Try and see,' he said.

Clover stepped closer, sank down to the sandy ground across the fire from him, then stretched out her arm. Their fingers closed on each other's.

'You're warm,' she said. His hand in hers felt as real as anyone she'd ever touched. 'How is this possible?'

'This land, this cave, is a space between the worlds,' Maxen said, not letting go of her fingers but allowing her to continue her marvelling. 'Here, we are both as solid as each other.'

Clover withdrew her hand, curling her fingers. She looked at Maxen for a moment, then dipped her eyes, feeling a sudden flash of attraction that confused her.

Seeing it, Maxen laughed, but the sound was kindly. 'Magic is a potent thing,' he said. 'Do not trouble yourself over the sensations of it.'

Clover shook her head. 'I'm sorry.'

'Don't be,' Maxen said, his voice gentle. 'All is well.'

His comment had Clover nodding, but she was distracted now, aware again of how lonely her life had been in some ways. 'I've never dated,' she admitted suddenly.

Maxen raised his eyebrows.

'Sorry,' Clover said. 'I don't know why I told you that. It's got nothing to do with why we're here.'

'It's on your mind, though,' Maxen said. 'Why have you never dated? You are lovely, I am sure any young man or woman would have been pleased to keep company with you.'

Clover blushed, her cheeks heating under the complement. 'It was me,' she said. 'It's too hard not to see things about another person. To know too much, and then that spoils everything.' She nipped a tooth at her lip for a moment, then shrugged. 'And I'm not good in crowds – or any social situation, really. Too much stuff swirling around.' She waved a hand in the air, the same one she'd touched Maxen with, then tucked it swiftly back in her lap.

Maxen was nodding. 'I can well understand that. Humans are notorious for letting everything hang out.'

The comment caught Clover's attention. 'Everything hang out?' she asked. 'What do you mean?'

Maxen laughed in the flickering light of the cave. It was cold in there, and he noticed that even their conversation could not keep the warmth in Clover's cheeks. So, while he decided how best to elaborate on his own flippant comment, he piled a few pieces of kindling on the fire and tucked dried moss under it, then waved his hand over it, drawing the spark of fire from the earth and setting the twigs and moss alight.

Clover stared at the fire in amazement. 'How did you do that?'

Maxen smiled. 'One question at a time – although that one is barely worth answering as I simply used the spark to light it.'

'The spark?' Clover shook her head. 'You're right. The first question, please – what do you mean that humans, how did you say it? Let everything hang out?'

Maxen shifted easily where he sat, the fire warming the cool cave air. 'I mean that they, for the most part, current company excluded, do not protect their energy. Everything flings everywhere. Humans are transparent in what they feel – they generally keep little in the way of energetic boundaries.' Maxen wrinkled his nose. 'It's part of what makes them fascinating, and it can be addictive.'

Clover was startled. 'Addictive?'

'For some faeries, yes. All that glorious energy, all that unbridled emotion?' Maxen shook his head. 'It's like food.'

'For Fae like you?'

Maxen shook his head. 'No,' he said. 'Not generally for

the Fair Folk. We are more likely to suffer disdain for such excesses, rather than slurp it up like soup.'

'But others?' Clover was appalled, but also unsurprised. Hadn't Morghan spoken of these entities, after all? Hadn't she herself seen them, clinging to the backs or heads of some people she passed on the street?

'I had hoped I was imagining it when I saw things like that,' she said.

Maxen shrugged. 'Unfortunately not.'

'Ugh. Let's change the subject,' Clover said.

'Let's do what we came here for,' Maxen suggested. Then he winked. 'Afterwards, perhaps, I can introduce you to a nice Fae lad – or lass, if that is your preference.'

Clover blanched, then blushed, again. She shook her head. 'I'm not going to be able to concentrate if you say things like that.'

But all the same. She remembered how warm Maxen's fingers had been in hers.

She cleared her throat. 'I don't have too much time,' she said, bringing herself forcibly back to the matter in hand – the true matter.

Maxen nodded, rearranged his long legs, then closed his eyes, began humming softly.

Clover listened, letting the sound fill her. It reminded her of the song of the trees, and she realised that's exactly what it was. Maxen sang of the world, of the trees and the mists and the mountains. Of the gentle hills, of rivers and streams, of deserts and dry winds.

She closed her eyes and turned her gaze inwards, the firelight bright against her cheeks.

Blackbird came and sat on her shoulder, his feathers

dark against the whiteness of the mist that surrounded them.

'What did you call this place?' Clover asked, her voice little more than a whisper.

'The flow in which the worlds are woven,' Blackbird replied, his little head bobbing against her ear.

Clover nodded. 'Which worlds are being woven?'

Blackbird opened his beak, pleased as always with his charge's responses. 'Where should we begin?'

Clover considered it. 'Back then,' she said. 'Show me Rhian. Show me what she was seeing. What magic they were weaving.'

Blackbird considered this, even having known that she would ask. 'Things are connected,' he whispered, his voice low under Maxen's song. 'The threads woven then are interlaced with the weaving of now.'

Clover nodded, only dimly understanding how this could be. It was like echoes, she thought. Or ripples.

But perhaps more deliberate. 'Show me what Rhian sees,' she said, and a coldness overcame her as the words left her mouth.

For even as she asked, she knew she was inviting visions that might never leave her. She swallowed, her throat dry.

'Show me what I most need to see.'

Blackbird bobbed in agreement, for now Clover had said that which was necessary to set what must be in motion.

He took a strand of her hair in his beak and tugged upon it, unspooling it into a thread which they followed deep into the whiteness.

Into the weaving.

46

Rhian stood in the water, the stream tumbling about her calves. She was there alone for once, and glad of it. The other girls – women now, like herself, chattered incessantly, and Rhian preferred to be still within herself, letting the worlds eddy through her much as the stream flowed now around her legs.

She bent and dipped her hands into the clear water, bringing it up to her face, wetting her cheeks and eyes.

'Let the blessings of your ceaseless flow enter into me,' she murmured. 'Let the song of your stories calm my heart.'

For in truth, her heart was burdened.

She straightened, and let her dripping hands fall to her sides as she gazed around herself – not at the stream bank where her gown lay on the grass as she stood only in her short shift, nor at the trees which crowded about, their roots dipping into the stream here and there like gnarled toes, nor even at the sky, which was unclouded, the colour of Finn's eyes, with whom, Rhian knew, Macha was much enamoured.

She looked at none of those things, considered not one of them. Instead, she looked at the web that crisscrossed over the land, shivering here and there with the heaviness that was come to the world.

Rhian turned her head, looking with eyes that did not see, towards the horizon, sensing the disturbance there. She shook her head slightly.

Disturbance lay now in every direction she turned her senses toward. It had been this way for almost the length of her remembrance.

Except dimly, she could remember past herself. Could remember another life even while she could not remember her beginnings in the present one, and there had been no such disturbance during that one. Her memories were vague, but those she had stood vibrant in her mind.

For the magic had been strong then, over all the land. Piece and weave of it. Part of everything, part of life.

'Rhian.'

She reeled in her senses and turned her gaze towards the voice on the bank of the stream.

And immediately bowed, staring at the water with eyes dazzled.

When she straightened, she gazed again at the sight of the Shining Ones who stood looking back at her. She felt, deep inside herself, a tug of recognition.

'It's you,' she said. Then struggled to make sense of her feelings. 'We know each other.'

She wanted to wade out of the water, climb the small

bank and stand with them, yet could not move. The stream gurgled around her.

'We delivered you here when you were only young,' the figure in the middle said.

Rhian looked at her. 'Where did you find me?'

Bryn had always wanted to know, but Rhian had never remembered.

'Or are you my mother?' she asked.

There was laughter from the figures on the shore. 'I am not your mother,' the one in the middle told her.

'Nor I,' said the second, and the third echoed her.

Rhian was silent.

'You are a foundling,' the Shining One told her. 'Found by us. Given the sight.'

'Why?' Rhian stared at them, heart pounding.

'For the task that is coming to you.' The woman in the centre nodded. 'Tell the Lady Ravenna the Queen seeks an audience with her.'

Rhian's eyes widened. 'The Queen?' she asked. Then, 'the task coming to me, or to us all?'

'To you. To you all.' There was a sweeping of bright fabric, and the figures turned from the bank of the stream. 'Tell the Lady,' the Shining One on the left said. 'We are drawing down a veil.'

Rhian sank down on her knees in the stream, watching as the figures disappeared into the shadows of the trees.

CLOVER STRETCHED, CAME BACK TO HERSELF, SMELT INSTEAD of stream water the scent of herbs that lingered in the cave, that had permeated the very stone of it.

'You are returned,' Maxen said. 'Did you find that which you sought?'

Clover squeezed shut her eyes, then blinked them open again. 'A piece,' she said. 'Like a puzzle.' She gazed over the fire at the Fae man. 'How old are you?' she asked.

Maxen lifted his eyebrows. 'It is not polite to ask my kind such a question.'

'Oh.' Clover's shoulders drooped. 'I'm sorry. I only...I only asked because perhaps you were there, when they...did whatever they did?'

'Who did what?' Maxen asked, amused.

Clover swallowed. 'The Shining Ones. The Queen. You.' She cast around for a way to express what she felt inside. 'When you drew the veil down,' she said at last.

That was what it was about. Wasn't it?

She drew breath. 'Were you there when the veil was brought down?'

Maxen regarded her steadily. 'I was.'

Clover nodded. 'And now it's being shredded, removed.'

Maxen didn't respond.

'Isn't it?' Clover demanded.

'It is.'

'Because humans must evolve,' Clover said.

'Or risk us all,' Maxen said easily, a smile on his lips. He liked Clover.

'But back then,' Clover mused, frowning now into the flames of the fire. 'Back then, the Queen wanted to see Ravenna.' She looked at Maxen again. 'It was to make the alliance that we live by now, wasn't it?' She paused. 'But why?'

Maxen shrugged and Clover threw up her hands. 'Why

does everything have to be a puzzle with you? Why can't you just speak plainly?'

'I believe you asked Queen Alastrina the same thing,' Maxen said mildly.

Clover cast her mind back, then sighed. 'Yes,' she said. 'And she wondered why we asked what we already know.'

'There you go, then,' Maxen said.

'But I don't remember!' Clover said, then shook her head at her outburst. 'Sorry,' she said. 'It's frustrating. You are fortunate — you get to live one long life, and so remember all of it. We do it piecemeal, and forget it all with every birth.' She frowned. 'Why is that, do you think?'

'Which?' Maxen asked, enjoying himself immensely. 'The many rebirths, or the faulty memories?'

'Both,' Clover asked.

'I do not know the answer to either,' Maxen said. He shifted upon the ground. 'But what I do know is that it all lives within you. Somewhere. The knowledge of how the world really works.'

Clover nodded, and closed her eyes, letting herself relax, feeling the warmth of the fire against her cheeks as she drifted.

When she finally roused herself once more, she stood, dusting the dirt off her jeans. 'I'd best go,' she said, and looked at the faerie man. 'Thank you for being with me.'

Maxen stayed where he was, looking at Clover's slumped body. He nodded and smiled at her. 'You are welcome,' he said. 'I think I shall stay here just a little longer.'

Clover looked at him, surprised, then nodded, and

stepped around the fire to the entrance of the cave and ducked out of it.

She blinked up at the blue sky, frowned at the warmth in the air, for hadn't it been cold, threatening rain later in the day when she'd made her way up here? She closed her eyes, opened them again, but the warmth hadn't gone away, and when she gazed down at the trees, she saw they were wearing crowns of green.

'Maxen,' she said, and turned back to the cave. 'I don't think I'm home yet.' Clover looked at him with panicked eyes. 'I don't think I am.'

Maxen shook his head and pointed across the fire with his chin.

Clover followed his gesture and saw herself, head tucked down, eyes closed, chest rising and falling.

'This,' she said slowly, 'has never happened before.' She looked again at Maxen. 'Am I safe?'

'Perfectly,' Maxen said. 'And shall remain so, under my gaze.'

Clover was silent a moment. 'What do I do, then?'

He smiled at her. 'Follow your impulse.'

CLOVER HESITATED OUTSIDE THE CAVE, THEN HEARD STEPS approaching. With a jolt, she recognised Rhian and Macha, and then for a moment all was dizzy spinning, and she was Rhian once more.

'You will hold the thread?'

'I will hold you within the beating of my heart,' Macha said, and Rhian looked at her through the mists that were already covering her vision, saw the flame of magic that

Macha carried within her, burning bright and strong, a light to guide them all.

A light and a heartbeat to guide her home.

'I am afraid, you know,' Rhian said, and felt Macha's touch upon her shoulder.

'I know,' Macha said, and then was silent.

Rhian nodded, grateful that Macha had said no more than that. For what more was there to tell than that?

She would wade out into the mists, the weaving, and she would perform her task, or she would fail.

'You won't fail,' Macha said, reading her mind.

'All you have to do is what you were born for.'

47

'CLARICE ISN'T HERE,' MINNIE SAID, STARING OPENLY AT THE two women asking for her. She squinted. 'Are you Rue and Clover?'

Ebony laughed, pointed a thumb at Rue. 'You've got one of us right,' she said. 'This is Rue. I'm Ebony.'

Minnie nodded, feeling suddenly, uncharacteristically shy. 'I like your accents. New Zealand is supposed to be amazing.'

Rue shrugged. 'It's home,' she said. 'Do you know when Clarice will be back?'

'Um,' Minnie frowned, a little confused. 'They've gone to London to get Erin. Morghan sent them.'

Ebony's brow rose. 'We thought they might be back by now. How do you know this?'

Now, Minnie gave them a broad smile. 'I'm part of the Grove,' she said.

'Whoa.' Ebony shook her head, glanced at Rue. 'It's really expanded since we were last here.'

Minnie was nodding, her heart singing at this sudden opportunity to meet these far-flung members of the Grove. She nudged her chin at the front window. 'Over there at The Copper Kettle, Lucy and Simon are too.' She thought a moment. 'There's Charlie and Martin as well, of course, out at the farm. Lynsey and Marshall, although they're more solitaries. And Henry and Jameel in Banwell, plus I guess there's Winsome.' She looked a little more hesitant at that one. 'Winsome's the vicar. Well, she was the vicar until the Church pushed her out, even though she'd done nothing wrong.'

'What?' Rue shook her head. 'What are you talking about?'

Minnie leant against the counter, settling in for a good confab. There was nothing else to do right that minute – the shop was empty except for Mr Roberts, who was trying to decide which car magazine to take home. The tractors were more his speed, but the one with the big article on the history of the Aston Martin had really snagged his interest.

'Well,' Minnie said, drawing out the word and folding her arms comfortably. 'You see, Winsome came here last year, to be the new vicar. Old Robinson died during the first wave of the pandemic – lots of old townsfolk did, down in Banwell, in the old folk's home there.' Minnie paused a moment. Where was she?

'Right, so Winsome came here, was an awesome vicar, everyone really liked her – except for Mariah and her niece Julia.'

Ebony put up her hands. 'Should you really be telling us this?' She didn't much go in for gossip. One of the things she'd learnt running Beacon, was the gift of discretion.

'Oh, of course,' Minnie said, unperturbed. 'You wanted to know about the Grove members – although you'll meet us all soon enough, I should say. Since we'll be getting together on the full moon in like a day or two.'

Ebony and Rue exchanged glances. 'Why would we be getting together then?' Rue asked.

Her question made Minnie frown. 'Well, of course we will. We get together every full and new moon.' She shook her head at the irrelevancy of the question. 'Anyway, Mariah reported Winsome to the Dean for praying to pagan deities and for being drunk in church.'

'She was drunk in church?' Rue was appalled.

Minnie shook her head quite violently. 'Of course she wasn't. Only, she'd done a secret mass for the souls of Robinson and the other oldies – she can see spirits, you know – and she hadn't grounded and so on properly, so was a bit you know, iffy and dizzy when she came out of the church and ran bang into Julia.'

Minnie heaved a sigh. 'Anyway, there was no convincing the Dean, especially when Winsome told him she could see spirits, so they closed down St Bridget's, and put Winsome out to pasture.' She nodded her head and gazed expectantly at her audience.

'Bloody hell,' Ebony said. 'That's some story.'

'Every word of it is true,' Minnie said, ready to be offended if they didn't believe her. 'We can go down and speak to Winsome if you like.' She heaved her hip off the counter, ready to hurry Mr Roberts along, shut the shop, and go trooping off to the vicarage.

'Okay,' Rue said, but she was shaking her head. 'I don't think we need to go and bother her.'

'She lives with Veronica, Erin's mum.' Minnie rolled her eyes. 'Not as you know, a couple. Just the vicarage is huge, and Veronica needed somewhere to stay when she shafted her cheating husband. Erin's cottage is tiny, see, and she and Stephan and Burdock live there already.'

'Burdock?' Ebony was almost afraid to ask.

'Their dog,' Minnie said easily. 'He's one of those huge Irish wolfhounds.'

'Right,' Ebony said. She looked around the shop. 'I think we'll just have a wander around,' she said.

Minnie nodded enthusiastically. 'If you go next door, you can see the space Krista has made for our art and dance clubs. Erin does the art lessons and Clarice teaches sacred dance.'

Rue turned and stared at Minnie. 'Clarice teaches dance? You mean, actually teaches people to dance?'

'Yeah. There are two sessions a week. It's real popular.'

Rue looked over at Ebony, shaking her head. 'Things have really changed.'

'They're gonna change even more,' Minnie said. 'Morghan's been asking us to come up with ideas about how we can open up the Grove to the public.'

Rue was aware of that, but seeing what was already happening was eye-popping.

'Do you know, she's already set up a care home and doctor's clinic? Just for the villagers?'

They had known, but still, when they finally escaped the shop twenty minutes later, they stood on the footpath looking at each other, feeling a little overwhelmed.

'God,' Ebony said. 'That was an experience.' She shook her head. 'That girl can talk.'

Rue laughed. 'No secrets around her, that's for sure. Which way shall we go, then?'

Ebony scanned the street, shrugged, and then the church farther up the road snagged her attention. 'Perhaps we could visit this Winsome?' she asked. 'I wouldn't mind talking to someone who can see spirits.'

'You want to just go knock on her door?'

Ebony shrugged, feeling a hum of excitement. 'Why not? She'll either say she's busy or she'll invite us in. What harm can it do?'

'Where's Morghan, do you think? I was hoping she'd be back by now too.' Rue looked around as though she half expected Morghan to suddenly materialise upon the street. Perhaps, for all she knew, she thought, Morghan could do exactly that. She seemed certainly to have been doing a great deal of other things.

'Okay,' she said. 'Let's go see the vicar who can see spooks.'

'GOSH, HELLO,' WINSOME SAID. 'I'VE BEEN WANTING TO MEET you two.' She peered behind them. 'Is your sister not with you?'

'No,' Rue said, stepping inside and looking around in surprise. 'She's at home resting. She's had a busy time of it, the last few days.' She looked back at Winsome. 'I'm sorry,' she said. 'I thought this was your home.'

Winsome looked around the large room, set up with computer stations and study tables and smiled. 'This is one of my pet projects,' she said. 'Teaching some of the oldies here to use the computer and so on. Not everyone here has internet either, so they come here to access it – and to hang out with each other. It's nice to have that social aspect to things.'

'Not everyone has internet?' Ebony wasn't sure what to make of that. She laughed. 'That hardly seems possible in this day and age.'

'And yet, it is,' Winsome said. She pursed her lips. 'I'm not sure how much good it's done us, though, on the whole.' She sighed. 'Which is why we're trying to make it a community thing. Come use the computer, read the news, weep, commiserate with your neighbours.'

There was silence for a moment, then Winsome perked up. 'What brings you to my door?' she asked.

'Minnie,' Ebony began.

'Oh,' Winsome said. 'You mustn't believe half of what that girl says.'

'It's not true, then?' Ebony was suddenly downcast. 'That you can see spirits?'

'Goodness,' Winsome said. 'She has spilled all the beans.'

'She rather got on a roll,' Rue said apologetically.

Winsome shook her head, then looked curiously at the pair. 'Tell you what,' she said. 'Come through and have a cup of tea with me. I was just about to stop for one anyway.'

They followed her willingly through the kitchen. 'This is a nice room,' Rue said.

'It's where we spend most of our time. This is such a big old house.' Winsome rattled about in the cupboard, then ran the water to put the kettle on.

Ebony was looking out the window at the church next door. 'Minnie said you used to be the vicar. I'm sorry for everything that happened.' She itched to mention again the spirits Winsome had supposedly seen but thought she ought to make some effort at a preamble.

Winsome nodded. 'It's been a difficult transition.'

Rue heard this and looked at her, sighing. 'I think we're in the middle of one of those,' she said. 'I'm not sure, when we go back home, that things are going to be able to be the same for us.'

Winsome put the cups on the table and smiled sympathetically at her. 'What do you do back at home?'

Rue picked up a spoon and fiddled with it. 'I run a business,' she said. 'A sort of sewing studio for people to learn to make their own clothes, ethically and sustainably.'

Winsome looked automatically at what she was wearing, then forced herself to stop. 'That sounds interesting and incredibly worthwhile,' she said.

'Successful too,' Ebony bragged. 'She's been able to open several studios in different cities.'

Rue wrinkled her nose. 'I have great people working for me. Ones who really believe in the difference we're trying to make.'

Winsome perked up. 'Gosh,' she said. 'You wouldn't think of doing a workshop while you were here, would you?' She laughed and shook her head. 'Of course not. I'm being silly. Ignore me of course.'

Rue found herself charmed by Winsome. There was something warm and open about her that made her glad they'd walked up the street to the vicarage. 'I might,' she said now. 'If I knew how long we were going to be here – or even why we're here, really.' She glanced at Ebony, who frowned. Rue looked back at Winsome.

'Things just seem a bit nebulous,' Rue said. 'When we were on our way here, I thought we'd get here, and something would happen, and we'd do something, and then we could go back home.'

'Loads of things have happened,' Ebony said.

But Rue shook her head, still looking at Winsome, who had the sort of face you wanted to open up to.

'Nothing I really understand,' she said. 'Clover...' Rue stopped, and the kettle whistled.

Winsome turned, flicked the electric kettle off and poured the water into the pot. 'I feel rather like a lot of strands are being woven right now,' she said seriously, bringing the pot to the table and sitting down to look at the two young women. 'Things are moving, shifting into a new position, particularly in the Grove. It's like everything is trying to line up at a new start line.'

She paused, frowning, thinking of the conversations along this line she'd had with Ambrose recently, and with Morghan. She tried to pick her words carefully. 'But,' she said, then hesitated, then started again, this time thinking of Erin, and the kerfuffle surrounding her, and of Morghan telling how Selena had suggested that Rue ought to be the next Lady of the Grove instead of Erin. It seemed to have been straightened out, but all the same, Winsome had been surprised at it occurring in the first place.

'But,' she said, looking more curiously at Rue, realising finally that this was Rue, Selena's preference for the next Lady. 'There always seems to be this something – this energy, for lack of a better term – that seems to push back, when new things are brewing. An opposite sort of force, that wants dissension and disarray.'

She could say, she realised suddenly, that in her case, this force wore the face of Dean Morton. Winsome was startled by the thought but couldn't find any fault with it.

Ebony was caught. She came to the table and sat down. 'Wants?' she asked. 'Consciously?'

Winsome considered it, then nodded slowly. 'I believe so,' she said. 'If I were still vicar, I would call it the presence of evil, I expect, and I do think that's what it is – an expression of oppression. Perhaps it can't help itself. Perhaps, it is the nature of this force to be made of dissension, but it doesn't change the fact of what it tries to do.'

The three of them sat and looked at each other, digesting this, then Winsome smiled and poured the tea.

'Of course,' she said finally. 'It's not the strongest of the forces. Usually, if we're consistent and determined enough, it's possible to push through, send it fleeing.'

She was glad she'd finally written back to Morton.

She touched the teapot to see if it was ready.

'And then things really start happening.'

'The true things,' Rue said, almost whispering.

Winsome smiled. 'Yes,' she said, feeling a final weight lift from her heart.

'The true things.'

48

'I'm going to go get Mum some of her favourite things before we go back.' Erin stood in front of the window the next day, looking not at the view outside — the sun had come out, the sky cleared, at least here in the city — but at her reflection. She'd taken the long woollen dress that had been Teresa's out of her suitcase that morning, the very first one that Erin had ever worn, in that first week in Wellsford.

It seemed appropriate.

She'd also taken the suitcase with all her old clothes that she never wore anymore, and put it in the walk-in wardrobe. She was going to leave it there.

That seemed appropriate too. This was the last time she'd think of running back to her old life.

Erin smiled, a little queasily, at her reflection. There wasn't any old life to run back to, anyway. All she could do was keep moving forward. One step at a time along this pathway she found herself on. One step at a time along the path of her purpose.

'We'll come with you,' Krista said. 'It's been ages since I've walked around the city.' She looked over at Clarice. 'Good idea?'

Clarice stared at her like a deer in headlights. 'Um,' she said. 'No?'

Krista laughed and smacked a kiss on her cheek. 'Of course it is. You'll be fine. We'll be with you, won't we, Erin?'

Erin turned around and nodded at Clarice. 'It'll be fun,' she said.

Clarice groaned. 'But it's so crowded out there.' She shook her head, knowing she was fighting a losing battle. 'Fine,' she groaned. 'I can do it.'

'We'll do it together,' Erin said, coming and looping her arm through Clarice's. 'Right?'

The three of them looked at each other and nodded.

The air around them hummed suddenly, and they knew they were agreeing to more than a quick walk around the city.

'We'll do it together,' Krista said.

Clarice nodded. 'Together.'

'And we'll be who we are,' Erin said. Her skin prickled in sudden nervous excitement. 'Who we really are, I mean.'

'Priestesses of the Grove,' Krista agreed. 'But more than that – we'll be the shining souls we are.'

'That we all are,' Clarice said. She paused only a moment.

'May the magic of our spirits shine bright.'

'Wherever we are, whatever we do,' Erin said.

They looked at each other, marking the moment that had passed between them.

'Thank you for coming here,' Erin said. 'For talking

everything through with me and being so supportive. Thank you so much. I don't know what would have happened if you hadn't.'

Krista glanced at Clarice, nodded. 'We did come, and we're glad we did – we're in this together,' she said, then grinned.

'Let's go get your mom some treats, then.'

'WHAT DO YOU THINK?' ERIN ASKED CLARICE, AS THEY STOOD in Trafalgar Square, the sky a bright blue above the city even while a cool breeze wrapped itself tighter around them.

Clarice shook her head. She was turning in a slow circle, taking in everything around her. She was opening her mouth to reply when something caught her eye. She pointed.

'Look at that,' she said, and stared through her sunglasses. 'That is not a pigeon.'

Erin looked where Clarice pointed, shading her eyes from the sun. 'Pigeons were moved on from the Square ages ago,' she said. 'They used Harris Hawks in the end, to scare them off.'

'That's not a hawk, either,' Clarice said, and looked at Erin.

'It's a raven,' Krista said, coming to stand beside her.

Erin stared at the bird, which perched across the other side of the square, its flat black gaze fixed on her.

'It's looking at me,' she said, and flung out a hand to grope at the air. 'I feel a little bit weird.'

Krista caught her arm. 'All right?' she said.

Another raven had joined the first, and another.

'There are more of them, look,' Clarice said.

She wasn't the only one to have noticed. Knots of tourists stood in the square, pointing at the birds, which now, to Clarice's eyes, numbered six or seven.

A couple people already had their phones out, filming them.

Erin's mouth was dry. Krista still had her hand, holding it firmly, which was just as well, because Erin felt as though the ground were shifting under her feet.

'I saw one the first day I was here,' she said. She cleared her throat, steadied her voice. 'When I was coming home from...from dinner. In a taxi. It landed on the car.'

'They're your birds,' Clarice said, and she was staring not at the ravens now, but at Erin.

'Not mine from home?' Erin breathed out. 'They couldn't have followed us all the way here.'

'I don't know,' Clarice said, then took a few steps closer to Erin when she looked back, and the birds lifted their wings. 'What are they going to do?' she asked. 'Why are they here?'

There were more of them now; Clarice counted twelve. She could hear the murmurs of the tourists, everyone around them turning to stare at the birds who were all looking in the same direction – at Erin.

'I feel odd,' Erin said, and she gripped Krista's hand tighter. 'I think I'm going to shift.' The world started a slow spin. 'I don't think I can stop myself.'

'You can't do that here!' Clarice stared at her in horror, then looked all around them at the crowds, which were growing larger.

'There are more ravens,' Krista said. 'Look. They must be coming from the Tower.'

Clarice snatched at her. 'We have to get Erin out of here.'

But Krista, her hand still gripping Erin's, shook her head slowly. 'I don't know,' she said.

'What do you mean, you don't know?' Clarice didn't like what was happening. The ravens were a large group now – perhaps fifteen or more, perched on the square's twin lions, on the bollards that surrounded the column.

And there were even more people. She liked that even less.

Most of them had their phones out.

Erin shook her hand loose from Krista's.

She had shifted, slid sideways until she wasn't herself anymore – or not just herself. Macha was inside her, an echo of herself, and Erin felt her calm certainty and straightened, opening her eyes to the sight of the birds – her birds.

Her ravens.

'What are you doing?' Clarice's voice grazed against her, fell away unheeded.

Erin didn't know what she was doing, but Macha was with her, and she trusted Macha, and the ravens were hers, weren't they?

And Macha herself — weren't the both of them really the same person?

Macha had always seemed like someone different to Erin, someone separate to herself, but now that changed. She could feel their twin wills overlapping each other, each woven to the same pattern.

They were the same person. Different bodies, different times. She breathed deeply. Same goals.

Same vows.

The world swirled around her, and she turned with it, tipping her head back watching the weaving of the web rippling slightly, seeing it glowing against the blue of the sky.

Yes, she thought, thinking the same thought as Macha. We are the same. I just didn't remember, that's all.

Until now.

Now, she said to herself, to Macha. I remember.

And she did. For a moment, she stood inside the cave at Wilde Grove, at the Forest House, head tipped back like this, keeping the beat that would bring Rhian back, while outside, everyone else stood, arms outstretched, pouring magic into the air. A spell, a weaving, a blessing.

'Blessed are we, the people of this world, who walk with bird and tree and stone, who breathe the wind, who sing the song of the trees, who follow the path of the North Star, who keep the old ways alive, who know the earth in our blood and bones and hearts.'

Clarice looked sideways at Krista, panic in her glance. Erin was speaking out loud, and the ravens, they were gathering closer to her.

And the people with their phones out, holding them up, video rolling. They had them pointed at Erin now, Erin who stood in the middle of the square, her long blue dress luminous in the cool light, her head tipped back, skin glowing, hair tumbled down her back.

She was strikingly beautiful.

And deep in trance.

Erin opened her eyes, and the ravens looked at her, lifted their wings, their feathers ruffling, black and oily, in the breeze that sprang up and scooted about the square.

She spread her hands towards the birds, and she was in the square and in the cave. She and the others were weaving the worlds, setting the spell, doing...something. Keeping a section of land sacred.

Then she was back in the square, seeing the ravens. She looked at them, and they looked back at her, and lifted their feathers.

As though they were waiting.

Waiting for her. She'd done this before, she thought, and hadn't it been making a choice then, too? Back at Ash Cottage, outside in the garden, lifting her arms for the birds to land upon, their wings a papery rustling, their bodies surprisingly heavy, their claws gripping her, firmly, gently.

'We have to stop her,' Clarice hissed at Krista.

But Krista shook her head. 'She's in trance, we can't just yank her out of it.'

'She's making a scene out here – look, everyone has their phones out. They're filming her.'

Several of the ravens had taken flight in a black cloud, flying the short distance to land on Erin's outstretched arms, on her shoulders.

Others moved, landed at her feet.

'What do we do?' Clarice asked.

'Do you remember what we said before we came out here this morning?' Krista said to her.

Clarice shook her head. Her gaze was fixed on Erin, standing in the square in her long blue dress, her red hair flowing free down her back, and her ravens perched on her outstretched arms.

Several people were running around to find better positions to film her, so they could capture her face.

'What did we say?' Clarice asked.

'We said we'd join her,' Krista said, and she straightened, took a breath.

'Join her?'

'We'll be who we really are,' Krista repeated from memory.

Clarice sank back. She remembered. 'Priestesses of the Grove,' she said, her voice low amidst the shouting and murmuring of the growing crowd.

'The shining souls that we are,' Krista agreed.

'Fuck.'

Krista smiled, reached for Clarice's hand. 'We promised. *Wherever we are, whatever we do.*'

Erin turned around and faced them as they spoke. Her face was calm, eyes open but unseeing. Inside herself, she felt Macha's presence, and other echoes behind it – the lives she'd lived. All the lives dedicated, sky to root.

Krista smiled at Clarice, then stepped forward, raising her hand to take one of Erin's. A raven looked at her for a moment, then hopped upon her arm from Erin's.

A bird from the ground took its place. Another leapt up to perch on Krista's shoulder.

Clarice watched, let out a breath, and stepped forward, skirts of her tunic flapping, to take Erin's other hand in one of hers, and Krista's in the other. The ravens were heavy on her arms, and she wished Sigil were among them.

For a minute, she thought about what they must look

like – the three of them in a triangle in Trafalgar Square, covered in ravens that must have come from the Tower of London – for surely the ravens that hung about Ash Cottage could not have made the trip down.

And Erin was wearing the long dress that Teresa had worn for rituals – Clarice recognised it. She looked, Clarice thought, every inch the priestess that she was.

With that thought, Clarice took a breath, and gave herself over to whatever it was that was happening.

'May the Goddess be with us,' she murmured.

Krista heard her. 'May the Goddess guide us.'

A serene smile spread over Erin's face, seeming almost to bathe her in light.

'We follow the shining path,' she said, and closed her eyes.

Macha's vow reverberated through her.

May the Goddess bless and lead me.

May the bindings of my choosing never weaken.

49

Stephan sat back on his heels, wiped his sleeve across his forehead. It was late afternoon now, and Krista and Clarice were still in London with Erin. He wondered how they were getting on. Felt guilty about not going there himself. Burdock got up and came to lick his cheeks.

'Stop, boy,' Stephan said, and pushed the dog gently away. 'Sorry, fella.'

Burdock whined and Stephan sighed, pulled the giant dog closer and leant against him. 'I know,' he said. 'I miss her too. And no, I don't know what's going on.' Standing up, Stephan tugged his phone from his pocket and gazed blankly at his screen for a moment, before it lit up in his hand.

'Erin?' his mouth was dry.

Things like this happened with the two of them – picking up the phone just before the other messaged or called was one of the more usual, but Stephan looked for a moment at his phone as though it might bite him.

He put his thumb on the answer button and lifted the device to his ear.

'Erin?'

'Stephan,' she said.

He closed his eyes. Her voice, he thought. It was gentle. Something had happened, something that had drained the stress and shame away. Thank the Goddess for Clarice and Krista.

'I'm coming home now,' Erin was saying.

Stephan nodded, looked down at Burdock who was staring hopefully up at him, able to hear Erin's voice on the phone. Stephan pulled gently at one of Burdock's ears, reassuring the dog.

'Now?' he asked.

'We're about to head out the door,' Erin said, then paused. 'But Stephan?'

He nodded, cleared his throat. 'Yeah?'

'Something happened,' she said. 'While we were in the city today.'

Burdock sat down, stared at Stephan, his doggy forehead wrinkling.

'What sort of something?' Stephan asked. He'd be alarmed, but Erin's voice – it wasn't strained. More...awed.

'I don't know,' Erin said. 'But there are videos of it posted online.'

Stephan frowned, not understanding. 'What do you mean?'

'Just search for *Trafalgar Square ravens*.' She paused. 'Or *priestesses of Trafalgar Square*.'

'What?' That didn't make any sense. Stephan reached out with his senses and touched Erin's energy. She was fizzing and excited and steady at the same time. Stephan was flooded with relief. Whatever had happened wasn't too bad then.

'Just look,' Erin said. 'I'm going to come home now. Will you be at the cottage?'

'You want me to be?' Stephan could feel that she did, but he wanted to hear her say the words.

'Yes,' Erin said.

'Come on, then,' Stephan said to Burdock, putting his tools away and brushing the dirt from his hands. 'Let's go home.'

And then they would see this video Erin was talking about.

Stephan would have looked already, but there wasn't any data on his phone. 'Trafalgar Square ravens,' he said to Burdock, who whined from the back of the van and stuck his head between the front seats.

'I don't know either, buddy,' Stephan told him. 'I thought they had pigeons at the Square, and ravens at the Tower.'

Ravens were Erin's bird though, so there was that. Had they found her there somehow? Followed her?

He shook his head. 'I dunno,' he said to Burdock. 'But we're going home to find out.'

They turned down the street towards Ash Cottage, Stephan feeling the familiar frisson under his skin as they crossed the unseen border into Wilde Grove land.

'What?'

The van came to a rolling stop in the middle of the lane,

and Stephan peered through the windscreen at the low wall that surrounded Ash Cottage.

It was covered in birds. Stephan counted ten or twelve of them. 'I haven't seen this many here since...' He tried to think.

'Since Erin first came here,' he said to Burdock at last.

Burdock wrinkled his snout at the ravens.

'Something is definitely going on,' Stephan concluded, and he got the van moving again, pulling into the driveway.

They made the dash through the rain that had just begun falling, fat drops and cold, to the cottage, pulling the door closed behind them, both man and dog heaving a sigh of relief to be back in their favourite place. Briefly, Stephan wondered what they would do when it was time to move into the big house, Hawthorne House, but he shook the thought from his mind. That was a long time away. Twenty years at the least. Morghan wasn't old, and she was strong, healthy.

Burdock had a noisy drink from his bowl, then went to his chair by the window in the sitting room and looked out at the ravens. He whined again, telling Stephan that they were still there, waiting for Erin.

He was waiting for her too, and he squinted at the birds, wanting to tell them to go away and come back later. But they stunk of magic, so he kept his growls in his throat, and tried to be a good boy.

Stephan leant against the kitchen bench and dragged his phone out of his pocket, bringing up the browser.

'Trafalgar Square ravens,' he typed into the search engine, then considered, frowning, as he watched the results click up. There was only one that dealt with actual ravens, and it was a video. He hit on that one, waited for it to load.

Then watched it in growing astonishment.

Then watched it again.

Finally, Stephan put his phone down and walked over to stand next to Burdock, both of them staring out the window at the ravens. The day was dim out, shrouded now in rain, but the ravens seemed unperturbed by either the darkness or dampness. Stephan put his hand on Burdock's strong neck and blew out a breath.

'I've got a feeling, Burdock,' he said.

Burdock twisted his head to look at him.

'Pretty strong one too,' Stephan told him.

Burdock chuffed agreement.

'We've crossed the Rubicon, or whatever that saying is.' Stephan shook his head.

Burdock didn't know what his words were, what a Rubicon was, but he knew what the ravens were, and he stiffened, looking at them again. Gave a small woof.

Stephan ruffled his fur. 'She'll be home soon,' he said and checked his watch, hoping she was driving safely in all that rain. The wettest autumn in memory. His, for sure.

'I'm going to have a shower,' he said. 'Get clean.'

Afterwards, Stephan prowled around the cottage as the day tipped steadily to darkness. He was restless, waiting for Erin, not knowing quite what to do with himself. He fed Burdock, who ate, went outside for three minutes, then came back in, wiping his feet carefully first, and resuming his seat watching the ravens and the lane – neither of which he could really see anymore.

Stephan threw together the makings of a soup, left it on

the cooker to simmer, then ranged around the house again. At last, he ducked outside, bending his head against the rain and making for the potting shed.

This was his place still, and the familiar smells of herbs and soil relaxed him immediately. He turned on the dim yellow bulb, then checked his watch again, drew a breath, and went over to the corner of the garden bench, the shadowed little spot he reserved for his altar.

It was a basic setup but it suited Stephan's purposes, and his temperament. Three statues, one of Bear, the sight of whom still could make him quiver in remembrance of their first meeting, and the second was Cernunnos, who Stephan had been seeing and sensing in his walks and travels through the forests both in the waking and other worlds. The third, of course, was Hare. Behind them, tacked to the wooden siding of the shed, was a painting Erin had done of the Lady of the Ways, and Stephan bowed his head to her now.

'My Lady,' he said, voice low. 'Keep her safe on her way back home. Let the road unwind in front of her without danger or detour.' Stephan closed his eyes for a moment, then opened them, searched around briefly among the herbs that were hanging to dry from the roof, and selected the comfrey, nipped off a leaf and held his lighter to it, then dropped the smoking incense into the metal bowl that was front and centre on his altar.

Closing his eyes, Stephan let his mind drift along the tree-lined paths of Wilde Grove, winding up and around the hills, feeling the dense magic of the place, hearing the song of the woods, the life of the land. He sank into it, letting it soothe him, for this was what the world was supposed to feel like, he thought. Alive and thriving.

'I bring my blessings to the land,' he whispered. 'I walk its ways and it blesses me.'

He drew another breath, sent himself searching for Erin in the darkness that gathered over the land, and found the touch of her spirit, its sensation familiar to him.

He smiled. She was well, almost home.

Opening his eyes, he wafted the smoke about the room with a hand, then bowed to Bear, and Cernunnos, and the Goddess of Ways and Paths.

'Thank you,' he said fervently, then made sure the herb had burnt itself out, and left the little potting shed, slipping out of the gate and going over to open the garage doors for Erin.

She arrived five minutes later, her headlights washing over him as she pulled forward into the garage. Stephan closed his eyes for a moment, relief washing over him that she was home again, back in Wellsford where she belonged.

Another car pulled in right behind her, and Stephan lifted a hand in a wave to Krista and Clarice. Then Erin opened the Mini's door and climbed out straight into his arms.

'I'm sorry,' she whispered into his neck, breathing in the welcome scent of him.

'Don't be,' Stephan said, and stepped back so that he could look at her in the light from the open car door. 'If that video is anything to go by, I think something is going to come from all of this.'

Clarice and Krista joined them in the shelter of the small garage.

'What will come from it remains to be seen,' Clarice said, an edge to her voice.

Krista patted her arm. They'd spoken of little else the whole drive home. She looked at Stephan now.

'Something,' she said. 'Something will come of it.'

They all nodded, and Erin heard the rustle and beating of wings over the rain. She looked at Stephan.

'Ravens,' Stephan said. 'A dozen of them, like they've been waiting for you.'

Erin gazed out into the darkness, the rain silvered in the light from the cottage windows. She thought she saw the black shapes of the ravens, flying in a spiralling circle around the house before flying away into the hills, and she drew in a deep breath.

'I feel like the next stage of things is beginning,' she said, then frowned.

'Whatever that might be.'

50

WINSOME DROPPED THE KNIFE SHE WAS HOLDING WHEN Veronica screamed in the other room. She ran into their shared sitting room and gaped at her, looking frantically for blood or a broken limb. Veronica though, seemed intact.

'What is it? What's the matter?'

Veronica had a hand pressed against her mouth and she shook her head, swinging it slowly, unbelieving, from side to side, not taking her gaze from the television.

Winsome sidled into the room, looking to the TV, wary of what she'd see on the screen – it was news time, after all, and the news was rarely good. They were waiting for the show afterwards. The Great British Bake Off had become a firm favourite with the two, leading to far too many trips to the kitchen for snacks, it was true, but everyone was so nice to each other on it that Winsome always came away feeling like she was right to hold high hopes for humanity after all.

She looked at the screen, eyes widening, and groped for a seat.

'But that's…'

Veronica nodded.

'Where are they?' Winsome sat on the edge of the sofa, gaze riveted on the screen.

Veronica found her voice, although it was little more than a squeak. 'Trafalgar Square.'

Winsome's mouth fell open. 'What are they doing?'

'I don't know,' Veronica said, and her face crumpled. 'It was just Erin to begin with — she was in some sort of… trance.' She's almost said *fugue,* but it had become obvious even to her over the last several months that Erin's little trips off planet were a lot more meaningful in ways that Veronica had never realised. But even so, Erin hadn't said anything about *this* when she'd called to say she was coming back home to Wellsford.

Winsome groped down the side of the sofa cushions for her mobile. She'd upgraded recently – for business reasons – and now had a smart phone on which she brought up the browser and searched quickly for the news site and the video.

'God help us,' she said. 'It's going, what do they call it? Viral.' She grimaced, copied the link, then messaged it to Ambrose and Morghan.

On the television, the clip played once more, from a different viewpoint, and Winsome stared at the sight of the three women covered in ravens.

'You can hear what they're saying in this one,' Veronica whispered, her hands grasped between her knees to stop their trembling.

It was true. The person filming had gone right up close.

'May the Goddess be with us,' Clarice said. Bold as

brass.

'May the Goddess guide us.'

That had been Krista, head tipped back, beaming at the sky, ravens on her shoulders.

And then Erin, who looked completely like a goddess herself, with her red hair and deep blue dress and overcloak of ravens, their feathers glossy, their heads dipped as though to catch the words Erin spoke.

'We follow the shining path,' Erin said.

And then the clip ended, and the newscaster came back on. Winsome and Veronica listened to their warbling speculation in silence. When the subject changed, Veronica picked up the remote and switched the TV to standby. She looked at Winsome.

'What was that?' she asked. 'What happened? Why did they do that?' She put down the remote and gazed at her hands. 'I'm shaking. Look at me. My hands are shaking.'

At Hawthorn House, Morghan stood in her bedroom with her phone in her hand. The video Winsome had sent her played out in miniature and when it was over, another came up of the same scene, and Morghan clicked on that one too. She watched five different clips of it, then dropped her hand to her side and stared frowning into midair while she considered it.

Astonishing, she thought. Whatever she'd expected would come next – whatever cog she'd thought was turning, whichever piece would fall into position, she'd never dreamt it would be anything along these lines.

On legs that were suddenly stiff, she took a couple steps

and sank down to sit on the side of her bed.

'This is going to change everything,' she said and shook her head. 'Everything.'

Her phone vibrated in her hand, and Morghan looked at the caller ID, then answered.

'Morghan,' Lucy said. 'I've just seen the most extraordinary thing on the news.'

Morghan nodded. There was a knock at her bedroom door, and she got up to open it. Rue stared wide-eyed at her, Ebony right behind her shoulder.

'I know,' she said to Lucy, and to Rue and Ebony. 'Winsome sent me the link. I've seen it too.' Then she corrected herself. 'Them. I've seen them. There are several of them online.'

'They've gone viral,' Ebony said.

Morghan was listening to Lucy. 'No,' she said. 'I don't know what we're going to do. Yes, it is going to change everything.' She listened a moment longer, then said goodbye, pressed end, stared at Rue and Ebony.

'Where's Selena?' she asked, stepping out of her room and closing the door.

Clover ducked under Ebony's arm. 'She's at Apple Tree Cottage. She said she might spend the night there.'

Morghan closed her eyes for a moment, her mind scrambling around this latest event. What should she do? What ought she to do?

She didn't know. This – this seemed completely outside her strengths. She looked at the women crowding around her door.

'Let's go downstairs,' she said.

A car pulled up outside as they entered the drawing

room to mill about. A minute later, Charlie and Martin blew into the room carrying a couple stray leaves with them.

'Did you see?' Charlie asked. She shoved fingers roughly though her hair, glanced at her husband, then zeroed in on the others in the room. 'Rue! Clover! – and Ebony! Oh my goodness I'm so glad you're here.' She pulled all three into an embrace, then looked around for Selena.

'She's at Apple Tree Cottage,' Morghan said.

Charlie frowned. 'What on earth for? That place is empty, isn't it?'

Morghan shook her head briefly. 'I had it cleaned up and furnished as a sort of retreat for her.'

Charlie thought about this for a moment, then turned as another car pulled into the gravel parking area at the front of the house. She went to the window.

'It's Lucy,' she said. 'And Simon.'

'I guess we're all thinking this is a big deal,' Ebony said. She had her phone in front of her face, scrolling through the videos of Erin, Krista, and Clarice.

Clarice looked ethereal, with her pale hair and skin, her light-coloured clothes. Krista and Erin looked like goddesses from exotic and ancient mythologies.

'I can't believe there are so many videos of this,' she said.

Lucy was almost breathless as she and Simon also blew into the room.

Martin caught Ebony's comment. 'There are fifteen of them. That I've been able to count.'

Morghan's eyes widened. 'Fifteen?'

'Trafalgar Square is a very public place,' Lucy said. 'And everyone videos everything these days.'

Morghan sat down.

Elise bustled in. She had been about to go home, but as soon as she saw everyone in the drawing room, she shook her head. 'I'll bring tea,' she said, and backed straight out, bumping into Ambrose, wincing at him, then scuttling away to the kitchen.

'Morghan,' Ambrose said, going straight to her. 'This...' He shook his head.

'Changes everything,' Morghan said. 'I know.'

'But what happened?' It was Rue who asked the question. She held up her phone. 'I mean, really? What is going on here? How and why?' She looked at Clover, who stood in the middle of the room, eyes glazed. 'Oh no, you don't,' she said, and clasped her sister by the arm.

Clover steadied, blinked. She was wading in the whiteness, close up in the weaving, Blackbird on her shoulder.

'Once,' she said. 'A spell was done to set us aside from the world.'

Morghan stood, Ambrose beside her, and looked at Clover. The room fell silent apart from the crackling of the fire which hissed and sparked for a moment, as if in warning.

Clover was gazing inwards, blind to the room, her vision filled with the whiteness of weaving. She couldn't see everyone looking at her.

'The veil was falling,' Clover said, 'for the world was no longer the same. Power was what was important to the world of men now. Power and dominion over everything, and they had fought the battle for this and won. The Fae retreated to the Fair Lands, the spirits in the trees and rocks and rivers stopped revealing themselves to all, and the veil was lowered.'

Morghan breathed out, letting herself relax into the body, her senses spreading out. All around her she could feel the press and chatter of those in the room with her, but she ignored them, sending her attention outwards from the room and the house, outwards to the land, the great criss-crossing of the web over it all, and to the barrier that she – and Ambrose beside her – had helped shore up each year.

A veil in its turn. She closed her eyes.

'This change came to the Forest House also,' Clover said, her voice like a bell in the room, her eyes open again, but unseeing except for what she saw in the deep world within her, where the past was just a ripple in an ever-flowing current.

Morghan nodded. She was examining the wards, sifting through them, all the strands of magic. Those that she had placed there, those that had been woven before her time. She stood among the trees, the oldest of them, the land under her feet, the air all about her, and examined the boundary between the Grove and the world on the other side.

Ravenna came and stood next to her.

'For most in the land,' Clover continued, 'this was welcome. For who needed to make allowances and alliances with creatures and peoples so different from oneself? When there was profit to be made instead.' She tipped her head to the side. 'Although service was still paid, of course, for memory did not die out overnight. That would take thousands of years.'

Clover paused, listened to Blackbird on her shoulder, looked deep into the weaving. 'This was what I lived then, and one of my reasons for being now.'

Rue looked over at Ebony who stood frozen, gazing at Clover with wide eyes.

Morghan stood next to Ravenna, outside on the great slope of the hill beside the Forest House. She looked at the sky, its stars hidden behind the blue, at the sweep of trees that surrounded them in all directions, turned her head toward the cave where Rhian had her visions even yet, plucking at the strings of the web, reading their vibrations in her fingers, seeing their visions behind her blind eyes.

'And we,' Clover said. 'We at Forest House stepped out into this new day and made our choice. We wove magic, sent it spinning over our small community, so that it would always and forever keep the veil from falling between ourselves and the truth of the world. An alliance had been struck, between us and the local court, the Fae Queen seeing the necessity of it, that a wedge be stuck in this closing door, so that at some point in the future when it would become necessary, that door might be opened once more.'

She paused.

'And perhaps the world saved.'

Morghan opened her eyes, strode across the room, and left the house, stepping outside into the drizzling dusk, her gaze uptilted, seeking the blue haze of the Wilde Grove wards.

She stood on the lawn, heedless of the wet, as the rest of the Grove – those who had gathered – followed her and looked also upwards, searching for what Morghan saw, looking for what Clover had told them was not actually there.

The veil that had never fallen over Wilde Grove.

51

WINSOME ANSWERED THE DOOR, SAW SEVERAL OF HER VILLAGE friends there, and stared at them wide-eyed, before holding the door open and ushering them in.

'You saw it, then,' she said.

Everyone nodded, then crowded around Winsome in a huddle, glancing down the hallway.

'Is Veronica here?' Cynthia asked.

'I am,' Veronica said, appearing from the sitting room.

'She is,' Winsome confirmed.

'I thought you might have gone to London, after Erin,' Cynthia.

Veronica leant against the door jamb and heaved a sigh. 'She'll be home. I haven't seen her, but she's back in Wellsford.'

'Did you know?' Emily Bright asked.

Veronica shook her head. She certainly had not known. 'I saw it on the television just like you all,' she said.

A hubbub grew at that, everyone talking at once.

Finally, Cynthia looked toward Winsome. 'This changes everything,' she said. 'I mean – have you seen the comments under the videos on YouTube?' She shook her head. 'I wouldn't be surprised if half the country's population are already packing their cars to trek here.'

Winsome nodded. She was rather afraid of the same thing because she had indeed been reading the comments under the videos on YouTube.

'How did they find out, though?' Sharon Johnston piped up. 'How did they find out where Erin lives?'

Veronica winced. 'People online are armchair investigators these days,' she said. 'And there's you know – facial recognition, and Erin has social media accounts.' She shook her head. 'It's not hard these days, unfortunately.'

'It's downright easy,' Minnie piped up, coming in the open door with her grandmother Rosalie. She had thought of going up to Wilde Grove, where she was sure a gathering very similar to this was happening, and she would in a little while, but first, she thought it would be useful to gauge the response among the good folk of Wellsford.

Cynthia sat down. She looked seriously around at the group, and everyone fell silent. 'This,' she repeated, 'is going to change everything.'

There were nods all around.

'It's going to put Wellsford on the map,' Melody said.

There were nods to that one too. Except for one person.

'It's going to put Wilde Grove on the map,' Rosalie said.

But Cynthia was shaking her head before the words were even out of Rosalie's mouth.

'Wellsford,' she said. 'Wellsford as well.' She spread her hands. 'Where are people going to come? They won't go traipsing up to Hawthorn House, or to Ash Cottage – or at least, not just to there.' She looked around the group, brows raised. 'This is what we wanted. It's exactly what we've been discussing, only now we don't have to worry about marketing. It's been done for us, thanks to Erin and Clarice and Krista.'

'I agree,' Winsome said, sitting down as well, along with everyone else. 'People are going to come here.'

'They're going to want to stay here,' Linda Wattle said, and she was holding up her mobile, waving the screen at everyone. 'There's already a discussion going on here about where there is to stay.'

'Banwell,' Fiona Davis said. 'Hopefully.'

But Winsome was shaking her head. She glanced at Cynthia. 'You're right,' she said, then straightened. 'We weren't thinking of anything to this degree, but it's still one enormous opportunity.'

'An opportunity?' Rosalie leant forward, and Cynthia nodded.

Minnie hid her grin. As far as she was concerned, what had happened was the most brilliant thing ever. Wellsford would be on the map, all right. What was needed was a reason to keep it there.

She had a feeling Winsome was about to give them all just that.

Cynthia nodded encouragement.

'Yes,' Winsome said, looking around the room. 'These people are all going to come here, seeking what? Some sort of miracle? Some sort of new way of life?'

'Hope,' Veronica said from where she still stood in the doorway. 'They're going to come looking for hope.'

It had been what she'd found in Wellsford, after all.

'Because there's precious little of that out there,' Melody said with a sigh.

'Yes,' Winsome agreed. 'Hope. And we should give it to them.'

There was a moment's silence, that Rosalie broke. 'But won't they be looking to Wilde Grove for that? To Morghan and Erin and everyone?'

'They will,' Winsome said. 'But they don't have the monopoly on it.'

'We're sort of part of Wilde Grove,' Melody said cautiously. 'When you think of it.'

There were nods all around, some less certain than others, some more so.

'I agree,' Emily said. 'We've lived alongside them for generations, most of us. We know their lore as well as our own.' She looked around the group. 'Goodness me, who among us hasn't crept up to the stone circle and watched the Fae come to dance on a summer solstice?'

There were murmurs of agreement.

'But,' Rosalie said, ignoring Minnie's elbow in her side. It wasn't that she disagreed so much as she wanted everyone to think through what they were saying. 'As true as that is – and we all know it's true – what does it mean for us in practical terms? How do we give people hope?' She shrugged. 'What do we actually do?'

'Well,' Cynthia said. 'That is what we will have to decide.' She glanced over at Winsome. 'We show them community. Our community.'

Emily nodded enthusiastically. 'We can showcase our community garden. And our grocery subscription.'

'And our care home.'

'Don't forget the new doctor.'

'And the vicarage and all that happens here. The men's group, the parenting classes – the buddy system, and our Adopt-a-Grandma-and-pa.'

Winsome nodded. 'We do have a lot to be proud of, here. And weren't we making plans for an ongoing craft and farmers' market? And to make this place Folklore Central?' She looked at Melody who nodded.

'What about the...spiritual aspect?' Fiona asked. 'Ought we to leave that to the Wilde Grove folks?'

'We could,' Cynthia said. She pursed her lips. 'But wouldn't it be nice if we had St Bridget's still?'

Winsome grimaced, shrank her shoulders down. Cynthia saw her and shook her head. 'No,' she said to Winsome. 'That's not what I mean.'

'What do you mean?' Rosalie asked.

Cynthia took a deep breath. 'Well,' she said. 'We've been doing a lot too – on that side of things.'

There were nods all around. It was perfectly true, after all.

'You see,' Cynthia mused. 'I just don't believe that community spirit as strong as ours has become, exists in a spiritual void.' She shook her head. 'I'm not saying that you have to be Anglican, or Druid, or whatever. Only that an awareness of the sacredness of life really does help. And that, you know, we have spirits, a deeper connection with each other and the world around us, that ought to be acknowledged, cherished, and talked about.' She shook her head and laughed, patting her chest. 'I sound like Morghan!'

'But it's true,' Rosalie conceded. 'Everything you've said is true.'

Winsome hesitated. 'But where does St Bridget's come into it?'

Cynthia shrugged. 'Just that I thought it would be nice to have a sort of hub for us.' She coloured slightly. 'A place of pilgrimage. I know Stephan suggested Apple Tree Cottage and the sacred spring there, but couldn't we have more than one? More than one sounds good.'

Her words sank slowly in.

'It is a beautiful building,' Fiona said.

'And has such an atmosphere,' Melody added.

Winsome agreed. It was and had both those things.

'It's coming up for sale,' she said. Then tried to think what the date was. 'Tomorrow, in fact.'

'Yes,' Cynthia said. 'I was going to ask when. You'd said it would be soon.' She looked about the group. 'Don't you think then, that this is provident timing?'

'How are you going to pay for it?' Minnie asked. 'I mean, don't get me wrong — I think it's a brilliant idea, but last I knew listed buildings and the like don't come cheap, even if it's the Anglican Church selling it.'

'And it will have conditions,' Winsome added. 'It won't be allowed to be converted, into a home for instance.'

'We don't want to convert it into a home,' Cynthia said. She turned to Veronica. 'Are you able to come up with a deposit?'

Veronica's eyes widened, and her brain stuttered to a halt. 'What?'

'We don't need the church building,' Rosalie said. 'Goodness me.'

'No,' Cynthia said. But then, wistfully. 'It would be lovely, though.' She waved her hands in the air. 'A spiritual sanctuary,' she said. 'I can imagine it quite clearly. A place for all to come and be quiet, to learn together – it could be a central point in the village.'

'How long do you think this influx will go on?' Sharon said. 'Surely only a few days, a week? Once Morghan sends them on their way, that will be the end of it.'

Cynthia turned to look at Winsome, and in her corner, Minnie tensed.

'Will she turn them away?'

Winsome, all eyes on her, shook her head slowly. 'I don't think so,' she said. 'I don't think she will at all.'

'There we go, then,' Cynthia said. 'So, we'd best get to moving all our plans forward.' She grinned. 'And extending them.'

Minnie slipped from the house, pulling her hoodie up to keep the rain out, and stepped onto the path between the trees at the back of the vicarage, standing in the dark a moment, indecisive.

Which way? She hummed at the question. Left towards Ash Cottage – Veronica had said Erin was home now, so Krista and Clarice likely were too. Minnie twisted around to look back at the lights shining from the vicarage window, and behind it, the winding lanes of Wellsford. Krista and Clarice hadn't been at Haven when she'd walked by with her gran. The lights had all been off in the shop, and in the flat above it too.

So, they'd probably all gone to Hawthorn House.

That settled it, and Minnie strode along the path, through the darkness, between the trees, taking the right-hand way that led to Hawthorn House.

Which was lit up like a Christmas tree, Minnie thought, coming out on the lawn. It looked like all the lights were on downstairs, and a few upstairs too. She pulled her phone out of her pocket and squinted at the time. Of course, it wasn't late. Only the time of year that made it seem so, with the sun slinking behind the hills by 6. And the rain, she thought. Don't forget the rain.

Minnie made the dash across the lawn, being very careful to skirt around the well in the darkness. She knew there was a grating over it, but still, the last thing she wanted was to twist her ankle and get any wetter than she already was.

She reached the shelter of the terrace and shook herself like a dog, sending water droplets every which way, then let herself into the house, to follow the hum of voices into the drawing room.

'Minnie,' Charlie said looking at her in surprise. 'You're soaking wet.'

Minnie grimaced, then grinned. 'Bit damp out,' she said.

'Come over to the fire and warm up,' Morghan told her.

Minnie nodded gratefully, took up a spot in front of the warmth, and sighed happily. The room was full, and everyone was looking at her.

'Wellsford is gathered too,' she announced.

Ambrose looked at her quizzically. 'Wellsford?'

'At the vicarage,' she said. 'Crowd of 'em, just like you.' She drew a quick breath, glanced at Morghan, then nodded. 'Everything's going to change, isn't it? That's what Cynthia and her lot think. They're already talking about how to take advantage of it.' She turned and looked properly at Morghan now.

'That's what you're doing too, isn't it? Talking about making the most of it?' Minnie hugged herself happily. 'You've been asking us how to open up Wilde Grove to the public – well, I think that's just happened, am I right?'

She didn't wait for an answer.

'So,' she continued without breath. 'How are we going to build on this, then?'

52

'I DON'T KNOW,' ERIN SAID, SITTING BACK DOWN AT THE TABLE with a second helping of Stephan's soup. She dug her spoon in it, glad to be home and warm and feeling okay again. When she remembered the scene in the quarry, she still felt everything – the shame and horror – but it was further away, as though she'd put some distance between her and it, some distance filled with other things.

Magic. Her magic. She glanced at the dark window behind her, the glass smeared with rain. Out there, she thought, were the ravens. Her ravens. She quivered at the thought.

'Well, I do,' Stephan said. 'It's all over the internet.'

'Yeah,' Clarice said, and she shuddered. 'But stuff on the internet never lasts, even if it goes viral. It'll be over in a day or two.'

'It was on the news,' Stephan said.

Erin blinked at him. 'What? What do you mean on the news?'

'I mean on the news. Regular television programming covered it.' He pushed his bowl away, finished. 'So, I don't think this is going to go away all that soon.'

Krista was also shaking her head. 'I'm in agreement. And we'd be fools not to take advantage of this – see it as an opportunity.'

Erin was wide-eyed, while Clarice dipped her head, groaned.

'Think about it,' Krista said. 'National attention. A chance to show the world how to shine.' She paused. 'And to warn them, perhaps.'

'Warn them?' Stephan drew himself up in his chair.

'That it's time to change the way we're in relationship with the world,' Krista said, resting her head on a hand. She was exhausted suddenly, and she thought perhaps they'd be in for a few big days. Maybe more than a few.

She pushed away from the table, wanting suddenly to get home, remove her prosthetic, lie down and maybe even sleep, despite that it wasn't even nine in the evening yet. She yawned.

'I'm beat,' she said, tapping Clarice on the shoulder. 'I need to take some weight off.'

'You can stay here tonight, if you like,' Erin said. 'I'd be glad to make up the spare bed.'

'Thanks for the offer,' Krista said, yawning again as Clarice got up and took their bowls to the sink to rinse. 'But it'll only take us a few minutes to get home.' She paused. 'First though, I guess we should call Morghan, let her know we're back. Make a plan for tomorrow.'

. . .

THE SUN CREPT BETWEEN THE BEDROOM CURTAINS, PRYING open Erin's eyes. She rolled over in the bed and squinted at it, then startled awake.

'We've slept in,' she said, sticking an elbow in Stephan's side.

He groaned. 'We were up half the night.' He grabbed the pillow and dragged it over his eyes.

Erin sat up, clutching the sheet over her breasts. 'What's that noise?'

Stephan's reply was muffled. 'What noise?'

But Erin just shook her head and leant over the bed head to peek between the curtains across the small high window.

For a moment, she didn't understand what she was looking at, and then the realisation sunk in, and she squawked, leaping from the bed and diving for her dressing gown, yanking it on and ducking her head down.

'There are people out there!'

Stephan peered at her from under the pillow, eyes puffy with sleep. 'Why are you hiding at the end of the bed?'

'Because there are people out there,' Erin hissed, and began scrabbling around in her drawers for fresh underwear and tights.

Stephan sat up, twisting around toward the window.

'Don't look!' Erin shook her head frantically at him.

'Then how do I know what's out there?'

'People are out there,' Erin said.

Stephan was baffled, still half asleep. 'Where's Burdock?'

Erin looked around. That was a good question. Where was Burdock and why hadn't he brought the roof down barking at the strangers out the front? She pulled the bedroom door open wider and stuck her head out.

'Burdock?' she whispered as loudly as she dared.

A moment later, she heard his feet on the stairs, and he appeared to look at her.

'What are you doing, boy?' Erin asked.

In response, Burdock brushed past her, jumped on the bed, and pushed aside the curtain with his snout.

'Argh,' Stephan said, one of Burdock's feet planted on his thigh. 'Gerroff.' He knelt on the mattress and stared out the window beside the dog.

'What on earth?'

Burdock growled in agreement.

Stephan let the curtain fall and pulled the dog away. Burdock resisted for a moment, then leapt from the bed and went barrelling down the stairs again, letting go a flurry of barks this time as though now that his people were up, it was safe to sound the alarm.

Stephan ignored the dog and stared at Erin in shock instead. 'I know we thought something would happen – that people would come,' he said.

Erin nodded, hopping on one leg to get her tights on. 'I know,' she said.

'But I guess I didn't expect them to be outside the house.'

'That's a TV van out there,' Erin said, almost whimpering. 'What do we do?'

Stephan shook his head. He had absolutely no idea.

. . .

On Wellsford's main street, Lucy braced herself. She glanced back at Simon. 'Ready?' she asked him.

'I'm not entirely sure,' he said. He glanced out the Copper Kettle's big windows and shook his head. 'There are people everywhere. Natasha says the Green Man's rooms are already entirely booked.'

'We can't wait any longer,' Lucy said. 'I have to open the doors.'

Simon nodded. 'Do it, then.' He moved back behind the counter while Lucy unlocked the door and turned the sign to open. She retreated quickly back to stand beside Simon.

'Good morning,' she said to the woman who had pushed through the door only moments later. 'What can I get you?'

'Do you know where the women are?' she asked, ignoring the food and the menu. 'The ones in the videos?'

'Oh,' Lucy said, even though she'd been expecting the question. Her gaze flicked to the view outside the shop, across the road where Haven for Books still stood dark.

'They live here, right?'

More people had crowded into the cafe behind her, and they were nodding their heads.

The woman in front held out her phone. Lucy recognised the front page of the Wilde Grove website.

'This is them, right?' the woman looked at her phone. 'Wilde Grove? That's the...coven, or whatever they belong to?'

'Grove,' Lucy said automatically. 'Not a coven, but a Grove.'

'Says it's a group that believes in community and living life deeply, following the path of the Old Ways and magic. Was it magic, that got the ravens to do what they did?'

There were murmurs all around, heads bobbing, people looking at their own phones.

Lucy shot a look at Simon, then stared back at the growing crowd. 'Yes,' she said after a moment. 'It was. The people who live here in Wilde Grove and Wellsford have a deep connection with land and spirit.'

She swallowed, cleared her throat. Tried a smile.

The crowd stared back at her. There were twelve or fifteen people in the little cafe, she thought, and more wandering about outside.

'How do we learn to do that?' the woman in front asked.

'That's right,' another said, a fella this time, phone in hand. 'Those birds — there were so many of them, all over her.'

'What else can they do?' a third person asked. 'Can you tell us all about it?'

Lucy took another breath. 'The website will give you an oversight,' she said, then opened her mouth to say more.

Someone interrupted her. 'It doesn't say much — not about that. It talks about...'

Lucy smiled at him and took the floor again. 'It talks about living deeply, ethically, and authentically. How magic comes from forming a relationship with the world.' She glanced at Simon, who nodded at her, then looked back at the crowd that had hushed to hang on her every word.

The silence lasted a little while longer while everyone digested this.

'Sounds like a lot of work,' someone said.

'All worthwhile things are,' Lucy said. 'And it doesn't really feel like work. Not while you're in it.'

'You're part of this Grove,' someone else said then. 'Aren't you?'

Lucy smiled. 'Yes. That's true. Many of us here in the village are. And even among those who are not, community spirit is strong.'

'Can we meet the ones on the video? We want to see them.' The woman who said this held up her phone, showing the webpage about Haven. Krista's photograph was on it. 'She's one of them. Is that the bookshop across the road?'

Everyone in the crowd swivelled to look.

'Will it be open later?'

Lucy lifted her hands against the growing murmurs. 'I'm sure Haven will be opening soon. I don't know if Krista is back from London yet, but the shop will open at the usual time as far as I know.'

'We weren't expecting TV people,' Erin said, standing well back in the shadows of the kitchen, a mug of coffee clutched in her hand. 'Were we?'

Stephan shook his head.

'This is unreal,' Erin continued. 'I just can't get it to sink in. Not properly.' She looked at Burdock who sat on his chair staring out the window, watching the to-ings and fro-ings and milling about with intense concentration. She wondered if he was visible from the lane. He was going to be famous soon, if so.

'We need to go up to Hawthorn House,' Stephan said at last, draining his mug.

'I'm not inclined to walk up there,' Erin said. 'I feel like they would just follow us.' She shook her head. 'I wish this had never happened. Why is it happening?'

'You caught their imagination, I suppose.' Stephan took her empty mug and rinsed it under the tap. 'And things are hard and uncertain at the moment, and there you and Krista and Clarice were — doing something astonishing and magical.' He gave her a sideways glance. 'Why did you do it, anyway?'

Erin stared out the window. 'I didn't know I was,' she said. 'I shifted, and then I was just...deep in the weaving, I guess.'

Stephan nodded. He'd asked the same question the previous night, before Krista and Clarice had gone home. Received much the same answer, except from Clarice, who had said simply *that's how it fell into place.*

Which, Stephan thought, was really saying the same thing.

'Come on,' he said. 'Let's get to Hawthorn House.'

Erin nodded, but didn't move. She glanced at her phone on the table, then at Stephan. 'I'm too scared to look and see what people are saying now online. I feel like I'll open up my phone and see Ash Cottage on it.'

'Probably will,' Stephan agreed. He opened his mouth to say something else when Erin's phone rang.

'It's Morghan,' Erin said after freezing for a moment. She dived for the phone and answered it.

'Yeah,' she said after a moment. 'There are people outside Ash Cottage too. And a TV van.'

Stephan watched Erin's cheeks pale as she listened to Morghan. When she pressed end finally, he shook his head.

'What?' he asked. 'What did she say?'

'She said she's going to do a press conference later today.' Erin's mouth was dry.

'And she wants Krista, Clarice, and me there.'

53

SELENA LET HERSELF OUT INTO THE DAMPNESS OF THE morning, locking the door to Apple Tree Cottage behind her, then standing and drawing in deep breaths of the fresh cool air. She wasn't quite sure she'd really meant to spend the night at the cottage, but it was, she had to admit, lovely to spend some time alone in a place that was special to her.

Lovely to take just a little time out for herself.

She patted her jacket pocket where Jakub's letter was, smiled to herself, then set off for the woods and the path back to Hawthorn House. The trees pattered raindrops upon her like blessings, and she wove between them, relishing their deep hush, their steadiness and sturdiness.

A grove of trees, she thought idly as she walked, was a good analogy for community. Deeply rooted, supporting everyone at ground level, each growing into their own space, providing a haven for life.

Selena smiled more widely, then stepped finally out

onto the lawn of Hawthorn House, her smiled fading at the commotion she found there.

Elise Palmer was outside flapping her hands at several strangers who seemed to be just milling about on the lawn. She herded them away around the side of the house, then reappeared, looking decidedly frazzled.

'Elise,' Selena said. 'What on earth is going on?'

Mrs Palmer's eyes were wide. 'Goodness me,' she said. 'It's turned into a zoo out here.' She paused. 'Or a circus. Probably that.'

Selena shook her head. 'What has? What's happening?'

'The girls – Erin, Clarice, and Krista – got themselves on the telly last night, and now the place is crowded with looky-loos and television people.'

Selena looked at her, the blood draining from her face. 'What?'

'In Trafalgar Square, they were. Praying to the Goddess and covered in ravens.'

Selena didn't understand her words to begin with. 'Did you say ravens? But there aren't any ravens in Trafalgar Square.'

'There were yesterday,' Elise said grimly. 'And now it's all over the news, and the internet, and people are all over the village.'

'Goodness.' Selena shook her head. 'What's Morghan doing about all this?'

Elise jerked her chin towards the house. 'They're in council in there right now. You'd best join them.'

Selena nodded. She best had, she thought, but her hand strayed to her jacket pocket again, and touched the sliver of paper in there.

She dropped her hand and went up the steps to the terrace and into the house.

WINSOME WALKED INTO THE KITCHEN TO FIND VERONICA already there.

'There are people wandering all over the church grounds,' Veronica said.

'What?' Winsome went over to the window to look.

'The village has been inundated,' Veronica said. 'Just like Cynthia said it would be.'

Winsome stared at the people milling about. At the couple of women who stood with heads bowed, one hand each pressed against the trunk of the great yew tree, as though talking to it. Or listening, she supposed.

An impulse took hold of Winsome, and she tried to make it go away.

'What's that face for?' Veronica asked, frowning at her.

'I think I want to open up St Bridget's.'

Veronica's brows flew upwards.

'Can you do that?'

'I have the keys,' Winsome said, thinking of them lying in her desk draw. She looked over by the door and saw Cù there, standing as though asking to go out. She flattened her lips at the sight of him.

'Yes,' Veronica said. 'But can you do that?'

Cù lifted a paw and scratched at the door, as though he were a real dog with urgent business outside.

Winsome looked at him, then turned her gaze to Veronica, who stared at her wide-eyed. 'Yes,' she said. 'Remember what Cynthia was saying last night about the church building? People are drawn to holy places – look at them there, wandering about the grounds. 'Everyone needs focal points, and...' She trailed off, an odd sensation bubbling up inside her as though she'd filled suddenly with air.

'What?'

'Stations of the Heart,' Winsome said.

Veronica gave her a quizzical look. 'What does that mean?'

'I don't know,' Winsome said, but she pressed her palm to her chest, above her own heart.

'Isn't that some sort of Catholic thing, the Stations of the whatsaname?' Veronica dredged the information from somewhere deep inside her.

'Stations of the Cross, yes,' Winsome said. She was looking outside at the people – not spirits this time, but real flesh and blood people, or at least for the most part – wandering around poking at the gravestones or communing with the trees. 'But it's a good idea.'

Veronica shook her head slowly. 'What's a good idea, though, Winsome? You're not making much sense.'

Winsome turned suddenly and beamed at her. 'I'm not, am I? It's just a seed of an idea,' she said. 'But I think it might grow.' She looked at Cù again, still standing patiently by the door, and nodded. 'I'm going to get those keys,' she said. 'Open up the building, and then later you and I can think about how I can buy it.'

Veronica stared at her as she left the room, then hurried after her. 'What do you mean, buy it?' She shook her head. 'That's a big investment. You can't just suddenly decide to do something like that. I can't even do that.' She paused. 'No matter what Cynthia thinks.'

Winsome was rummaging around in her desk for the keys. 'No,' she said. 'Of course not. That's why we'll talk it over. With Morghan too, if necessary, which it probably will be.'

The keys were shoved at the back of the drawer and Winsome drew them out, cradling them in her palm for a moment, feeling the weight of them. She'd been bitterly ashamed when she'd pushed them out of sight, but now there was that buzzing, fizzing lightness inside her again. She closed her fingers around the keys.

'Veronica,' she said. 'Will you make a Thermos of tea for us? I want to get started, but I haven't had tea or anything yet.'

Veronica trailed her back out of the room. 'Get started on what?'

'The Stations of the Heart,' Winsome said. 'Or perhaps it ought to be Stations of the Spirit.' She wrinkled her brow. 'Or Soul.' Then she shrugged and pushed open the kitchen door. Cù bounded outside and she followed him. 'We can decide later, I suppose.'

Cù went straight to the church door and Winsome followed him, glad that Wen had been keeping the church lawn short. What with all the rain, it was in danger of turning into a quagmire. She selected the right key and slid it into the lock with an indrawn breath.

'Excuse me,' someone said from behind Winsome. 'Are you the vicar?'

Winsome turned and smiled. It was one of the women who had been talking to the yew tree. 'No,' she said. 'I'm afraid this building is no longer consecrated to the church and doesn't have a vicar.'

'Oh.' The woman nodded. 'We wondered why there was no information on the sign board.'

Winsome glanced over at it, her plan forming more completely in her mind. She smiled. 'You're quite right,' she said. 'We need to update that.' She pushed the heavy door open, then turned and did the same with its twin, pausing as Cù walked inside into the dimness.

'May we come in?' the woman asked. 'Only we love old churches, don't we, Heather?' She turned back to Winsome. 'So many have such great atmospheres.'

'This one does,' Winsome agreed. 'And yes, do come in and spend a while in meditation, if you like.' She led the way inside. 'Although I will be making a bit of a ruckus getting the old girl cleaned and dusted.' She smiled apologetically. 'It's been a while since she's had any visitors.'

Cù was sprawled out on the steps to the sanctuary, his lips peeled back in a wide grin. Winsome rolled her eyes at him and stood in the aisle, hands on her hips, gazing about, building on the vision that had come to her.

'Bridget's Sanctuary,' she whispered. Glanced back at Cù, then nodded her head.

The building had already been stripped back to its bare essentials. The altar table had no cloth or candlestick, and the vestry cupboards were empty of wine bottle and cup.

Winsome blinked at the thought of the cup, and her travelling in which Ceridwen had bidden her to drink from it.

'Yes, well,' she murmured, and somehow, suddenly, that seemed completely appropriate.

The tapestries were also gone, as well as the ceremonial cross that had stood on the altar. There was only the building, and the pews, and the softly coloured light that streamed in from the small stained-glass windows.

Also the baptismal font at the back of the pews. Winsome turned around to look contemplatively at it. She nodded to Cù. 'That could be something, don't you think?'

Cù, as usual, said nothing, but his tail thumped soundlessly against the floor.

'I'm sorry, I didn't catch that?'

Winsome smiled at the woman who stood gazing about. 'I was talking to myself, I'm afraid.'

The stranger nodded. 'What are you going to do with this building?' she asked. 'It's lovely.'

'Well,' Winsome said. 'That's a good question. First, we'll give her a good clean, I think. Poor thing's gotten very dusty.'

The yew tree woman wandered away, rejoined her friend, and stood whispering with her at the back near the very font Winsome had been contemplating.

Veronica came in, looking around, then glancing at Winsome. She carried a Thermos, and behind her Cynthia followed her in.

'Winsome,' Cynthia said. 'Veronica tells me you've come up with some sort of a plan?' She smiled at the visitors then leant closer to Winsome. 'Didn't I say the village would fill with pilgrims?'

'Not Christian ones,' Veronica pointed out.

'This isn't a Christian church anymore,' Cynthia said rather sadly. 'They gave us up.'

'It's still a holy place,' Winsome said. 'Or can be, anyway.'

'It does still feel sacred,' Cynthia agreed.

Veronica sneezed. 'And dusty.'

'Yes.' Winsome nodded at her. 'Pour me a cup of that tea, Veronica, and I'll get the cleaning supplies.'

In a couple hours, with a brief stop for more tea and some sandwiches that Fiona and Rosalie went into the vicarage to prepare, St Bridget's was sparkling clean – or as clean as stone and wood allowed.

'It looks lovely,' Winsome said, allowing herself a wide smile.

'I like the spare look of it,' Fiona said. She and the others had turned up not long after Cynthia, and stopped to pitch in. They'd moved the pews from their rigid rows and set them up in more conversational and contemplative arrangements. Some of them they'd taken away altogether, and there was semi-serious talk of bean bags.

The new layout made a feature of the beautiful old baptismal font in a way that particularly pleased Winsome even as it made her nervous. She had removed the lid, and the water in the bowl reflected the blue and red glass of the window. It was beautiful and reminded Winsome strongly of all Morghan's talk of wells, and their symbolism.

Rosalie looked mildly apprehensive. 'We'll have to find a way to buy it now,' she said.

Veronica came in the door in time to hear what she said. 'It's done,' she said, allowing an edge of triumph to make it into her voice.

'What do you mean, it's done?' Winsome asked.

Veronica spread her arms. 'I've just been up at Hawthorn House – where TV vans are camped out, might I add – and Morghan has secured the place. For the village.'

She shook her head, unable to completely believe what she'd made happen that morning.

Cynthia clapped her hands and laughed. 'I don't believe it!'

'I'm not sure I do either,' Winsome said. 'Veronica, I thought you weren't sure about it?'

'Morghan's bought it, as a gift to Wellsford, or slapped the deposit down at least, but I think we're all going to be responsible from here on out.' Veronica gazed around the old building. 'But I thought that we couldn't risk someone coming along and buying it, doing goodness-knows what with it, when it should be a village asset.' She shrugged. 'Morghan Wilde agreed with me, and so – it's ours.'

'Tom,' Cynthia said.

Fiona's brow wrinkled. 'Tom?'

'Tom Bower. He's a signwriter,' Cynthia said. 'And we need a new sign.' She drew a breath. 'What shall we call it? It can't very well be St Bridget's still, can it?'

'Bridget's Sanctuary,' Winsome said.

'That's what we should call it.'

54

'ARE YOU SURE?' AMBROSE ASKED. HE WATCHED MORGHAN shake her head, smooth a hand over her hair.

'I'm not sure of anything,' she said shortly. 'Only that this has happened, and the opportunity given to us.'

'I feel woefully unprepared,' Ambrose said.

'I don't know how we are supposed to be prepared,' Rue said, shaking her head.

'Of course we're prepared,' Selena said, and she frowned at Rue. 'I'm surprised by your attitude, Rue, and yours, Ambrose. You ought both to know better – weren't we all expecting this, after all?'

Everyone looked in astonishment at Selena, who had arrived half an hour earlier and quickly been brought up to speed, and who, deep inside, did not feel at all astonished by the turn of events. She nodded her head, gazed around the room.

'This is exactly what we have been heading for,' she said. 'For quite some time.' She turned to Erin, held her gaze for a moment. 'I was wrong to ever suggest that Morghan had made a mistake in considering you to be the next Lady of the Grove.'

Erin's eyes widened and she glanced quickly at Stephan, Clarice, and Krista. 'You were?' she asked Selena.

'I was.' Selena smiled at her, then turned to Rue and Clover, and Ebony standing behind them. 'Because now it is clear that we are not to be part of this Grove except by extension – we are to become the beacons instead.'

'Beacons?' Ebony asked. Then glanced at the others. 'That's the name of my shop. My esoterica shop.'

'Beacons,' Selena agreed. 'All over the world, there should be beacons of the Grove, so that light can spread, hold the darkness at bay.'

'And eventually,' Morghan said. 'So many beacons that the world is made brilliant once more.'

Clover closed her eyes, seeing her vision of the future – of the possible future, she reminded herself, then winced. The one they were heading towards, but also the one not yet certain.

There could be another, she thought.

Another, where life was held as a gift, where the world was a treasure. She breathed slowly, deeply, and for a moment, the whiteness inside her was brilliant with colour.

'We get to go home?' Rue asked, glancing at Ebony then looking back to Selena.

'We must,' Selena said. 'Once your faces have become known here.'

Rue's eyes widened.

'We must do what the Grove here must do.'

'Which is?' Ambrose asked, looking at Morghan, who nodded, already knowing the reply.

Selena turned to Morghan. 'Do you remember, all those years ago, when you first came here?'

Morghan's lips twitched. 'Yes,' she said.

'Your first travelling,' Selena said, helping herself to another cup of tea, feeling within her a settling certainty that, although tinged with sadness, filled her also with a welling purpose.

She would not stay here at Wilde Grove, would not spend her days walking her beloved paths and trails, biding time until she would die in the same bed that Annwyn and countless other Grove priestesses had.

Nor would she venture to Poland, to rekindle her romance with Jakub. As much pleasure as that would bring her – and it would bring her a great deal – it was not to be. Not this lifetime.

She smiled slightly. Perhaps, she thought. Perhaps in the next lifetime, or the one after that. Or maybe they would settle for the ones they'd already had.

'My first travelling?' Morghan asked, then nodded. 'Of course.'

Erin looked at her curiously. 'What happened? What happened during it?'

Morghan looked around the room. At the priests and priestesses of the Grove. Their faces shone back at her.

'There is a place in my travellings that I have called the Silent Village. The way to this place is by horse, through a great and eerie forest, where lost souls bury themselves to hide in the undergrowth.' Morghan tapped a finger on the arm of her chair and thought about it. 'This was the first place I was shown when I came to the Grove. A horse took me between the trees, through the darkness, and we came finally upon a small village where not a single soul came out to be seen. There were only buildings from which no one emerged, and no one's steps rang upon the cobbled streets except those of the horse and myself.'

Morghan closed her eyes, feeling herself sway slightly as she considered this place in her inner world. 'This first time I came to it, leaves were strewn everywhere, and I knew somehow that it had become perpetually autumn in this part of the world.'

Clover nodded. Unlike the eternal summer in the world the Fae had fashioned for themselves, then.

Morghan opened her eyes, but she was seeing the silent village, not the room in which she sat by the crackling fire.

'There is a square in the shadow of the houses,' she said. 'Buildings lean over it, and once it must have been beautiful. Once, the fountain at the centre of this square must have run with fresh and clear water, into a pool neither stagnant nor clogged with leaves and muck. Once, the buildings must have rung with laughter and footsteps, and the bell in the church tower would have tolled to call each person to remember the beauty of their souls.'

She shook her head. 'But the place was silent. There was no laugher, no joy, and the water of the fountain did not run, and the fountain itself was filthy, neglected.'

She'd dismounted from the horse that first time, she remembered. 'I walked past the fountain on that first travelling and on impulse entered the building directly behind it.'

Erin stared at Morghan, holding fast to the details of the story, already imagining them drawn upon a page. This, she thought, had to become one of her cards. Maybe two of them – or three. The forest of lost souls. The fountain...she waited to hear more about the building.

'Upstairs,' Morghan continued, 'was the room of a scholar.' She smiled at Ambrose. 'Books lined one wall, and when I picked a volume up, curious, I saw that whatever was written in it was in a language I didn't understand, but the illustrations were perfectly clear.' She glanced at Selena, and they shared a smile between them.

'They were fairy tales,' Morghan said. 'Tales of an older world, of animals that talked, of woodcutters who cherished the forests they tended, of sacred wells and springs and the maidens who rose from them to offer nourishment to the passerby.'

Morghan lifted her hands. 'I was shown all this, then taken home. Not given the meaning to any of it except to puzzle it out myself.'

'What does it mean?' Erin asked. 'Did you ever work it out?'

'Of course,' Morghan said. 'The village is the illustration of our lives.'

Erin sat back, glanced frowning at Stephan.

But it was Selena who spoke next. 'We must gather up our lost souls,' she said. 'And return to life. True life.'

'The fountain must flow once more,' Morghan said. 'That is the task of each of us.' She got up and walked across the room to look out the window, where a few strangers still lingered.

'And we must make sure that everyone possible, everyone who is willing to listen and learn, has access to the books in the scholar's library, to the church bell, to the tools with which to clean the fountain, to someone willing to lead them out of the forest.'

'That's no small task,' Clarice said.

'No,' Morghan agreed. 'And yet, it is the one we have been set.'

Erin shifted slightly. 'I'm still not entirely sure I know how we're supposed to do this,' she said, her tone apologetic.

'Me neither,' Rue said. She caught herself about to cross her arms protectively over her chest then reminded herself of the promise she'd made. To follow her path. To be what she'd really trained to be.

To shine.

'I know,' Morghan said, turning around. She looked at Ambrose, and Selena, then around the room at everyone present. 'We let people know of the way,' she said. 'And we teach them to walk it, if they will.'

'Yes,' Erin said. 'I understand that, but how do we do it?' She winced an apology.

But Morghan laughed, lifted her hands. 'We've been trying to answer this question for a year.' She gestured at the window. 'And now we've been given our first students.' She paused. 'Our first beacons, back at the Forest House, at Wilde Grove.'

'We'll need a curriculum, or something,' Ebony said, warming to the idea. 'And we'll teach it back at home, too.' She gazed into the air, plucking out ideas. 'It has to be really accessible, though.'

Stephan's eyes widened. 'Oh my god,' he said. 'I could teach about plant spirits.'

'And I could finish my card deck,' Erin said. 'It's about

the soul's journey.' She leant over and looked at Clarice. 'You have to continue your dance classes – and you could teach about the Fae.' Her face clouded and she looked back at Morghan. 'The Fae,' she said. 'Don't we still have to do something about them?'

'Yes,' Morghan said. 'The ones at the quarry particularly, to begin with.' She drew a breath. 'But that is only one facet of a bigger issue we have to confront – and help people confront.'

'Their relationship with the land,' Stephan said, nodding.

'Yes,' Morghan said.

'We've got our work cut out for us,' Rue said.

'I don't know,' Ebony said, putting a hand on her shoulder. 'Most people – the people you see walking down the street worrying about the state of everything – they would be glad to learn to live more deeply.'

Rue nodded. 'You might be right,' she said. 'After all, look what I've been able to do with the Stitch Studio. That's slowing life right down and making it meaningful.'

Morghan nodded. 'That's exactly what we want to do. The sort of thing we want to facilitate.'

Erin thought about this. 'Do we have the right, though?' she asked, shaking her head. 'I mean, my mother once thought Wilde Grove was a cult. I don't want anyone else to think that.'

Selena laughed. 'Did she really? Your mother?'

Erin felt her cheeks burn. 'I'm afraid so. And it was actually kinda hard to argue against it. Every time I tried to explain it, she said well, that's what cults do too.'

'We're not going to be taking anything from anyone,'

Morghan said. 'Not money, or property, or anything. We're not going to be demanding allegiance, or even saying that we have the only truth, or that our path is the only way. We will simply be making our knowledge and experience accessible.' She lifted her shoulders. 'That's all we can do.'

'Show the horses there is water,' Ebony said. 'And hope to the goddess that they drink.'

'Lots will,' Krista said. 'Perhaps even enough.'

Morghan shook her head. 'It doesn't even really matter, how many,' she said. 'Only that we perform our task. It will make a difference, or it will not, but still we must do it.'

Clover nodded, feeling Blackbird upon her shoulder. She looked down and saw her great lion lying at her feet, then swept her gaze around the room. Everyone in the room was illuminated, she saw. Shining. Each with their kin nearby. She nodded. Morghan's wolf, at her side as always, Erin's fox, sitting in the folds of her skirt. Her fellow next to her, Stephan – he had a big white hare, and so it was around the whole room. Clover closed her eyes, looked deep into the weaving within her, that she seemed to carry around with her all the time now, and looked upon the strands of it, knowing that if she waded far enough out into them, patterns would become visible to her.

'I agree that we all have to be part of the press conference later,' she said, flicking her eyes open.

Rue shook her head. 'Not you,' she said. 'That won't be necessary, surely?'

Clover looked at her. 'It's okay,' she said. 'You don't have to protect me from this.'

Rue looked at her without speaking, unsettled.

'I agree,' Ebony said, breaking the awkward silence. 'We all need to be, so that the news will follow us back home.'

Clover nodded. The pieces were slowly coming into focus.

'Yes,' she said.

'I see it in the weaving.'

55

AMBROSE SET DOWN HIS TEACUP AND SHOOK HIS HEAD. 'I'M still in awe that you have organised buying the church.'

Morghan laughed. 'Things are moving swiftly, aren't they? Thank goodness for Henry.' She looked over to where Jameel was talking, head bent, to Clover, and felt a rush of affection for all the people in her life.

There were a surprising number these days.

She turned back to Ambrose and shook her head. 'Where are we going to have this press conference?' she asked, tapping her fingers against her hip.

'I assumed here,' Ambrose said. 'Probably on the turnaround outside on the drive.'

'Hmm,' Morghan said. 'I wonder.'

'What do you wonder?'

Morghan tilted her face up and closed her eyes, feeling around for inspiration. It came, dimly at first, then grew and shone.

'I think I'm going to slip down and see Winsome,' Morghan said to Ambrose.

'What about them?' Ambrose asked, nodding his head at the window and the lingering few people there.

'I'll sneak out the back,' Morghan said. 'It won't be a problem.'

Ambrose nodded, turned his attention to Morghan. 'What are you thinking?'

But Morghan just shook her head, a slight frown knotted between her brows. 'How many people do you think will come?' she asked. 'To the press conference?'

'Lucy said there's a good fifty or so milling about the village. Some are even staying at the Green Man tonight.' Ambrose glanced toward the window again. 'Then there's the television crews. Two of those; one local, one from London. They're staying in Banwell, if they need to.'

'Erin and Stephan said there were at least twenty people outside Ash Cottage.'

'So,' Ambrose shrugged, 'perhaps a hundred all up?'

'I'm glad the reporters are here,' Morghan mused, then looked at Ambrose. 'How is Molly?'

'Molly?'

Morghan nodded.

'Well, she's hanging in there.'

'Good,' Morghan said, mind ticking along. 'I hope she'll be able to come to Wellsford soon. I've a feeling we're going to need someone like her.'

'Someone like her?' Ambrose frowned.

Morghan nodded. 'Someone who can write.' She smiled. 'Now, I'm going to go have a chat to Winsome. Do you want to come?'

Ambrose paused a moment. He did want to go, felt the tug in the centre of his being that he always felt when he thought about Winsome.

'What's the matter?' Morghan asked, seeing the hesitation on his face.

'I'm not sure about seeing her there, in the village,' Ambrose said.

His answer made Morghan pause. 'She mentioned her... ambivalence about being public with your relationship.'

'We've discussed that, and everything else that has been going on for her, and she's asked me to be patient with that side of things,' Ambrose said, pushing his fingers through the flop of hair on his forehead. 'But I would like to see what is happening in the village, nonetheless.'

Morghan patted his shoulder. 'Come with me,' she said.

THE SUN HAD BROKEN THROUGH THE CLOUDS AND MORGHAN tipped her face towards it, grateful for the unexpected warmth. The walk through the woods had been damp and chilly.

'What are they doing?' Ambrose asked at her side.

Morghan looked, and a wide smile spread across her face. She glanced at Ambrose, eyes shining, then strode across the vicarage lawn to join Winsome and her knot of friends in front of the church sign.

'Morghan!' Winsome said, then saw Ambrose coming behind her and flushed. 'Ambrose.'

'You've been busy,' Ambrose said, wishing he could reach out and smooth back the honey-coloured strand of hair that was stuck to Winsome's cheek.

'Doesn't it look fantastic?' Minnie said, shaking her head at the newly painted sign. 'Winsome's brilliant, she is.'

Morghan looked at the sign and felt a flood of warmth all through her body. She nodded. Yes, she thought. Things were falling into place.

The sign, freshly painted, was simple and uncluttered in its message. *Bridget's Sanctuary,* it said on the first line.

'Winsome came up with the name,' Cynthia said, putting an arm around Winsome's shoulders and giving her a quick squeeze. 'It's perfect, really.' She nodded.

'It is,' Morghan said. 'Our Lady Brigid will be pleased.' She looked at Winsome. 'What does the second line mean?'

Winsome glanced again at Ambrose, then looked back at the sign.

Stations of the Heart, it read in neat green print. Tom had done a perfect job with his paint and brush.

'I'm not really a hundred percent sure,' she said. 'But it felt just right.'

'And obviously, the rest of us agreed with her,' Cynthia said.

'Stations of the Heart,' Morghan read, letting the phrase seep into her. 'I think it's perfect.'

Winsome nodded, her cheeks warming with pleasure. 'Can you believe all this?' she asked, gazing around in astonishment. 'It's like the village has suddenly woken up. We're serving tea and chats in the vicarage. The charity shop is doing a raging business. People are streaming in and out of Lynsey's wool shop, where she's also practically sold out of the dresses she'd made like the one Erin was wearing in the videos, and I don't think poor Simon has left the kitchen at the Copper Kettle all morning.' She turned to face Morghan.

'And you bought the church for us.'

Morghan shook her head. 'How could I not?' she asked.

'It brings me to tears,' Winsome said, but she smiled, then looked at Ambrose, her smile growing both wider and shyer.

Morghan turned her gaze back to the church's – the sanctuary's, she corrected herself – new sign.

Stations of the Heart. It resonated deep within her, and she wondered at it, a plan growing.

'Winsome,' she said. 'We've told the television crews that we'll give something of a press conference later.'

Winsome nodded. She'd moved to stand next to Ambrose, sliding her hand into his and leaning against him in her first public display of affection.

'That's a good idea,' Cynthia said.

'Where are you going to have it?' Minnie said, tugging her grandmother closer to listen. She noticed that the visitors to the churchyard were also drawing nearer, perhaps to listen, perhaps just to stare at Morghan, who, Minnie thought, radiated presence and a sort of gentle power wherever she went.

Minnie stood straighter, breathed calmly in and out, despite her excitement.

'That's the thing,' Morghan was saying. 'I would like, I think, for it to be at the village green.' She looked at the assembled group of Wellsford folk. 'If that is all right with everyone.'

'Are you sure?' Rosalie asked. 'I rather thought you'd

have it up at Hawthorn House, since it's Grove business, so to speak.'

'But it's not,' Cynthia said, and she nodded at them all. 'If it were, why would we have just done all this?' She waved a hand around at the church, the sign. 'And anyway, Grove business has become Wellsford business, thanks to the pandemic when we all decided to pull together.'

'I agree completely,' Morghan said and looked around at the growing crowd. It wasn't just strangers to the village now, but more of the inhabitants themselves, come to see what was happening, what was going on.

But the visitors to Wellsford, the strangers, they were drawing closer too, looking curiously at her, trying to hear, she thought, what they were talking about.

Except, they weren't strangers, she thought, and shook her head slightly. Not strangers at all.

They were pilgrims. Seekers.

Behind her eyes, Morghan saw her vision again, and she stood on top of the tor, watching a procession of people spiralling their way up it, each carrying a torch, a lantern.

And singing. They'd been singing too, a song of the trees, a song of the stations of the heart.

'Morghan?' Winsome touched her lightly on the arm.

Morghan opened her eyes, nodded, her lips curving slightly. Yes, she thought. They were beacons and wayfarers.

'Do you remember your first Samhain in Wellsford?' she asked.

Winsome frowned, wondering why Morghan was changing the subject.

'I do,' Minnie said, making herself stand still and tall when she really wanted to run screaming with excitement around the village. This, she thought, was turning out to be a very good day. 'I remember it perfectly – Mum, Tiny, Robin, and me, we'd just moved here, hadn't we, Gran?'

Rosalie nodded.

'We had a big bonfire and dancing and so on,' Wen said from the back of the group. 'It were a real fine evening.'

'Oh,' Winsome said. 'Yes, I do remember.' She swallowed and saw suddenly where Morghan might be leading with her question. 'You lit a series of beacons. It was very affecting.'

'We should do it again,' Wen said, enthusiastic already at the thought. 'I could get the blokes to build 'em, and we can wait until dusk, and it will be very effective, I reckon.' He glanced around at the milling strangers. They looked like alright sorts, for the most part. 'We'll give 'em a bit of a show.'

Morghan was nodding at him. 'Exactly my thoughts. Do you think we can make it happen?'

'No problem at all,' Wen said, certain of it now he'd come up with the idea. He flushed happily under Morghan's approval. 'An' we'll put up the bandstand again an' all. That's still in storage in Bob Riley's shed.' He had another stroke of inspiration and grinned widely. 'Perhaps you'll get that Stephan and his mates to give us some music?' He shook his head happily. 'We could make a real night of it.'

'We'll need food,' Fiona said, but she was nodding vigorously. 'Get the grills going.' She paused, frowned, looked up at the sky. 'But will the weather hold? It's been doing nothing but rain lately.'

'It's very risky,' Veronica said, scowling at the sky. 'Doing anything that needs a fair evening.'

Morghan too, looked upwards. 'Nonetheless, I think we'll go ahead with it. Gather up as many gazebos and the like that anyone has and set them up.' She looked at Wen. 'You're sure about the fires? Even if it rains?'

She had a feeling it wouldn't.

He grinned broadly at her. 'You just leave it with me.'

'Whoa,' Minnie said, growing excited the more she thought about it. 'That is an amazing idea. Talk about drama! You want to keep the drama up too, right? I mean, after what Erin and the others did in London, it's only right.' She gazed about the churchyard, where people were milling, going in and out of Bridget's Sanctuary. 'They want the magic. That's why they're here. We'll give it to them.'

Morghan nodded. Perhaps, she thought, she wouldn't have put it quite like that, but Minnie was right. People wanted the magic. Needed it.

And so, they would give it to them.

The air rippled around her, and overhead, the great web crisscrossed the world, connecting everything.

MINNIE BOUNDED UP THE STEPS TO HAVEN, PLUNGED THE KEY into the lock and turned it, her smile stretched almost from ear to ear. She pushed the door open, aware of the people behind her, impatient to get into the bookshop and look around.

Even, Minnie thought, even if what they really wanted a glimpse of was Krista, who had been so amazing at Trafalgar Square, then that didn't matter. They'd find that Haven had some interesting stuff, besides the popular books and magazines, and the stationery stuff. There were the talismans – Minnie had a feeling they were finally going to sell some of those, for sure. And they had a decent if smallish collection of esoteric books and tarot decks, that sort of thing.

Plus, she thought, switching the lights on. There was Erin's artwork. That would make people ooh and ah.

She slapped the pile of flyers down on the counter, then went around dividing them up among the small tables around the shop.

'This is today?' a man asked, immediately picking one up.

'Yep,' Minnie said, plucking one from the pile and taking it to the front window, sticky tape in hand. 'You'll want to be there, for certain.'

'Are you part of this Grove?' another asked.

Minnie turned around and looked at the woman who had spoken. She grinned at her. 'Sure am,' she said.

'What...' the woman paused. 'I'm Marielle,' she said. 'What do you do in the, you know, the Grove?'

Six or seven people had followed Minnie into the shop and all of them were looking expectantly at her now.

Minnie beamed under the attention. 'We learn magic,' she said.

'Yes, but what do you mean by that?'

Minnie spread her arms. 'We learn how to live deeply in the world.' Now, she touched her heart and became serious. 'We learn to heal our wounds and those the land around us has suffered.' She took a breath. 'We learn how to look after each other.'

She was impressed with how like Morghan she sounded.

'That doesn't seem a lot like magic to me,' an older man at the back said, disappointment in his face.

'Doesn't it?' Minnie asked. 'Do you feel strong, grounded, and whole as you walk through your days? Do you feel supported and nourished? Are you able to care for others because you feel cared for yourself?'

The man frowned at her.

'What about the birds?' someone else asked. He was a tall guy, maybe early twenties, Minnie thought, and easy on the eye. She smiled brilliantly at him.

'What about them?' he asked.

'That's easy,' Minnie said, and reached up to twirl one of Krista's evil eye talismans in a blur of silver that caught the light. She tried to choose her next words carefully. 'We all have kin,' she said, dropping her hand and looking seriously at the small crowd hanging on her every word. 'Animal and spirit kin, who walk with us on our path. We build a relationship with these kin, and sometimes they come to us in ways that you saw Erin's ravens come to her.'

'But why?' another asked, a woman jiggling a baby on her hip. 'Why did they?'

Minnie smiled widely again. 'To get your attention, of course,' she said. 'It's time, you see.'

'Time for what?'

'Time to step up and remember who we are.' Minnie nodded, then started moving away. Feed them a tasty morsel, she thought, then leave them to chew it over. 'Feel free to look around. We've some beautiful prints of Erin's artwork, and the silver evil eye talismans are made by Krista.'

'What about the other one?' the woman with the baby

asked. 'Clarice, isn't it?' She looked around as though half expecting Clarice to appear pale and shining out of the shadows. 'They're all back here, now, aren't they? For this meeting later?'

'They are,' Minnie said, stepping behind the counter and bouncing on her toes with excitement. 'We're all here. You'll meet us later.'

56

MORGHAN AND AMBROSE LEFT THE VILLAGE AND WENT INTO the woods. It was still cool, but the clear weather was holding, and the only splashes of rain were droplets from leaves still damp from the rain during the night.

'Will it stay clear, do you think?' Ambrose asked, peering up through the canopy at the sky.

'I hope so,' Morghan said. 'It won't be quite the spectacle we're going for if we're a gathering of bedraggled rats.'

Ambrose looked at her properly. 'Are you sure about all this?' It was the second time he'd asked.

Morghan shook her head. 'Of course not,' she said. 'I'm throwing the pin cushion and following it, remember? That's all any of us can do.' She turned back to the path and mused upon the story Ambrose had told them all – so long ago now. 'That would make a good lesson, wouldn't it?'

'Wouldn't what?'

'How to follow the pincushion.' Morghan drew breath. 'How to walk the path one step at a time knowing where you're heading, but not exactly how you'll get there. Being open to where the path leads you, how the world unfolds in its challenges and beauty.'

'We're thinking in terms of lessons, now?' Ambrose asked.

Morghan looked at him, surprised. 'Are we not?'

Ambrose shook his head, but he was considering it. 'I suppose we are,' he said at last, watching as his booted feet found the best steps along the trail seemingly without him having to pick or choose. He chewed the idea of lessons over. 'That scares me rather,' he admitted after a minute's silence between them.

Morghan reached out and touched his arm. 'It scares me too,' she said. 'It felt quite enough when it was just Erin and Stephan, don't you think?' She shook her head. 'I've no idea how we're going to go about it.'

Ambrose paused, then put forward a tentative suggestion. 'Molly has been planning a book, you recall,' he said in preamble.

Morghan nodded.

'Well,' Ambrose said. 'I think I'd like to try my hand at that.' He cleared his throat. 'At writing.'

Morghan beamed at him. 'But that's wonderful,' she said. 'I think that's a marvellous idea.'

'We don't know that I can write well enough,' Ambrose said.

'We don't know that you can't, either,' Morghan laughed. 'What will you write about?'

Ambrose shook his head. 'Everything,' he said. 'Perhaps.' He looked at Morghan, expecting her to tell him that was a bit vague.

But she only nodded. 'I like that idea very much,' she said. She turned on the path towards the stone circle, away from the house. 'Erin is making her oracle deck, and I'm very interested in how that is working out. And now, we've someone who will put our teachings in book form.' She looked at him with raised eyebrows. 'Isn't that what you meant?'

Ambrose nodded.

'I like that,' Morghan said. 'This is all a big lift, I think, what's being asked of us, and I've still no real idea of how we should structure things.' She paused, then carried on, the leaf mould crunching under her boots. 'But I do know that we're dedicated to it now, thanks to Erin. We're truly dedicated to it now.'

Ambrose, who had been walking deep in thought, looked around them. 'Why are we detouring here?' he asked.

'I don't know,' Morghan said. 'Only that recently so much has been happening, that I've barely taken a moment in it all, and I want to give thanks.'

Ambrose nodded and remembered suddenly the way Winsome had slipped her hand into his. It had been warm, her hand, and although put there shyly, it had held his firmly, and stayed put.

The first time she'd publicly acknowledged – in the village, anyway – that they were a couple.

'I'm going to ask her to marry me,' he blurted.

Morghan stopped walking and turned to look at Ambrose. 'You are?' Her lips curved in a smile.

'Why? You don't think it's a good idea?' Ambrose pressed his palms against his trousers.

Morghan laughed. 'I think it's a wonderful idea.'

Ambrose tucked his chin down, contemplated the leaves stuck to his boots. 'I think so too,' he said, his voice low, husky. He nodded, looked at Morghan, at her clear grey eyes. 'I think so too.'

Morghan smiled at him, put her hands on his shoulders and kissed his cheek. 'I'm glad for you,' she said. 'More than I can say.'

She turned back to the path. 'Now we have even more to be grateful for.'

THERE WAS MAGIC SWIRLING ABOUT THE STONE CIRCLE AND Morghan, lips twitching, glanced at Ambrose.

'Can you feel that?'

He nodded and raised a hand, fingers spread, as though to sift the air. 'A sort of electricity,' he said.

Morghan nodded and stepped into the circle, breathing out as she did so, emptying her lungs and her mind, becoming automatically even more consciously grounded, present. She crossed to kneel at Grandmother Oak's roots, taking from the bag around her waist a small twist of herbs and a lighter. She touched a flame to the dried herbs and let the smoke waft up into Grandmother's branches.

'My greetings and my gratitude to you, Grandmother,' Morghan said. 'Your roots teach me to be grounded, the beautiful thickness of your body teaches me to stand solid in the world, and your branches speak to me of spreading wide, of reaching out, of being part of the great glorious web of life.'

There were sudden tears in Morghan's eyes, and she

didn't blink them away, but let them catch in her lashes, as she knelt among the damp leaves and listened to Grandmother's whisperings.

Ambrose stood, one hand on the tallest of the stones, and watched as Morghan slipped into trance. He bowed his head in a prayer of his own.

The North Star guides me
along the path of my soul.
I am here to live
my love for the world.

When he looked about again, Morghan was before him, eyes with that strange, far-away gaze that let him know she stood with one foot in each world. She held out a hand to him.

'Come with me,' she said.

He looked down at her long fingers, confused by the offer. They seldom travelled together.

Morghan smiled at him. 'Come,' she said.

Her fingers were cool in his, and her touch sent him immediately beyond the boundaries of his body, his spirit unfurling and stepping free. When he looked at Morghan again, she wore an antlered headdress, and spirals were painted upon her cheeks.

'Where are we going?' he asked, then saw past Morghan to Grandmother Oak and gasped.

Morghan swung around and looked at the tree, from whose branches hung a hundred gleaming crystal eggs, dangling from ribbons. She touched the egg that swung from its own string around her neck, beside the leaf and acorn she wore, and gratitude welled up in her, catching tears between her lashes again.

'Take one,' she said to Ambrose. 'Take one and put it around your own neck.'

He hesitated only a moment, then stepped forward and grasped one of the gleaming eggs, lifted it from the branch and put it around his neck. The stone glowed against his chest and when he touched his fingers to it, they warmed against the egg.

Morghan was looking away into the Wildwood, at Snake who slithered down a path into the woods. She followed, bringing Ambrose along with her. Wolf pressed close to her side.

A great golden eagle landed upon Ambrose's shoulder, and Morghan smiled.

All was well.

They followed the path, deep through the woods, onwards and farther, the air scented lightly with something that reminded Ambrose of oranges, perhaps, or orchids. It was soft against his skin, and he settled into the rhythm of their steps, watching Morghan's Snake, seeing sometimes the brief shadow of other animals, a glimpse of the White Stag that roamed this part of the world.

But onwards they went, until a meadow opened out in front of them, and beside him, Morghan looked this way then that, the antlered headdress gone from his vision now – although, he considered, if he looked hard enough, he thought he would see it there still.

'Where are we?' he asked.

Morghan settled her breath. 'I recognise this place,' she said. 'We wait for Epona.'

A horse? Ambrose nodded, letting it be whatever it

would be, and let the sensations of the world slip over him instead.

'It is quiet here,' he said.

It was too quiet.

Before, on their long walk to this place, the woods had been alive with rustlings and singings and sightings.

Now, it was silent, except for the soughing of the wind in the long grass.

And then, the thudding of heavy hooves.

Epona came, just as Morghan had said she would, and then, as she tossed her head in the wind, Ambrose realised finally where they were.

Where they were going.

Morghan looked at him, saw his understanding, and nodded. 'You recognise this place,' she said.

'From your retellings,' Ambrose agreed, and straightened as Epona came to a stop in front of them, nose flaring, ears flicking back and forth.

Morghan stepped up to her, touched a hand to the animal's neck and leant briefly against her. 'How lovely to see you again,' she said. Then, when she stepped back. 'Will you carry us both?'

Epona nodded her head up and down, then tossed her mane and stamped a hoof, eager to be on their way. She bent her front legs to kneel on the ground.

Eagle lifted from Ambrose's shoulder, his great strong claws digging in momentarily before letting go. He joined Morghan's Hawk circling high in the sky.

Snake disappeared into the grass.

Morghan swung herself onto Epona's back, reached

down to grasp Ambrose's hand, held fast while he heaved himself up behind her.

The ride through the Forest of Lost Souls was swift, for they were not here, Ambrose realised, to find and gather the souls of the wandering. Their destination was farther onwards.

It was the village, and Epona's hooves clip clopped on the cobblestones as she wound along the lanes then came to a stop near the square. Morghan and Ambrose slid from her back and stood in the street, mouths agape.

'The fountain still doesn't run,' Ambrose said, amazed to be in a place he'd heard of only from Morghan's travellings. But there he was.

Morghan shook her head. 'No,' she said. 'It doesn't.' She paused, looking around. 'Yet.' Switching her astonished gaze to Ambrose, she looked at him with hope and slow-dawning joy. 'They're here because we showed them, Ambrose,' she said.

He nodded and Morghan looked back at the street, which had forever been deserted when she'd come to this place previously.

It was not now. There were several people on the cobblestone street, their gaze and steps purposeful.

'They're moving in,' Morghan said, wonder tinging her voice. 'They're taking up residence in the houses.' She shook her head again. 'The village isn't going to be deserted anymore like it was in my first travelling here.'

'Do you remember the one you had after that?' Ambrose said. 'Your most recent?'

Morghan nodded. 'Epona took me up the steps in the bell tower where I hung the egg of the soul to spread its light.' She swallowed. 'That was prescient, wasn't it? Everyone came to watch.'

Ambrose nodded. 'People are returning to this place, and they will clean and sweep it clear of shadows and neglect.' He turned to Morghan. 'We have put the light in the bell tower,' he said. 'And now we must do so in our world also. I have been sceptical until now that this is something we could do, but coming here convinces me.' He turned back to the street where the people going hither and thither – so far only five or six of them – paid him no mind, as if he were invisible. 'We can make this place thrive again. We've already begun.'

Morghan looked at him, at his shining face, the enthusiasm and delight plain upon his features. She smiled too.

'You realise, don't you,' she said. 'That this place is real but mostly as a reflection of my task in our world?' She looked about. 'It feels real to me because I have memories of being here, and because here we are, but I believe mostly, it's been a way of teaching me. Showing us.' She paused, musing upon it. 'Rather like I got Erin to make an imaginary garden, so that she would learn to tend all aspects of her life.'

'Which was a brilliantly simple and effective way to do it,' Ambrose said, glancing at her. 'You realise that it doesn't matter at all? Whether this place exists solely in your inner world, or if it has some objective reality here in the Otherworld?'

Morghan looked about her. The light was still dull, brownish, and the buildings still had an air of resigned neglect, but there were bright patches. There were people.

Not many, not yet. Soon though, if they continued with

their task, then there would be more and the streets would be swept, the houses dusted and brightened.

And the fountain, she thought. The fountain would run again, and light would shine from the bell tower.

'No,' she said. 'It doesn't matter at all.'

57

'I'M SO NERVOUS,' ERIN SAID, SQUEEZING HER HANDS together and tying her fingers in knots. 'I don't think I've ever been this nervous in my life.'

Ebony was pacing about the drawing room. It was sixteen steps from end to end. She shook her head. 'I don't think I'm nervous,' she said. 'But I'm impatient to get it started.'

'We need to be doing something,' Krista said, feeling the old desire to go outside and run itching deep within her. To run and feel the wind in her hair, her heartbeat against her ribs, the trail under her feet.

'I'm not sure,' Clarice said. 'I'm inclined to stay put right here from now on.'

Ebony snorted, then apologised. 'I'm sorry,' she said. 'The way you said that; it was funny.'

Erin tapped her foot, leaning over her lap. She didn't even have Burdock to pat to calm herself down. When the room had emptied out, everyone going every which way to organise things, she'd brought him inside.

But then he'd seen Clover for the first time and gone straight to her.

And not left her side since.

Fortunately, Erin thought, the fascination had been mutual, and when Clover had decided to go to her room for a rest before the show began, she'd asked if she could take Burdock with her.

Erin hadn't had the heart to say no. Clover, she thought, with a tiny, amused smile, had also thought Stephan rather fascinating, so the dog was definitely the lesser of the two evils.

'When do you think you'll be heading back to New Zealand?' she asked Rue, who sat on the chair opposite and looked just as nervous as Erin felt.

Rue shook her head. 'I've no idea. I suppose when we've decided how we're going to go about it all.'

Erin nodded. Of course. They still had to figure out exactly how this new Wilde Grove was going to work.

But Morghan and Ambrose had come back from the village full of action and resolution. The press conference was now going to be so much more than that.

A celebration.

A beacon-lighting.

Erin understood why this was necessary, why it was a good thing, but still, this enforced waiting around was getting to her. She stood up, looked at the others.

'I'm going home for a couple hours,' she said. 'If I sit here any longer, I'm going to go bonkers.'

'What about the people everywhere?' Clarice asked,

very glad that she and Krista had decided it was best to stay away from Haven for now. She would do her part that evening – and likely every day afterwards – but that was then, and this was now.

But Erin just shrugged. 'Morghan said the camera crews had agreed to stay in the village, so they won't be planted outside the house anymore, and I'll just slip in, hopefully unnoticed.'

Hopefully.

'But I can't just sit around for the next few hours. I need to do something. I don't even have my sketchpad with me.' She shook her head. 'I'll be back for Morghan's rehearsal.'

Stephan had gone to round up the people he jammed with every now and then, to convince them to play later. They'd have to set everything up as well, so that would be him busy for the rest of the day. Erin glanced out the window. So far, the weather was holding, the sky a grey-blue and no sign of rain.

Rue looked up. 'Can I come with you?'

Erin stared at her in surprise. 'Oh. Ah, of course.'

Rue smiled at her. 'Thanks. I'd like to see Ash Cottage again.'

Her comment made Erin's eyes widen. 'I'd forgotten,' she said, putting a hand over her mouth and shaking her head. 'You knew my grandmother.'

'Teresa,' Rue said, smiling sadly. 'Very well, in the end. She came over to visit us in New Zealand, and of course we came here. We spent a fair bit of time together.' She looked over at Ebony. 'It's hard to believe she's gone.'

'I wish we'd been able to come before she died,' Ebony

said, coming to lean on the back of the sofa. 'She was terrifically funny.'

'Funny?' Stephan had given Erin the impression she was more grumpy than anything else.

'Well,' Ebony said. 'Deep down, under the seriousness and the practical streak that was a mile wide. Under all that, she was pretty hilarious.'

'She was,' Krista agreed. 'She had this earthy sort of humour – and I don't mean crass or anything.' Krista giggled suddenly. 'She told jokes about dirt; she didn't tell dirty jokes.'

'I wish I'd met her,' Erin said, thinking it for the thousandth time.

'You'll meet again one day,' Clarice said.

Erin nodded, then looked at Rue. 'You'd be welcome to come,' she said. 'You and anyone else.'

The others all shook their heads.

'I'll stay here,' Ebony said. 'In case Clover needs anything.'

Rue shot her a grateful look.

'I'm just going to stay here and work on getting my nerve up for later,' Clarice said.

THEY WALKED IN SILENCE FOR HALF OF THE WAY, ERIN shooting Rue curious and surreptitious glances every now and then.

'I'm sorry about what Selena said, about me being Lady of the Grove,' Rue said finally, as the path wound down the hill towards Ash Cottage. It was strange, she thought, taking this path and knowing that she was going to Teresa's home, but there would be no Teresa.

'That's all right,' Erin said. 'She probably had a point – I haven't been here long.' She pursed her lips as the memory of the Fae woman's taunting flashed large inside her, making her wince away.

'Are you okay?'

Erin drew breath, made herself think instead of the scene in London, the way the ravens – her ravens – had gathered around.

She stopped walking.

'What is it?' Rue asked, coming to a halt too.

Erin shook her head slowly. 'No,' she said. 'That couldn't be, could it?' She closed her eyes for a moment, running through it. 'No,' she repeated.

'What?' Rue asked again.

Opening her eyes, Erin looked at Rue. 'Well,' she said. 'When I went to the quarry the day you arrived, I had rather an awful encounter with the Fae there.' There was a lump in her throat that she had to speak around.

Rue nodded. She'd heard the story, if not the fine details.

'Well,' Erin said. 'I was so upset I decided to go to London – for some time out.'

Rue nodded again. She was very familiar with this bit. And the bit that came next.

'We all know what happened then,' Erin said. 'Since we're dealing with the fallout from it now.'

'Agreed,' Rue said. 'So?'

Erin shook her head. 'Well, I know I'm wrong, but I just had this thought – what if the Fae at the quarry did everything that they did, just to push me to the edge like that?'

She shied away from exactly how close to the edge they'd shoved her.

'So that you'd go to London and what would happen there would happen, you mean?' Rue asked.

Erin nodded. 'Well, yeah. Except that it's not the case, I know that. It was just a thought.'

'How do you know that?'

'Because they had no way to know I would go to London. Also, other people have committed suicide there, at the quarry.' Erin was silent for a moment, then took a breath, moved on. 'Stephan and I am sure that it's because of them. The Fae.' She paused. 'Or at least, I was, sure, that is.'

Rue considered this and decided to skirt delicately around the question of just how close Erin had come to doing the same as she'd said others had. 'Was it, though? Or could it just be that it's – the quarry – a suitable place?' She shook her head. 'I mean, it was pretty awful the day we went there. Completely bleak and wounded. An absolute scar in the land.' She lifted her shoulders in a shrug. 'So, what you're suggesting could be possible.'

But Erin shook her head. 'I don't think so. I mean – that faerie woman was brutal. Wouldn't there be better ways to make me go to London?' She huffed a laugh. 'Like, you know, ask?'

Rue thought of Clover. 'I think sometimes, those of the Other Realms don't have the same care and sensibilities as we do. They're not precious about our feelings the way we are.'

'You mean, they don't care about our feelings,' Erin said. They'd begun walking again, and Erin shrugged down into her jumper. It might not be raining for once, but the day was still chilly. Perhaps she'd be glad of the bonfire later.

'I mean that our soul family, those who sit in council trying to work things out for us all, they have a much bigger and longer view of things than we do,' Rue said. 'When you're seeing wide and far, small things like passing emotions might not register as much.'

'Well,' Erin said, considering this. 'It was a risky move, if so; I can tell you that.'

Rue thought about it some more. 'You know,' she said after a minute. 'It could be both things.'

Erin stopped walking and peered out through the trees. They were at the spot on the path where it was possible to look down and see Ash Cottage. The house, the garden. There wasn't anyone wandering about or lingering in front on the lane, or anywhere. They'd gone away with the TV crew, she imagined.

She turned her attention back to what Rue had said. She thought she might like Rue, given more time to get to know her. She had an energy unlike any Erin had felt before. There was a thread that ran through it, she thought now. A strong thread, a backbone of steel or something like that. A thread that drove her onwards, that dictated everything she did.

Erin shook her head briefly, and drew her senses in. 'What do you mean, that it could be both things?' she asked.

'Well,' Rue said. 'The Fae at the quarry could have been acting according to their own agenda, but that doesn't mean that theirs didn't fit in with a bigger one, or someone else's, in the scheme of things.'

Erin frowned. 'Doesn't that mean that someone somewhere has to know the future?'

'Clover's seen the future,' Rue said. Then she shook her head. 'A possible future, anyway. But even if not all of the future can be known, I do think it's possible to swim in the flow of it in some ways – I mean, you've had prophetic dreams, right?'

Erin nodded. 'How do you know that?'

'I don't,' Rue said. 'Only you see, just about everyone does.' She warmed to her subject. 'And we have also seen the past – those people we were right here in Wilde Grove, for example, somehow they still live.' She shrugged. 'So, time, it can't be only what we see of it. And I think our kin – I think they play the odds all the time, and I think they influence it in their favour as much as they can.'

Erin was silent for a minute, digesting this. She shook her head. 'That feels like such a big idea.'

'The Weaving,' Rue said, thinking of Clover again. 'It's everything there is, right? All the worlds?' She huffed out a breath. 'Well, it's time too, then.' She laughed suddenly.

'What?' Erin asked. They were at the end of the path and slipped now out of the woods across the grass to Ash Cottage, Erin already reaching into her pocket for her key. She made for the side gate, wanting to get out of view of the lane as quickly as possible, just in case anyone still lurked about.

'I've been away from this sort of thing for a while,' Rue said. 'Well, as much as it's possible to be, when you live with Selena and Clover.' She shook her head, following Erin into the garden and stopping to look around in astonishment.

'It's changed,' she said, seeing the new arrangement of the garden beds.

Erin stopped and looked too. 'Oh,' she said. 'I guess it has since you were last here. Stephan and Teresa did this a few years back.' She pointed to the beds, most of which were mulched down for the winter already. 'It's the Wheel, see? Coming out from the well in the centre? And all the plants are in beds according to their properties and which element they align to.'

'It's amazing,' Rue said. 'Teresa designed this?'

'She did,' Erin said. 'And Stephan keeps it up.'

58

'What were you going to say?' Erin asked after a minute while Rue looked around in astonishment. 'I feel like you were going to say something important.' She looked at Rue, at Rue's short, stylish haircut, the brown eyes underneath it.

Rue nodded. 'I was thinking about how I've drifted away from this life.' She thought about it, choosing the words that felt the most truthful. 'I always wanted my own business, you see – or to work as a fashion designer or similar – and even though I had dedicated myself to taking care of Clover, I thought I could do both.' She paused. 'And I have.'

Erin nodded, waiting. She felt Rue sorting through something, and that there was something waiting for her at the end of this.

'I don't regret it,' Rue said, and she walked down one of the aisles between the garden beds to the well at the centre. She looked back at Erin. 'I don't regret it for a moment. And I won't stop, either.'

Erin nodded again, keeping quiet.

'But now I see that in doing all that, I maybe wasn't as focused on the rest of it as I should have been.' She paused. 'I've been through a sort of dry spell.' She laughed at the choice of words. 'Dry spell – still a spell, do you see? Only not a fruitful one. Which kind of gives me the idea I did it to myself. I made the spell.' Rue lifted the lid of the well and breathed the scent of the water. It smelt to her of mysteries and depth.

'I still greet the day and so on. But mostly I've left that sort of thing to Clover and Selena – and Ebony for that matter.' Rue paused again, then looked at Erin.

'But now, it's time to rededicate myself to it. To my path into the wilderness of the worlds.' She smiled. 'There's got to be a way to follow that, and still be a businesswoman, right?'

'I'm sure,' Erin said. 'I actually think that's really important – living this way while also working, making a difference, feeding and housing ourselves and all the rest of it. Although who knows where the path will really lead us, particularly these days.'

'That's true,' Rue said. 'And it's not at all like we only just stepped onto it, is it?'

Erin shook her head. 'No.' She joined Rue at the well, looked into the dark water. 'Macha,' she said. 'You know who Macha is, right?'

'Yes.' Rue hesitated. 'I've seen her in my visions. She followed Ravenna to the Forest House. Way back when.'

Erin nodded. 'She did something back then, that I think the rest of you did too.'

Rue looked at her.

'She dedicated not just her life then to the Way of the Wheel or the Weaving, or whatever we called the Ancient Way back then when it wasn't so ancient.' Erin paused, got back on track. 'But every one of her lives. She dedicated every lifetime to it. Hers, mine, all the ones in between, all the ones to come.'

Rue breathed slowly out, thinking about this. 'Yes,' she said finally. 'I think Clover and I did the same. And Morghan, and Selena.' She fell silent, thinking.

'You know,' she said at last. 'I don't think it's such a big thing as it sounds. I mean – it is, and it isn't. We think it is, and it probably was too, when Macha and Bryn did it, but in the end, aren't everyone's lives dedicated to it? When we start out, I mean. When we first begin our lives here on this earth, and between them? For most of us, anyway. Those who haven't gotten lost along the way?'

'Maybe,' Erin mused. 'But how come so many of us have become corrupted then? Even those of us who don't consciously choose meanness and greed, we've been brought up to be consumers.'

'You've answered your own question, Erin,' Rue said, and she rested her hands on the rim of the well. 'We've been brought up to be consumers, rather than in a reciprocal relationship with the land.'

'You think it's that simple?'

Rue sighed. 'Maybe. In words. In action, however, it's the whole structure of our civilisation we're talking about.'

Erin dipped a finger into the water and touched its dampness to her forehead. 'Blessed water through the worlds,' she murmured. 'Flow too through my spirit.'

Rue watched her, heard the words, and did the same. It

was a simple act, and yet, for some reason, her throat grew thick and her heart full.

'Do you dance?' she asked abruptly.

Erin looked at her. 'Dance?' Then, more slowly. 'What sort of dance?'

Rue shifted on her feet, drew down the lid to the well and looked around the garden. There was space to dance, barely. She cleared her throat.

'Sacred dance,' she said. 'You know, the dance that is sort of a prayer and a slipping between the worlds as well.'

Erin laughed. 'Yes,' she said. 'I'm trained by Morghan too, remember?' Her smile widened. 'I guess she got you to dance as well, then?'

Rue grinned, feeling suddenly, for a moment, lighter. 'She did. It was awful to begin with, thinking you could dance as prayer, or dance your way out of a mood and into joy.' She shook her head. 'I was so self-conscious, I hated it. For a little while, and then I got the knack.'

'I love it,' Erin said, and she looked at Rue. 'Would you like us to dance? We can dance you stepping back under the light of the North Star and following your way.' She touched Rue lightly on the arm. 'I think it might be a good idea.'

It would be good for her too, Erin thought. Dance brought her back into alignment. While she danced, she was different – she was herself, and she was more, her eternal self. She was there, in her garden, and she was in the Other Realms as well, in a place she had gone to spontaneously one day, and which she recognised from Morghan's teaching, as being her personal place in the worlds.

The place where she could stand and span the Otherworld and the Ordinary world.

'Do you have a place in the Otherworld?' she asked Rue.

Rue pressed her lips together, shifted slightly. 'Yes, but to tell the truth, it's been ages since I've thought about it, let alone been there.'

'Perhaps it's a practice you should start again,' Erin said. 'I'm going to double down on it, I think.' She nodded. 'It will help me feel stronger, because the me that is there isn't quite the me here. She's bigger, older, wiser. If I can feel that me within this me more often, I think I won't be quite so afraid.'

Rue looked at her curiously. Selena, she thought, had seriously underestimated this young woman. Erin was very serious about following the Ancient Way. But of course, Selena hadn't then had the opportunity to get to know her.

'Do you often feel afraid?' she asked.

Erin looked at her. 'All the time,' she said. 'If I let myself. Don't you?'

Rue nodded. 'All the time,' she said, then echoed Erin's words with a smile. 'If I let myself.'

Erin smiled at her. 'Then let's dance,' she said. 'Let's call in our dragons and dance the worlds together.'

Rue's brow rose. 'Dragons?'

'You have a white one,' Erin said. 'I can see it, inside my mind, when I look at you.' She paused, feeling for it. 'I do too. It rose from a loch I once lived near, and it's been close to me ever since, I think.'

'Grainne had a dragon too,' Rue said, then blinked. Grainne's memory was still too near, here in Wilde Grove. Teresa's too, for that matter.

'Maybe everyone does,' Erin said. 'Morghan calls them the protectors of the golden treasure of our hearts, and I like that. In which case, wouldn't we all have one?' She smiled more widely. 'But come on, let's dance.'

There was enough space, just, and they faced each other, Rue feeling the old awkwardness again, and pushing it from her mind with effort borne on a long breath. They steadied themselves, letting their minds and bodies relax, their spirits expand with each exhaled breath.

Erin smiled. The Fae woman had been wrong, she thought. This was where she belonged, and she was doing exactly the thing she was supposed to be doing. She felt the hot sting of shame touch her again, bringing heat to her cheeks at the knowledge that she could have been so easily pushed about. She felt it, then forgave herself, head bowed slightly, heart filled with compassion for herself.

The shame cooled, drained away, and a joy took its place. Joy, and hope, that here was another minute in which she could be true to herself and her path. She seized it and breathed, raised her arms.

'I hold myself in honour to you,' she said. 'Earth, sea, sky.'

A pause, feeling herself between all three, connected.

'I walk in balance between you, world to world to world.'

She nodded then, smiled at Rue, and began to dance, a swaying, a stepping, a prayer to the elements, to the world.

'Blessed water, blessed earth, air, and fire,' Erin sang, feeling her breath, feeling herself expand into the worlds.

'Spirits of the north, east, south, and west. We greet you, in peace and blessing.' She smiled at Rue, who reached out so that for a moment, their fingers were linked.

'We are called,' Erin continued, 'to weave the world with you. We are called to keep the weaving safe.'

They were quiet for a moment after that, feeling the gravity of Erin's last words sink into them.

'To keep the weaving safe,' Rue murmured, and she stretched and breathed, feeling the truth of it settled deep inside her.

'May we be in peace,' Erin said. 'May we be in peace.'

They danced then, both sinking into the light trances that they'd learnt, Erin over the last year with Morghan, Rue much longer ago.

RUE FELT HER BREATH, AND THE GROUND UNDER HER FEET, and between her half-closed lids, she could see Erin if she looked, but she could feel her gaze turning elsewhere. Why, she wondered vaguely, deep inside herself, did she not do this more often?

Because I don't make the time to, she told herself, then let it go with the resolution to change that. Instead, she turned her vision inwards, seeking something.

Someone. Bryn. Rue took a breath, held it, let herself shift, until her dancing steps took her back into her own deep past.

Bryn stood on the grassy bank below the buildings of the Forest House. She was gazing at the trees, her breath quick in her chest. Too quick. She was worried for Rhian.

Rhian ought to be with them, she thought. Not in the cave, not with only Macha to take care of her. She shifted her footing, half turning to leave their formation, to go to Rhian. Had not the Fae themselves put Rhian into her care?

They had, and she ought to be with her now.

Ravenna put a hand on her arm. 'No,' she said. 'Your place now is here.'

Bryn shook her head. 'Rhian,' she said.

'Rhian is well,' Ravenna told her. 'She follows her destiny. Macha is with her.'

'But I should be the one with her.'

Ravenna looked at Bryn without blinking. 'You have served her well,' she said at last. 'But Rhian is no longer a child.'

Bryn wanted to protest, but the look on Ravenna's face made her silent.

'The path of your destiny leads you here,' Ravenna said. 'To this spot. Hold your place.'

Bryn bowed her head. Was it true, she wondered? Did the threads of their purpose together – she and Rhian – unravel here? At this moment?

There was a pang of loss inside her, and then she realised that Ravenna had not yet moved on, retaken her place in their line. Instead, she was gazing still at her, as though waiting for the moment when Bryn would straighten, accept the way forward.

Bryn swallowed, nodded, and made herself stand tall. She looked towards the trees.

Ravenna watched her a moment longer, then touched her shoulder. 'My daughter,' she said, and stepped back to her own place in their line.

Bryn waited, heart thumping, thoughts falling away from Rhian as the Fae Queen stepped finally from between the trees.

Ravenna stepped forward, the swirls painted on her cheeks glowing in the light that seemed to shine from the

Queen's aura. As Bryn watched, barely daring to breathe, Ravenna slipped to one knee and bowed her head.

The move sent a ripple of shock through Bryn, who had never seen their teacher from across the sea do any such thing to any person before. She heard a rustle from the others about her and saw that they too had knelt. Even Finn and the other men had done so.

She sank down to one knee also. Then stood once more upon the signal of Ravenna's rising.

The Queen Alastrina was taller than Ravenna, and made Ravenna look almost swarthy, although, Bryn saw, others of the Queen's retinue were not so pale of skin, but ranged in their looks. All, however, were tall and fine boned.

She wondered if any were those who had handed Rhian to her all those years ago. Their gazes grazed over her without recognition.

They wore expressions that seemed foreign to Bryn. They gazed around the circle of humans with a detachment that almost bordered, Bryn thought, on disinterest.

And yet, she knew they were not disinterested, for were they not here, in this time of crisis?

Bryn blinked, and was Rue once more, mid step, and Rue stopped her dance, gazed upwards at the sky, at the web, and knew that whatever their task going forward, it had been set in motion long ago, and all she had to do, was to follow the thread and walk – and dance – her purpose.

59

THE DAY WAS DIMMING, AND CLOVER COULD FEEL THE
excitement rising in Wellsford, almost like it was a cloud,
something she could stretch out to reach.

Something had been brewing in her all day also, and
she touched her chest now with chilled fingers, feeling as
though whatever was inside her would shortly be
demanding to be seen.

At least, she supposed, she hadn't gone actually blind as
she'd feared. The white mist was still only inside her.

That was enough.

She stepped into the shadows of the village, drawing her
energy close so that she could slip almost unnoticed past
the visitors that thronged the main street and wove in and
out of the shops.

It was almost time for Morghan's lighting of the beacons,
and Clover knew she didn't have much time left to herself
before it began, and yet she couldn't stop the feeling that
another seizure – another vision – was coming on.

One that she'd been expecting.

The one that would connect the last of the dots. Show her the way forward.

When the church building's new sign rose out of the darkness, Clover breathed a sigh of relief. Of course. Bridget's Sanctuary.

She felt a sudden certainty that for a few minutes at least, it would be empty.

And a few minutes might be all she needed.

She slipped into the silent church, feeling the echoes of its history pressing against her. But Clover ignored them with the ease of long practice. Someone had left an electric candle burning and Clover stopped inside the inner sanctum of the church and looked about in surprise. It was not arranged at all how she expected a church to look.

'Of course,' she said to the building. 'You're not a church anymore, but a sanctuary.' She smiled. 'It suits you.'

The baptismal font called to her. Of course, it was no longer a baptismal font either, and Clover stood in front of the bowl of water, feeling the scent and shape of its energy and knew that it had been blessed by Winsome, whom she'd liked very much when they'd met. She smiled in the gloom and dipped a finger into the water and touched her forehead with damp fingers.

'May the Goddess bless and keep me,' she whispered. 'May she guide and teach me. May I walk ever in her presence and service.'

She took a deep breath, closed her eyes for a moment, and looked at the great whiteness inside her. Now, however, it didn't seem made of nothingness. Emptiness, perhaps, but one of such pregnant potential. The flow of the world,

Blackbird had called it. The flow from which all is woven. Clover remembered that, and remembered too, Rhian's white eyes, that, contrary to being blind, saw much.

So much.

Was she in the right place, Clover wondered? She'd thought she felt one of her visions coming on, but now that she was away from the crowds, she felt perfectly fine, not wobbly on her feet at all.

Clover walked up the centre of the sanctuary, slipped between the railings where once people had got on their knees before their god and took the symbols of his blood and body into theirs. She'd never quite understood how that worked, even as a metaphor, but that didn't matter any longer. This building belonged to Brigid now, saint and goddess, and it was her energy that filled it as Clover stood before the lone candle burning on what had once been the altar table.

Clover's lips twitched in a smile as she thought of a very old prayer she'd once converted from Christian to pagan. That had been during her poetry phase, which had also coincided with her guitar phase. The guitar had stuck, the poetry not quite so much.

But the prayer – it seemed the perfect place and time for it. Clover looked at the candle, wished it were real for a moment, fire flickering in air, then straightened, tipped her head back slightly, and prayed to Brigid.

Goddess be a light
to illumine and guide me.
Brigid, as a shield,
overshadow me.

Your spirit under me,
over me,
beside me,
on my left and on my right.
This day be within and without me,
be in the heart of each to whom I speak,
in the mouth of each who speaks unto me.
Brigid as a light,
as a shield;
Brigid beside me,
on my left and on my right.

CLOVER PAUSED, THEN CONTINUED WITH A PRAYER MORGHAN had taught her, drawing breath, seeing now not the candle flame, yellow in the dimness, but the whiteness inside her.

The flow of all things. She bent her head.

The flow of all things from which the world is woven.

'May the strength of your heart be with me,

'Wherever I need to go.

'May I be guided through the wilderness,

'Protected through the storm.

'May I follow your path

'Through the eternal forest.'

Clover paused, breathed, slipped into the mist.

'May healing and blessing be mine,' she murmured, then changed the last words slightly.

'May compassion for me be in your heart.'

· · ·

THE BATTERY-POWERED CANDLE FLAME BECAME A FIRE, BESIDE which she sat, and her heartbeat that of a drum, and she smelled the air heavy with burning herbs. She knew without opening her eyes where she was.

Who she was.

Rhian.

She stood sure-footed upon the ground, the fire warming her cheeks, and knew that it was Macha who stood on the other side of the cave, her drum in her hands, making the opening in the world for her to slip through.

And back, with the blessing of the Deer Mother.

How long had she been here, in this cave, her vision turned inwards? She no longer knew.

Nor why it was Macha who drummed for her, rather than Bryn.

Except, that was not the truth, was it? She knew, tipping her face up to where she felt Macha standing. Macha, whose beat was steady, who did not falter, or wish the path was otherwise, who did not share Bryn's protective feelings.

Once, those had been essential to Rhian's wellbeing.

Now, she was grown past that.

And unlike Bryn, Macha would let Rhian risk her life to do what was necessary.

There was movement within the flow and Rhian turned her attention towards it. She watched as the whiteness began to separate, to stream in ribbons, this way, and that, forming an intricate pattern she knew she could never hope to replicate in even her best weaving with thread.

Blackbird hopped upon her shoulder, his weight negligible but comforting, nonetheless.

One of the ribbons seemed to glow brighter than the

others, and Rhian followed it, walking out onto the grassy bank beneath the Forest House and looking down at her fellow priestesses arrayed across the slope. They were on their knees.

Rhian gazed at the figure to whom her sisters were giving such an honour, and the Queen of the Fae glanced up at her, held her gaze for a long moment before nodding her head slightly to her, and returning her attention to Ravenna, who was greeting her.

Bryn turned her head and looked behind her, up the slope to where Rhian stood watching, but when she saw nothing, she turned back.

Rhian closed her eyes and still she saw everything.

The decision was being reiterated below her. Ravenna, Alastrina the Queen, making certain they understood each other, for what was coming could not easily be unmade.

Rhian knew, however, that all had already been agreed to. It was there in the threads of the Weaving, in the strands of the Web, the great interlocking pattern of the worlds.

She looked further, past where it had already been agreed to, to where the deed had already been done, and the consequences of it stretched out into the flow of time, and Rhian followed the threads, saw where they thinned, thickened, tangled, were straightened.

The world spun around her, vast, intricate, no outcome certain until reached in the flow.

When it was time, she opened her eyes again and watched.

The drawing down of the veil. It whispered like gauze across Rhian's consciousness.

The separation caused her pain, and she screamed out

in horror at the loss of so much of the world, then pressed her hand to her heart, ripped the veil from her self, from her sight.

And then, her purpose. She tore the veil also from the Forest House, so that there was no separation between spirit and heart, between faerie and human. Not in this small pocket of the land. Not there, at the Forest House, not in the span of land about it.

The effort cost her footing, and she dropped to the ground, curled into a ball, spent.

Lay there for who knew how long, until finally, into the whiteness came a sound and Rhian lifted her head, listened.

And let Macha's heartbeat bring her home.

IN BRIDGET'S SANCTUARY, ALEX CHERROW PUT HIS CAMERA down. He'd come into the church – sanctuary, he corrected himself – to get a bit of atmospheric footage down. The stuff he thought he was about to get on the green would be brilliant, but he knew, if he stitched it together with some scenes from around the village, it would be even better.

Hence, coming in here.

It had been a stroke of luck that he'd found one of the Wilde Grove girls making good use of the place. Praying, it had looked like. He'd recognised her, since she was wearing one of their long dresses, looking like she'd stepped out of the Middle Ages, or some time even earlier.

Which was all part of the show, he expected, and while the *press conference* was yet to begin, the show was for sure already on.

For starters, there were all the birds. Ravens, everywhere, just like in that damned video from Trafalgar Square. Which was one of the more astonishing things he had seen in his 24 years.

Alex could appreciate a good show. Still, he wondered how they were getting the birds to stick about around so many people. There was an owl too, but he thought that was obviously tame, since for a while it had been perched on the shoulder of one of the dudes playing in the band up on the stage set up in the green.

But the ravens. They had Alex Cherrow baffled.

Likewise, the bird that had perched on this girl's shoulder. Much smaller than a raven or crow, but still, it had looked amazing on film. He'd caught it flying into the building, landing on the girl, then eventually, flying back out.

Harry, his boss, would be ecstatic.

Hell, he was ecstatic.

She hadn't even seemed to notice it. The bird, that was. Alex wondered over that, camera still over his shoulder, filming in the dim light. It wouldn't be ideal, the lighting, but it was atmospheric, Alex reckoned, and that would go a long way.

'Hey,' he said suddenly, noticing the girl come back to life, shivering and unsteady. 'Are you okay?'

Clover turned and stared at the stranger, startled, and disoriented. She'd travelled hard, deep into her past, and the landing back in the present was never easy even in the best of circumstances.

This wasn't the best of circumstances.

'Who are you?' she asked, and her voice was raspy, her throat dry.

'Ah, I'm Alex,' he said.

Clover stared at him, her thinking sluggish. Then she narrowed her eyes. 'Is that a camera?'

Alex cleared his throat, looked at the offending item, then nodded, took a few steps forward up what used to be the aisle. 'Yeah,' he said.

'Were you filming me?'

'Yeah,' he said again, then shook his head. 'Don't tell me to get rid of the footage either, because it was brilliant.'

Clover, her hands gripping the edge of the altar table, stared at him in confusion. 'Why?' she asked. Watching her sway there with her eyes closed – what would be awesome about that?

'A bird flew in,' Alex said, reliving it over again, shaking his head. 'Right into the church, and it landed on your shoulder. You didn't even notice.' It finally occurred to him to ask. 'What were you even doing?'

Clover didn't know how to answer that. With the truth? Telling this guy she'd popped back to a past life to see where the threads woven then would lead her now?

She decided to ignore the question.

'Was it a blackbird?' she asked instead.

Alex's eyes rounded in the dim light. 'How was there even a bird in here? How are you guys doing this shit with all the birds?' He glanced back towards the door. 'It's night out there now – no birds ought to be about.' They went to bed – to nest, rather – he supposed, or whatever it was that birds that weren't nocturnal did at night.

He was no nature photographer. He worked on whatever hot topic was going to be news that day, trailing around after Harry, following the stories.

Although, come to think of it, more and more the hot topics were to do with weather, so that was a sort of nature, wasn't it?

Nature at its most pissed, generally.

'I need to sit down,' Clover said, and she raised her hands experimentally from the table. Yes, she decided. She could probably walk. What she really needed was something to drink. Maybe even one of Morghan's chocolate biscuits.

There was a commotion at the door.

'Oh,' Winsome said. 'I didn't realise there was anyone in here.'

'Winsome,' Clover said.

Peering past the fellow with the camera, Winsome squinted at Clover.

'Clover?' she asked. 'Are you all right?'

Clover sighed. 'I am, actually, but do you have any water on you?' Her mouth was so dry. She licked her lips. 'Maybe a chocolate biscuit?'

Winsome heard the question and bustled past the camera man. She knew exactly what had happened here, and grasped Clover gently under the elbow.

'Come to the vicarage with me,' she said. 'I'll make you some tea – and I've plenty of chocolate biscuits. There's still time before things start.'

Alex turned and watched them leave, frowning slightly, feeling like something was going on that he had no idea about. He wondered who the girl was – she had a different accent, so definitely wasn't from around there. For a moment, he looked around the old church and felt a breeze stirring, remembered the bird that had flown in and landed on the girl's shoulder.

She'd been right.

It had been a blackbird.

60

'IT'S AMAZING WHAT CAN BE DONE IN SUCH A SHORT TIME, isn't it?' Winsome asked.

'I'm just gobsmacked that the weather has held,' Veronica answered.

They stood on the green, where Stephan and his friends had spent the afternoon putting the finishing touches to the bandstand, their faces shining with excitement, and were now playing joyously to the crowd. Wen, along with his cronies, had also been busy, stacking dry wood in the precise shaping that would make the bonfire catch and burn easily and safely when the time came.

Joe, from the grocery, had wheeled out his barbeque and cranked up the grill. Winsome's stomach rumbled.

'Goodness,' she said, pressing her hand flat against her middle. 'Those sausages smell good.'

'They must be good, they're very popular,' Veronica answered. She looked around for Erin, but of course her daughter wasn't anywhere about. She'd come soon, the star attraction.

What was going to happen, Veronica wondered? When Morghan and Erin and the rest of them turned up?

'What sort of show do you think they'll put on?' she asked.

'Who?' Winsome asked absently. She was marvelling at the atmosphere on the green. The very air, she thought, was coloured with excitement, anticipation. Everyone – visitor and villager alike – were buzzing with joy. Everyone, she decided, liked a good celebration, and it had been so wet and dreary that it was lovely to get out and get together while the clouds held off. And they were, she thought, squinting up at the sky. It was grey, but to her eye, no rain threatened. Perhaps someone had done a weather spell. Winsome giggled at the idea.

Then she thought of Clover, who had recovered quickly from her travelling in Bridget's Sanctuary, who had seemed relieved, even excited by whatever it had been that she'd seen unfold in her vision. She was with Ambrose and Morghan now.

'Morghan,' Veronica said. 'My daughter.'

Winsome's attention swung back, and she looked at Veronica. 'Do you still not approve?'

Veronica dragged in a deep breath and let it out in a whoosh between parted lips. 'I wouldn't say that, exactly,' she said, then relented. 'Or at all. Even I can see that Erin is at home here.'

'I should hope so,' Winsome laughed. 'Since you're also here, part of it all.'

Veronica relented and nodded, stepping out of the way

as a couple of children raced past, holding sausages wrapped in bread, tomato sauce smeared about their mouths. She was, much to her surprise, and probably Erin's as well, still in Wellsford, four, almost five months after turning up unannounced and with no intention of staying.

'It's funny how things work out, isn't it?' she asked.

Winsome gave her a squeeze. 'Yes,' she said. 'It is.'

DUSK HAD SHROUDED ITSELF OVER THE VILLAGE BUT IN THE green, lights were shining. Someone had strung up hundreds of Christmas bulbs and they glowed in bright specks of green and white and blue and red. The effect was magical.

The music wound down, hushed, and the crowd turned their bright faces to the bandstand where Stephan, looking tired but happy, grinned at the crowd, then moved back off the stage, pushing his hair off his face while he went to take his place.

The spotlights went out and the crowd murmured, shifted on their feet. The cameramen bent to look through their viewfinders, adjusting the focus.

Alex Cherrow discovered he was holding his breath.

Ambrose stepped up onto the dais beside Morghan and Selena, his gaze immediately going to search the upturned faces, looking for Winsome's. He found her even in the dimness, and the sight of her warm smile went some way to calming the flock of birds in his stomach. He nodded at her, and watched as she pressed her fingers to her lips and blew him a discreet kiss.

Beside him, Morghan stood, hands loose at her side, and

he tried to feel whether she was as nervous as he, but when Ambrose reached out with his senses, he found nothing but calm. Morghan had pulled a veil over her energy, and stood there contained, letting nothing show of how she felt inside. When he glanced at her face, she saw the movement and smiled slightly at him.

He hadn't especially wanted to be up there on the stage with them, but Morghan had insisted. Just as she'd insisted that Stephan join the upcoming dance she'd taught them – Ravenna's dance, along with Ben and Chris, Charlie and Martin's sons. The Forest House, she'd said when he'd asked why, had been a women's house, but Wilde Grove would be open to anyone of any gender.

Ambrose had to admit, when he looked down at the group ranged on the ground at their feet, standing in a curving crescent, it looked good that they had Stephan, Ben, and Chris standing there with Erin, Clarice, Krista, Rue, and Clover. He winced at the thought of how it might have seemed without them – Morghan had been right. Without the men it would have looked, well, he decided, slightly distasteful perhaps, with he and Morghan above, and their women ranged in front of them. He nodded slightly, trying to take his mind off everyone staring at them. It had to be all women, or if he was there, then the other men as well.

He was startled, actually, at how Morghan had choreographed everything. She'd surprised him, although now, as he thought about it, he wondered why. Anyone who led ceremony, he decided, probably had a flair for drama. And Morghan had been leading their ceremonies and rituals for a long time.

Selena also looked perfectly comfortable, he thought,

standing waiting, a slight smile to her lips, while her white hair curled down over a silver-grey gown.

Behind them, against the back wall of the bandstand, a film flickered to life, and Ambrose tried not to turn around to watch it. It was the video of Erin, Krista, and Clarice in London, standing in the Square, ravens flocking to them. It was remarkable footage, Ambrose knew, and the reason why everyone was in the village today, and it playing life-size behind them would, he knew, look quite astounding. He glanced across at Morghan, but she was still, contained, and he felt the depth of her, even from where he stood.

That was when he decided too, to be quiet, to stand straighter and to breathe, to become who he was, a magician, priest, and shaman. Morghan smiled at him.

The video played on the white sheet strung across the back of the tent. It was in black and white, flickering, soundless. Martin, back in the shadows, began playing his drum, deep slow beats that reverberated in the bones.

The crowd on the grass stared, transfixed, gazes torn between the video playing, and the fact that the women in it stood in real life on the green with them, the Christmas lights making them seem only half real.

Morghan, dressed in a dark red tunic, Celtic styled embroidery decorating the coat, stepped closer to the microphone and spoke over the heartbeat of the drum.

Ambrose watched, not knowing what she was going to say. She'd told him that she would decide in the moment.

Morghan looked out over the crowd, saw the lights shining in their eyes, gazed with pride at the people of Wellsford, who were coping perfectly well with the influx of seekers the video of Erin, Krista, and Clarice had brought to their streets.

How glad she was, to be part of this. Wellsford, she thought, was extraordinary.

It always had been.

And so, she knew, could other communities be. Because in the end, it was people who made a community.

But right now, she reminded herself, there was a spectacle to make.

'Once,' she said, and the microphone carried her voice over the crowd. 'Once, there was no veil between the worlds. Once, magic was part of our lives, as near and natural as our own breath.'

She paused a moment, looked out over the crowd, and something stirred in the sky, and Morghan smiled, blessing the spirits who did not let them down, who had brought them to this time and place and did not desert them now.

Sigil was a pale blur of wings in the dusk, and the crowd gasped as she swooped down low to land upon Clarice's outstretched arm.

'Once,' Morghan continued, feeling Ambrose step nearer to her. 'Once we could do many things. We could bring down the weather.' She glanced at the sky, lips twitching. 'Or keep it at bay.' Another pause. 'We could draw down mists. We could part them. We could bring forth fire, stir air, call forth water to gush from the ground. We could move stone.'

She was silent for a moment, and a breeze gusted through the green, ruffling people's hair, bringing with it the scent of the trees.

Then it was gone.

'There was no separation in that time,' she continued, listening to the hush of the crowd, the beat of the drum, and beyond it, the song of the trees, the twinkling of the North Star. 'No separation between the world of spirit and the physical realm. We lived then in full awareness of both.'

From away in the trees that surrounded the village, the breeze brought the sound of a flute, lilting silver on the air, and Morghan drew in a deep breath, closed her eyes, and thanked Maxen in her mind. She would recognise his playing anywhere.

The crowd moved, rustling upon their feet, and even if they thought it was only showmanship, still Morghan could see that they were moved, caught in the song of flute, in the beat of drum, in the image behind her, frozen now, of Erin, arms outstretched between Krista and Clarice, ravens sitting upon her shoulders and around her feet.

And as if on cue, from somewhere in the deepening gloaming, a raven cried out, its harsh cawing recognisable to everyone. The crowd shifted again, murmured.

'Everything sang,' Morghan said. 'Everything roared, dreamt, spun magic. Every frog, every leaf, every stone.'

The raven cawed again, joined by a friend. On the air was a beating of wings, a streaking shadow overhead before things quietened again, and there was just the lamenting flute, the heartbeat of drum.

'Every tiger,' Morghan continued, her voice clear as a bell. 'Every wolf, sandpiper. Every human.' She drew breath.

'And then there was a shift. A turning. Towards domination. Power. Possessions. Greed. And a veil fell between the worlds of spirit and humanity, and without effort, we could no longer see our place in the great weaving of the worlds.'

More beating of wings in the sky, the two ravens joined by their friends.

'The faeries retreated to the other side of the veil. The songs of the trees grew muted, silenced as they were felled in their thousands, living beings, no one thanking them for their sacrifice. The world turned and the universe spun.'

Morghan paused a moment.

'And magic was lost.'

'It's not lost here!' someone called out from the crowd. 'Light the beacons!'

Morghan smiled, lifted her hands. 'Welcome to Wellsford,' she said. 'When the veil fell all those millennia ago, only then did the priestesses of this place – to whom we trace our direct lineage – tear it from their sight, the land blessed and kept instead for all this time, a place where magic still moves us, where spirit still speaks, where the only separation is the veil we bring down over our hearts.'

The crowd had hushed once more, listening. Even the children were still.

Morghan spread her arms, standing in front of the image of Erin, whose arms were similarly wide. She paused for a moment on an indrawn breath.

'Welcome to our community. Welcome to Wellsford and Wilde Grove, where we keep the magic and reverence for the world in our lives. Where to live deeply is to live our soul's true purpose, to love each other, and every part of this wondrous place.'

She nodded to Wen, standing over by the bonfire, waiting. He fumbled his phone a moment, then made the call.

'Now,' he said.

'Let us each,' Morghan continued, 'be the light that

brightens the world. Let us each hold the darkness at bay.'
She held out a hand, and in the far darkness, a light
bloomed.

'Let us each be a beacon.'

With that, Wen lit the bonfire in the green, standing
back in satisfaction as the flames bit and caught and grew.

The villagers, knowing what to expect, remembering
from Halloween a year before, watched, then turned and
looked across the hill beneath the village, taking the visitors
with them, and under their gaze another beacon was lit,
brightening in the darkness.

A fourth flared to life a breath later.

Wen had outdone himself.

The television cameras swung around to take note also.

Alex Cherrow couldn't help it; he grinned even as he
peered through his camera.

For a long, suspended moment, everyone was silent,
seeing the beacons, only four, but feeling inside themselves
a string of them across the land, lighting up the darkness.

Then the drumbeat changed, and another joined it,
became not just a heartbeat, but music, and in the green,
Erin, with bells around her ankles, and Stephan took each
other's hands, joining their line into a circle with the
others, Sigil still upon Clarice's shoulder, and they danced
Ravenna's dance together, the crowd moving back to watch
as they wove and dipped around each other, across and
back again, around in the shape of the Wheel and magic,
their pale clothes glowing in the dimness, and then they
broke apart and swirled between the onlookers, and the
music swelled, grew, and the light from the bonfire brightened also, and for a moment in which everyone threw

back their heads to look, the very air shimmered with blue.

With the weaving of a great and beautiful blessing that rose and settled in the sky over the village.

THEN EVERYONE WAS DANCING, WHIRLING AND WHOOPING IN the light of the beacons and under the beating wings of the ravens who flew backwards and forwards overhead.

61

MORGHAN LIFTED HER HAND FROM ERIN'S SHOULDER. 'COME,' she said kindly, seeing Erin's pale face. 'Let's do what we came here to.' She looked to the carpark and saw that the others had arrived. 'We'll go greet them,' she said, speaking to Ambrose this time, and the two of them walked across the gravel with Selena to meet the men climbing from their vehicles.

'Are you all right?' Stephan asked after they'd gone.

Erin nodded, holding on to her composure with grim determination. 'I'm fine,' she said. 'Or I'm going to be.' She looked over at Clover. 'Are they here?'

Clover didn't have to ask who Erin meant. She nodded. 'Over there on the far side.'

Erin closed her eyes. Took a breath meant to be steadying but was as shaky as she felt.

'They can't hurt you again,' Ebony said. 'That was a one-time deal.'

Erin nodded. She knew that. 'I just hate this place,' she said.

Rue sighed. 'Except you can't,' she said. 'Hate this place, that is. You can't heal what you hate.'

It was a simple observation, and Erin knew it was true. She tipped her head back and looked up at the sky.

It would rain again soon.

'I can hate them,' she said, talking about the Fae. 'For what they did to me.' She paused. 'Tried to do to me.'

Rue shook her head. 'No,' she said. 'Not them, either.' She glanced at Clover, who stood composed and at ease. She'd been different since the beacon lighting. More certain of herself.

'Why not them, either?' Erin asked, and had to make herself stand straight when all she wanted to do was to tuck herself into Stephan's side and hide in his strength.

'If we hate them, we're just the same as them,' Clover said, and she glanced over at where Morghan, Ambrose, and Selena were greeting the suits from Banwell. Her gaze flicked to the television cameras and sought out the guy who had filmed her in Bridget's Sanctuary.

His footage of that and the beacon lighting was still being played everywhere, a week later. Even Clover had to admit, the bit where Blackbird flew into the church and perched on her shoulder was spooky cool.

The vision she'd had that night had changed things. She smiled slightly and gave Alex Cherrow a tiny wave before looking away. She wasn't a glitch, she'd realised because of it. There was a purpose to her gifts, her ability to see into the deep and wide, count the threads of the weaving.

Wherever she was, there was no veil. Others could step into her space and experience that, if she wished.

She could teach them to.

WINSOME SMOOTHED DOWN THE FOLDS OF HER WOOLLEN coat, her hands brushing over the Celtic style embroidery down the front of it, and she smiled at Ambrose as he walked past with Morghan and Selena.

'Can you believe this?' Cynthia whispered next to her.

It was hard to take in, that was for sure, Winsome thought, nudging one of the plants they'd brought for Ackerman and Bidden to plant after the blessing ceremony.

She nodded at Cynthia. 'The beginning of a new era,' she said, and felt the air shimmer about her with magic.

'COUNCILLOR,' MORGHAN SAID, SHAKING HIS HAND. 'IT'S good of you to come.' She smiled at him, all the while still feeling the gaze of the Fae at her back. They had sharp sight, she knew, and would be able to see her, even from the distance where they stood.

'I'm pleased to be here,' Colin Ackerman said. 'Still a little nonplussed by it all, but pleased, I think.' He smiled for the cameras. 'It's a new era, I guess.'

'That it is,' Morghan said, and introduced Selena to him. He'd already met Ambrose, the day they'd sat down in his office in Banwell to organise this.

Colin Ackerman nodded, his public smile firmly pasted on to hide the fact that he felt more than a little confused by everything. He introduced everyone to George Bidden, who nodded blandly, and held out his arm.

George wasn't sure why he was attending what promised to be a rather bizarre ceremony, but it was his company who owned the quarry, and he would be relieved to attend to the last of his responsibilities towards it and move on. If this went any way to rebuilding his reputation, then it was worth a bit of mumbo jumbo and arm waving.

Especially as the TV channels, not to mention the whole internet it seemed, had blown up over these Wilde Grove people, and goddamned if he didn't find he had to play along or risk continuing to be thrown into the limelight as the bad guy.

'Ms Wilde,' he said, touching her fingers.

Councillor Ackerman rubbed his hands together, nodding at the trail of cars coming up the road in a cloud of dust. 'Looks like the public is arriving now.' He nodded approvingly at the first vehicle to pull up. 'Good. And the photographers are already here.' He glanced at Morghan Wilde, checking what the woman was wearing, what sort of image it would make for the local paper, then looked behind her at the others of her group.

She had a good sense of drama; he'd give her that. She looked every inch the new spiritual leader of the day, while being just on the right side of normal so as not to look a flake.

And who really knew, he thought. Perhaps these Grove people really were onto something.

'Shall we get set up, then?' he asked.

Morghan walked back to her group, took in Erin's pale

face, and nodded at her. 'It will be all right,' she said. 'We'll do it just as we discussed.'

IT WAS JUST A BLESSING, ERIN REMINDED HERSELF. THEY WERE just here to do a blessing, exactly the same as she and the others had done the other day, standing on Hawthorn House's lawn and spinning out a great blessing over the land, and Erin had felt Macha stir at her shoulder, knowing their actions echoed almost precisely those that had been performed thousands of years before.

Morghan and Ambrose had gone around beforehand and dismantled the wards, unweaving the magic, so that Grove and village were once again a fully sacred space.

Erin cleared her throat, gave Stephan as reassuring a smile as she could manage, then took a deep breath and began the work of centring herself. This was important, she knew. There could be no wandering off, no misstep. She had to be present and inside her power.

She had to own her magic.

Morghan's gaze was on her, and she looked toward Morghan, who was dressed in a silver green tunic that matched her aura. Erin smoothed her hands down her own deep green dress and nodded at Morghan. She was ready.

As ready as she'd ever be.

The council guy was giving his speech, the quarry owner shifting uncomfortably behind him. Erin didn't look at the journalists and photographers come to witness the scene. They were almost as disconcerting as the Fae over the other side of the quarry.

Were they still there? She was about to find out.

Ambrose's drumming started up.

Erin closed her eyes, stuttered inside her head for a moment. 'Goddess,' she murmured. 'Give me your grace and your strength.'

Behind her eyes, Fox came to sit at her feet, and Raven landed upon her shoulder. She waited for the stirring of air behind her shoulder that would signify that Macha was there. It didn't come, but instead, something moved within her, and she felt Macha's presence inside her, an echo of her own self.

They were the same soul, after all.

She opened her eyes and looked over at the line of Fae at the far edge of the quarry. In the middle of the row was the woman who had taunted her. Erin stared at her, remembered what Rue had said about being unable to hate them, and she took a deep breath, Ambrose's drum beating in time to her heart.

The faerie woman smirked at her, gave a mocking bow. Erin closed her eyes, remembered being there at the quarry, on her knees in the dirt, hands scrabbling, breath heaving.

There was a touch on her shoulders, and Morghan's strength poured into her.

'Gather her up,' Morghan whispered, as though she too could see that part of Erin who still cowered near the edge. 'Gather her up and bring her home again.'

Then Morghan's touch was gone, and Erin looked at herself, face wet with tears, streaked with dirt, and she smiled at her, reached for her.

'Hush, my love,' she told herself. 'Everything is well. Come back to me and I'll strengthen you.'

All else was dark in her vision but for the sight of herself on the edge of the cliff, hauling herself upright, turning to the great chasm behind her and spreading her arms as if to fly.

'No,' Erin said, and strode over to her. Touched her on the shoulder. 'Erin,' she said. 'They're using your fears against you. Why are you listening to them?'

The part of herself who still stood on the edge, too ashamed to move, turned to look at her and shook her head.

Erin smiled at her, spread her arms wide. 'Come back to who you are, my love,' she said. 'Let us be whole once more.'

'But...'

Erin shook her head, realising the truth of what she was about to say. 'No one can take the treasure of our own hearts from us. It is precious no matter how we might stumble.' She drew the wounded piece of herself to her, and made herself whole once more, then looked over at the line of Fae on the far side of the quarry and tipped her chin up slightly, pulling her shoulders back, arms at her sides.

Her heart was open, even to them, she decided. Her fear had drained away, and nor was there any hate, for how, she wondered, could she have anything but compassion for someone who could not see the preciousness of the heart, of all life?

'We will sing this place back to life,' she told them. 'We will tend the earth, invite the spirit of place back to it. Heal its wounds, make precious once again this place and all such places, inside and outside of ourselves.'

Erin looked up and saw the great silver blue blessing, woven in the web from the prayers of those gathered there, as it spread out over the wounded land, glimmering in the light, a thing as fine and beautiful as any she'd ever seen, and then joined in its song as it settled down over the quarry, over the dirt and rock and water, a blessing and a promise.

To rewild that which had been wounded.

For as hearts could be healed, so too could the land.

For all was sacred in the world.

And the torches of the beacons had been lit.

To be continued in
THE HOLLOW PATH

PRAYER OF THE WILDWOOD

May my way open before me.
May my resolve be strong, my heart
    true.
May I find the wisdom necessary for
    the tasks ahead.
May compassion guide me in all I
    need to do.
May my allies not forsake me.
May wind bring me clarity,
water bring me depth.
May the earth grant me steadiness,
may fire kindle my resolve.
May my spirit touch always the truth
    of the heart.
World to world to world.

JOIN THE GROVE

Subscribe to the Wilde Grove mailing list and community to be part of the magic. Find out more at www.katherinegenet. online

ABOUT THE AUTHOR

Katherine has been walking the Pagan path for thirty years, with her first book published in her home country of New Zealand while in her twenties, on the subject of dreams. She spent several years writing and teaching about dreamwork and working as a psychic before turning to novel-writing, studying creative writing at university while raising her children and facing chronic illness.

Since then, she has published more than twenty long and short novels. She writes under various pen names in more than one genre.

Now, with the Wilde Grove series, she is writing close to her heart about what she loves best. She is a Spiritworker and polytheistic Pagan.

Katherine lives in the South Island of New Zealand with her wife Valerie. She is a mother and grandmother.

Printed in Great Britain
by Amazon

40323691R00330